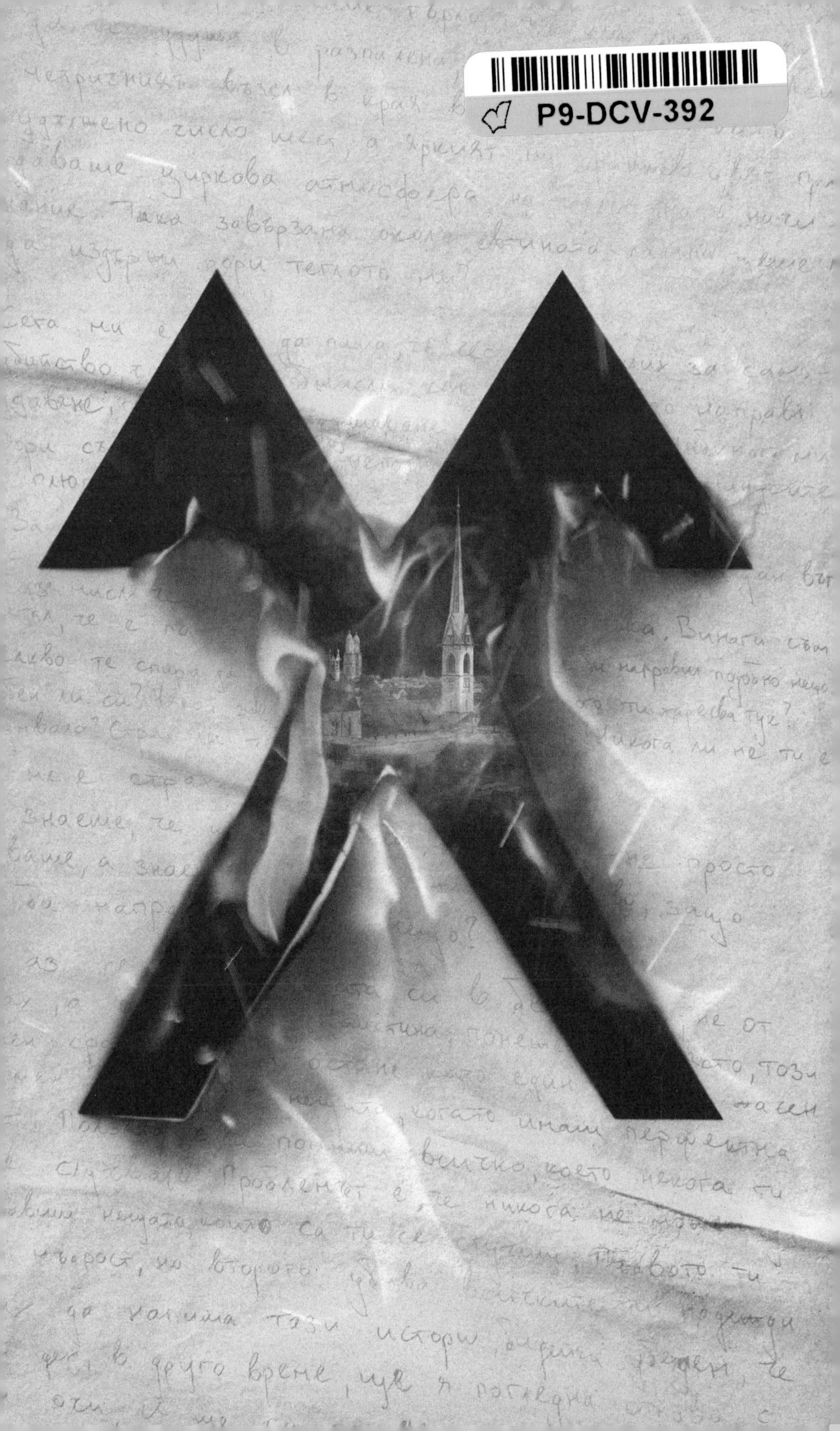

THE

REINCARNATIONIST

PAPERS

THE REINCARNATIONIST PAPERS

D. ERIC MAIKRANZ

BLACK
STONE
PUBLISHING

Copyright © 2021 by D. Eric Maikranz
Published in 2021 by Blackstone Publishing
Cover and book design by Sean M. Thomas

Previously published by Barbary Press,
an imprint of Parallax Publishing,
as *The Reincarnationist Papers* by D. Eric Maikranz,
copyright © 2008 by D. Eric Maikranz

Printed in the United States of America

ISBN 978-1-0941-5495-4
Fiction / General

1 3 5 7 9 10 8 6 4 2

CIP data for this book is available
from the Library of Congress

Blackstone Publishing
31 Mistletoe Rd.
Ashland, OR 97520

www.BlackstonePublishing.com

AUTHOR'S EXPLANATORY NOTE

This manuscript came into my possession while living in Rome at the turn of the millennium. I noticed the three plain notebooks in an antique shop on the medieval Via dei Coronari, just off Piazza Navona. At the time I was conducting research for my first book, *Insider's Rome*, a travel guide to some of the city's more obscure but interesting sites. The notebooks seemed out of place in an antique store, weathered but not quite old enough. Idly picking up the first notebook, I was surprised to find it filled with Cyrillic handwriting. Being a Russian speaker, the pages intrigued me and I purchased them for a meager twenty thousand lire, about ten dollars US, at that time.

Despite lengthy efforts, I could not fully translate the text of the notebooks and eventually determined that they were Serbian, Bulgarian, or Ukrainian, but definitely not Russian.

Following a hunch, I first went to the Bulgarian Embassy on Via Pietro Rubens in Rome. I struck up a conversation with a receptionist, and she confirmed the handwriting was Bulgarian.

Intrigued by the first few pages, she agreed to help me translate it. Over the summer, Marina Lizhiva and I set to work. She translated aloud to my typing accompaniment. We became enthralled as the story unfolded in those summer evenings in my apartment on Caio Mario near the Vatican. When the translation was finished, I set to work to verify what I could of Evan's claim. That research is detailed as footnotes to the text, the only editorial work required after translation.

D. Eric Maikranz

FIRST NOTEBOOK

"As the stars looked to me when I was a shepherd in Assyria, they look to me now a New Englander."

Henry David Thoreau, 1853

1

The noose looked ridiculous. Fashioned from a braided extension cord, it was likely too stiff to be an effective neck breaker anyway, and I would end up strangling in a flailing, pantomimed panic. The asymmetrical loop at the end hung off to the right like an elongated number six, and its bright-orange color lent a circus air to the entire endeavor. Would it even hold my weight, wrapped around the cheap light fixture like it was?

It's easy to write about it now, that I'd often thought about killing myself, that I'd thought specifically about how I might do it: drowning, overdose, asphyxiation—immolation is a personal favorite. I've even talked about the virtues and pitfalls of different methods with strangers on the bus.

"Why would you do such a thing?" was always a popular response. But I think that is the wrong way to look at it. I've always thought the better question was "Why *not* do such a thing?"

"What prevents *you* from doing such a thing? Do you like it here that much? Are you in love? Do people depend on you being here? Did it never occur to you? Are you afraid?"

I am not afraid.

If you knew you would come back. If you knew you would live again, not just believed it, but knew it, why would you not do such a thing?

But I didn't put my neck into that noose, not out of fear, but out of courtesy really, because this place, this type of desperate end would be too horrible to remember. That's the trouble with having a perfect memory. The benefit is that you remember everything that has ever happened to you. The drawback is that you can never forget anything that has ever happened to you. The former imparts wisdom, but the latter robs you of hope. I decided to write down this story with the certainty that I will look on it again with different eyes in a different time and remember who I'd been.

I LEFT MINNESOTA THREE YEARS AGO because I started to remember. I left to find myself, only to find myself here, in Los Angeles. Nobody's exactly what they seem in LA. Everyone has an ulterior motive for leading their everyday lives. No one's just a doctor, or a student, or a salesman. Instead, they're a doctor and an art collector, a student with an audition next week, a salesman with a screenplay. In this place, more than any other I've found, there is anonymity in being more than you seem. And that, more than anything else, explains why I landed here.

It was still in the low nineties outside when I left for the club. When it's hot at night and there's no wind, all of downtown LA's visceral smells hang thick in the air, assaulting as you pass. But still, it felt good to be outside, anywhere but in that room.

I'd been cooped up in my room for three days straight, knowing the management wouldn't put a padlock on the outside of the door if there was still someone inside. I had lived, if you can call it that, in the Iowa Hotel[1] for five months and every time I was

---

1. The Iowa Hotel stands at the corner of East Seventh and Ceres.

even a day late with the weekly rent, those bastards put that same blue, spray-painted padlock on my door. If you didn't pay the rent by the end of that week, they would remove the lock along with all your possessions. That hadn't happened to me yet but was only four days away. Leo, the manager, was already scurrying through the drawer in search of the blue lock when I passed by the front desk on my way out.

There was a line outside the Necropolis Club. It seemed there was always a line. Thankfully, the doorman let me in without waiting. I was supposed to meet Martin at midnight; it was ten forty-five when I arrived.

The once-quiet Necropolis had been my bar of choice for the past year, but with one write-up in the *LA Weekly*,[2] the amateurs started pouring in from as far away as Simi Valley and Chino. But for all its newfound popularity, the bar itself hadn't changed. The Egyptian-themed club sat in an old movie theater, and all they did to modernize it was to remove the seats, level the floor, put bars along the front and back walls, and build a stage in front of the silver movie screen, which showed vintage films behind the bands. The bar tops along each wall were lit by blue-white neon underneath thick, frosted glass, making it look as if they served nothing but iridescent blue liquors to the patrons. The walls had been stripped clean, painted black, and covered in twenty-foot-tall, white bas-relief portraits of strange-looking Egyptian gods.

"Hello, Evan," a familiar voice said from behind the bar.

"Henry," I said, smiling at him as I took the last empty seat at the back bar.

"What can I get for you?"

"Give me a beer."

2. The *LA Weekly* is an alternative local paper with club listings.

"That'll be two bucks," he said, nodding to someone holding up an empty glass at the other end of the bar.

I had less than a dollar on me. "Run me a tab, will you, Henry? I'm going be here for a while," I said, lighting a cigarette. Henry smiled and went down toward the man with the glass.

By midnight the place was buzzing. The second band of the night took the stage while an angry Godzilla silently destroyed 1958 Tokyo on the screen behind them. The dance floor seethed with motion that appeared in stop frames from the overhead strobe lights. I could see the door from my seat at the back bar. The doorman was still letting people in at twelve thirty.

I had given Martin directions to the Necropolis and told him to be there early because of the increasing crowds; told him to mention my name and to tip the man at the door. I told him to look for a six-foot-tall, twenty-one-year-old white man with blue eyes and short, straight blond hair wearing a black shirt. Looking around now, there were three dozen of us matching that description. Martin had started to describe himself over the pay phone, but I told him I would know who he was; I would, and he wasn't there.

Henry came back with another beer in hand. "Here you go," he said, placing the glass on a fresh napkin. "Hey, check out the mark." He pointed over my shoulder into the crowd toward a middle-aged balding man in a camel hair sport coat and cream-colored khakis. He was apologizing as he made his way through the crowd.

"Oh," I chuckled, "he's with me."

"Yeah right," said Henry, turning away.

I walked straight up to Martin.

"Evan?" he asked, gasping, a dazed look on his face.

"Yes, Martin, you're late."

"I know. I had trouble at the door."

I looked him up and down, from his balding head to his penny loafers. "I can't imagine why."

"This place is different all right, just like you said. Pretty cool. Why did you have me meet you here?" he asked.

"Because if you were a cop, a wire would be useless in a place like this," I shouted as I reached inside his sport coat to run my hand over the sweater vest, feeling for a recording device. "Right?" He squirmed at my touch.

He regained his composure and ran a comforting hand over his lapels as I took my seat again. "Is this an old movie theater?" he asked.

"Yes. How did you hear about me again?" I took a long draw off my beer.

"Preston. He said you could help me."

I nodded.

"Can you help me?" he asked, raising his eyebrows in an attempt to solicit a response.

"Yes, I can. Did you bring the money?"

He reached inside his sport coat and produced a white unsealed envelope which he placed on the luminescent bar next to my beer. "I'm glad to get rid of it. I get nervous carrying around that kind of cash on this end of town."

I didn't acknowledge his remark as I looked at the envelope. It lay on the frosted glass, half an inch thick. I picked it up carefully, as if it might break. Fanning through it, I found twenty-five one-hundred-dollar bills, a handwritten address, and a key. "I get the other half when it's done."

"Yes, I know. Preston told me," he said.

Henry came over again and shot me a curious look, then sized up Martin. "Another?"

I nodded.

"And what'll you have, Dad?" Henry asked sarcastically.

Martin looked at me. "What, is he making fun of me?"

I shook my head and stifled a grin.

"I would like a white wine, please."

Henry grunted and grabbed a fresh glass.

"So how do you want it done?" I asked Martin.

He hunched over instinctively and leaned close to me. "Well, it's got to look like an accident or it's just no good."

"Besides that," I said, dismissing his comment, "is there anything else I need to know?"

"The key is to the alley entrance, it's a heavy steel door. You can't miss it."

"Are there any windows?"

"Yes, on the second floor, but there are none on the first floor, they were bricked up years ago."

I smiled and grabbed the fresh beer. "It'll be done in a week. Meet me here again, at midnight, the Saturday after it's done," I said, folding the thick envelope of cash into my front pants pocket.

"Are we finished, then?"

I looked at him sideways. "No," I said sternly. "We are finished after we meet again."

"Okay then, until we meet again." He held up his wine glass to make a toast.

I clinked my glass against his and drank deeply, letting the cold beer calm the excitement I felt at being flush with cash again. He gathered himself, shook my hand, and nodded a curt good-bye. He took a first step away, but I grabbed his shoulder before he could go and whispered in his ear. "Make certain you're insured," I said, unsuccessfully trying to suppress a laugh.

He smirked, unamused, and walked away quickly as though he didn't want to acknowledge his involvement. They're always like that the first time.

"Who was that?" asked Henry.

"Not sure really, let's find out," I said, holding up his eel-skin wallet. I fished out the driver's license. "Martin Shelby, it says."

"Nice pull," he beamed. "Are you working again?"

"Yes, a new job."

"Why did you lift the wallet? Wasn't there enough money in the envelope? Hell, I saw it. It was that thick." Henry held his index finger and thumb an inch apart.

I reached up, placed my hand on his, and adjusted his measurement by half. "*That* thick. And no, it's not the money. See, this guy only has eight bucks in here, but the rest of this stuff might come in handy."

I pulled the eight dollars out of the billfold before I put it in my pocket and retrieved my lighter and cigarettes. "Henry, Mr. Shelby would like to buy me another beer."

"Whatever Mr. Shelby wants," he said, replacing my glass.

"I might need your help in a couple of days. The usual stuff at the usual rate. You up for it?"

"For you, man, always. Besides, I could use the money. Just call me when you're ready. Another drink?"

I reached into my pocket, grabbed the envelope, pulled out the handwritten address, and unfolded it. "No, this is my last one. I'm going to take a walk."

GARBAGE AND BROKEN WINDOW GLASS covered the sidewalks in Martin's warehouse neighborhood. Only one in four buildings looked occupied. I counted down the numbers on the transoms and door frames of the passing buildings: 2678, 2674, 2670. Martin's building was brick and had been painted, the last time in gray. It stood two stories high, with four tall, narrow, unbroken windows running along the street side of the second floor. The two large picture windows in the front of the second floor had long been boarded over with plywood that had turned the same color gray as the paint from the assailing smog-soiled rain. A lonely floodlight at the back of an occupied warehouse halfway down the alley cast long shadows at the rear of the building. The door Martin had mentioned was large, four feet wide, eight feet high, and made of metal with riveted steel straps running horizontally across it. It looked more at home in a prison than it did on a warehouse.

I looked around and picked up a discarded newspaper. Folding it so that it fit the inside contours of my left hand, I pulled out the key with my right. I placed my hand on the large iron door handle, being careful to keep the newspaper in place around it so that I left no fingerprints, and gently placed the key into the dead bolt housing. It turned with ease and made no sound as it unlocked.

The poor lighting from the alley penetrated only a few steps inside. A dim glow from the second floor windows illuminated an old wooden stairway leading up along the back wall. I took out my vintage Russian cigarette lighter, slapped it three times against my hand, and lit it. The small flame threw sparse light around the back room and up the stairwell to the rafters of the second floor. To the left was an open door to a dingy bathroom. Directly in front of me, the ground floor opened up into a dark expanse.

I stepped into the main room on the first floor, careful not to overstep the small circle of illumination the lighter provided. The ceiling was a cross-hatched pattern of floor joists, cross beams, and electrical conduits, and no sprinkler system. The ground floor was a concrete pad painted battleship gray like the outside brick. Eight roughly hewn square wooden posts supported the weight of the second floor. There was no sign of light or life anywhere as I retraced my footsteps to the staircase in the back.

Decades of footfalls had worn the rough-cut stairs smooth in the centers. I climbed into brighter light with each step. The tall windows I had seen from the sidewalk opened to the streetlights on one side, projecting long rectangles of light onto the hardwood floor. I walked along the wall next to the side street, checking each window in vain with a newspaper-covered hand to see if it would open. The gray paint on the outside bricks ran wildly over the wooden window frames, locking them tight. The ceiling looked exactly like the one below, with no sprinkler system in place. I turned away from the wall and surveyed the second floor. "It's going to have to start up here," I said to the awakening voices in my head. "Let's figure out how to burn this place."

2

Holding the steps together in my head, I practiced and executed this latest arson job over and over as I walked back toward downtown. The sun lurked just below the horizon as I reached the Iowa Hotel. I pushed open the front door and walked into the empty lobby, realizing I had never seen it in the early morning. Usually, it was crowded with broken men sitting on broken furniture. The black-and-white television mounted in the upper corner of the room was off for the first time in memory, and the threadbare couches by the counter looked even more so without occupants. The lobby looked strangely peaceful, like a leftover scene in a run-down theater long after the actors had walked off. I quietly walked over to the vacant front desk and enjoyed the silence for a few moments before repeatedly pounding the bell on the counter, sending shocking waves of unrelenting noise through the dirty brown curtain into the manager's room beyond. I continued striking it three times a second like a fire alarm until that familiar bald head peered around the curtain.

"Good morning, Leo," I bellowed. "Take the fucking lock off my door. I'm going to pay the rent."

The grubby manager emerged from behind the curtain,

picked up the small dome-shaped bell, and threw it past my head into the empty lobby with a motion so sudden and unexpected that I didn't have time to flinch at its proximity. It landed at the base of the far wall with a combination of muted rings and thuds.

"Give me the money," he said in a gravelly voice.

I pulled two bills out of my pocket and placed them on the clean spot on the counter where the bell had been. "That's for this week and next week."

He picked up the pair of hundred-dollar bills the same way he'd picked up the bell, and I half expected him to throw them at my head. Instead, he produced his receipt book and began scribbling.

He walked to the stairway leading to the second-floor rooms as he searched for the blue key on his oversized key ring. He turned to face me after he had unlocked my room, but kept his narrow, bloodshot eyes fixed on my kneecaps. "Don't ever fucking touch that bell again." Each of his words hit me squarely in the chest like a stone.

I didn't say anything as he walked past me back down the hall. I stepped inside and went straight to sleep.

I DIDN'T KNOW WHY I STAYED AT THE IOWA. I didn't know where I was supposed to be going or why I wasn't going there. Each day in that room passed into the next without reason or purpose, and I found myself wondering more and more often if I shouldn't just step off and start fresh again. The stiff orange noose was still hanging from the ceiling lamp, still willing. I wondered if it would be different next time, if I could forget that I can remember.

I got up and looked out my window onto the dark street below. The clock at the bank across the street flashed nine thirty.

It has to be p.m., it's dark outside, I thought as I rummaged through the English and Bulgarian newspapers on the kitchen counter, looking for the Los Angeles master bus schedule. I sat on the bed and planned my getaway from the warehouse back to the club as I flipped through the coffee-stained booklet, cross-examining routes.

The hotel lobby was full of men when I went down to use the phone. Leo sat on a stool behind the counter and strained his eyes to see the snowy television screen hanging in the corner. Red, Murphy, Cotton, and a fresh old guy were playing gin at a card table set up behind one of the couches.

"Hey, kid, did ya scrape up enough money for rent?" Red shouted across the lobby. He chuckled to himself as he went back to his conversation.

The Iowa hadn't been a hotel in the conventional sense in ages. It was the kind of place that draws two types of men: those who don't feel comfortable making plans so they live week to week, and those who stop here temporarily on their way to the street. I hoped I was in the first group.

I stepped over to the pay phone and dialed the club.

"Henry!" I shouted over the background noise on his end. "It's Evan. Hey, let's do this thing tomorrow."

LOUD KNOCKING WOKE ME FROM A DEAD SLEEP. I answered the door, rubbing at my eyes.

"Good morning, sunshine!" said Henry, chuckling.

I motioned for him to come in.

"Charming. Is that a noose?" he asked sarcastically.

"No, it's just how they decorate here," I said behind the bathroom door, trying to think up something. "It's a new motivational tool the city is installing in these Seventh Avenue flophouses."

Henry looked around. The room was cleaner than usual. "Man, you really need to do something about this place. This is like county jail—no pictures, no art, no amenities, just books, clothes, bed . . . and a noose. Why don't you throw up some curtains at least? Do you know what this place needs? Plants, something green and alive."

"Are you finished?" I asked, annoyed. "Let's go. Did you bring the truck?"

Henry nodded. "Can you read this?" he asked, picking up a Bulgarian paper filled with strange Cyrillic letters from the table.

"Yes." I locked the door behind us. He was right about the room, and it bothered me. There was no reason to live like this, in a place like this, other than habit. But if I had better habits, I'd just have to get a regular job to support them. Besides, what's the point in a better standard of living if you're not standard?

When we reached his white pickup truck, I hesitated to open the passenger door and looked at him through the open windows. "Don't worry about the noose. I put it up just to mess with the management."

"Where to?"

"Sierra Chemical Company near Riverside and the 2.[3] I'll show you."

HENRY MADE THE TURN INTO THE PARKING LOT of the chemical store and left the motor running. "So do you just go in and buy it, or what?"

"Yeah, they sell chemicals here, it's no big deal. They don't know what it's going to be used for."

I had no trouble buying the industrial alcohol and emerged minutes later with a white five-gallon can.

"That was quick," Henry said.

"Quick and easy. Let's go."

Henry pulled into the alley and stopped by the door of Shelby's warehouse. "Take off after I unload the stuff, and come back

---

3. Evan mentions he got his supplies from Sierra Chemical Co. He probably means Sierra Color and Chemical on North Coolidge Ave.

in an hour. I'll leave the door open if I'm ready to go. If it's not open, come back in another hour. It shouldn't take any longer than that." I put on a pair of black rubber gloves and jumped out of the cab of the truck. In less than fifteen seconds, I had opened the warehouse door, unloaded the truck, and closed the door behind me.

My heart raced, and I sat for a moment on the steps to keep my legs from shaking. There was more light now, and I could easily see up the stairs. I pulled out a cigarette and smoked it down to the end. I crushed out the remainder and placed it in my pocket before unwrapping the roller pan and mop head. *You're not thinking clearly, you should have removed these wrappers before-hand. Concentrate.*

I placed the clear plastic in a pile by the back door so I wouldn't—*couldn't*—forget them. *Concentrate.* I carried the equipment up the stairs in one trip. The temperature was in the midnineties again outside and seemed to rise by five degrees inside with each stair I climbed. The second floor looked smaller now in the brighter light of day, and I had completely missed two small boxes next to the back support post in the darkness of two nights ago. The heat upstairs was stifling.

I opened the container of alcohol, filled the paint roller pan, and let the mop head drink its fill before beginning to methodically coat the floor, starting in the front corner opposite of the stair-well. The methanol went on easily in thin coats that dried into the thirsty wooden floorboards. I worked rapidly, staying away from the uncurtained windows by making longer strokes from the sides.

My first coat stopped at an imaginary diagonal line between the last window on the far wall and the top of the stairs. I had three of the original gallons left when the first coat was finished. My shirt was soaked through with sweat, and the biting smell of the alcohol hung in the stagnant air of the second floor.

The vertical support beams were next. The rough, unfinished posts easily drank two coats apiece. I set the mop down and took out my lighter and a cigarette in consolation to my frayed nerves. I slapped the lighter twice, then thought better than to light it in the alcohol-charged air of the upstairs.

The air in the downstairs bathroom was refreshingly cool. I lit a cigarette and barely recognized my own reflection in the dirt-streaked mirror. My blond hair appeared brown and clung to my sweaty forehead in narrow points. I looked pale even in the dim light of downstairs. I drew long on the cigarette and followed it in with a deep breath. The red end of the cigarette highlighted my face in the mirror. I moved closer so that I could see myself clearly through the grime.

"This is the worst of it," I said out loud. "It's almost over. Concentrate." I took the cigarette from my mouth with black-gloved fingers and blew the smoke at my reflection as I spoke. "See you soon, old friends."

HENRY SCREECHED HIS PICKUP TO A STOP, and I threw the steel door open, tossed the stuff in the back, and jumped in the cab.

"Step on it, let's get out of here," I said, slamming the door closed.

He looked at me with a sense of urgency on his face. "Why, is it gonna blow?"

"No, it's not gonna blow. Let's just get away from here." Sticking my head out the window, I ran ungloved fingers through my hair in an attempt to dry it. I looked back at the building as we drove off. "Everything is set."

Halfway back to the Iowa Hotel, I pulled out two hundred dollars and gave it to Henry.

"What's the extra fifty for?"

"My alibi for tomorrow night."

"Cool. You were there all night."

"I'm going to come by tomorrow night and sneak out early so I can be back by last call and get a ride home with you."

He pulled up in front of the hotel. "Like I told the man, you were there all night. I think this is your stop."

"Let's hope the man doesn't ask. Thanks for the help today."

"Thanks for paying me. See you tomorrow."

I WAITED UNTIL HENRY HAD GONE around the corner before I turned my pocket inside out and dumped the dozen or so inch-long cigarette butts onto the sidewalk. I crossed the street and walked through the hotel lobby and up to my room without speaking to anyone.

The perspiration had dried out of the shirt, and it clung to my chest like shrink-wrap. I peeled it off and took it into the cool shower with me to try to rinse some of the sweat out of it. I got out of the shower without drying off, letting the water drops evaporate in an attempt to cool myself.

Henry was right; this place was becoming more and more like a prison cell every day, and I was becoming a model prisoner, never banging my cup on the bars or burning toilet paper in protest against my condition, but accepting it, more and more every day. I felt like this room was beating me the same way it must have beaten the others who'd lived here before. I stepped around the noose and opened the window, letting the sounds of the street fill my silent cell.

3

Empty liquor bottles littered the alley behind the hotel. I walked the alleys on my way to the club and found four intact bottles and four stones before stopping at a liquor store for my final items: a large bottle of cheap vodka and two packs of generic cigarettes. I put the full bottle in my rucksack next to the empties and put the generics in my jacket pocket.

There was already a short line in front of the bar when I turned the corner. I walked to the head of the line and nodded to the doorman as I went inside and waited for Henry.

"What do you want?" Henry asked as he stepped behind his bar.

"A beer and a shot of Old Grandad."

Henry raised his eyebrows, "Drinking with Grandad, nice. We're hitting the ground running tonight, aren't we?" he said, reaching for the bottle of brown whiskey behind the bar.

I put a cigarette in my mouth and waited for him to light it. "Do me a favor, would ya? Take my backpack and put it behind the bar."

"Sure," he said, striking a match. "I'll run a tab for you too. I thought we'd close it out at about one thirty or so."

"Timestamps. Good idea."

"Yep, you'll be here all night. I'll talk to you in a while. I've got to clean this place up before it gets packed."

He filled the sink and started to work on the leftover glasses from last night. I tilted the beer glass and drank, holding the bitterness in my mouth for an instant before swallowing. The blue-white light from underneath made the brown whiskey look like green swamp water. I studied it for a few moments before downing the shot in one quick motion. Its warmth slid down my throat as I clinked the small glass on the glass top of the bar.

"Another?" he asked, not looking away from the soapy water.

"Yes," I said in a flat voice. "You better keep those coming for a while."

I drank at a steady pace, and Henry immediately refilled my glass no matter how busy he was. By ten o'clock I was feeling the effects and slowed my pace. He came over, bottle in hand, as soon as I placed my glass on the bar again.

Henry leaned on the bar and placed his head close to mine. "Hey, I've set 'em up like this for you quite a few times now and I was always curious about why you're so careful in the planning only to get blasted the night you actually do it."

I looked up at him from the shot glass full of green whiskey and measured my response, knowing that I would have to remember it. "Courage."

He looked at me for a long time before he spoke, as though he were trying to discern the real reason. "I could see that," he said finally. "Clouds your judgment enough to do it, huh?"

"Something like that," I said before turning to catch a view of the band that was tuning up below a lab-coated Vincent Price. "Hand me my gear, I've got to go."

"This way," Henry said, leading me behind a black curtain into the storage room. "Go out this door. I'll leave it propped open for you until we close."

I quickly walked to the bus stop at the side street and waited on the empty bench for the number thirty-seven to come. I caught myself tapping my foot in nervous expectation and placed both feet flat on the sidewalk to stop them. I closed my eyes and visualized the flames licking at the support posts.

The bus stopped in front of me, and I entered, handing the fare to the female driver without making eye contact. I walked back and took a seat across from the rear door as the bus left the curb. There were six other people on board.

My foot started tapping again, and I could feel the tension rising inside my chest. I wanted to yell out at the top of my lungs what I was about to do. I wanted to shock these six people into my reality. I was about to commune with who I had been, but I really wanted to commune with them, with anyone. I stared at each one in turn, my foot hammering now. They didn't care. They just sat there, ignorant, distant, dead.

I hadn't told anyone the truth about myself since I'd left home. I'd thought about telling several friends and lovers along the way, but always held back in the end, and it always seemed to drive them away. I can't lie to myself, I've missed having someone close to me through these three years, someone who could know me. I've almost told Henry several times, but like all the rest, I chose to keep him in the dark, but keep him around nonetheless, as long as I could. I have always preferred an ignorant friend to an enlightened, yet unbelieving, confidant. I had felt like this many times since I left Minnesota; I had felt like screaming at strangers because I didn't have the courage to hazard a friendship. But somehow I have always resisted attacking them with my story. I have resisted telling them that all penitent sinners and good little boys don't go to heaven when they die; sometimes they go to LA. I've resisted telling them that no one up there gives a damn if they've been naughty or nice anyway. I've resisted screaming at them to quit their dreary jobs and change their dreary lives because if they don't remember, then this is all they'll ever get. I never tell them because I want to keep up the facade, for my own sake, so that I might still pretend to be like them. In the end, I always take my facade home and tell myself the stories again just to make sure I haven't forgotten them. I forget nothing.

THEY MUST HAVE ALL TIRED OF ME resisting temptation because the bus was empty when it reached my stop. The back doors opened, and I stepped onto the curb of the dark and deserted LA street without looking in the driver's direction. The bus pulled away and disappeared around the corner, taking all signs of life with it. I've always felt at home in this type of desolation, as though these abandoned neighborhoods beckoned me to release them from their shame and solitude.

The lone light down the alley behind the warehouse was still on and shone just brightly enough for me to find the key. I put on the gloves, took off the backpack, and stepped inside. A faint air of solvent crept down from the second floor.

I sat the rucksack at the base of the stairs, removed both packs of generic cigarettes, and opened them, taking out four from the full flavor pack and two from the mild. I put the six cigarettes in my mouth, primed the lighter, and lit all of them at once, being careful not to draw the concentrated smoke into my lungs. The six burning tips glowed bright red in the darkness. I left the lighter burning and placed it on its flat base on the fourth step, then sat each cigarette one by one next to the lighter with their lit ends hanging over the edge of the step so they could burn down to their filters. When they burned as far as they would go, I crushed out each one on the gray-painted floor of the back room. I imagined the arson inspector walking through the charred remains as I removed two bottles and tossed them onto the concrete floor of the back room. The wine bottle broke, and the gin bottle bounced and landed next to the bathroom door.

I then picked up the lighter, not disturbing the flame, and went upstairs to repeat the same process with the remaining cigarettes. I placed the two black folding chairs across from each other near my point of origin in front of the center post. Each time I crushed one out on the methanol saturated floor, I had to be careful to keep my rubber-soled shoe on it long enough to keep it from igniting. Sitting in the chair facing the lit windows, I took the last three bottles out of the rucksack, setting the full one next to the burning lighter.

The light from the flame refracted through the liter bottle of vodka and threw several small spectrums of color across the polished floor. I picked up the bottle, turned it back and forth in front of the flame, and watched the tiny rainbows as they danced around the dark room. Cracking the seal, I removed the plastic cap and placed the open mouth next to my own, letting the quick liquid race over my tongue and down my throat, burning as it went. I gritted my teeth before taking a second swallow, then a third. Standing up, I held the bottle by its base and threw long lines of vodka across the floor toward the front of the building. Three, four, five long arcs of liquid splashed to the floor like fingers reaching out from where I stood. With the last of the bottle, I carefully connected all the near ends of the streaks back to my point of origin. When the bottle was empty, I placed it next to the two others and kicked them across the room. I moved the chair back and got down on all fours next to the puddle, then took the still burning lighter down from the other chair in my left hand and with a gloved forefinger drew a line of wet vodka out of the center. After several strokes, I had stretched it out a full two feet. It was no more than an inch wide but was as deep as the puddle itself. I switched the lighter to my right hand and held the flame inches above the end of the narrow line, then stopped and studied the lighter in my hand for a moment. Its strange Cyrillic letters and red starburst background were easily visible by its own light. My eyes looked at the small flame and defocused as it began to dance in my shaking hand.

DURING MY JUNIOR YEAR IN HIGH SCHOOL, I knew that I was different, it just took me a while to understand how. My teachers would often catch me daydreaming in class. They reprimanded me constantly for this, but, as their reports later stated, it had little effect. I would "check out" without warning or pattern. These *spells*, as they were termed, came alone and in connected series, some lasted only a second, and others as long as several minutes. At the time, I didn't know where I went. The sensation could best be described as watching a movie. At the time I wouldn't have called it remembering, for how could someone remember something that had never happened to them?

They came on subtly at first, appearing as ten- or twenty-minute short features, but by the end of that year they were multihour epics that ran constantly and crowded normal thoughts out of my teenage head. Several of them played over and over, while others played only once then went back out of circulation, but after a while, all of them, short and long, began to share something in common, and it frightened me.

The first scenes were panoramic. They were pastoral, peaceful, even boring at times. Only later was there action, along with strange people coming on and going off camera, often in many different scenes. Oddly, there was no main character, no main focus to bring these strange people together. Only when they began triggering emotional responses consistent with the visual, auditory, and tactile sensations I saw, did it start to make sense to me. All the scenes were set around a central character, an unseen actor that starred from behind the camera in every scene. After sentience, came thoughts, reasoning, and finally identity. He was the focus, everyone interacted with him, everything happened to him, and this meant everything happened vicariously to me because of this strange first-person point of view.

In time, with practice, I was able to summon these movies at will, experiencing them over and over in an attempt to form a timeline. I found, after a while, the more often I viewed a particular clip, the more intimate I became with it and the more confidence I had to emulate the actions I was empathically experiencing in my head.

This unseen actor was a farmer, a soldier, and a prisoner. Eventually I learned every detail about this man, down to his favorite brand of cigarettes, and I became adept at all these things he could do, but that other alphabet came first.

In the fall of that year, I began to write and understand the strange language I'd seen him use. The *N*s were backward, as were the *R*s, and in addition to several new letters, several familiar ones were not used. I practiced for a full year before I could functionally read and write it without having to slip back into the past of the man who haunted me. In time, I came to know his name, Vasili Blagavich Arda.

The story of my miraculous new ability to read and write in what I had now identified as Bulgarian, was more difficult to prove to my parents.

I wrote page after page of text and read aloud to them from Bulgarian books I'd sent for from the University of Minnesota, but all to little more than idle fancy. They were amused at my claim when I first made it, but when I told them it would make sense to any other Bulgarian who read it, they became concerned. When I told them that I knew the language from another man's memories, they became annoyed, and when I told them that I remembered another life in another land in another time with another family, they became angry, especially my father.

I wanted so badly to tell them, to tell anyone and have them understand, but the more I told them about my memories, the angrier they became, until I finally fell into a more comfortable silence. That was the last chance I gave anyone to understand me.

With only two months of high school to go, I told them I was leaving and wouldn't be back. After all the other shocks I had given them, this one went almost unnoticed. Almost.

When they accepted that I was really going, my father attempted a half-hearted reconciliation, and my mother gave me the lighter. She must have recognized some of the same Russian Cyrillic letters on its worn surface and thought it was the same as the Bulgarian letters I'd shown her. Two nights before I left, she pressed it into my hand after supper. She didn't say anything when she gave it to me. Instead, she held me tightly, stroking my blond hair as she rocked us both back and forth at the table. I went up to my room, packed my things, and cried all night.

The animosity between my parents and I had ended, but the new memories unfortunately did not, and the next night, my last night there, I burned the barn down with my new lighter.

WHEN MY EYES REFOCUSED IN SHELBY'S WAREHOUSE, the lighter was shaking, still inches above the line of vodka. *Concentrate.* I drew in a lungful of smoke from the cigarette in the corner of my mouth and blew it at my shaking right hand like a shaman exorcising a demon. I moved my head down next to the floorboards in order to watch the miracle up close. The summoning is always the most exciting part. People carry flame around and use it every day, but only a few ever realize its potential to consume and rage like a monster.

I slowly moved the lighter closer to the edge of the narrow, wet trail of vodka. I love to summon the monster. The monster that brings the truth back over bridges from the past, the monster that eats little boys, the monster that brings deliverance. I moved the lighter even closer, beckoning it until it came. When the distance to the floor was close enough not to cause injury, the little flickering sprite in my hand leaped from the lighter to the floor and began to run along the length of the inch-wide strip. It had been yellow in my hand but turned blue with a faint yellow outline when it hit the floor and started running. It reached the large puddle and flashed a brilliant blue, lighting up the entire second floor before running silently down each of the long fingers. The room began to fill with light, it was coming.

I got to my feet for a better look at it. It ran out to the end of each finger and hesitated, still flashing brilliant electric blue around the room. Then slowly, so slowly I almost couldn't see it, it began to creep outside the lines of vodka onto the methanol-coated floorboards. I could feel it coming to life. The flames burned in blue and violet as they consumed the vodka and caught on the accelerant. It spread slower than I had anticipated, but it was spreading. And then, like a miracle, it was there in the room with me. The fire got up on its knees and grabbed hold of the center post next to the point of origin. The tiny flames licked at the wood and inched ever upward, turning orange as they began to consume the wood of the post. Fire can do its work once it gets up on its feet and starts moving around. I found this out the first time I summoned it.

MY LAST WEEK IN MINNESOTA, another disembodied memory hit me. It was stronger than all the others and was different in that it couldn't be controlled. It happened in Macon, Georgia, in the 1970s. He was a young boy named Bobby Lynn Murray. I didn't inherit many memories from Bobby, and this one, seen through a child's eyes, is the strongest.

I watched the small flames climb the post all the way to the top where it met the rafters. I looked at its progress around the room and realized I was the ghost in here; this was for young Bobby.

He was amazingly industrious for a boy of six, and on that last day he built a tower out of his wooden toys that was taller than he was. The tower stood in the corner of his small room by the window. Its skeleton was made of brightly painted thin wooden rods, joined by round wooden wheels with drilled holes. It had taken him all day to build it. He returned to his room after supper to play with it and reorganize the sticks on the sides so all the colors matched. His mother, Judith, came in at eight o'clock to put him to bed, against his protests. He had wanted to stay up and build his tower even higher. He lay in bed looking over at it, wondering if he would have to move it outside to make it as tall as he wanted to.

His tower stood silhouetted in front of the curtains. A street light beyond his bedroom window shined every night. Bobby got up and walked over to the tower to reinspect it in the dim light. There were two cords that opened and closed the curtains, but the one within his reach only closed them tighter. He could see there was work to be done, but he couldn't tell which rods were which color, and construction couldn't continue unless it followed the same color code as the rest of the tower. Turning on the light never worked because somehow his mother always found out he wasn't in bed.

Bobby had seen his mother's new boyfriend, William, use matches as a light at night when they all traveled in the car to Atlanta. Bobby had taken a book of matches from the dashboard and kept them to use in case the comforting street light ever went out. He went to the footlocker at the end of the bed, opened the lid, and slid his small hand down one side and into the corner of the trunk until he found the paper matchbook. He walked back over to the tower, took a single match, and tried to strike it by imitating what Will had done. After several attempts, one sparked and lit. The red tip flashed and was completely consumed in a second. Bobby was too busy watching the process of the match burning to notice the light the flame gave off. He was fascinated by the flickering of the blue-and-orange flame and watched it change the blue-gray paper of the match into a blackened, shriveled, and twisted cinder. When it burned down to his small thumb and forefinger, he dropped it and put his scorched fingers in his mouth. The match went out before it hit the green carpeted floor.

He carefully lit another one, this time studying the colored rods on the floor. He picked up a yellow one and held it and the match close to the tower to check if he was on the yellow side. The flame miraculously jumped off of the match and onto a support rod in the tower. He stood there, puzzled at how this little sprite could jump on its own. The flame raced up the yellow rod, blistering then blackening its paint before jumping over the unfinished connecting wheel on its way to the next highest rod. Young Bobby stood there, hypnotized by the metamorphosis happening in front of him. In minutes, the entire skeleton as well as the edge of the curtains behind it were aflame. The polyester in the curtains dripped burning globs of plastic onto the carpet, igniting it. By the time the flames on the tower had died down, and Bobby noticed what was going on, it had spread to the wood paneling on the walls and ceiling surrounding the window.

THE MONSTER ALWAYS ACTS THE SAME whenever it is summoned. It had already moved out across the floor to the front wall and was on its way to the corners. I retreated back from the point of origin toward the top of the stairs. The flames had engulfed the center and forward posts and were halfway up the rear one. By the time I retreated, the yellow flames were three feet tall on the floor. The foot-thick rolling flames on the ceiling were bloodred and much cooler than the ones on the floor, due to lack of oxygen in the upper air.

Soon the color of the bottom ones would get darker, orange then red, and then just before it got drowsy and bored, I would free it.

I stepped farther back from the wall of flames and toward the window. The heat was becoming intense. My leather jacket helped to shield some of its attack. The fire crackled and popped as it took hold on the wood itself. Not much time left. The flames at the point of origin leaped higher than the surrounding ones and formed a symmetrical, volcano-shaped mountain that reached almost to the quiet flames of the ceiling. As the cone rose, it changed from yellow to orange to red at the top. Almost time.

My mouth hung open, and I drew the thin air in long gasps like a trapped miner. I unzipped the left pocket of the jacket and removed one of the baseball-sized stones I'd taken from the alley. The volcano slowly shrank back from the ceiling, taking the darker hues back down with it. Suspended in between the two layers of flame, a foot-thick band of gray smoke undulated softly. I was becoming drowsy and had to fight to keep my eyes open. I bent over at the waist and breathed deeply from the heavier air at knee level before straightening and throwing the stone at the tall window pane next to me.

The stone struck the surface and continued through normally, but the splintering glass exploded inward as the fresh oxygen was sucked inside. I turned away from the blast of air and flying glass. The monster roared angrily as we both breathed deeply, and I looked up in time to see that the stone I'd thrown had sent a ripple across the flames on the ceiling. The flames were still bloodred at the leading edge of the ripple, but were bright yellow and scrambling hungrily downward in its wake. The thick layer of gray smoke burst into turbulent swirls as it fed on the fresh air. In its changing shapes, I could see Bobby.

THE BOY STEPPED BACK toward the center of his bedroom. The burning carpet under the tower sent crackling flames racing through its fragile superstructure. The monster hissed as it ate at the thin veneer on the walls. Bobby watched his tower lean to the left and fall over after a few seconds.

"Mommy!" he shouted in response to the destruction of his work. "Mommy!" he cried out again as he ran toward the door only to find the top half of it already engulfed in yellow and orange. He stopped in his tracks and looked at it as it crawled down the door and the wall surrounding it. His young emotions went from anger to fear when he realized what was happening.

"Mommy! Mommy! Mommy!" Bobby screamed until he became winded in the thin air of the room. He stood there breathing heavily and watched the flames eat at the door, little yellow teeth taking small bites in front while the orange back teeth chewed violently. The heat pushed him away from the door, and he walked back to the footlocker at the end of the small bed.

It had spread across the ceiling and three walls but was only a quarter of the way across the floor. He sat down on the toy chest and fought to keep his eyes open against the smoke as his head began to swim.

"Mommy," he said softly. The word came out in a weak exhale, barely audible over the crackling of the paneling.

"Bobby!" shouted a voice beyond the door down the hall. "Bobby!" shouted his mother louder and closer to the closed door.

Bobby, breathing heavily, looked up in time to see the door-knob twist. In a motion that was too quick to see, the door flew inward and slammed against the flaming paneling of the rear wall. His mother, Judith, stood in the open doorway, framed in dark-orange flames, and she looked down curiously at her open hand where the doorknob had been a fraction of a second earlier. She raised her eyes in search of her son just as the monster raced toward the fresh air in long yellow tongues. The flames caught instantly on her threadbare blue-and-white cotton robe.

The intense heat pushed Bobby off his seat and onto the floor. He crawled under the bed to get relief and looked out after the flash subsided, only to see his mother's thrashing figure aflame in the doorway.

That was the last memory from Bobby.

THE ANGRY YELLOW FLAMES BOILED DOWN from the warehouse ceiling, knocking me to my knees. I ran a gloved hand over my hair to make sure it wasn't burning. It wasn't, but I kept the cool leather of the palm side of the glove on my scorched neck for a second to ease the pain.

I'd made a mistake. The burn on the floor was going exactly as planned, but I hadn't expected it to spread this far back on the ceiling so quickly. The bloodred flames had crept silently and unnoticed all the way across the ceiling, and setting the fire free had almost trapped me. The flames edged downward like a giant, oppressing hand.

I crawled on my hands and knees toward the top of the stairs and stood up only after I'd scrambled, headfirst, two-thirds of the way down. I stopped for a second to collect myself and to listen to the roaring above me. It sounded like a jet was landing on the second floor. I turned, ran down the stairs, and opened the deadbolt. The door opened quickly, and I was met by an onrush of garbage-fouled air. I left the door open and walked quickly down the alley and across the street, stopping beside the building that faced the burning warehouse. Two more windows had melted in the heat, and yellow flames boiled into the night sky. I turned away and stepped into the welcoming darkness of Los Angeles, leaving my monster raging inside the empty warehouse, still looking for the boy it once knew.

I was halfway down the alley when the spotlight hit me in the back. Turning around, I saw a police car parked at the end of the

THE REINCARNATIONIST PAPERS

alley behind me. I continued walking down the alley, stalking the elongated shadow in front of me. My heart raced, my mouth was dry, my neck hurt. *Calm down, they don't know it's me, they can't know it's me. Take it easy, keep walking. They'll question me, maybe take me in, but they can't put me at the scene except for* . . . I ran my still-gloved hand over the front pocket of my jeans and felt the outline of the key to the warehouse door. *Fuck, Fuck, Fuck!*

"Stop walking and turn around with your hands in the air!" called an authoritative voice over the cruiser's public-address system.

I took off the right glove and shoved it into my pocket after the key.

"Now, asshole!" shouted the voice.

I was three-quarters of the way down the alley when I took off running.

4

Yearning for the darkness once more, I turned the corner at the end of the alley and glanced over my shoulder to check the position of the police car. It was gone from the alley entrance, but a tall police officer, silhouetted by the burning warehouse, was already halfway down the alley running toward me. I missed a stride as I fished the key out of my pocket and threw it onto the roof of the building on the corner. My high-top sneakers made little noise as I ran, allowing me to hear the footfalls of the cop's hard-soled shoes behind me. He had gained slightly when I ditched the key but was slowly falling behind as we ran down the sidewalk past closed shops and empty storefronts.

I first heard the distant sirens when I took off running and finally saw their source as two white fire trucks raced up the street toward us. Their blaring prevented me from listening for the police cruiser or my pursuer's steps. The cop chasing me was still falling behind but had taken his pistol out. It jerked up and down in his right hand as he ran. He tried to shout something but stopped as the sirens closed on us. The lead engine was half a block away when it swerved to the right in anticipation of a left-hand turn at the cross street in front of us.

I took a long stride off the curb and onto the asphalt of the cross street, committing myself to beating the lead fire engine across the street. The white truck swept wide into its turn, committing itself to making the corner. The driver's eyes widened as they met mine, and his companion pulled feverishly at the air horn cord. The blast from the horn mounted in the middle of the grille hit me squarely in the left ear, and I lengthened my stride as the heavy chrome bumper neared to within inches of my leg.

I continued running in longer strides and looked back to see the tall cop tentatively cross the street after the second truck had passed. He saw me looking back at him and he leveled his semiautomatic pistol at me. "Stop, or I'll shoot!"

I ran on and measured a turn into the next alley behind a stone church. A shot rang out behind me, sending a chill down my spine.

"Stop now! Last warning!" He'd stopped running and stood still with his gun aimed at my back.

A few more feet and I'd be in the alley. My legs seemed to move in slow motion, and each stride seemed more difficult than the last. I veered sharply to the right, into the warm, welcoming darkness of the alley.

I felt it before I heard it, a sharp pain in the heel of my left foot, like someone had hit it with a baseball bat. The echo of the shot followed. The next stride brought my left foot forward, which collapsed as soon as my weight shifted onto it. I stuck out my arms to break my fall as I crashed into a low railing and flipped over it, falling down a flight of dark stairs to the garbage-covered landing of a basement door below street level.

My fall was broken by a foot-deep pile of old newspapers, boxes, and other trash. The pain in my foot was blinding. I placed my right hand on my heel and felt an inch-wide gap ripped into the rubber sole at the back of my sneaker. I could barely see my hand in front of my face in the shadows of the sunken stairwell, but I could feel that it was coated in warm, slick blood, a lot of blood.

I heard the police car stop at the end of the alley and I moved farther into the dark inside corner of the landing, pulling newspapers and other garbage up around me. I curled up under my camouflage and gnashed my teeth in silence against the pain. Car doors closed and two sets of hard-soled footsteps started down the alley.

"You didn't shoot him, did you?" a voice asked above me.

"No, I shot *at* him. I think I missed," answered the same voice that had shouted at me.

"Jesus, Willard, what were you thinking? He was just running."

"Running from a felony crime scene, you mean."

"We don't know that!"

"I know that. If he wasn't guilty, why was he running?"

"Great logic, Willard, just fucking great. Say, do you still have a day job in case this cop thing doesn't work out for you?"

"Just help me look for some blood or something, all right."

"You don't want to find this guy, at least not if he's shot."

"Just help me, will ya. He ran down this alley."

I cradled my heel with my right hand and thought invisible thoughts as I lay curled up underneath the garbage. The alcohol was wearing off, and I began to shake with fear and shock. It was all I could do to remain motionless and control myself at the same time. I tried adjusting my foot to ease the pain, but any movement I made, no matter how slight, made it worse.

I heard them pass over me and imagined them scouring the alley with flashlights and pistols drawn. My hands were slimy with blood.

"He's gone, you missed him. Let's get the hell out of here, I'm hungry."

"I bet you five bucks that fire turns out to be arson," said Willard.

They were walking back to the car and getting closer to me again.

"He got lucky," continued Willard.

"Him, lucky? Shit, if you'd have hit him, he'd have really been lucky. This is California, man, he'd have sued the department for millions. You got lucky, Willard."

"That's bullshit, it's arson. You'll see." They were right on top of me.

I peered upward through a crack in the garbage and saw the bright beam of his flashlight as it darted quickly over me then disappeared. My foot throbbed in time with my racing heartbeat. I felt lightheaded and desperately craved a cigarette. I heard their voices grow more distant over the sound of my own breathing, which now came in staccato huffs, along with violent shaking. Both car doors shut, but it was five long minutes before it drove away, five minutes of more bleeding and fearful shaking.

I poked only my head out at first, half expecting Officer Willard to be at the top of the stairs, waiting for me to give up the charade. I heard nothing but the usual sounds of the city at midnight, along with the distant sirens still at the fire. He wasn't at the top of the stairs. I looked around the dark stairwell as I gently removed the trash from on top of me. Fourteen concrete steps led up to street level. The back wall of rough-cut limestone blocks above me stretched high into the night sky. I had landed at the back door of a church. The door next to me felt like wood. The tall windows in the back wall of the church were made of stained glass and glowed faintly with green, red, and yellow from a dim light source inside.

I readjusted my position and grimaced as I sat on the concrete floor and leaned back against the steps. The throbbing ache in my foot was a tremor that rocked me with every heartbeat. I reached into my pocket and took out my cigarettes and lighter. The pack had been crushed when I fell, and I had to pull out five broken ones before I found one intact. I looked down at the shaking white cigarette as it flared red and noticed it was brown with blood on the ends. I left the lighter burning and looked down at my hands. They were covered in blood. Bending over slowly, I held the lighter next to my left foot. The bullet had torn through the rubber sole of the shoe and into the fleshy part of my heel. Blood dripped from the open wound onto the newspapers. I closed the lighter, closed my eyes, and leaned back again as I drew on the cigarette.

I reclined against the stairs with my smoke and thought about what my options were. I couldn't walk, I couldn't limp or even crawl. If I got help, I'd need to go to the hospital without a police report of when, where, and how I was shot. *I'm damn sure not going to bleed to death in a city of four million from a gunshot wound to the foot,* I thought as I gingerly fumbled around in the trash until I found an unbroken bottle. I grabbed it and began pounding rhythmically on the wooden door as hard as I could without bumping my foot. The solid wood absorbed most of the blows. I clenched my teeth as I put more force into each successive blow.

"Open up!" I shouted, stopping the blows only long enough for my words to carry. Minutes passed, and the bottle began to feel heavy in my hand as I continued to pound on the wood. The outline of the door started to blur, and my blows began to glance off irregularly as I fought to keep my bearings. I lost my balance, and the bottle slipped out of my hand, landing in the trash behind me. I slapped my empty hand against the wood several more times before turning over and resting my back against the door. I closed my eyes to control the tilting, spinning staircase. The thought wasn't that funny, but I couldn't keep from laughing. I thought about the scared priest huddled behind the door, about Henry watching for me at the back door of the Necropolis, and about what Officer Willard was eating just then.

I calmed myself down and got my laughter under control just before the door opened and gave way behind me. I opened my eyes, and everything had stopped spinning except me. I put my hand back to brace myself on where I thought the floor should have been but instead vaulted down another short flight of steps to the concrete floor of the church basement. My bloody left foot banged hard against a white-painted step and then caught my full weight at the bottom.

The bright lights inside seemed to dim the longer I screamed. When they went bright again, I was sitting on the floor bent over holding my left foot with both hands. Blood coated my hands and clothes. I had turned my foot slightly so I could see it when I felt the nudge of a cold gun barrel at the back of my head.

I froze, my foot still held at a painful angle. I couldn't see the gunman behind me. I was nudged again as I heard the hammer pull back. "Father?" I asked, closing my eyes tight against the pain and fear.

"I'm not your father," said a female voice in an accent.

I turned my head slowly to the right until she came into view. She was Asian, perhaps as young as me, and very beautiful. Her dark almond eyes penetrated like those of a stalking feline. She wore a black silk robe with two scenes of mountain brooks embroidered in gold thread that ran down from her shoulders before joining at her waist and continuing down one side to the bottom. The robe was loose fitting, and the bottoms overlapped slightly below the waist, exposing the tan skin of her bare legs from the inside of her upper thighs out over her knees to her small feet, which were wrapped in white, cloth-laced wooden sandals. Her hair looked long, even pulled up as it was. She looked like she could have come from feudal Japan, aside from the large caliber black revolver in her small hand.

"Start talking," she commanded coldly.

I obeyed and opened my mouth, but realized I hadn't thought up anything to say.

"Now!" she shouted, shaking the gun barrel in my face.

"I . . . I've been shot," I said meekly.

"I can see that. Who shot you?"

I clicked through several options in my head. "These guys drove by and shot me," I said, looking down at her feet. I felt the dizziness coming on again.

"I don't believe you. I saw the police searching for you in the alley." She took two steps back and continued. "You know what I think happened? I think you are on the run, a fugitive from justice. I think you were shot by the police and then broke in here, where you were shot and killed as a burglar. That's what I think happened."

I looked back up at the gun. She had distanced herself from me and closed her left eye, lining me up in the gun sights with the right. It was the end. I knew it. So this is also what the end of a life looks like. *Better than the orange noose waiting for me.* It was a strange thought, yet very clean and concise. I knew she meant to kill me. I could see it in the subtle features of her small face. A dizzying rush came over me. It was a combination of this realization, alcohol, blood loss, pain, fear, adrenaline, and finally anger. My vision flashed red as I began to shout.

"Do it. Do it! Do it! Do it, you fuckin' bitch, you crazy, psycho bitch, kill me! Yeah, that's it. Stand back so you don't get any blood on you. Come on! Come on!" I screamed as I crawled toward the black muzzle.

"Pull the trigger. Go on, pull it. I fucking dare you." I spat the words at her. "I'll probably just come back again anyway," I said, running out of breath. "I'll probably just come back again anyway." I trailed off quietly over and over until I began to cry.

I wept uncontrollably, like a child, not knowing or caring if or when the release might come. I looked up after several minutes. She was still there, only now the gun shook in her trembling hand, and tears ran down from the corners of her eyes. I fought unsuccessfully to stop crying and collapsed again facedown on the floor. I heard her uncock the revolver and felt her hand on my shoulder.

She laid the gun on the floor and took my right hand in hers. She placed her hand palm down in mine exposing a postage-stamp-size black tattoo on the back of her hand between the thumb and forefinger. The tattoo captured my attention and refocused my senses. Its shape was striking and looked like three joined peaks, two above one larger one, or two crossed Egyptian flails like so:

She turned my hand over and ran the fingers of her left hand over the blank web of skin on the back of my hand where her tattoo had been. She looked into my eyes and searched for something in them. She broke her concentration and spoke. "I'm going to call an ambulance. It'll be okay. You're not injured badly."

"No, please don't," I said, lifting my head. "Please stop," I pleaded as she started to walk away. "You were right about the police shooting me. If I go to a hospital tonight, I go to jail. I can have a friend pick me up. Please, help me, just let me use your phone," I said, smearing blood under my running nose as I wiped it.

She stopped and turned. "I have a better idea. I'll be right back." She walked up a set of stairs in the back of the basement and returned with a short, elderly Hispanic man. He looked to be in his sixties or early seventies but walked proud and straight as a soldier. His thick, snow-white hair and mustache contrasted dramatically against his dark-brown skin.

"*Ayudame, Antonio*," she said to him and pointed to my right arm, which he grabbed. She grabbed my left, and together they lifted me to my knees.

"What's going on?"

"We're taking you upstairs to get you cleaned up," she said.

I nodded and adjusted my arms around them as they raised me onto my right foot. She was only about five and a half feet tall. Antonio stood just over five feet tall, and I had to hunch my back in order to put weight on their shoulders.

We struggled up the stairs into a utility room, where my undersized aids rested before carrying me through an open door, into a bathroom filled with antique fixtures.

"We're going into the tub—mind your foot," she cautioned before speaking at Antonio in Spanish. He stepped into the tub first and began lowering me in once I'd braced the back of my left knee on the lip of the claw foot tub. I grabbed its rolled edges and lowered myself down painlessly.

Antonio disappeared back into the utility room.

"What are we going to do?" I asked, being careful to speak in the plural.

She walked over to the sink and started running hot water. "First, I'm going to clean and dress that wound of yours. I haven't decided about what comes second," she said, washing the blood off her hands and wetting a fresh washcloth. "Here," she said, handing me the warm, wet rag. "Wash your face and hands, you're a mess."

I cleaned myself up as best I could before the cloth became pink and useless. Antonio came back in and handed her a small pair of scissors. She walked over to me and bent over to look at my foot hanging over the edge of the bathtub. It bled and throbbed less in this elevated position. Antonio brought a chair over and placed it perfectly behind her as she sat down without looking. She placed her thumb and first two fingers on a clean part of the white toe of the sneaker and raised it gently, allowing a better view of the heel. "Does it hurt when I move it?"

I nodded, even though it didn't hurt, as she had moved it so gently.

"I'll have to remove the shoe. I'll be as careful as I can. Are you ready?"

I nodded.

She slid the bottom blade of the scissors under the first cross lace nearest the toe and deftly snipped it in two. The other seven laces went as easily as the first. She slid the bottom blade inside the canvas upper next to my ankle bone and cut through the tough cloth, down to the rubber sole.

I kept a white-knuckle death grip on the rolled edge of the tub in anticipation of the pain that never came. She worked slowly on the shoe, being careful not to move it.

She cut the canvas on the opposite side and placed the bloody scissors on the tile floor. "This is probably going to hurt," she said, taking hold of the dangling rear canvas and the red-and-white toe. She pulled steadily on the rear canvas until the rubber sole bent slightly ahead of the heel and then pulled it straight off painlessly. My white sock was light red along the sole and up to the ankle. "That wasn't so bad, was it?"

"No," I said defensively. I looked at her and couldn't help but wonder who she was, what relation she had with the church, and what she was going to do after she'd finished with my foot.

She set the shoe down, picked up the scissors, and leaned over to get an angle on the top of my sock. She cut quickly down to the top of my toes, sat upright in her chair, then peeled the entire sock off, again, painlessly.

"Let's get a closer look at you," she said, pulling my foot up by the big toe. She said something in Spanish to Antonio, who took over her grip on my toe. I felt her place a thumb and forefinger on either side of the gash as she opened it gently. Gentle didn't matter here. I cried out in shock at the slight pressure she applied. Her hand was gone before I had regained my composure.

"Sorry about that," she said sheepishly. "From what I can see, it looks like a clean wound. The bullet didn't hit any bones, and I don't think it hit any tendons."

"So what are we going to do?" I asked once I'd caught my breath.

"Well . . . I'm going to sew you up, and you're going to enjoy yourself."

I winced at my throbbing foot. "I doubt that."

She stood up and spoke. "Don't worry, you've landed in the right place." She left without closing the door. Her wooden sandals echoed loudly in the next room.

Antonio still had a hold on my big toe, probably because she hadn't told him to let go. He was obviously a servant and looked to be the type that would carry out any order no matter how bizarre. I looked at him and felt awkward and embarrassed at having a stranger impersonally touching my foot. He looked at me, and I could tell he felt the same way. The tension between us eased as I motioned for him to let go.

"Do you speak English?" I asked slowly.

"A little."

"I speak a little bit of Spanish. Your name is Antonio, right?" He nodded.

"Tell me, Antonio, what is her name?"

He shook his head vigorously. "You must ask her that."

"Okay," I said, backing off. "Is she a nun?"

He shook his head again. "Please, señor, you must—"

The door creaked behind her as she walked silently up to

us. She had changed clothes and now wore a blue work shirt, paint-splattered jeans, and dirty white sneakers. In her hand was a small, well-worn brown leather case.

"*Muy bien, Antonio*," she said, unzipping the case.

Antonio looked at the case and rolled his eyes to the tin patterned ceiling. "*Aye, dios mío*," he said before leaving the room.

I understood and sat upright in the tub. "Where is he going? What is that in your hand? Why did he say that?" I didn't like his reaction or her prolonged silence.

She slowly opened the case as she approached. I grew more nervous with each step she took. Her hand slipped inside the case and brought out an old brass syringe. "He doesn't like needles," she said, taking her seat again.

"Are you a doctor?" I asked in a concerned voice.

She smiled as she admired the syringe. "I used to be, a long time ago."

"Do you know what you're doing? What if the tendon is damaged?"

"Then you'll walk with a limp," she replied as she screwed together the antique syringe.

I thought about her quick answer and watched her remove a glass vial half filled with a light-brown tinted liquid.

"I don't like needles either."

"Then would you rather I do this without anesthetic?"

I looked at her and quickly went over my ever-shortening list of options. "No."

She smiled and continued to fiddle with her medical antiques.

She poured a small amount of rubbing alcohol onto a cotton ball and cleaned the needle before screwing it onto the main body. The syringe was old. It was made of brass and was as big around as a roll of dimes. The shaft of the plunger had a large brass ring at the end for the thumb. After she had cleaned and assembled it, she placed the needle down into the clear vial and pulled back on the plunger, siphoning liquid up into the syringe. The level of fluid in the vial went down by half an inch.

"How much do you weigh?" She removed the needle from the vial and turned it up to remove any air bubbles.

"One hundred sixty-five pounds," I answered.

"That's about what I thought," she said, looking at the fluid level through the narrow graduated glass window that ran the length of the syringe's polished brass body. She recorked the vial and replaced it in the case. "Would you like a cigarette before we begin?"

I nodded solemnly. She acted with such confidence that I began to think she really could do this. Perhaps it was wishful thinking. Even if it were, it beat her calling the police and having to answer questions about running from a burning building.

She pulled out an orange-and-white pack of cigarettes and placed one between my lips. I recognized the brand from the distinctive color of the pack. They were Lendts, a Turkish brand that used to be very popular there. And I remembered, they were also distant Vasili's favorite brand.

She struck a match and held it to the end of the short, unfiltered cigarette. "Centuries of flavor," I said matter of factly, recalling the Lendts slogan from Vasili's memory.

She gave me a surprised look as she lit hers. "You've smoked Lendts before?" she asked, exhaling a plume of smoke.

"In another life." I laid back and rested my head on the edge of the tub. It was a stronger smoke than I was used to. We said nothing for a long time as we smoked. Her beautiful, catlike black eyes never wavered no matter how long she stared at me.

"Thanks," I said, breaking the silence.

"For what?"

"For the smoke, for the help."

"Well, wayward one, as I said, you landed in the right place. Speaking of help, I'm ready to begin. Close your eyes, please— this may sting a little."

She placed her left hand around the top of my ankle and squeezed harder than I thought she could have. Syringe in hand, she pierced a bulging vein on my instep. It stung at first then was followed by a warm orange-cream colored wave that slowly crawled up my leg. It was hard to describe other than to say that it felt orange and peaceful, and that everything the wave washed over was going to be okay.

I opened my eyes and looked at my foot, expecting it to be orange. It looked normal but didn't ache any longer. It really was going to be okay. The wave rolled up to my hip then turned down the other leg and up my torso at the same time. She removed the needle, and I noticed half its contents still showed in the glass window. She swabbed the needle with another soaked cotton ball and checked it again for air bubbles. The wave slowly reached my upper chest then raced up my neck and over my face and head in a few heartbeats. Everything was going to be okay now. She readjusted the seat and readied the syringe again.

"I really don't think I need another one." I heard the words slowly drawl out of my mouth in a long orange-cream-colored line, but that was okay. I had to fight to keep my eyes focused.

She laughed at me. "You're really cute," she said as she turned the syringe on herself. The needle entered a vein on the back of her hand, and she depressed the plunger, emptying the contents. That was okay too.

THE MINOR SURGERY THAT FOLLOWED WAS QUICK, fuzzy, and pain- less. She placed the stitches in my heel and wrapped my foot and ankle in a white bandage. The effects of the drink, the fire, the adrenaline, the shock, and the syringe were taking their toll by the time she had put on the last wraps. I felt myself drifting toward sleep and had to fight to keep my eyes open.

"How do you feel?"

I couldn't tell whose voice it was. It seemed to come from everywhere in the room. "Better. Sleepy." My words had almost returned to their original color.

"I'll have Antonio prepare a guest room for you. Rest. I'll be right back."

I fell asleep in the tub and awoke to being lifted up by my arms. My head still swam with whatever she had shot me up with, and I had trouble keeping my balance on one leg. They carried me through a large room into a small bedroom on the other side of the church. They spoke to each other in Spanish as we went. A single bed waited inside the guest room with covers pulled back invitingly. I fell asleep as soon as I hit the pillow and dreamed rare and unwelcome dreams.

5

A mother and son sat across a kitchen table from each other. It was Bobby's mother, Judith. She was young and looked the same as I remembered her before the fire. The thin blue-and-white cotton robe was gathered tight around her small waist.

I looked around the room, if you could call it that, for it had no walls that I could discern, only a vast expanse of white. Glowing ivory light illuminated the room from all angles, if there were any angles. The faint, yet distinct sound of dripping water persisted in the distance. We looked at a blank game board before us, then at each other.

"I get to go first this time, Bobby," she said, eyeing the lettered game pieces in her tray. She looked up and smiled sweetly.

"I have my word." She began to place the tiles down one by one in a line across the center of the board. W-E-E-V-I-L.

"Weevil," she said, "like the bugs we had last summer. You remember, don't you, Bobby?"

"Yes, Mommy, I remember." The voice that escaped my mouth was that of a child. I looked down to check my body and found my normal long legs stretched underneath the table before me.

"Let's see, that's four plus one is five, six, ten, eleven, twelve, then doubled because of the pink square is twenty-four. Pretty good start," she said, writing on the table without pen or pad.

"But, Mom . . ." I stopped for a second after hearing my normal tenor voice. "But, Mom, there's no *we* in *evil*."

She raised her pale-blue eyes slowly until they met mine. The edges of her cotton robe and the ends of her brown hair blended into the ambient whiteness of the room. The water drip chirped like a metronome in the background.

"Hmm," she said, cocking her head as she looked at the word on the board, "we'll have to check on that." She looked into my eyes again and pointed to the edge of the board. "Aren't you going to open it?"

I looked down and saw a letter on the left side of the board and a wood-handled steel letter opener on the right.

"Go on, open it," she prodded.

I placed my hands on the letter and the letter opener at the same time, and when I did, the room took shape around us. She didn't notice the change, but we were now back in the living room of our small Georgia home. I looked around and everything was the same, the green carpeting, the cheap wood paneling, the pictures in the hallway.

"Well, what does it say?" she asked impatiently.

I moved the blade of the letter opener under the flap and started to tear at the seal, when it began to shake uncontrollably in my right hand. I dropped the letter to the carpeted floor and gripped the opener with both hands, trying to control its now wild and dangerous jerks.

"Bobby?" she asked, concerned.

I gripped it tight and struggled in exaggerated corrections, trying to counter the unseen force moving the knife.

"Bobby, stop it, this isn't funny."

THE REINCARNATIONIST PAPERS

I couldn't muster the clarity to speak or the strength to subdue whatever was now wielding the blade.

"Bobby, you're frightening me."

I lost my balance and was knocked out of my chair and onto the floor by those unseen hands. My grip on the opener released when I hit the floor, and the blade flew unnaturally far across the room, landing ten feet away on the green carpet.

Mom began screaming loudly. Her long shrills came in steady, predictable bursts between short gasps of air. I didn't take my eyes off the blade that lay motionless on the carpet, its sharp tip pointed at me. I was on all fours staring at it, looking for any sign of movement. I could hear my own breathing over Mom's shrill screams. I turned my head slightly toward her while keeping both eyes focused on the letter opener. When I turned my head so far that it was in view of only one eye, the letter opener moved. I froze and watched it with that one eye. The point of the blade rose up three inches off the carpet and hung there abnormally, quivering ever so slightly each time I exhaled. Mom's loud screaming was becoming as monotonous as the dripping water had been. The blade still trembled menacingly with each exhale.

I knew what I had to do. If I could only concentrate hard enough, I could make the knife stop moving. But I couldn't focus with that damn woman screaming like that. I stared and concentrated on the knife until it stopped quivering. When it did, she stopped screaming.

"Bobby, honey, don't play like that, it's dangerous," she said in that sweet, motherly voice I'd known as her child.

I involuntarily turned to look at her and saw the silver flash of the blade as it whizzed past my eyes on its way to the far wall where it plunged two inches deep into the wood paneling.

She smiled at me with a mildly scolding, coy look that was

almost seductive. I could see the knife wriggling free from the wall out of the corner of my eye.

I spun around and ran for the front door hoping the opener wouldn't catch me. My hand found the doorknob, and I turned to check but saw only the empty slit in the paneling where it had been. Standing still with my back against the door, I frantically searched the room with my eyes. *Concentrate.* I turned the handle and cracked the door open to hear the sounds of an engine racing and tires squealing coming from the driveway.

"Don't go out there," Mom said sternly.

"It's okay, Mom, I'll be right back," I said as I threw the door open and walked down the three steps to the driveway. It was a beautiful, sunny Georgia day outside.

The source of the revving and tire screeching was a small, red four-door sedan racing counterclockwise around our circular driveway. It raced so fast that it almost tipped over at several points along each circuit. The driver and passenger in the front seat were too busy laughing to notice me, but there was someone in the back seat who did. I watched the car make several laps. Each time they passed, the young man in the back seat looked at me with excited, familiar, pale-brown eyes. Each lap they made was faster than the one before it, and each time by, the man in the back seat became more threatening, until he thrashed wildly, screaming and clawing at the glass in a violent attempt to get at me. The hair on the back of my neck stood up the last time they went by, and I turned away, unable to look at his grimacing face again.

I ran back into the house to check on my mom. She wasn't in her seat, but I could hear her rumbling with something behind the first door on the right side of the hallway. I took cautious steps toward the sounds, but they stopped at the same time I heard the tire-screeching, glass-shattering crash of the car outside.

She appeared from behind the door and closed it behind her. She looked startled at my presence back in the house and began talking nervously.

"I was just locking up the shotguns. You know, it's not safe to have weapons lying around at a time like this." She made her way over to the couch and sat down. There was a slight difference about the gait of her walk, but I couldn't quite put my finger on it. I turned around to look for the letter opener and noticed the half-opened letter at my feet. Picking it up, I ripped open the seal and removed the tri-folded sheet inside. The white page was completely blank on both sides. I looked up from the letter in time to see Mom walk into the hallway again from the first door on the right where the rumbling had been. She looked at me with a menacing confidence.

She appeared much different now, dressed in a pink tube top; short, shiny, black vinyl skirt; thigh-high fishnet stockings with a hidden garter belt; and pink, four-inch-high spike heels. Her hair was permed into tight, dark-brown curls around plastic dangly earrings and excessive makeup. She gripped a pump-action shot-gun in her small hands.

I stood before her in disbelief, then turned toward the couch, only to see the feeble figure of the original mother slumped down, twitching her left arm and leg as she gazed mindlessly at the floor.

I looked at the page in my hand again; it was still blank. Then I looked at the mom in the hallway walking toward me.

"Weevil," she said softly, as she quickly worked the action of the gun, jacking a shell into the chamber.

"Weevil!" she squealed, drawing out the *e* until it sounded like an injured animal. She walked toward me and leveled the barrel of the shotgun at my face. I blinked, disbelieving, and looked past the muzzle into what should have been her soft pale-blue eyes. They were instead solid black from corner to corner.

"WEEVIL!" she screamed as the muzzle flashed and the gun bucked in her hands.

I BOLTED UPRIGHT IN BED and scanned the room in a panicked and sleepy stupor. The Asian woman sat in an antique wooden chair beside me, smoking. I felt weak and hot. My face was covered with sweat. "My God, is there no pardon anywhere?" I mumbled.

She stoically watched me turn my head around the room several times until I remembered where I was.

"Better now?" she asked.

I nodded. I felt nauseated.

"Are you hungry? Would you like some breakfast?"

"I feel sick," I said, using barely enough breath and energy to get the syllables out. I felt short of breath, and my mouth was filling with saliva, a bad sign.

"You smelled strongly of alcohol last night, so I had Antonio bring in a basin in case you need to vomit. It's on the floor next to you." She spoke with a matter-of-fact tone.

An antique wooden nightstand stood next to the bed, in front of it on the floor was an old, white-enameled metal washbasin like the kind used before the advent of indoor plumbing. I—or rather Vasili—had used these in Bulgaria. Leaning over the edge of the bed to look at where she had pointed was enough to start me gagging, on my way to throwing up three times in rapid succession.

"There's a towel on the nightstand for when you're finished. I'm going to check on Antonio and breakfast." She left before I could clean myself up. I threw up once more before Antonio came in. He wiped up the mess and handed me a clean, warm washcloth before leaving with the dirty towel and full basin. After he left, I laid back down and tried to reconstruct everything that had happened the night before. I lifted the covers and brought my left foot up so I could see it. A line of red dots tinged the white gauze wrapping.

"How does it feel?" she asked, carrying in a tray of food.

"It feels fine."

"Do you need another basin?"

I shook my head and pulled the covers back up to my chest as she approached. I was naked.

"I thought you might be in rough shape this morning, so I instructed Antonio to fix an appropriate breakfast: scrambled eggs, toast, and tomato juice." She placed the tray in front of me and began peeling an orange for herself as she sat in the chair next to the bed again.

I took the fork, swallowed the excess saliva gathering in my mouth again, and began to eat. I felt better in minutes and ate everything on the plate as she peeled, segmented, and ate the orange.

"Thank you for breakfast, for letting me stay here, for everything. You were right about the drinking. I must have been really drunk, I don't recall how I got out of my clothes. I don't even remember your name."

She looked at me as she chewed. There was something unnerving about the way she eyed me. Usually, when someone stares, you can see the determination and effort in their expression. Hers was one of total relaxed confidence. She swallowed and cleared her throat. "My friends call me Poppy."

"What do your patients call you?" I countered.

She smiled and held her small hand out to me. "Hello, my name is Poppy."

I leaned over, placed my right hand in hers. "Evan Michaels."

"Yes, I know. I took your clothes off last night after you went unconscious. Your wallet fell open on the floor when I folded your pants. I hope you don't mind, you had a lot of blood on your clothes, and I didn't want to ruin the bedding."

I nodded. "Thanks. You don't look like a nun," I said, still confused.

"Thank you, I think. Is that supposed to be a compliment?"

"This is a church, isn't it?"

She smiled. "Ah, it used to be, a long time ago. It is my home," she said, looking at the old wooden walls. "I'll show you the place when you're up and around."

I wondered if she intended to let me stay until I'd healed. The charity I had received so far seemed out of place, even from a church. And now, knowing that it came from a stranger, I felt wary.

"How much do you remember from last night?" she asked.

"I'm not sure. I remember the gun, I remember the tub, and I remember the stitches. What did I miss?"

"Nothing really," she said, then fell into a confident silence.

"Do you live here alone?"

"No, Antonio lives here as well."

"But it's just the two of you."

"Yes."

"Why did you help me last night? Why didn't you call the police?"

She looked up at the ceiling as if looking for an answer. "I don't like the police, I've never had much use for them. And you, I helped you because you looked like you needed it, and you remind me of someone I used to know."

"Lucky for me. Say, do you have another one of those Lendts?" She pulled out the orange-and-white pack, handed me one, and lit it. "How many stitches did it take?"

"Twelve, it should close up nicely. I don't think you should have any problem with it healing properly."

"How long should I leave the stitches in?"

"Five days or so, we'll change the dressing soon. If we keep it changed, it will heal quicker."

"Good," I said, wondering how soon the change would be and how soon I'd be gone. I was just happy to stay off my foot as long as I could. "You said last night that you used to be a doctor, where?"

She pulled out a cigarette for herself as she spoke. "Lots of places, but I don't want to talk about me, I want to talk about you, Evan. Where are you from?"

"A farm in Minnesota."

"Do you have any brothers or sisters?"

"Nope."

"And why exactly did you come to Los Angeles, Evan Michaels?"

I liked the way she said my name. "I traveled around a bit after I left Minnesota, I just liked it here, I guess. It felt comfortable."

She smiled. "Yes, it has that effect, doesn't it? It's the anonymity."

I nodded. I felt strangely comfortable talking with her about myself, like I could trust her, even though, out of habit, I wouldn't allow myself to. "What else would you like to know?"

"What do you do for money?" she asked.

"Just about anything."

She laughed. "I like that answer. Where do you live?"

"In a hotel near Slauson and Crenshaw."

She cocked her head toward me. "That's a fairly rough neighborhood, isn't it?"

"Yes, it is, but it's cheap. This area doesn't seem that safe either."

"Well, it's not what it used to be. Time can do that to a place. What were you doing here last night?"

I took a long drag on the Lendts and began thinking up a story.

She spoke first and interrupted my train of thought. "Before you tell me a lie, remember that I didn't call the police last night and I'm not inclined to do so now. Last night when I undressed you, I noticed the hair on the back of your head is singed, and the skin on your neck looks scorched."

I almost swallowed my tongue at her warning. Her unnerving stare looked right through me. "What if I don't feel comfortable telling you?"

She thought for a second before she answered. "That wouldn't reflect well on my hospitality, now would it?"

She had me cornered. She was good. "Could I have another cigarette?" I asked, crushing out the old one in the ashtray on the nightstand. I took a long draw off the fresh one and leaned back against the headboard. "I was at a fire last night."

"Yes, I thought so. I heard the fire brigades go by last night. It looked like the old Lynnman Warehouse over on Marion."

"It was," I conceded. I couldn't believe that confession had come from my mouth.

"Hmm," she murmured. "Do you have a wife or any children?"

"No," I answered quickly, relieved that she'd changed the subject. "I have to go to the bathroom," I said, changing it again.

She smiled warmly. "I hadn't thought of how to handle that. Let me see if I can find a pair of crutches for you to use," she said, leaving the room.

I sat up carefully after she'd gone and moved my legs sideways over the edge of the bed. My foot began to throb as soon as I lowered it to the floor. I scooted sideways toward the low footboard and looked over the edge at the chest she had glanced at periodically during the conversation. On it lay a pair of underwear, a different pair than the ones I'd worn the day before, my leather jacket, wallet, and the hundred and fifty dollars I had carried.

I leaned over, grabbed the underwear, and slipped them over my legs, being careful not to touch the bandage. I put the money and wallet in the jacket before moving back to the head of the bed.

She returned with a single crutch that looked like it had just been taken from a Civil War soldier. The top part that fit under the armpit was a large, roughly carved block of wood, and the

THE REINCARNATIONIST PAPERS

lower part was nothing more than a polished and partially twisted tree branch. It didn't have a hand grip, and I assumed that you just gripped the branch at wherever your hand landed.

She looked down at the underwear I'd donned then back up to my eyes. "Good for you. Are you ready to try it?"

"Oh, yes, I'm ready." I had to urinate badly.

"I'm sorry, but I could only find one." She presented it to me, and I stood up, putting some weight on it. I realized immediately that it wouldn't take much usage for the discomfort in my armpit to make me forget about my foot. My hand fit nicely into a worn twist in the branch about halfway down.

"This is an antique, isn't it?" I asked, taking a tentative step as I braced myself on her shoulder.

She looked at it for a moment before she answered. "Yes, I suppose it has gotten old, hasn't it?"

Her words echoed in my head as I took the next step. *I guess it has gotten old, hasn't it?* It sounded like something I might say if I wasn't paying attention. It sounded hauntingly familiar. A funny thing happened to me after I'd completely assimilated Vasili's and Bobby's memories, I lost almost all perspective of time. It happened so subtly that I didn't realize it for the first few years, and I sometimes still misplace things in my own history. I would remember important events in history that happened during Vasili's lifetime, like the opening of the Panama Canal or the first flight of the Wright Brothers, then would pick up a newspaper to see that it was the fiftieth or seventy-fifth anniversary of the event. Only then would I realize, hey, that was a long time ago. Vasili's and Bobby's memories are as clear to me as my own, and though I can always tell who the memories belong to, they appear to me as an uninterrupted timeline. Events that happened during their lives happened to me as well, and quietly got older while I wasn't paying attention. *I guess it has gotten old.* I kept thinking about how familiar it sounded and how strange it felt coming from someone else. She probably misspoke.

The door to my room opened into the nave of the church. The room I had traversed in the drugged darkness before was enormous in the light. The long sides of the room were covered in rich wooden panels that rose a full fifteen feet before slanting inward to meet the ones of the other side in a high vaulted ceiling. The vast hardwood floor was devoid of the original pews, except for two lonely ones directly in front of a short stage where the pulpit had once been. The back wall of the room was the exterior stone wall I had seen the night before. The rough-cut stones held three tall stained glass windows ending in Gothic arches at the top. The colors of the glass shone through softly, but I couldn't make out the scenes in the dim twilight. I turned to look at Poppy. "What time is it?"

She looked up and pointed to a clock on the wall above me. "Eight thirty p.m."

The unexplained time loss made me feel even more disoriented. "Wow, what was that you shot me with?"

"Laudanum.[4] It can knock you out for a while if you're not used to it."

She obviously was. The crutch clicked against the wooden floor with every step I took, echoing throughout the large room.

"It's the last door on the right, it's the same bathroom you were in last night. I'll wait for you out here," she said, walking over to the near church pew.

I reemerged in minutes, and she helped me back to the bedroom. I was unable to walk without putting some weight on my foot and by the time we'd reached the bedroom, it was hurting again.

---

4. Poppy's use of "laudanum" described here is more likely morphine or heroin. Laudanum, a type of opiate diluted with alcohol into a tincture, was popular in the nineteenth century as an analgesic. Her usage of the term here might be euphemistic.

"Are you in pain?" she asked.

"Is it that obvious?"

"I can tell you're favoring it more than when you first got up."

"Yes, it's sore. I'd like to lie down again." I hovered in the doorway and looked around the main room. I sat down on the bed and eased my legs up, sighing heavily. Poppy stopped in the doorway.

"I hope you'll forgive me, but I must leave. I have some business to attend to. I'll have Antonio bring down some fruit and a few selections from my library. Get some rest, I'll see you in the morning. Call for Antonio if you desire anything."

"Thank you. Good night," I trailed off as she left. I hadn't trusted anyone in a long time, but I felt the strange and unfamiliar stirrings of trust when near her. Despite this, I couldn't ignore the question of why she would go out of her way to help a total stranger that had just been shot by the police. It wasn't normal. *I would like to meet the person I reminded her of*, I thought, looking at the white plaster ceiling.

It's pathetic to think that suspicion would be the first reaction I should have to any kindness shown me. I don't think Vasili would have had the same reaction in his day. If altruism still exists in the world, I've never seen it in this town.

6

Raindrops resonated on the roof and echoed throughout the nave of the church and each flash of lightning exploded into brilliant hues through the stained glass. Antonio was warmer to me when he brought in the fruit and books. He handed me three aged volumes: *The Critique of Pure Reason* by Immanuel Kant, *The Collected Poems of John Donne*, and *Some Dogmas of Religion* by J. M. E. McTaggart.[5]

I remembered most of Kant's work from Vasili, who had taken an interest in philosophy in the latter years of his life. I picked up *John Donne* and read several poems as the approaching thunderclaps punctuated the mood of his poetry.

The third book, *Some Dogmas of Religion*, was the newest. It looked like a fifties-era college textbook and the title suggested it would be dry enough to put me to sleep. I hadn't heard of Dr.

5. J. M. E. McTaggart, a Hegelian philosopher of some respect in his native England and a committed atheist, pursues some interesting facets of perceived reincarnation in *Some Dogmas of Religion*. Specifically he theorizes that interests, aptitudes, and skills are inherited from our previous incarnations. This would have no doubt been of interest to Evan Michaels.

McTaggart, but by the time I was a hundred and twenty pages into the text, I was already searching the bibliography for related titles.

The first sections on religion and dogma were as dry as I'd expected. The next section on human immortality reawakened me, but the following section on human preexistence blew me away. McTaggart was a metaphysician and lecturer at Cambridge around the turn of the last century. He was also a believer in reincarnation.

I had read many books about reincarnation since I'd realized I was unique, but everything I found was written in the context of Eastern Philosophy. Some parts of Hinduism and Buddhism made sense and were very appealing, but I could never embrace them fully because of my inability to accept their major tenet of karma. Nothing in my experience through three lives has ever supported the idea of karmic debt.

McTaggart was different. He argued,

> But even the best of men are not, when they die, in such a state of intellectual and moral perfection as would fit them to enter heaven immediately...This is generally recognized, and one of two alternatives is commonly adopted to meet it. The first is that some tremendous improvement—an improvement out of all proportion to any which can ever be observed in life—takes place at the moment of death...The other and more probable alternative is that the process of gradual improvement can go on in each of us after the death of our present bodies.

I thought if this second, more probable of McTaggart's alternatives were true, then we have to contend with a plurality of lives instead of a single one. And a plurality of lives must mean at least three; the present one, the one before it, and the one after it, though it is more likely that there would be a series of past lives.

He supported his plurality of lives and preexistence argument by explaining innate skills or propensities as skills known or practiced in an earlier life, and that a man's character is directly shaped by the unremembered experiences of these previous lives.

I laid back on the bed, held the book close to me, and relished the vindication in its pages. The storm had eased, but by the time I'd finished, I was too excited to sleep.

It felt claustrophobic in my room and I decided to continue reading in the main nave. I hobbled silently to the pew and carefully settled in to read. The type on the pages was barely visible in the poor light. Dawn was breaking outside. I had read all night.

I sat bathed in the faint, multicolored twilight that filtered through the three tall windows, wondering why she had chosen those three volumes for me to read, especially the McTaggart. She could have scanned a library of tens of thousands of books and not found one as perfectly suited as that one. It seemed to me it would hold little interest to anyone normal, and certainly not enough interest to merit selecting it for a guest. I made a mental note to ask her if I could keep it.

The light outside grew brighter, and I began to make out different shapes and scenes in the colored glass in front of me. There were nine different panels set into the three windows. I sat and studied each in detail as they took shape in the morning silence. One after another, they burst into vivid reds, blues, yellows, greens, and whites and took on a life of their own. I studied their beauty, a bit bewildered, for half an hour or so until I recognized the pattern. There wasn't any. None of the panels, as near as I could tell, had anything to do with the Bible. I was very familiar with Vasili's Eastern Orthodoxy, somewhat familiar with Protestantism, and I found it hard to believe that Catholic icons could be so different, if this had even been a Catholic church.

The first two panels shared the same character, a young American

Indian man. He was slim with medium-length, straight, black hair. In the first scene, he sat at a workbench admiring a piece of jewelry. The middle panel on the left window showed the same young man sitting on a cliff above a southwestern pueblo, kissing a young girl.

The third and fourth panels at the bottom of the left window and the top of the center one featured a different character, a young, tall black boy. In the third, he was riding a white horse through open country, and in the fourth, he was dancing around a fire as part of a ceremony in a Pueblo village similar to the one in the second scene.

A Middle Eastern woman was set into the center panel. She stood alone, clothed in a red dress and adorned with gold necklaces and headbands that held down a patchwork of crimson scarves. She had eyes that looked out of the glass right into your soul. Below her was a white man in a rowboat sculling away from what looked like a burning island. The same man was in the top panel of the last window, only here he looked a little older and was being pursued through an old European city at night by a cloaked figure holding a dagger. The deep blues, purples, and grays of this nocturnal panel gave it a particularly rich feel.

The next panel was my favorite—it showed a pale, thin man in royal French costume, complete with powdered wig and painted mole. He looked straight ahead and clutched a flintlock pistol in his right hand. The pistol, pointed up, was held next to his head in position for a duel. Behind him, in a blossoming cherry orchard, I could make out the outline of his opponent. The artwork was incredible. I could see the urgency in his face and sense his emotion. There was no doubt that this man was fighting for his life. His face showed confidence, but not an ounce of fear, and if you looked at him long enough, he almost seemed to be suppressing a smile. The last panel showed the same duelist blowing and shaping an orange glass ball in a workshop.

I sat and looked at the panels in different orders trying to make sense of them. The sun had broken over the horizon and shot directly through the panels, sending hundreds of colored beams onto the hardwood floor around me. I looked down at the books on the pew and realized I was awash in the colors as well.

"It's beautiful this time of the morning, don't you think?"

"Poppy?"

"Up here."

I looked up out of the colors to the balcony in the back of the room. I had noticed its underside earlier but hadn't realized that it served as her bedroom. Poppy looked down at me from behind the railing, the black silk robe fastened around her narrow waist.

"Yes, it's very beautiful—"

"Which is your favorite?" she asked before I could finish my sentence.

I turned and looked at the different scenes. "Him," I said, pointing to the right-hand window. "The duelist, definitely the duelist."

"Mine too."

"Who are they?" I said, keeping my eyes locked with the duelist's.

She was silent until I turned around and looked at her again. "Minor characters in history. I cut, colored, and set the pieces myself. I always get up with the sun to see this.

"You made these? This is impressive, Poppy," I said, turning to admire them again. "Where did you get the ideas from? I mean, why these characters? These pieces seem so personal . . . so real."

I turned and looked up at her. She stood at the balcony railing, arms folded across her chest, staring at me. "Wait there, I'll be right down."

I grabbed the crutch and the books and hobbled toward the

front of the church dressed only in my borrowed underwear. I had taken only a few steps when Antonio came out of his room. He was unshaven, and his thick, white hair lay on his head in random disarray. He wore a fresh white shirt, the Cuban kind that you're not supposed to tuck in, but it had been buttoned hastily and was askew by one buttonhole, giving him a noticeable list to the left. A look of astonishment graced his face when he saw me.

"Good morning," I said, smiling.

Antonio turned to Poppy as she emerged at the bottom of the staircase and spoke to her in Spanish.

"Are you hungry?" she asked me.

I nodded enthusiastically.

"What do you think about poached eggs, croissant, and coffee?"

"Sounds good," I said.

"I'll have Antonio get you a robe. Breakfast should be ready in about ten minutes." She finished the sentence and walked back upstairs, speaking loudly to Antonio in Spanish as she went.

I carried the books back to my room and waited for Antonio to bring me something to wear. "Breakfast in five minutes," he said warmly.

I put on the robe and headed for the kitchen. The sound of clanging dishes rattled through the kitchen door as I walked toward the front of the building. In daylight, with my head cleared, I could see details in the building I hadn't noticed before.

The large wooden doors of the church hung in the front of a traditional vestibule, complete with a carved stone baptismal font that, now unused, looked like an empty bird bath. The balcony above me was supported by a round wooden pillar, and the ceiling in this front area was a normal height. The stairs that led to the loft were to the left of the front doors.

Antonio was filling the water glasses for the three places at the kitchen table when I walked in. He motioned for me to sit in the chair nearest the door.

"How many?" he asked, holding up a carton of eggs.

"Three, but scrambled like yesterday, please."

He nodded and went back to work at the gas stove. The kitchen was equipped with modern appliances throughout. It wasn't the type of thing you would normally notice, except that the kitchen seemed to be the only modern room there.

She walked in as Antonio poured the juice. "Good morning."

"Good morning," I replied.

"How is your foot? Does it hurt?"

"Yes, a little, but it's better."

"Here." She handed me a prescription pill bottle. "I found these upstairs. They should help with your pain."

"Thank you." I placed the bottle down and picked up a fork. We had eaten the majority of our meal before she spoke again.

"How did you sleep last night?"

"I didn't, really."

"Why? I hope the storm didn't keep you up."

"I don't like lightning, but that wasn't it. I read all night."

"Then I take it you liked the selections."

"Yes, very interesting. I meant to ask you why you chose those books."

"They were the last three books I read."

I nodded thoughtfully as I chewed my eggs.

"So were you in a mood to read, or did something in particular interest you?"

"*Some Dogmas of Religion* was fascinating. I read some poetry too, but McTaggart kept me awake." I studied her face for any reaction.

"That's interesting; I wouldn't have thought you'd have liked that one. What did you find so fascinating?"

I put the last large forkful of eggs into my mouth in order to buy some time for my answer. "It was unlike anything I've ever read in Western philosophy." I knew that answer sounded lame.

"Have you read much philosophy?"

"Yes, some. Kant, Hegel, Hume, and others." I reached for the pills. "How many of these should I take?"

"Two," Poppy said, sounding slightly disappointed at the change in conversation. "You look tired, Evan, would you like to lie down?"

"Yes, I would. I wanted to ask you if I could take a bath later."

She tugged at the corners of her delicate mouth with the white linen napkin. "The Spanish have a saying, *mi casa es su casa*—that means this is your house too."

THE CHURCH SEEMED VACANT WHEN I GOT UP and went for a bath in the afternoon. *If this is my house too, then I have a wonderful place,* I thought, walking through the empty church. It was the kind of home I'd always dreamed about; not a church per se, but someplace, some beautiful edifice like this that I could call my own. The thought of this being my house, even if only a courtesy, made me feel proud.

The hot bath felt wonderful, and I was just drying off when a knock came at the bathroom door. I put the robe on as Poppy opened the door and handed over my clothes.

"Antonio just finished drying these. I thought you might need them."

"Thank you," I laughed. "It seems like that's all I ever say to you."

She smiled. "Well, you'd better not get tired of saying it just yet. We need to rewrap your foot."

"Good idea."

"Get dressed. I'll be right back."

I dressed and removed the old bandage before she came back.

"Great," she said, looking at my bare white foot sticking out of the black pant leg. "Let's get started. Hold your leg up, please." She got on one knee and inspected my wound. "It's already starting to close. Brace yourself, this may hurt." She applied a small amount of white salve to the stitches, stroking her finger gently along the seam as she looked into my eyes for a reaction. "Does that hurt?"

"No, not at all."

"That's a good sign."

I broke away from her stare and looked around the room. "This is a wonderful place you have, Poppy. How did you get it?"

She unrolled two feet of fresh gauze. "Brace yourself again, I'm going to wrap this tightly." The first three wraps hurt and she answered as she continued to unwind the gauze around my foot. "I inherited it, along with a large sum of money."

"That's what I suspected. I mean, I didn't think a woman as young as you could afford a place this large. I'm sorry, that sounded horrible. What I meant to say was—"

She smiled. "I understand. You're correct about a young woman like me not normally enjoying such luxuries. I've been comfortable in this way for so long that I often forget how different it must seem. It's ironic though, I almost make enough from my trade to maintain all this anyway."

"What trade is that?"

She made several delicate wraps next to my toes. "Evan, you are looking at one of the only authentic stained glass artisans left in the world."

"What do you mean *authentic*?"

"That's a good question." She continued wrapping. "Stained glass you see today, when it is glass at all, is mass produced in large plates and is colored with standardized industrial dyes. It tends to be rather flat and lifeless when compared to glass made and colored with older, more traditional techniques.

"Glass used to be made by hand, blown to be exact, and no matter how experienced the craftsman, there are imperfections in unpolished, blown plate glass. It is these now extinct imperfections along with base element dyes that produce the quality of glass you witnessed this morning."

"It was incredible, I admit, but is there really that much money in it?"

"The market definitely is small, but the number of suppliers is even smaller. When a thirteenth-century cathedral needs replacement panels, who else is going to do it?" She shrugged her shoulders quickly. "There is no one else."

"How did you learn this extinct trade?"

"From my benefactor, along with the building. There. It's done," she said, securing the end of the bandage. "How does it feel?"

"Tight, but I'll be okay."

"Take a few more painkillers. The tighter it is, the easier it should be to walk on. Speaking of walking," she continued, "I hope you feel good enough to go outside today. I took the liberty of having Antonio prepare a picnic basket for us. It's beautiful outside."

"That sounds wonderful."

"It's settled then. I'll let you finish cleaning up. Antonio's toiletries are, of course, at your disposal."

I nodded at her.

She hesitated in the open doorway. "Evan, I don't mean to imply anything, but would you like some help with your hair?"

"Is it that bad?" I asked, running my hand over the back of my head. The burned patch felt coarse and matted like the coat of some neglected, wire-haired dog.

"Well it's already wet, let's see what we can do with it." She picked up a pair of scissors and a comb from the sink and walked back over to me.

"Hold these for a second," she said, inspecting the burned

hair on the back of my head. She eased her slim fingers under the matted hair as far as they would go. I closed my eyes and concentrated on her touch.

"I think it's going to be pretty short, probably half an inch long in the back."

"That's fine, my hair is normally close to that length. The only reason it isn't that short now is that my barber for the last few years died three months ago, and I haven't found a new one."

She affectionately stroked my hair in different directions. "Looks like you might have found a replacement."

"Yes," I said, my eyes still closed.

"Hand me the scissors, Evan."

She snipped at the strands between her fingers. The tension on my scalp eased as small sections of the mat came free.

"You have nice hair. Just a second . . . there. That's all of it," she said, removing a napkin-sized chunk of hair. "Hand me the comb, please." She combed through it until all the smaller tangles were gone, then she began to shorten the rest of the unaffected hair.

"Here," she said, handing me a pack of Lendts and a lighter. "Light me one too, please." She continued to snip and play with my hair. I took one of the two cigarettes from my mouth and handed it to her.

"Where are you from?" I asked.

"I was born and raised in Osaka, Japan, but my citizenship is Swiss."

"And you came here because this place was left to you?"

"Basically," she said, trimming around my ear.

"You're quite the enigma."

"What do you want to know?" she asked.

I was careful not to move as she cut. "Who was this benefactor?"

"Watch your leg," she said, throwing a leg over both of mine, straddling me. She sat on my thighs facing me and looked at each ear in turn before starting to work on my bangs. Her face was inches from mine, and she looked intently at the scissors as she cut.

"She was a relative," she said softly. "This home has been in my family for eighty years."

"I see."

She moved forward on her seat and began work on the top of my head. The soft skin of her neck brushed against my cheek as she cocked her head around mine to see what she was doing. It wasn't necessary, I could plainly see what she was doing. Her breasts pressed against my chest as she wriggled and repositioned herself. I could feel myself becoming aroused by her weight on top of me.

"Hang on just a minute longer. I'm almost done," she whispered into my ear.

"I'm fine," I said defensively.

She looked away from the scissors and into my eyes. "There," she said, making a final cut before stepping off of me. "So you liked the McTaggart, huh?"

"Yes, very much."

"I have some other material along the same lines. If you're interested, I could let you read them as well."

"Yes, I would be very interested in seeing them. Does the topic interest you?" I asked.

"I'm interested in a lot of things," she said, combing through my hair. "There, it's finished."

"How do I look?"

She stood in front of me with her arms crossed. "You look good, very handsome. Have a look for yourself." She pointed to the mirror above the sink.

"Hand me the crutch, will you?" I asked.

I got to my feet and walked to the mirror. "You did a great

job, thank you. We'll have to work something out for future haircuts."

"Hmm, we'll see. Antonio's shaving supplies are behind the mirror. I'm going to change, I'll be down in a bit. Antonio put your shoe at the end of the bed."

She left, and I looked at myself in the mirror again. She had done a great job. I looked good. I ran some water, grabbed Antonio's shave cream and razor, and finished my makeover. I couldn't stop thinking of Poppy as I shaved. The more I knew about her, the more mysterious she became.

Antonio had cleaned my shoe. It sat lonely on the floor in between the bed and the nightstand. I put on the sock that I found stuffed inside it, laced up the sneaker, and hobbled out toward the front doors of the vestibule. A wicker picnic basket sat on the floor at the foot of the stairs that led up to the loft. I walked up and almost stumbled over it as I bent down to peek inside. Two bottles of wine, one white, one red, lay next to a brick of cream cheese, a package of sliced roast beef, a tube of rye crackers, and a tin of caviar. I looked up when I heard light footfalls on the stairs.

"Do you think it's enough food?" Poppy asked.

"Yes," I said, somewhat stupefied as I looked up at her. She had worn jeans and a cotton shirt when she'd cut my hair but came down the stairs wearing a short, shapely black-and-white dress, black high-heeled shoes, and a white hat with a black fishnet veil pulled down over her face. She carried a small black purse in one hand and an ornate cane in the other. She walked slowly down the stairs and stepped carefully around the basket at the bottom.

"Here," she said, handing me the cane. "This is for you. I found it this morning and thought it would be easier for you to use than that unwieldy crutch."

I took it from her outstretched hand and looked at it. The shaft was an inch-and-a-half-thick rod of smooth, dark-stained wood that tapered slightly into a worn brass end cap. The handle was a dragon's head, meticulously carved from the same type of dark wood as the shaft. The artwork and detail were incredible. Each tiny individual reptile scale was carved out and defined from the others. The open snarling mouth held rows of small, pointed, ivory teeth set into the upper and lower jaws. Two faceted, button-sized blue gem eyes looked out at me, and a mother-of-pearl inlaid band collared the beast where the polished shaft joined with the carved neck.

"Poppy, this is beautiful." I turned it over and looked at it from all angles.

"Well, I would say that I hope you get many years of use and enjoyment out of it, but let's hope you only need to use it for a few weeks. After that let's hope it's for decoration only."

I held the cane in my hands, disbelieving. "I'm not sure I understand; you mean, you're giving this to me?"

"Yes, it is yours."

"I . . . I don't know what to say. I mean, these, these eyes look like—"

"Sapphires?" she prompted.

"Yeah, sapphires."

"They are."

"I don't understand," I said, confused.

"Try it out, see how it fits," she said, motioning for me to walk around the room like a model. I obeyed her subtle command in my stunned state and walked around the baptismal font. The cane felt perfect and made it much easier for me to get around. It was just the right height, just the right weight, and fit my hand perfectly.

"It looks good on you," she said, admiring me. "The eyes match yours, very nice."

"Poppy, why are you doing this?" I asked, looking at her as seriously as I could. She gave back a similar stare. "I figure you patched me up and let me stay because you felt guilty for almost killing me, but this," I said, holding up the cane, "this is far beyond that. I want to know why you are doing this."

She broke off her stare, lifted her eyes to the ceiling, and let out an exhale before looking at me sincerely. "Let me show you why."

7

"Easy with the steps this time," Poppy said as she slipped on a pair of dark, horn-rimmed sunglasses under her veil, grabbed the wicker picnic basket, and opened one of the large doors to the world outside. I stepped through behind her and pulled the door closed. The afternoon sun shone brilliantly, and I had to shield my eyes from the rays reflecting off the polished granite steps that led down to the street. Ten steps down, I turned to look at the facade of the building I had lived in for the past two days. The two heavy doors were set in a twelve-foot-tall Gothic arch of rough-cut limestone. One large, circular stained glass window looked out from high in the wall. A square bell tower stood on the left-hand corner of the church and stretched twenty feet taller than the highest part of the wall. Wire mesh screens covered the small open arches of the belfry to keep birds out.

Poppy was halfway down the steps when Antonio got out of the driver's side door of a long, glossy, black vintage Cadillac. It was an early sixties model in perfect condition. Antonio quickly walked the shorter way around the front of the car and took the picnic basket before opening the back door for Poppy. He wore black slacks and shoes, the same white short-sleeved Cuban shirt, now buttoned correctly, and a black chauffeur's hat that covered most of his white hair. He kept his hand on the open car door and watched me as I slowly descended the steps. I eased in and sat on the large bench seat next to Poppy as he closed the door.

The car was large inside. The back seat was set five feet back from the front and was obviously designed for chauffeuring duties. The gray leather upholstery and gray carpet looked brand new, as did the burled walnut inlays in the armrests and the dashboard.

Antonio placed the picnic basket on the front seat and sat down behind the wheel. Poppy gave a one-word command in Spanish as he started the engine and drove away from the church toward downtown LA.

We had traveled about a mile away when Poppy took a four-inch-long black cigarette holder out of her purse along with the familiar orange-and-white pack of Turkish cigarettes. She looked over at me behind the opaque lenses and held out the open pack, offering me one. I took one and watched as she placed hers in the end of the slim, silver-tipped holder. She then slipped the slim end of the holder through the wide gaps in the fishnet veil, opened a polished cover in the wooden armrest of the door, and depressed the cigarette lighter. I shifted the cane to my left hand and depressed the lighter on my side.

I couldn't help but feel a small amount of remorse for questioning her gift of the cane and wondered if she thought I was questioning her hospitality as well. I was, of course, but didn't want her to think so. The point was moot now—I'd said my piece. I made up my mind to remain silent until we reached the picnic spot or until she spoke to me, and I wondered in the silence about what answers would come at the end of this ride.

Poppy's lighter popped up first. I watched her profile as she lit her cigarette. She was the epitome of elegance and enigma. My lighter clicked, and I looked out the window as I smoked. It was a beautiful day. *I need to call Henry tonight. I should have called him last night. He'll never believe this story*, I thought, replacing the lighter and closing the cover.

ANTONIO DROVE SLOWLY through residential areas and stayed off of major thoroughfares except to connect to the next neighborhood. Poppy looked straight ahead and spoke to him only once more. I looked straight ahead, too, sneaking glances at her when I could. Her right hand was placed on top of her left and showed the tattoo I had seen earlier. It was flat black and stood out dramatically on her fair skin.

We drove alongside the short fence that bordered the large Evergreen Cemetery.⁶ Three small, monument-covered hills rose above one another beyond the green. Antonio slowed almost to a stop as he turned right into the cemetery.

I turned back to Poppy and opened my mouth partially, but found she was already looking at me. I wanted to say something but stopped. One corner of her mouth curled into a smile as she spoke. "We're almost there. I hope you're hungry."

"Yes, I am," I said, regaining my presence of mind. I looked out the window and continued waiting. *A picnic in a cemetery. Different*, I thought.

Antonio drove at a respectful ten miles per hour.

The headstones got older the farther back into the cemetery we went. Two groundskeepers on large, three-bladed riding lawn-mowers drove next to us and kept up for a second before peeling off together like formation fighter planes weaving quickly in and out of a long row of granite monuments. The first section of the

---

6. The Evergreen Cemetery, east of downtown at the corner of First and Evergreen, is Los Angeles's oldest and matches Evan's description of being an oasis of quiet within the city.

cemetery we drove through was dotted with the light-brown rectangles of fresh graves, along with fresh flowers and mourners, but
on this back part, on the third hill, everything was green. Old
gray soldier's crosses, headstones, and large vaults stood lonely and
vacant like the remnants of a lost city. There were no flowers or visitors in this oldest section, only groundskeepers, birds, and squirrels
to keep the dead company. Looking around this deserted area with
all its green grass and trees, the idea of a picnic seemed less strange.
This was probably the most peaceful and secluded spot in the city.

We drove out of sight of the mowers into a section of large
tombstones and vaults with dates from the late nineteenth
century. Antonio eased the Cadillac down a narrow lane between
the plots, and then stopped in the middle of several medium-sized
family vaults.

"We're here," Poppy said, crushing out her cigarette.

Antonio got out and opened the door for her, then for me.
"This is a beautiful spot, Poppy. I wouldn't have thought of this," I
said, adjusting the cane underneath me. The sounds of the faraway
city were barely audible.

"Follow me," she said to me as she took the basket from Antonio. "It's over here." She said something to Antonio in Spanish as
she looked over at his watch. I followed Poppy into the cemetery
as he drove off.

She walked briskly out in front of me. The soft ground under
the grass made it difficult for me to walk with the cane, and I
felt like shouting to her to set the basket down so we could eat
here and I wouldn't have to walk any farther. She walked toward
one of the larger vaults, a weathered and rain-streaked gray one.
Two thick columns stood vigil on either side of the wrought iron
double doors. Two squirrels scampered off as she approached. The
vault was the size of a small carriage house. As I got closer, I could
make out more detail. The same symbol Poppy had tattooed on

the back of her hand was carved into the marble above the arched doors where the family name should have been. It hadn't occurred to me until then that we might be going to a specific place in here.

I continued my slow, steady pace as she set the basket down in front of the doors and turned to look at me. Fresh purple flowers sprouted from two metal vases in front of the columns. The surrounding tombstones were large and ornate. I glanced at them as I passed; Phillip Clairmonte 1820–1892 was carved into the base of an eight-foot-tall obelisk, Regina Duncan 1888–1889 lay underneath a weathered and worn, life-sized, kneeling baby lamb.

"This is a very special place for me," she said when I was about twenty steps away.

"Why is this place so special?"

"It is the resting place of my benefactors."

The outfit she wore made sense to me now, and I felt awkward at being dressed in jeans and a T-shirt. At least they were black. The purple orchids in front of this vault were the only flowers in sight. "Do you visit here often?"

"I come here when I want to think," she said, removing a black skeleton key from her purse. She unlocked the doors and opened them one at a time.

The room inside was lit, to my surprise, by two small skylights. One shaft of light slanted down onto the center of the floor and the other landed on the left-hand wall. Polished brass plaques lined the left and right walls above two simple stone benches, one on each side.

She grabbed the basket and walked inside. I took a step behind her but stopped in the open doorway. She placed the basket on the bench and sat down beside it as she lifted the veil and removed her sunglasses. "Aren't you going to come in?"

Now was my chance to press the issue. "You were going to tell me about this," I said, tapping the brass end cap of the cane on the stone floor.

"Why don't you ask them?" she said, pointing to the plaques on the opposite wall.

Them? I thought as I stepped inside. The air inside was cool. *Them.* I turned my back to her and looked at the plaques. The second square of sunlight perfectly framed and highlighted one of the brass markers, making the others hard to see. The plaque was two feet wide and a foot and half tall. The only thing on it was a name and year of birth and death, Graciela L. Cruz 1889–1977.

"Graciela Cruz, was she your— Is she the one you spoke about?" I asked, turning to look at Poppy.

Poppy had already placed two wine glasses on the bench next to the basket. "Yes, she bought the church. What do you want to start with, red or white?"

"White, please."

"White it is. I thought we'd start with caviar and cream cheese."

"Hmm," I murmured. "Was this cane hers?"

"No, it belonged to Louis."

"Who?"

"Louis, on this side," she said, pointing to the darker wall behind her.

It took several seconds for my eyes to adjust from the shiny sunlit brass of the other side. Six plaques were set in two rows of three. Names and dates showed on all the plaques. The one she pointed to was in the middle of the bottom row, Louis Lucas de Nehon 1657–1723.

I looked at it for several seconds, reading the date over and over. I gripped the cane next to my right leg and did the math, over two hundred fifty years old. I thought the cane was old, but I wouldn't have guessed it was that old. The dragon head seemed to get hotter in my hand as I thought about the significance of such a gift, and I was more determined than ever to find out what was going on.

My eyes wandered to the neighboring plaques as I formulated

my next question for Poppy. The one to the left of Louis's read Marco Parcalus 1630–1657, the one to the right on the bottom row read Colleen Korin McGregor 1723–1761. I started to see the pattern in the dates and stood straight up to look at the ones above. Nez-Lah 1506–1524, Bando 1524–1540, and Bahram Al-Malick 1540–1630 looked back at me from left to right. The cane clicked on the stone floor as I turned to look at the plaques on the other wall. Diana Marie Duggan 1761–1824 was on the top row on the left and Dr. Hans M. Roder 1824–1889 was in the middle. Graciela still shined in the sunlight on the right. The three plaques below were all blank.

My eyes unfocused as I thought about my own timeline, three lives, uninterrupted from 1892 till now. It all began to make sense: the enamel basin, the crude crutch, the McTaggart, and the cane. I ran my hand over the warm brass of Graciela's monument as fragmented thoughts coalesced in my mind. She would have been three years older than Vasili. I turned and looked at Poppy. She was staring at me again, but I had expected it this time. "I think I understand," I said, my voice almost cracking.

"I think you understand too," she said. Her facial expression warmed as she continued. "You're like me, aren't you?"

I nodded after several unblinking moments. I was too stunned to speak. *You're like me, aren't you?* The words echoed in my head, echoed in the vacuum where my reality had been seconds before. *You're like me.* I never thought I'd be like anybody. I mean, I never thought there would be anyone like me.

Poppy uncorked the bottle and filled the glasses. "Here," she said, patting her hand on the bench, "sit down and have some wine."

Sitting down, I held the wine glass with two hands to keep it from shaking. I drank half the glass, but it was little help for my dry mouth. "I don't know what to say," I said, placing the glass down on the bench, again using both hands.

"It's all right, Evan, I understand what you're feeling. I've been in your position before. Take your time, we have plenty of supplies," she said, opening the basket.

I remained motionless and must have seemed catatonic on the outside. But inside, I was a turmoil of activity. I felt nervous about confiding in anyone after all these years and yet joyful about the possibility that this could be true. I was anxious to find out more and I felt uneasy about a new reality in which I would no longer be unique. *You're like me.* In the past three years, I'd often fantasized about finding someone else like me, someone else who remembered.

I stirred back to life after several minutes. "Do you remember all these people?" I asked, looking at the nine plaques around me.

"Yes, sort of, I don't tend to look at it as remembering them. I *was* them, each of them. They continue to live in me. One person, the same person in new bodies, including this one," she said, admiring her skinny outstretched arms. "This body will go right there." She pointed to the blank plaque on the lower left side.

I reached down and grabbed the forward edge of the stone bench in a vain attempt to keep my world from spinning off its axis. If she was like me, I began to question who or what I was. This all started when I began to remember Vasili and Bobby. I had always thought of them as precursors to me, it had never occurred to me that I could be a continuation of them.

"Evan?" she said, lightly touching my right arm. "Are you all right?"

I looked at the blank brass plaques on the bottom row which would serve as future memorials. "I, ah, never thought of it that way, the way you put it. It changes everything when you put it like that."

"What do you mean?"

I turned around and looked at the oldest plaque: 1506–1524. That would mean she remembered back almost five hundred years; she was five hundred years old. "I don't know what I mean yet. This is all so . . . This, ah, wasn't what I was expecting today, Poppy," I laughed nervously.

She lightly stroked my arm as she refilled my glass. "I'm obligated to tell you this," she said, motioning around the vault with the mouth of the wine bottle. "I wanted to tell you as soon as I was sure about you. Evan, I know what it's like being in the dark."

"What am I?" I asked.

She smiled for several seconds. "The clinical term for you and me is *palingenesist*."[7]

"What does that mean?"

"It's derived from Greek, it means to be born again, in a literal sense. But we think of ourselves as reincarnationists, people who remember their past lives with complete recall."

I nodded automatically as I contemplated whether she remembered, really remembered, the people on these plaques.

"How old are you?" she asked.

"Twenty-one."

"No, not this," she said pinching my forearm. "You are not the age of your body. You are as old as your mind." She raised her hand and touched her finger to her temple. "I mean this." Her dark eyes burned with intensity.

I knew what she meant, but my thoughts were still too cluttered to do the math. "Since 1892."

"How many trips?"

"What?"

---

7. Poppy's use of this term is interesting. The word palingenesis is an arcane term used to describe the metaphysical doctrine of the transmigration of the soul, or, in lay terms, reincarnation.

"I'm sorry. Lives, how many lives do you remember?"

"This is my third."

She rummaged through the basket and brought out the caviar, the rye crackers, and the brick of cream cheese. "How long have you known you're different?"

"Three or four years."

She looked at me curiously. "That can't be. Seventeen sounds about right for you to begin to remember, but you said this is your third trip."

"Yes."

"Didn't you realize what you were when you came back in your second life?" she asked.

Came back. There was that point of view again. "No, I didn't. I started to remember both lives three or four years ago."

"Fascinating," she said, squinting into my eyes. "How old were you when you died?"

I looked up at the ceiling as I searched for the numbers. "Sixty-four the first time and six the last time."

"Ah, that explains it. You never got old enough to remember on your second trip so you remembered both in this trip. Very interesting."

"Trips? That's a very odd term. Why do refer to it as trips?"

"It starts to seem that way after a while. As the years pile up, you begin to realize the transitory nature of these physical bodies," she said, looking me up and down. The way she looked at me when she said that was unnerving, like I was some kind of walking cadaver.

"You said I wasn't old enough to remember the second time. What do you mean?"

"You said your physical age is twenty-one years, yes?"

I nodded.

"Three years ago means you changed when you were eighteen."

"What change? I'm not sure I understand."

"I'm talking about the change that happened when you began to remember who you are, or who you were before, depending on how you look at it. That's what happened to you, right?"

I nodded.

"That's normal, it happens when the body reaches physical maturity, usually between sixteen to eighteen in each incarnation. The change would have happened on your second trip if you had survived to that age."

That's normal. Normal hadn't applied to me in a long time. *You're normal like me*, I thought, watching her remove the metal key and open the tin of caviar. "Why does it happen that way?" I asked.

"Who knows," she said, shrugging. "Not me, that's for sure, and I've been trying to figure it out for hundreds of years. It's always the same though. You lead a normal childhood, playing and carefree until your body begins to mature, then you're hit with a barrage of memories from the past. Sometimes it takes several years to get them straight in your head, other times they fall into place more easily. Each time it gets a little easier because you remember being in this same confused state in your earlier trips. Was it a difficult time for you when you began to remember the other lives?"

"Yes, I thought I was going crazy."

"It is always such a confusing time. You just get used to the changes in your teenage body, and then those memories come flooding back, and you are not sure of who you are or who you are going to become."

"I am still wondering who I will become," I answered.

Poppy continued, "I like it that each time there is always an intermission, an amnesic period, I like to call it, from when you come into a fresh body until you begin to remember. I don't know, it's sort of nice to feel innocent and free for a while before you have to face your past again. Were you happier before you began to change?" she asked.

"Yes," I said without thinking; I didn't have to.

"Hmm, I suppose I am, too, most times. Have you ever tried Iranian caviar before?" she asked, placing a dollop of tiny black eggs on a cream cheese covered wafer.

"No."

"Really? Over one hundred years old and you've never had this," she said, handing it to me. "You *are* lucky I found you."

I took a small bite. It tasted strongly of fish and salt. "It's good."

"Another?"

"Please. Speaking of finding me, how did you know I was like you?"

"I knew the first night."

I raised my eyebrows in surprise as I took another cracker from her.

"Yes, the first night. I suppose after so long, I know what to look for. You may not remember—you were in pretty bad shape after you fell down the stairs—but you basically told me. Just as I was about to shoot you, at your request I might add, you told me that you would probably just come back anyway."

"I remember, but could you tell from just that?"

"I suspected after that. I knew after I gave you a cigarette. You don't speak, write, or read Turkish, do you?"

I was lost by her line of questioning. "I know a few sayings. I had lived in Istanbul for a while, before this life I mean."

"That's what I thought," she said excitedly. She reached inside her purse and removed a fresh pack of Lendts. "Can you read what this says?" she asked, pointing to the small Turkish script under the English.

"No, I can't read it. I've never been able to read it, but I know what it says."

"Do you?" she asked, challenging me.

"It says *Centuries of Flavor.*"

"That's when I knew. It used to say *Centuries of Flavor*. They changed the slogan in the late 1960s, before you would have been born this time. I was pretty sure after that, but I used the book to bait you even further. I had no doubt after your reaction. I don't think there is anyone alive who would stay up all night reading McTaggart unless they were like me. The man's writing style is so stilted and dry, it can be maddening to read even a single chapter."

I guess she did know what to look for. I had no idea I had given any clues. "What does it say now?" I asked, pointing to the pack of cigarettes.

"*The Pride of the Turks* or something like that. I can't read it either, but I remember when it changed. These have been my brand for a long time."

"You know, I started to sense something was up after Antonio brought the books down. Your bait, as you called it, seemed too much of a coincidence." I was beginning to feel much less at a disadvantage.

"You saw that coming, huh?" Poppy smiled sheepishly.

"A little bit." I returned her warm smile.

"I also had you checked out, just to be sure," she added defensively.

"What are you talking about?" A lump of concern began to rise in my throat.

"I researched your medical records for any history of mental illness. Confiding your true nature to anyone normal could easily get you diagnosed as schizophrenic, delusional, or any number of other things. It wouldn't be the first time it had happened."

"What did you find?"

"Nothing, no history. Should I have found something?"

"No, I never told anyone except my family."

"And now me," she said, placing her soft hand in mine. "Tell me about Istanbul." Her eyes lit up as she squeezed my hand.

"All right, but I should go back a little farther to preface the story. Pour me some more wine, would you?"

Poppy refilled my glass and prepared more crackers as I began. I was anxious to tell my story to someone, anyone, and not see my own face reflected in a mirror, mouthing the words.

"I was born in 1892 as Vasili Blagavich Arda in a small Bulgarian farming village northwest of Varna. He was—I was—an only child of a farmer, so there was never any question as to my future. I worked with my father until I was twenty-three, when Bulgaria entered the war against the allies and all the single men in my village were pressed into service. I was in the army until the Great War ended.

"My father and I worked together for two years after the war, until he died. The land was mine after that, and I found a wife the following year, Vanya. She and I lived and farmed peacefully for the next twenty-five years until the end of the next war when the communists forcibly took our land and put us both in prison. She didn't survive. I was released in 1948 and managed to reach the Turkish border later that year. I lived in Istanbul for the last years of that life."

"Did you and Vanya have any children?" Poppy asked as soon as I took a break.

"No, we were unable . . ."

"What did you like about the city?"

"Life in Istanbul was a shock after coming from rural Bulgaria. It's a lot like LA, I suppose. Everybody's hustling or working some kind of angle, and it's very much a cultural mixing pot. I think that helped with my initial loneliness. There was a large Bulgarian expatriate community in the oldest section of the city next to the strait, that's where I spent most of my time. I remember there were lots of boats around—small fishing boats mostly."

"If you were so attached to Istanbul, it makes sense that in this life, you were drawn to LA," Poppy said.

"Once you've seen Istanbul, you'll never forget its skyline. The city is built around seven hills, each topped with an opulent mosque. From where I used to live, the entire skyline consisted of tall minarets and colorful domes. At night and in the early morning when the city was quiet, you could hear the muezzins calling the faithful to prayer."

"Sounds beautiful."

"Yes, it was nice, but anything was nice after prison."

"Would you like to go back there again someday?"

"Yeah, I'd like to see it again, go back to where I lived and see how things have changed. Knowing Istanbul, I bet they haven't changed very much. But where I would really like to go is back to Bulgaria. I want to read street signs and speak with other Bulgars. I miss the language."

"I've never been to Bulgaria. What's it like?"

I ate another cracker and thought about her question. "The farmland looks a lot like Idaho."

I took the bottle and refilled her glass. "That's enough about me. I want to hear something about your history."

"All right," she said, looking up at the skylight. "I was first born five hundred miles east of here in a small pueblo village. It's in Arizona now." She stopped for a moment to take her glass back, and I used the break to pry deeper.

"Have you ever gone back there?"

"Yes, twice." She pointed to the Bando plaque on the wall behind her. "I went back in 1540, on my second trip, to rejoin them, and I went there again in 1854 when this area of the world was being settled."

"What was it like to go back?" I asked as I thought about my old Bulgaria.

"It was bittersweet—things change, you know." She paused and took a drink. "Anyway, the first two times, I died so quickly

I didn't have a chance to do much. The third trip I tried hard to live a normal life. I was married into an affluent family in Persia before I was old enough to realize who I was. But the fourth trip is the one that changed me forever." She stopped, dipped her middle finger in the wine, and ran it around the rim of the glass. A haunting high note began to sing from the glass on the second revolution. "It was then, as Marco, that I learned about glass."

"Wait a minute," I interjected, "you've been both male and female?"

"Yes, of course. It's all up to chance," she said, chuckling.

"I didn't mean to distract you, it's just that, I haven't . . . so it never occurred to me that it was possible."

"Don't worry, you'll come back as a girl too—the odds will even out. After you have been both a man and a woman, things like gender tend to become more fluid, less defined by hard lines. You'll see in time. It's cool to be both. It offers an interesting perspective."

I'd often thought about the idea of coming back again and remembering this life the way I remembered the others, but the matter-of-fact way she said it like it was a foregone conclusion made me begin to think about it more as a probability than a possibility. If we were alike, she had been in this situation many more times than I had, enough times that it had become a foregone conclusion. The ringing from the glass continued for a few seconds after she removed her finger. "Please, continue . . . You were talking about Marco."

"Yes. I was born for the fourth time, in 1630, as Marco Parcalus on the island of Murano. Murano is a small island near Venice and was home to the city's glassworks.[8] I was born into a family that had lived and worked on the island for generations,

8. Venice was a world leader in glass manufacture until the eighteenth century, but the glass is actually manufactured on the nearby island of Murano. Venetian glass furnaces were moved to Murano in 1291 due to safety concerns after several devastating fires.

each father passing the secrets of Venetian glass to his son. The finest glass in the world came from that island, and I became the best craftsman that ever worked their furnaces."

I could tell that Poppy remembered this life fondly, and I wanted to know more. "How old were you when you began learning glass?" I asked her.

"My father started teaching me when I was old enough to hold a blowing tube—five or six, I think. He taught me about plate glass, leaded glass, colored glass, mirrors, and *cristallo*, like this," she said, looking at me with one eye through her wine glass. "At sixteen, I was already a master craftsman. I could achieve any color, thickness, texture, or shape, and could make plates of glass half again as large as anyone else on the island.

The families of Murano were very close. They had to be, because once you were born into a family, you were also born into the art of glass, and you were never allowed to leave the island."

"Never?" I asked, dumbfounded by the idea that a whole society would abide by such strict rules.

"Never. I stayed for a while, but you must keep in mind that I had just spent a long, frustrating life trying to pretend I was normal. The idea of doing it again left me no choice but to risk escape."

"Wait," I said, looking around the vault. "These people are the same ones in the stained glass scenes at your church aren't they?" I asked as I made the connection.

"Yes, but as I said before, I *am* those people, the scenes are from my own lives."

"Right, Marco is the one rowing away from the island."

"Yes, I eventually escaped on a small boat. Only official Venetian ships were allowed into the port on Murano. The ships brought supplies to us and carried away vast inventories of window glass, mirrors, and *cristallo* to Venice for trade and export. There were ten or fifteen soldiers on each ship that checked for stowaways when they counted the cargo in port, and it was the job of the island governor to get a head count of all the island's inhabitants after each ship left. On the two occasions that there were escapes, both men were eventually hunted down and killed by assassins hired by the Doge of Venice.[9] They brought back their bodies tied to the prows of the ships so that everyone on Murano would know what became of them. This stranglehold on the island kept a European glass monopoly in Venice for centuries, but it also allowed me my chance at fortune and comfort later."

Poppy paused for a sip of her wine, then continued. "The whole plan took about a year. There were two main ships that visited the island for pickups. They alternately came every two weeks, except for special projects."

I nodded, completely enthralled in her story.

"Loading cargo was not my assigned duty, but the porters never seemed to mind an extra hand down at the dock. I helped with the loading for months, until my face was known to everyone on both crews. It was only then that I made my next move.

"The crews used the same crates over and over, and we would always unload the empty crates back into the island's warehouse so they could be used again for the next outgoing load of finished glass."

She paused for a moment, looking off into the distance as if overtaken by the memory. "My main duty was to blow and shape glass, which I did with extreme care and craft. I made museum-quality pieces by the dozens; flowers, orbs, vases, statues, then carefully packed them in straw-filled crates so that each piece lay exposed on top. I then secretly placed all of these crates

9. Venice did indeed have a death penalty in place for any Murano glassworker who left the lagoon. This was in order to maintain their treasured glass manufacture monopoly in Europe. This is well detailed in many editions, specifically *Mirror, Mirror* by Mark Pendergrast.

in an unused part of the warehouse and waited for my ship to come in.

"When the church bells announced its arrival, I made my way to the dock like normal, unloaded the empty crates like normal, smiled and said hello to the crew members like normal. Then, when it came time to load the ship, I brought out my master-pieces. I carried every fifth crate that came out of the warehouse, only I grabbed mine off of my special pile in the back. The crates the other four carried had a layer of straw on the top, but mine were open to the sun which brilliantly illuminated each piece. I studied the face of each guard as I passed with my crates. After the sixth trip, I knew which guard it would be. His eyes lit up, and he craned his neck to look at each piece as I went by. He stopped me on the next trip and picked up a large purple-tinted swan I had completed just four days before.

"I talked with him for several minutes and told him that I had made the pieces he had been admiring. He praised my skill and said he would like to see more of my works the next time they came to port. I knew what to do after that.

"During the day, I worked on the regular quota of mirrors and plate glass, and at night I would fire up the furnace alone and work on my own pieces. I worked alone at night for the next month. The final product was nineteen pieces, including an incredibly difficult mirrored glass ball about the size of an orange. When the boat returned, I carried my special crates from the back of the warehouse again. The guard stopped me on my first pass and told me to place my crates in the back corner of the ship's hold. He went below and inspected each piece in every crate as I carried them in. He admired each work covetously and seemed blind to his position and responsibility while he held them. I sat down and made my pitch after I carried in the last crate.

"I offered him nineteen pieces of better quality than the ones he had arranged on the crates around us, in exchange for a small boat to be brought to me at midnight three weeks from that night at the west end of the island. He would pick up his pieces when he delivered the boat. He looked at the glass around him. We both knew it was worth a king's ransom in any other Mediterranean city.

"I reached into my jacket pocket and pulled out the mirrored ball. His eyes glazed over when he saw it. 'Three weeks from tonight at midnight. Don't be early, don't be late,' I said to him as I placed the ball in his hand.

"I completed a piece a night, every night, until the night I left. The twenty pieces fit in five crates, which I hid in some underbrush at the shore. I had told my father and the other blowers that I was experimenting late at night. They grew used to seeing the furnace smokestack belching red embers into the night sky and usually left me alone. On my last night on the island, I stoked up the furnace as usual but left my tools in their racks. I sat on a high stool in front of the furnace and pulled on the rope that moved the bellows. The only possessions I had with me were my clothes, some small pieces of gold from the shop, and the journal I had kept through my seventeenth and eighteenth years.

"In those years I had begun writing down the scraps of memories and experiences that came to me when I began to remember, in hopes that I could make some sense out of them. I did, of course, realize again what I was. I stoked the fire until I had enough light to read. The heat from the hearth was intense. I untied the leather straps that bound the loose pages and read each one before throwing it into the mouth of the furnace.

"I was waiting in the bushes next to the crates when I heard the sound of oars breaking the water. I called out to him several times before he came to shore. By the moonlight, I could tell he had a companion that rowed the second boat. He greeted me warmly, then inspected all twenty works by holding them up to a lantern. There was no question about their quality. To this day they were the most exquisite things I have ever produced.

"The two men left quickly, and in the darkness, over the sounds of their rowing, I thought I heard him yell back 'Buona Fortuna.' I followed the light of their lantern until I picked up the outline of the Italian shore in the morning sky, then veered west and went ashore and on to what I thought would be freedom beyond Venice." She finished the last of her wine and placed the glass next to me.

I opened the red bottle and refilled both glasses. "That's an incredible story, Poppy. In the stained glass, there was a man with a knife stalking Marco, was he an assassin?"

"She," she corrected, "was an assassin and killed me in the streets of Prague three years later. It didn't matter in the end. In my next life, I took the secrets of Murano and made a fortune. I still live off that fortune today. I've worked with stained glass since then just to keep in practice."

I nodded and handed her the glass, noticing the tattoo. "I have another question for you, Poppy."

"Yes."

"That symbol tattooed on your hand, it's above the doors on the outside of this vault too. What is it?"

"Oh, this," she said, turning her hand so that she could see it, "this is called an *Embe*. It's a tradition with all of us."

8

"Of us?" I asked, confused. "Us *who*?"

"The others like you and me."

"There are others?" I asked, raising my voice.

"Yes," she nodded, "but much older."

I didn't know what to think. I couldn't think. My mind reeled with the possibilities. "How many more?"

"Twenty-eight, including me. I'm one of the younger ones."

Twenty-eight. Each question she answered prompted ten more. "How old are they?"

"Well, we all know from experience that if you come back once, you will continue to come back. It's the same for all of us, so some are quite old." She looked up as she did the math. "The oldest one dates back to the first century AD, forty or so incarnations. The rest started at all dates between then and now. You would definitely be the youngest."

"Tell me about them," I demanded.

"I cannot," she said firmly. "Evan, I know it's cruel to be so close to the truth about yourself and not be able to touch it, but there are good reasons—"

"What, what good reasons?" I asked, irritated.

She sat calmly and looked up at me. "As I was saying, all of the members of this society, all twenty-eight of us, are sworn to secrecy by each other. I suspect most of them will only share their identity with you once you are accepted."

"Accepted? Into what?"

"That's one of the things I *can* tell you. The twenty-eight of us are an extended family of sorts, we all formally belong to a society formed centuries ago by the first ones like us to find each other. This society is called the Cognomina. It's a Latin term that means to remember the same name.[10] The tattoo," she said, rubbing a thumb at it, "is worn by all of us in each successive life after we go through the Ascension."

I gave her a questioning look.

"The Ascension is like a trial all of us must go through in each successive incarnation before we reenter the Cognomina. Basically, you have to prove to the others that knew you before that you are the same person in this new body, hence the name, *Cognomina*."

"Then how can you be accepted if they don't know you?"

"Well," she said, laughing, "it's certainly easier than it used to be. In the old days, before my time, the members would face the candidate and one would run him through with a spear. The candidate would only be accepted when he came back in his next life, if he came back, and identified his murderer. These days you simply have to convince a panel of judges that you have lived before; names, dates, places, things that can be verified. It's most difficult the first time."

"What happens if I fail, I mean, what happens if you fail the first time?"

---

10. Poppy's use of Cognomina here appears to be an archaic reference to the Roman naming convention of a third "known as" name called a cognomen. This name could either be inherited or adopted.

"Don't worry, Evan, you'll do fine. Besides, I'll be your advocate."

"What does that mean?"

"I'll tell them about how I found you."

I couldn't help but think about what these others would be like. Twenty-eight people who would know what this type of life is like. Twenty-eight people that I wouldn't have to lie to in order to be close. Twenty-eight people to know now and in the future. "Poppy, tell me about this society. Tell me as much as you can."

"All right," she said, taking some more wine. "This society, the Cognomina, was established by the first six of us in 839 in the then small Swiss confederation village of Zurich, but the tradition of the first of us coming back in successive lives and meeting one another dates back to the third century AD. The first two that found each other started meeting each year on the summer solstice at the pyramids of Giza in Egypt. They met this way every year so that if one died, the other knew he would eventually return to the same spot in a new body and greet his friend. After a few lives, they began to mark themselves with the symbol of their assigned meeting place to make identification easier when meeting each other in fresh incarnations. That's what this symbol evolved from," she traced the outline of the tattoo with her finger, "the three peaks of the pyramids."

I nodded.

"One Egyptian summer, on that longest day of the year, one of them came back as a fresh young man after an eighteen-year absence and met his old friend, only to find two others with the same Embe symbol on their hands standing next to him. The first one had discovered a new one who already knew another. This is how we began, at least that's how the story goes. I entered in 1649."

"Are they still alive?" I asked, trying to fathom what it must be like to be that old.

"Yes, they are still around. Like I said, if you come back once, you always will. It's the same for all of us, it always has been," she said in a voice that sounded almost sad.

I thought about them, hundreds, even thousands of years old, the memories, loves, skills, and torments piled up on them unwillingly like an odd assortment of bricks shabbily assembled into haunted temples. I had lived in such a temple for over three years, alone. The idea of living in it alone for one day longer seemed too much to bear. I looked over at Poppy as she unwrapped the roast beef, and it all began to make perfect sense. They had to stay together, for sanity's sake if nothing else.

"It sounds like they were already well rooted in Egypt, so why move to Zurich and reestablish there?"

"Well, this condition we share has always afforded us the one luxury of practical immortality, though I've always thought the term *immemorial* more appropriate for us than *immortal*, for we all die, we just remember having died. I say *practical* because we were able to bequeath wisdom and experience to ourselves in each successive life, but we were never able to reap the benefit of any wealth or lands that we acquired because we could never pass it on to ourselves.

"Back when there were five of us, the odds were very high that there would always be at least one of us alive, *alive* in the sense that they were old enough to be aware of their nature and aware of the others. Since then, there has always been one designate who keeps the holdings of the ones who have died and returns them to the new incarnates upon their reemergence. The Ascension became the way of verifying identity. If the designate died, all of his assets and the assets of the others were passed on to an alternate or second designate that was still alive. It still works that way today. The fact that we have to depend on and trust one another makes us a very close family. The home you stayed in, the car you rode in, my other homes around the world, my twenty percent stake in one of the largest glass manufacturers in the world, were all left to me by my benefactor," she said, motioning to the plaques, "by me, the same person." She handed me a small sandwich of roast beef and cheese between two crackers. "Here, have a sandwich."

I took it without speaking and thought about family as I ate. I thought about what the word meant to me. Its meaning had changed forever when I had changed. Since then, there had been three families: mine, Vasili's, and Bobby's. Before I left, I spoke to my parents about this, but the memories of the older families drove my current one apart, turning it into a memory as well. It wasn't until that moment in the vault with Poppy that I realized what I had been unknowingly yearning for—a family, but not an ordinary family. I yearned for a family that wasn't transitory, fragile, or misunderstanding like the ones I'd known, but one in which I could be accepted as I am. "What would this Ascension be like for a newcomer like me?"

"I'm not sure I understand what you're asking."

"What would I be required to do? Are there initiation ceremonies? You said you would be my advocate; is there a trial?" I stopped to take a breath and soften my tone. "Poppy, what you are telling me, this society, these people, is beyond my wildest fantasies. For years I've wondered why I was different and what made me this way. I've battled with myself daily about whether or not to tell the people around me. I've held all-night conversations in my room with imaginary people who could understand what this is like and now I find these people, and they're real. Poppy, I want to know what I have to do in order to meet them."

I fought back tears as she took my hand. "I know what you're feeling, Evan. I am the one who found you. It is my responsibility to introduce you to the Cognomina, and I will tell you everything that I am allowed to tell." She stroked the back of my head fondly.

"The Ascension could best be described as a trial," she continued. "There will be a panel of five members that will have the
final say on your status, and you will have an advocate to help
you through the process. You will be asked to recount your life
histories first. Then you must answer questions from the panel
about those histories. There will be an emphasis on dates, places,
people, anything that can be verified to corroborate your claim.
This process can go on for days, even weeks. There is often a
break in the proceedings while certain facts are verified. After all
the questions are answered and names and dates verified, the five
members of the panel confer and give their decision. That's when
the fun starts," she said, breaking into a warm smile. "There is a
huge celebration after a confirmation, where the newcomer takes
a name for himself that is known only by the others. All the
members that are alive are summoned to a new confirmation
party, and after you take a name, you will be introduced to all in
attendance, one by one."

"You speak with such confidence about how I'll do."

"Of course I do; I'll be your advocate."

"Really?" I asked, feeling the excitement rising inside me.

"Yes, it's normal for the one who finds you to be your advocate." She stopped and looked at me seriously. "It would be my
honor, Evan."

"Great, how many have you done?" I asked, squeezing her
hand again.

"I've never been an advocate, but it's not that difficult. I'm
basically there to help you with the procedures, all the answers
are yours."

"Where is it located? In Zurich? Is there a permanent building?"

"Again, that is something I cannot tell you yet. I've told you
too much as it is. But I can tell you that I told some of the others
about you, and I took the liberty of arranging a flight for us to

Zurich on Sunday night, so you won't have to wait too long for the answers to your questions. I assume you *do* want to go?" she asked, looking at me for a response.

I didn't have to think very hard about it. One simple answer now could answer a thousand other questions. "Yes, I want to go."

"Good. I'll let them know so preparations can begin."

"What do I need to bring?"

"Nothing special, just normal travel gear. Do you have any suits?"

"No, do I need one?"

She emptied the last of the second bottle into my glass. "As your advocate, I'd recommend you get two or three. Do you have enough money to buy them?"

"I think so. I should after tomorrow. Oh, by the way, I need to use a telephone sometime tonight."

"No problem, I just bought one of these new portable ones," she said, taking a cell phone out of her purse. "You can use it now."

I shook my head. "It's too early, he doesn't get in until nine."

"What's going on tomorrow?" she asked.

"This guy I know owes me some money, and I have an appointment to meet him at a club tomorrow night to collect. Would you like to come?"

"I'll think about it. We should go, it's getting late. Are you ready?"

I nodded as I finished the last of the wine. She turned on the slim cell phone, punched in a number, and looked at me as she spoke into the receiver, "*Listos, Antonio.*"

I LEFT AND WALKED AHEAD as she locked the doors to the vault. Antonio was waiting with the car doors open by the time we made our way to the road. The sun sank behind orange, red, and purple clouds. I listened to the birds chirping and thought about what my life would be like from now on. I'd always felt like a cast-away, walking alone on my island, but now instead of finding one strange set of footprints in the sand, I found twenty-eight.

Antonio looked at me differently as I walked up to the car. He knew that I knew and acted as submissive to me as I'd seen him act with Poppy. He held some mysterious reverence toward her that hadn't made sense until now. She got in the car, and Antonio slowly started the Cadillac on the narrow, winding road out of the cemetery.

"Can you tell me why everything about this Cognomina is so secretive?"

She took a moment to answer. "There are two reasons. One is practical, and the other historical. You see, all of us have been around long enough to know that we have little in common with normal humans. The only people we can relate to are each other. We are all so old with so many memories and experiences from our lives that outsiders, those who do not remember, could never fathom what our existence is like. There seems little purpose in sharing something that can never be understood or appreciated. Surely, you already know that."

There was no longer any doubt in my mind she was like me. "Yes, you're right," I conceded.

"The second reason goes back to tradition. It all started shortly after everything was relocated to what is now Switzerland, around the turn of the first millennium. The seven members at that time had already amassed a fortune that rivaled many nearby king-doms. One of the oldest members, upon becoming the trustee, decided, without permission from the others, to tell all the villages within several days' ride about the Cognomina. She later claimed she did this in an attempt to establish a new kingdom with the seven members acting as a royal family that could rule in succes-sive incarnations. Word of the *tattooed devils* spread across the land like wildfire, and within a fortnight, the villagers killed all the members and looted the treasury of everything. Since then it's been a tradition to maintain secrecy about ourselves."

Antonio stopped in front of the church. I got out and started up the stairs. My foot was sore from walking in the cemetery.

"I have to go upstairs and take care of some business. I'll be back down in a while," Poppy said.

I watched her calf muscles flex as she walked up the stairs before I went straight to the guest room for the painkillers. They started to work in minutes, and I felt much better as I walked to the bathroom. Antonio was reading on the pew next to the bathroom when I passed. I came out and sat down beside him. "Is she still busy?"

He nodded and closed his book, an English language bible. "She is on the telephone."

"You read English?"

"I try to practice but I don't understand too much," he said, looking at the book. "She took you out to the vault today. That means you are the same as her, yes?" He spoke softly and kept his eyes cast down. I wondered if this was some kind of test she had put him up to.

"What do you mean?"

He drew in a deep breath. "I knew her before. Graciela Cruz hired me forty-five years ago. I have lived in this church since the 1950s, and in all that time she has never taken anyone else there. She always goes alone. I think you are special to her." I could tell something was burning inside him. "She hasn't even taken the other ones like her that have visited."

"You've met others?" I asked in an excited whisper.

"Three have come here to visit since I've been here. Two of them come back every few years."

"How did you know they were like her?"

"The tattoo," he said plainly. I felt like an idiot for asking such an obvious question. "But I would know anyway," he continued. "There is something about them that is unmistakable. I think I would know one anywhere now, even without the tattoo."

"What is it?"

Antonio looked up at me. "Power. They hold power over you, especially with their eyes."

He was right about the eyes, at least I thought so from what I'd seen of Poppy. She probed you with them and knew exactly what you were thinking, or let you know exactly what she was thinking. "Why are you telling me this, Antonio? I'm sure you're aware of how secretive Poppy is about this."

"She is secretive with the rest of the world, not with her own kind. You are lucky," he said, getting up. "I wish I was like her."

I didn't speak as he left. His words seemed to hang in the air until I digested them one by one. I had never thought of being lucky. I never saw anything particularly lucky in being alone, but the more I thought about it on that pew, the luckier I seemed. I would live beyond the annihilation of death. I would eventually be able to live in the same style Poppy did, and I would never lose this identity, this self that I have, that I am now. Like Poppy said, it was the closest thing to immortality anyone could ever find. I realized then that I always knew I would come back again and again, and that I'd lived in fear of it, like a roller coaster that never stops so you can get off. Until today I had been on that roller coaster alone. I was lucky not because I would come back, but because I would now come back to someone, something, someplace that was home.

The images of Nez-Lah, Bando, Marco, and Louis grew dim and faded to black as I sat alone. I eagerly looked forward for the first time in years. The questions were finally finding their answers.

POPPY CALLED OUT FOR ANTONIO, who was already halfway up the stairs to the loft before her last Spanish syllable was spoken. He came back down the stairs in less than a minute, turned right, and walked out the front door without a word.

"Is he gone?" she asked from above.

"Yes."

"I'm finished with my business. Come up if you want to use the telephone." I could see her now. She was dressed in the robe again with her hair pinned up like before. "Do you think you can navigate the stairs?"

I nodded. I could only see her from the chest up because of the rail, but it looked like her robe was open.

"Consider it physical therapy. Doctor's orders."

I smiled as I got up and climbed the stairs to her.

"You can sit on the bed. The phone cord reaches that far," she said, motioning to the black, bedspread-covered, king-size bed.

The high headboard and low footboard were a maze of vines and leaves reproduced in black wrought iron. A red, white, and black Persian rug blanketed most of the hardwood floor. Two old, brass oil lanterns lit the room from their perch on the large, ornately carved wooden bureau across from the bed. A life-size stone bust stood next to the mirror in the center of the bureau. It was a woman smiling. Her hair flowed wildly down onto her shoulders as though a strong breeze had just overtaken her. A crudely made necklace of hammered silver plates and leather straps hung around her delicate stone neck. I walked around and sat on the far edge of the bed nearest to the railing where I had seen Poppy standing.

"Here we go." She brought out a 1940s-style chrome-plated rotary phone. "Help yourself," she said, placing it on the bed, "I'd let you use the portable phone, but it doesn't work inside these stone walls. I'm going to ready a fresh dressing for your foot. I'll be back up in a bit."

I hung the cane on the railing and leaned back across the bed to get the phone. I could see another stained glass window above the stairs from where I lay. It was fifteen feet across and was divided into six pie-shaped wedges surrounding a small round panel in the center. It was too dark outside to make out much detail, but I assumed they were scenes from the rest of her lives.

I dialed the number to the Necropolis from memory and held for a few minutes until Henry came on the line.

"Henry, it's Evan."

"Evan! Where the fuck are you? I've been turning this town upside down trying to find you. I was worried the cops were sweating you out in some hole downtown. Ah, fuck, you're not calling from jail, are you?"

"No, I'm not in jail, and I'm okay, at least for now."

"What happened?"

"I got shot in the foot running from the job."

"Is it bad?"

"No, it's not that bad. I already got it sewed up, but man, I gotta tell ya, this has been the weirdest few days of my life. I'll tell you about it tomorrow night. I have to meet Shelby and get paid."

"You could've fucking called me, you know. You got a butt kickin' coming, big time."

"I know. I'll talk to you about it tomorrow. Save me two seats, will you, I might be bringing someone."

"Two seats? I knew there had to be a woman involved."

I laughed. "I'll see you tomorrow. I gotta go." I placed the receiver back in its cradle.

"Are you finished?" Poppy called up to me.

"Yes."

She returned with an old and worn black-leather medical bag in her hand. "That bandage is probably dirty from walking around outside today. Let me have a look," she said, dragging over a chair from in front of the bureau. "Scoot over here and give me your foot." She cradled it and quickly unwrapped the dirty gauze. "Better?"

"Yes." It felt good to get it off.

"I think we should leave it unwrapped tonight," she said, squeezing my calf. "The fresh air will help it heal, and you'll need to be one hundred percent soon. We leave for Zurich on Sunday."

"Really?"

"Yes. I called some of them after we got back today. Everything is set for it to begin. They are very excited to meet you."

I sat and watched her apply the salve to my stitches. *They're excited*, I thought. Through the excitement I'd felt about all that had happened, I hadn't thought about what anyone else would feel. Of course they would be excited. "Is it a rare occasion to have someone new come into the Cognomina?"

"Yes, it is, but it's not as rare as it used to be, probably because the world is becoming an increasingly smaller place, and finding lost brothers like you is easier than ever before. We always suspect there are more out there like us, so we are always on the lookout for them, like I was for you."

"How long has it been since the last one?"

"About sixty years, but he wasn't young like you. As a matter of fact, he was older than me. You know, you're lucky you found us so soon in your life. Some aren't found for centuries. Can you imagine what that existence is like? There could still be, and probably still are, scores of others, centuries old, perhaps, who are wandering around unaware that there are others like themselves. That's why we keep vigil."

"Is that what you meant when you said you were obligated to tell me about yourself?"

"Exactly," Poppy answered.

"How old were you when you were found?"

She laughed. "I was younger than you, much younger. It was in my second trip, so I would have been about thirty-six."

"That means you were lucky too."

"Hmm, I suppose so. I know that I was the youngest ever to be found, though I didn't enter the Cognomina until my fourth trip, as Marco."

"Why did you wait so long?"

"My second trip ended shortly after I was found, and in my third trip, I wasn't allowed to leave Persia." She stopped applying the ointment and thought before she continued. "The truth is, I could have left Persia if I'd wanted to. I didn't go because I didn't want to have any contact with the person who'd found me. I had to in the end, of course. He was summoned to my Ascension, but seeing him in a different body after a hundred years made it easier for me."

"Was he your advocate like you will be for me?"

"Never!" she barked vehemently, startling me. "No, I refused, and someone else was appointed to me, someone who since has become very special to me."

I could tell by the tone in her voice that she didn't want to talk about whatever had happened. "Was your Ascension difficult because you requested a different advocate?"

"It could have been, but my first Ascension took only two days due to special circumstances. The one who found me was there and had to testify to knowing me two trips before.

"After the first time, most Ascensions usually go like that. You have memories with other sitting members who can corroborate your claim. The first time is always the most difficult," she said, running her hand up my pant leg to the knee then dragging her fingernails down the back of my calf.

"Yes, I see what you mean." I lay back on the bed as she stroked my leg and untied my right shoe. It was happening. I wanted her. I had wanted her since seeing her that first night in the basement.

Learning about her, what she was, made me want her even more. I closed my eyes tight and moved my leg against her hand. *Oh, please let this be happening*, I thought.

Poppy withdrew her hand from my pant leg the same time my shoe hit the floor. I heard her walk away and I sat up on my elbows to see her pull the brown-leather syringe case from the top drawer of the dresser.

I had always been wary of heroin. I remembered how prevalent it was in Istanbul and how many people I'd seen it destroy. I'd experimented with marijuana and cocaine. I don't think you can live in this town without doing those. This week was the first time I'd ever had a needle in my veins. "I'm not in any pain," I said, preempting her.

She turned and looked at me with the case in her hands and burst out laughing. I sat up farther and tried to figure out what I'd said that was so funny. My erection showed no signs of going away. She unzipped the case and quickly assembled it. "It's for me," she said, still laughing. She grabbed the syringe and vial and climbed on all fours onto the bed next to me. "But you could be in pain." She whispered the words as she ran her tongue along the outside edge of my ear. "What would happen if I were to accidentally bump you in a moment of passion?" she said, nudging my left leg with hers.

I recoiled, even though I felt no pain.

"See what I mean? I won't use as much as last time," she whispered seductively. "Make a fist." She pulled away and switched the vial to her left hand, which she placed squarely on the now visible outline of my erection under the jeans. She kept her hand on me, squeezing as she uncorked the vial with her thumb and forefinger. She submerged the needle and drew half an inch of brown liquid up into the brass syringe. I felt my excitement getting stronger and my objections getting weaker as I balled my hand into a fist and held it out in front of her.

She recorked the vial, placed it on the bed, and gripped my wrist the same way she had done with my ankle the first time. I couldn't watch as I felt the needle enter. The same warm, orange-cream-colored wave rolled over me when she released her grip.

"Now you do me," she said, holding her left fist out in front of me. There was still more than half left in the syringe. I placed my hand around her delicate wrist and squeezed until tiny blue veins surfaced under her soft skin. She pierced one and emptied the syringe. I released my grip and watched, fascinated as the hole closed up and the blue vein disappeared under the surface of her skin like a long fish swimming out of sight into the depths of a muddy pond.

I laid back and mentally followed the wave as it crossed my body from left to right. Poppy placed the brown-leather case back in the bureau. Her robe opened slightly as she turned to me, and I could see she was naked underneath. She stood at the foot of the bed and looked at me. The velvet cord around her waist was still tied, but the lapels of the robe were uncrossed and lay close to her skin, hugging the outline of her breasts and exposing the small inverted triangle of dark hair just below the knotted cord. She studied me as she removed her hairpin, letting her hair down for the first time. It fell over her shoulders in silky, raven-black waves. The drug was taking hold of me, and I felt myself sit up as though someone was pushing from behind and below. I reached out and grabbed one of the tassels at the end of the velvet cord. She bent over, placed her hands on my shoulders, and kissed me hard on the lips. My mouth opened, and she thrust her tongue deep inside as she ground her lips against mine. She moved her head vigorously from side to side and her teeth clicked against mine as I hungrily tried to follow her lead. She didn't just kiss, she pressed, sucked, probed, and bit all as one motion. I struggled to anticipate her movements and keep up with her before finally surrendering and letting her take me where she wanted.

I was unprepared for the jolt of her violent shove against my shoulders and I felt like I left my body as I recoiled back onto the bed. I floated in an orange limbo as she worked feverishly at the zipper on my jeans. I raised my hips and helped her slip them off. I protruded underneath my red-and-white-striped boxer shorts. She reached out toward me and grabbed at my T-shirt. "Off," she said, tugging at it quickly, letting it snap back into place. I took it off as Poppy slowly ran her hands up the insides of my thighs and under the open legs of the boxers. Her fingers glided over my skin, touching only the thick patch of hair around my sex. Each tiny hair she touched sent a small shock wave of excitement through my body. I arched my back, yearning for her to take hold of me, yearning for this to begin. She removed her hands and pulled on the bottom of my shorts. My length caught under the elastic waistband and sprung back, slapping against my stomach as it came free.

She spread my legs apart and knelt between them. She probed me with those feline eyes, only now they wandered and searched my body. I was naked and I *felt* naked, like the naked you feel lying with a lover for the first time. Delicately, she untied the cord around her waist and eased the robe off her shoulders, letting it fall to the bed. The drugs made me unsure of my actions, and I lay motionless, searching her body with my eyes.

Her hair fell over her right shoulder, covering her breast. Her skin was a light tan from her face to her feet. I reached out and touched the skin of her thigh, savoring it's softness for only a second before she moved in a motion too quick for me to antic-ipate. Before I knew what was happening, she had straddled me, feet flat on the bed in a crouch just inches above me. Her eyes locked with mine as she reached for me. I let out a low groan as she squeezed me with her small hand. She shifted her weight, and I was inside her effortlessly. She took her hand away and placed it on my chest for balance as she began rising and falling in a slow rhythm, keeping her feet on the bed so that I touched her only on the inside. The sensation was intense, like being teased and satisfied at the same time. She steadily increased her pace, throwing her head from side to side in waves of black hair. I could feel the crescendo she was pounding toward. I closed my eyes and held back as long as I could, opening them at the last minute as I released. She threw her head straight back and dug her fingernails into my chest then slowed her movements until I stopped shuddering.

I lay on the bed dizzy and motionless for minutes or hours—I couldn't tell. Time seemed not to exist. The lazy, soft flickering light from the lanterns sang to me like a lullaby. I might have fallen asleep. Poppy spoke first.

"Whew, that was fun," she said, getting up for the cigarettes on the dresser. I watched her get up out of the corner of my half-closed eyes and caught the passing flash of green and bright orange on her back. I sat up to get a better view and rubbed my eyes to make sure I wasn't still hallucinating. She stood with her back to me as she unwrapped a new pack. I couldn't believe I hadn't seen it until now. It started at the top of her hips and ran all the way up to her sculpted shoulder blades, seven bright, blaze-orange poppies, each about the size of my hand, in full bloom atop long, spindly, dark green stems. I had never seen a tattoo with such brilliant colors before. It looked like a photograph embossed directly onto her skin. The lines were so sharp and the detail so crisp that the flowers looked three-dimensional, like I could reach out and pick one right off her back.

"Where did you get that?"

"Get what?" she asked, putting two cigarettes in her mouth.

"The poppies, Poppy."

"Ah, these," she said, looking over her shoulder at herself in the mirror. "I got them in Osaka from an old friend of mine. He does all the work for the top Yakuza in Japan."

"When did you get it done?"

"Right after I turned eighteen. It took about two months" she said, putting down the lighter. "Do you have any tattoos?"

"No."

"Well, what do you think of this design?" she asked, offering a cigarette in her right hand so the Embe symbol was facing toward me.

"I could live with that one," I said, smiling as I took the smoke.

She turned the wick of the lamps down until there was barely enough light to see her face when she laid down next to me. There was a long silence before she spoke. "You'll probably be very popular with the others at first."

"Why, because I'm new?"

"That's part of it. You are new to us, but you're also young. More specifically, you act and think young, and most of them will find that very attractive. You see, most of them are creatures of habit, and old habits at that. Someone as young as you will remind them of what it was like to be normal, and we were all normal once. It's not a bad thing, but I've seen it happen before and I want you to be prepared for it," she said.

"You mentioned *normal* earlier, but I don't feel normal at all. I walk around this town and see crowds of people all the time. Each time I look at them and wonder if any one of them is like me and each time I feel so different, so abnormal that I can't help but see myself as an alien, some kind of stranger among them. The thoughts they have, their motivations, fears, and desires all seem so contrary to my own. I always saw *them* as normal."

She drew in long on the cigarette, the dull orange glow highlighting her face. "Maybe you're not as young as you seem, Evan."

"Are you a creature of habit?" I asked after a long silence.

"Yes." I felt her roll over next to me. "But all my habits are bad," she said in a husky voice before biting me on the shoulder.

I took a last harsh drag off my cigarette and rolled toward the nightstand by the rail to put it out. The cane still hung on the railing, and one of the blue jewel eyes caught and refracted the low flickering flame of one of the lamps. I felt her hand run over my back as I watched my dragon wink at me. "Poppy, tell me the story behind that cane."

"Sure," she said, looking up at the ceiling. "It was France, and I was Louis Lucas de Nehon.[11] I remember an unrelenting rain hissed against the insides of the smokestack and into the furnace . . ."

---

11. Poppy's reference to being Louis Lucas de Nehon can be directly cor-roborated from several sources. Louis Lucas de Nehon is also spelled Néhou in some texts. In 1999 French author Jean-Claude Lattès worked with the Compagnie de Saint-Gobain to compile a comprehensive history of the company. Louis Lucas de Néhou was detailed as having been director of St. Gobain twice. There is even a photo of Néhou displayed on p. 21 of *From Sun to Earth, 1665–1999: A History of Saint-Gobain.*

9

Unrelenting rain hissed against the insides of the smokestack and into the furnace. Louis checked the iron pot inside the fiery hearth then realigned the flat, square copper forms on the dark-green granite work table.

"Monsieur, Monsieur!" shouted his valet, Serge, from behind the door.

"Not now!" Louis growled as he bent over the forms.

"But Monsieur, it is Madame Ruebal to see you," he said apologetically through the workshop door.

"Ruebal . . . Ruebal . . ." Louis said softly to himself as he readjusted his adjustments. "Ramsay!" he exclaimed, straightening up and knocking the whole work table out of alignment. "Damn. Damn it to hell!"

"Sir?" Serge asked, poking only his head around the door.

"Well, show him in," Louis said, throwing up his arms in disgust. "Sir?"

"Her, I'm sorry. Show her in."

"Very good, sir." His head disappeared behind the door, and a moment later she stepped through. She was a small woman, standing less than five feet tall and weighing about ninety pounds. Her doll-like red-velvet dress was unbuttoned at the top and spotted with dirt.

"Ah, the lovely Ms. Ruebal. Always a pleasure," Louis said, taking her childlike right hand in his as he kissed the black Embe tattoo on her fair skin. "That will be all, Serge."

"Yes, sir," he said as he closed the door.

Louis stepped back and looked at her from head to toe. She had fair, milky-white skin; warm, disarming brown eyes; and brown hair tucked up under a dirty black-velvet hat that lay crooked on her head. "My goodness, you look like hell."

The muscles in her jaws tightened and rippled slightly as she folded her arms forcefully in front of her small chest. "You never were very suave, were you? I'll have you know I just finished an all-day carriage ride from Trianon to bring you a message."

"Oh yes, what did he say?" Louis asked.

She stood in front of him shaking her head like a petulant child. "Drink first."

"Oh my word, you're right. Where are my manners. It's brandy, isn't it?"

She nodded.

"I think I have some around here somewhere. Ah, here we go," he said, pulling a black bottle and two silver cups out of a toolbox. He uncorked the bottle and filled both cups to the top. "Ramsay, old man, it's good to see you again. It's always good to see you, but I don't think I'll ever get used to this ridiculous body."

She turned up the cup and drank deeply. "You only have to look at it, imagine trying to live in it. It could be worse—at least I'm cute."

"That you are," he said, smiling. "What did Le Brun say?"

"He will receive you a week from tomorrow, though he confided in me that he sees little purpose in it."

"Hmm," Louis said as he sat the bottle down, "don't worry about that. If I can see him, I can get the contract."

"Well, Louis, you're in. Here's to your success," she said, offering a toast.

They emptied their cups at the same time. "What's Le Brun like?" Louis asked, reaching for the bottle.

"He is a fantastic talent: painting, sculpture, architecture, etching, all top notch. He's not the official portraitist to the king by accident. He's very powerful within the ministerial peerage, mainly because he despises most of the others for the talentless lackeys they are. That could work to your advantage. From what he told me, you'll have to dazzle him. The person most likely to win the contract for the Galerie des Glaces is a Vaux glassier named Joubert. He's talented, so I'm told, and all the rage in Paris and Versailles."

"Why's that?"

"It's quite ingenious, actually. He makes what he calls *skinny mirrors*."

"What?" Louis asked.

"Skinny mirrors. He manufactures them with a slightly concave surface that makes one appear thinner than normal. It's even rumored that His Majesty has one, though he certainly doesn't need it. Joubert's star is on the rise, my friend."

"Rubbish. Ha! Skinny mirrors, what nonsense. Don't those society cows realize that they're still their actual size when they walk on the avenues and sit in their opera boxes?"

"That's not the point. The point is, he's on the inside and you're not. But as I said, Le Brun has a good eye and appreciates skill. That reminds me, I was thinking about it on the way here, isn't a normal mirror like any other? What are you going to do to dazzle him?"

"Ah," Louis said, walking over to an unused bench along the

wall, "take a look at this." He pulled a small plateglass mirror the size of a medium book out of its leather sheath. She took it and held it out in front of her face. "What do you think?" he said, folding his arms.

She looked at her reflection for several seconds before answering. "It's remarkable. There aren't any imperfections. It reflects like a metal mirror, only with more detail. How did you do this?"

"It's cast instead of blown. That's what gives it the true surface. The bad news is, I can't produce them any larger than that, but I'll be able to soon.[12] Do you think Le Brun will appreciate this?"

"Probably, it is remarkable," she said, turning her head from side to side as she looked at herself. "Huh," she sighed. "I don't think I will ever get used to this face."

Louis laughed quietly. "I don't know, I kind of like it. Somehow it suits you."

She smiled sarcastically at him as she handed over the mirror. "Pour me another."

LOUIS LOOKED NERVOUSLY across the carriage at Serge, who held the leather satchel containing the only six specimens of cast glass mirrors in the world.

"What do you think our chances are, sir?" asked Serge, fidgeting nervously under Louis's watchful eye.

"Chances of what?"

"Of you making mirrors for the king?"

"Good, I think. We'll know tomorrow," he said as the carriage rolled to a gentle stop in front of the town square. Louis opened the door and stepped out. "Hand me the glass," he said, leaning

12. Poppy's retelling of her glass-casting innovation in a past life seems to be corroborated by author Mark Pendergrast in his book *Mirror, Mirror*, in which he details Louis Lucas de Néhou casting very large panes of glass, few of which survived the annealing process.

back inside. "I'm going to secure a room. I want you and the driver to go around and casually find out whatever you can about a local glassier named Joubert. How does my wig look?" Louis asked, posing for Serge.

"Good, sir."

"Do you have enough money?" Louis asked.

"Yes, sir."

"Good. Go then. I'll see you tonight."

IT WAS DARK WHEN SERGE AND THE DRIVER walked into the inn's small, dingy dining room where Louis ate alone. "Sit. Help yourselves," Louis said. The two young men ate like lions at a kill. Louis watched for a full fifteen minutes before breaching the subject. "Well, what did you find?"

Serge swallowed a large mouthful. "He lives here in Trianon, but his shop is in Vaux. He's about forty and he's very well connected in royal circles."

"How do you know that?"

"Just the way people speak of him. I can tell he commands respect."

"Don't forget the wife," the young driver interjected, his mouth full of food.

"We saw his wife on the other side of the square."

"And?" Louis prompted impatiently.

The two young men looked at each other and fought back laughter. "And she's enormous," Serge said, as they both burst out in long, laughing howls.

"Enormous?" asked Louis, studying their contorted faces.

"Yes," said Serge, calming himself, "enormous. Larger than the three of us together."

"Surely you jest, man."

"No, Monsieur, it is no jest. Jean here is a witness, he saw her too," Serge said, pointing to the driver who nodded as he chewed. "And that dress, I've never seen so much yellow in one place in all my life."

"I've seen smaller tunics on cavalry mares," Jean said, chuckling.

"All right, what else?"

"He has no children and lives a short ride west of town."

"Did you see his place?"

Serge nodded. "It's about the same acreage as yours, near as I could tell, but with a larger house."

"Anything else?"

Serge shook his head.

"Good work, lads. You're both in room two. I'll see you at sunrise," Louis said, getting up from the table.

SERGE AND JEAN WERE ALREADY WAITING by the carriage when Louis stepped out into the morning sun. He wore a pastel-blue jacket and pants with white leggings and black shoes. A tightly curled powdered wig covered his brown hair. "How do I look?" he called out to Serge, who walked toward him quickly.

"Marvelous, Monsieur," Serge said, circling him as a worker bee attends a queen. "Oh, a little bit of hair showing. Just let me tuck . . ." He slipped a lock of brown under the wig. "There, you look perfect, Monsieur."

"Let's go," Louis said nervously as he handed the leather case to Serge and stepped inside.

The ride to Versailles took less than an hour. The palace grounds buzzed with activity. Construction of all sorts was underway in every part of the grounds. Serge hopped out and placed the black-lacquered step stool under the carriage door. "Do you want me to come in with you, Monsieur?"

"No, just have the carriage ready to leave. I'll find him myself."

Louis straightened his jacket, grabbed the mirrors, and walked up the wide marble steps leading to the main hall. An attendant met him halfway up and escorted him in.

In a time of wigs and makeup, Le Brun wore neither. The long, black, wiry hair bordering his round face fell down almost to the desktop he was leaning over.

"Monsieur Le Brun," the attendant said softly, "a Monsieur Louis Lucas de Nehon to see you."

"Yes, thank you," he said, looking up at Louis.

"I've looked forward to meeting you, Monsieur," Louis said, offering his hand.

Le Brun took his hand normally, then did a double take as he saw the tattoo. "Say, this symbol on your hand, Madame Ruebal has the same one. What is it?"

"It's an Egyptian good luck symbol that we both saw and fancied during a trip together. We decided to keep it as a remembrance."

"Interesting. I always wondered what it was, but never thought it appropriate to ask a woman about . . . Well, you know how it is. I'll make this plain from the start, Monsieur . . ."

"De Nehon."

"Yes, of course, Monsieur De Nehon, as you can see from the chaos outside, I'm a very busy man. I agreed to meet with you only because Madame Ruebal mentioned your skill as a glassier and said something vague about a new process."

"Well, let's get directly to business then," Louis said, opening the case. "Madame Ruebal was correct about a new process. As you no doubt know, glass and mirrors are made by a blowing, shaping, and cutting process that leaves ripples and imperfections by even the finest craftsmen. But this," he said, removing a mirror, "this is made differently and has no imperfections."

Le Brun set his notepad aside and delicately took the

mirror from Louis. "It's thin," he said, looking at it on edge before admiring his round, fleshy face in its depths. He turned the mirror to different angles, then walked to the windows overlooking the courtyard and compared the surfaces. "This is cast, is it not?"

"It is."

He turned and walked quickly toward Louis. "This is marvelous!" he said excitedly. "How did you do it? No, never mind that, can you make more of these?"

Louis reached inside and pulled out the other five, one by one, placing them edge to edge on the desk so that they made a larger whole. Le Brun placed the sixth on the desk to complete the rectangle. "I can make as many as you need, Monsieur. In fact, I was hoping to produce several thousand of these for the Hall of Mirrors concession."

LeBrun's eyes fixed on Louis. "Interesting idea, Monsieur De Nehon, very interesting. Tell me, please, can you make larger ones?"

Louis swallowed hard. "No, Monsieur, this is as large as I've been able to produce yet, but I've only been producing these pieces for five months. I'm sure with a little more time, I could—"

Le Brun held up his hand to cut him off. "I understand. You'll have your time. I want to use pieces of this quality in the project, but there is another problem that may take time. There is someone else who has been promised the concession, but his pieces don't come close to these," he said, looking down at himself in the six mirrors.

"Joubert."

Le Brun looked up at him and raised his eyebrows in surprise. "Yes, Joubert. Do you know him?"

"I know of him."

Le Brun nodded. "Here's what I can offer you, Monsieur. The project starts in about six months, as soon as the carpenters and masons are finished in the hall. In that time, you may have access to the glassworks at Tourlaville to improve your process.[13] I will check your progress, and if it appears we can get pieces of sufficient size, the concession is yours. If not, it goes to Joubert. Is that fair in your opinion?" LeBrun asked.

"When can I start at Tourlaville?"

PER LE BRUN'S DIRECTIONS, Louis was given access to all equipment as well as a private shop and office. Louis's past life experience from Murano was centuries beyond anyone else's at Tourlaville. But the first enthusiastic weeks stretched into months with only minor improvements in plate size. Tension began to show in the lines of Louis's face and seemed to increase after each excuse-filled appointment with Le Brun.

"Perhaps we should take a break, Louis," Serge said, rubbing at his tired, red eyes.

"No, we're behind schedule as it is. Check the furnace again and see if it's ready," he said, bending over to align the copper forms.

"It's ready!" Serge yelled from across the room.

"Okay, I'm coming. Ready the pot."

Serge put on his heavy protective leather breeches, sleeved apron, and gloves. Louis buttoned up his apron as he walked over to the furnace. The heavy iron pot used for melting the rough glass stock had specially made thick leather covers that slipped over the handles and allowed them to carry and maneuver it. They both gripped their sides and walked carefully over to the forms. They

13. At the time, Tourlaville was a small village in Cherbourg, Northwest France. A fledgling glass blowingindustry (all previous glass blowing in Europe had been confined to Venetian Murano) sprung up around the town due to the availability of natural resources (i.e. timber for fuel and sand for glass stock) and river transport. Later this factory would move to Saint Gobain. (*From Sun to Earth, 1665–1999: A History of Saint-Gobain.*)

walked in synchronized steps like dancers, from the hundreds of carefully choreographed trips with the pot empty. If either one fell, one or both could receive fatal burns from the molten glass.

They stopped above the short worktable and gently eased the pot over, filling each of the six forms with the angry orange liquid.

"Okay, that's it, set it down. Mark the time," he commanded to Serge, who turned over the hourglass next to him. "Good, good, good, good," Louis mumbled to himself as he threw his gloves off and started in his notations again.

"We're going to have a hard time making the deadline, aren't we, Monsieur?"

Louis ignored him and continued writing feverishly in his notes. Serge watched until he stopped writing. "I told you about the invitation for tomorrow night's ball, didn't I?"

"Twice," answered Louis.

"Yes, you're right. I asked around, and everyone who's anyone will be there."

"Ready the light-blue outfit for tomorrow night."

"Yes, sir," Serge said, yawning. He looked over at the hour-glass. "It's time."

Louis looked up from his notes and walked over next to Serge. The forms were twice the size of the examples he had shown Le Brun but still just over half of what was needed for the Hall of Mirrors project. The cooling, wheat-colored glass miraculously cleared before their eyes in the order they were poured. Louis held his breath as he watched the bottoms of the polished copper molds begin to show through, then exhaled as the first one cracked into four pieces. The other five followed at fixed intervals. Louis closed his eyes and dropped his head after the last one cracked.

"It's late, Monsieur, perhaps we should begin again in the morning."

"No. Draw more glass stock. Let's do it again."

THE LONG HOURS SHOWED ON LOUIS'S FACE as the attendant checked his invitation in the antechamber. "If you wait until the end of this waltz, I can introduce you, Monsieur," the attendant said.

"No need," Louis said laconically as he walked into the main ballroom. Couples whirled and skipped across the polished marble dance floor, while onlookers chatted and fanned themselves. The gilded faces of the numerous statues against the wall sparkled under crystal chandeliers.

I don't know why I bother to attend these functions, Louis thought as he surveyed the room. *I should be working. No. No more work, not tonight. Tomorrow. Start fresh tomorrow, maybe even the day after. It is too late to make the deadline now. Perhaps I should just find some young diversion to take my mind off of it until tomorrow.* He reached out and took two glasses of champagne off the tray of a passing host.

The waltz ended, and everyone on the side of the room closest to the door turned as a high-tone bell rang, noting new arrivals. "His Majesty the King's minister of finance, Monsieur Colbert[14] and his wife, Marie." The couple entered to mild applause. "Madame LaMae du Gascon and daughter Michelle." Louis was setting down his first empty glass and missed a look at her. "The Viscount Joubert and wife, Emil." Louis stood on his toes to get a view over the lightly applauding crowd. He was tall, gaunt, and more elegant than Serge had described. He walked in confidently, nodding to several people in the crowd, but his wife was exactly as Serge had described. She wore a billowing brilliant purple dress that resembled a sheik's tent.

Louis felt a soft poke in his ribs and looked down to see who

14. A legend in French royal politics, Jean-Baptiste Colbert served as King Louis XIV's minister of finance after the disgraceful exit of his predecessor Fouquet. Colbert was also appointed the king's overseer of buildings and was charged with complete control over the Versailles project. (*Versailles* by Jean-Marie Perouse de Montclos, 1991.)

it was. "I can't see. What's she wearing?" asked Ramsay, looking up at him with a smile.

Louis smiled and looked out at Emil again to make sure he wasn't hallucinating from overwork. "Purple, a mountain of it."

"Typical," said Ramsay.

"My goodness, I can't believe it. She is huge," Louis said.

Ramsay laughed. "Their carriage had to be specially built with double doors and heavy springs."

"A woman like that could bathe in a tub using only a wine glass full of water," he said, before tilting his glass up.

"Don't be cruel, it doesn't suit you." Ramsay said, scolding. "Le Brun tells me you're having a hard time out at Tourlaville."

Louis sighed and looked around the heads for another walking platter of glasses. "It's more difficult than I thought it would be."

"Important things are never easy."

Louis put his empty glass on a tray and took two more fresh ones. "That's good. I'll have to remember that one," he said snidely.

"Oh, come now. Why the long face? I'll catch up with you later," she said, disappearing into the crowd.

Louis sank into a corner for six more waltzes and four more drinks before wandering back into the crowd in search of Ramsay.

"Pardon me, Monsieur," came a voice from behind him. Louis turned to see who it was. The old man wore a long white wig and a pince-nez. "I know everyone here but you. Please allow me to introduce myself. My name is Mansalles, His Majesty's administrator of this palace. And you are?"

"I am," Louis slurred, "pleased to meet you. My name is Louis Lucas de Nehon, master glassier." Louis offered his hand.

"So, Monsieur," Mansalles said, taking his hand but not shaking it for fear of toppling him over. "What brings you to Versailles?"

"I'm working at Tourlaville on special new mirrors for the Galerie des Glaces project."

Mansalles stiffened and drew his hand away, almost pulling Louis over as he did so. "I think you must be mistaken, Monsieur. I know the man who is making the mirrors for the hall. He's only just arrived. His name is Monsieur Jouber—"

"Don't mention that man's name to me!" Louis shouted. "His name doesn't deserve to be mentioned in my presence. I am an artist, a craftsman, and he . . . he is nothing more than . . . than an opportunistic socialite." A crowd began to gather around them, trapping Mansalles, who looked around, skittishly trying to get away. Louis fought to keep his eyes focused as he spoke loudly enough to draw more people over.

"Monsieur, please. Calm down, people are starting to stare," Mansalles said through a nervous smile.

"People! What people, these skinny people. Made skinny by your Joubert. Ha! He is nothing more than a purveyor of novelties, a man living off a gimmick."

"Monsieur," Mansalles said, loud enough for the crowd to hear, "I must insist that you stop speaking about him in this manner. I won't stand for this sort of rudeness."

"Rudeness! Rudeness!" Louis said, spitting the words in Mansalles's face. "You know why he devised those skinny mirrors, don't you? So his oversize wife would have the confidence at home to put on that outrageous purple dress. That's rudeness!" The crowd gave a collective gasp followed by a few giggles. Mansalles went white as his wig. A hand came out of the crowd behind Louis and tapped him on the shoulder. Louis wore a slight smile and chuckled to himself as he turned. The outburst had relieved some of the tension and frustration that had built up in him over the past grueling weeks.

The openhanded slap across his face wasn't hard but was enough of a surprise to knock Louis off balance. He looked up sideways from the floor. Above the black shoes, the white stockings, the gray leggings, and jacket, was Joubert, rubbing at his stinging right hand. Joubert peered down his nose at Louis with an arrogant look on his face. Louis had gotten up to his knees before someone grabbed him under the arms and helped him up. It was tiny Ramsay.

"You've done it now," she whispered in Louis's ear.

Joubert threw his head back proudly. "Sir, I don't know who you are, but you have slandered me and insulted my wife," he said as Louis straightened up in front of him, "and I demand satisfaction." A stunned Louis stood, rubbing his left cheek. "I can plainly see that you are drunk, sir, and I offer you the opportunity to recant before this crowd," he said, smiling smugly as he looked at the faces grouped around him. Louis stood as still as he could and collected himself. Ramsay poked him in the ribs and gave him a stern look as if to say *go ahead.*

"All right, Monsieur, but first, please tell me, is it true what they say?" Louis said motioning to his wife.

"Excuse me," said Joubert, confused.

"Oh, come now. Surely, you must know. It's been rumored for hundreds of years by several cultures that when a large woman, a woman of your wife's girth, for instance, approaches sexual ecstasy, she will begin to squeal like a pig with delight."

The crowd shrieked in unison and burst out in stifled laughter. Joubert stuttered with a stupid look on his face. His wife fainted and collapsed into a purple heap on the floor as several onlookers frantically scrambled out of her way. Ramsay's brown eyes rolled up into her small head. Mansalles managed to escape the crowd and the embarrassment in the commotion. Louis stood smugly in front of Joubert, his hands tucked into the waistband of his trousers. "I won't hold it against you if you don't know," Louis continued before Joubert could retort. "After all, as I can plainly see, she is a lot of woman to love."

Joubert, now completely red, was visibly shaking. "You . . . you . . . I demand satisfaction! I demand it!" he said, stomping his feet uncontrollably on the floor. "I am within my rights to demand a duel to defend my honor and the honor of my wife. You may choose the weapon."

Ramsay tugged hard at Louis's jacket to get his attention. "Pistols . . . pistols," she hissed quietly at him between clenched teeth.

"Pistols," slurred Louis loudly, his voice carrying throughout the ballroom. "The day after tomorrow."

"Fine," Joubert said sternly. "Have your second call on mine tomorrow at my home. It's at—"

"I know where it is," Louis hissed.

"Day after tomorrow then, at sunrise," Joubert said as he stooped to comfort his wife.

Louis nodded and stumbled through the crowd toward the door. "Here, let's take my carriage," Ramsay said as they left the ballroom.

"Why pistols? I've never even held a flintlock before, much less fired one," Louis asked.

"If memory serves, you've never held a rapier before either, have you?"

"No."

"Then a pistol is your only chance. Stay at my chateau tonight, and we'll practice tomorrow after you've slept it off," Ramsay said.

LOUIS WAS PASTY WHITE and winced with the report of Ramsay's first shot. "How's your head this morning?"

"It's been better."

"I'll bet it has. Here, it's reloaded," she said, handing it to him. "You try it."

Louis took the pistol in both hands. "What do I do, just point it and pull the trigger?"

"Pull back the catch, like so." She pulled the hammer back

until it locked in place. "Now, point it carefully and gently squeeze the trigger."

"Okay. What am I aiming at?"

Ramsay looked around the barnyard. "That chicken over there by the fence, if you hit it, we eat it for lunch."

"It's a bet," he said as he closed his left eye and drew a bead on the unsuspecting bird. He winced again at the report and peered through the fading white smoke to see the chicken clucking and scurrying about, clearly startled by the shot, but unscathed. "I think I missed."

"Yes, you missed. Here let me reload it for you." Ramsay took the pistol and dumped a measure of powder down the barrel. "Tell me, why did you go through with that outburst last night? Why didn't you apologize when you had the chance?"

Louis sighed. "I was frustrated, I guess. I've been working for months trying to perfect larger and larger mirrors, while that talentless buffoon stands to make a fortune, and all because of a gimmick. It's infuriating."

"Here, it's ready," she said, handing it back to him. "Well, if by chance you kill him tomorrow, the contract would almost certainly be yours."

"That thought has crossed my mind this morning," Louis said before he fired again. Again, the smoke cleared to show the chicken running about, still unharmed. Louis looked at the bird, looked at the end of the gun, then back at the bird. "That damn chicken is too dumb to know it's dead."

"This task might be more difficult than I thought," Ramsay said. "Let's try it again."

"Even if I prevail tomorrow, I wonder if I haven't burned all the bridges that might lead me to Versailles. I was a bit much last night."

"You certainly were, but you said things many people have wanted to say for a long while. If you do win tomorrow, I'd bet that you'll be forgiven and accepted back. You should kill him and make it clean."

"Do I have to do that? I've never killed anyone before."

Ramsay looked up at him. "Never? In all these trips?"

"No, never," Louis said, shrugging his shoulders. "I don't know if I like the idea of starting now."

"Well, it's a little late to be getting cold feet, don't you think?" she said, handing over the pistol again.

"No, that's not what I mean. Can I just wound him so that he can't work?"

"For god's sake, man, you can't even rattle a motionless chicken at fifteen paces and you're talking about wounding a man on purpose. That takes skill."

"Oh, yeah, watch this," he said, aiming and firing. The smoke cleared, and again the chicken was still alive, mocking him. "Damn!"

"Do it again," Ramsay said with a sigh.

THEY WERE STILL PRACTICING when Serge returned from Joubert's. Louis's marksmanship had not improved.

"What happened?" Louis shouted to Serge, who was running up to them.

"It's set—tomorrow morning, an hour after sunrise, in the royal cherry orchard."

"That's perfect!" Ramsay exclaimed.

"Why is that?" Louis asked.

"Because I have a plan that might just save your hide," she said, recocking the pistol. "But first, I want something to eat." She aimed the gun barrel at the white bird.

"I think the sights are off. That's why I'm having such a hard time," Louis said.

"Hmm. If you shoot a pheasant or a chicken in the head,

it leaves both breasts undisturbed," she said as she squeezed the trigger. "Got 'im!" she cried before the smoke cleared.

"Tell me about this idea of yours," said Louis, looking through the smoke at the headless chicken flapping wildly as it tried over and over to get to its feet.

"Bring him in," Ramsay said, walking to the house. "We'll talk over lunch."

"HERE'S WHAT I'VE BEEN THINKING. You don't want to kill him because of your conscience," Ramsay said sarcastically. "But if you wound him, say in the arm or the shoulder, he would be unable to work and would have to forfeit the concession at Versailles, right?"

Louis nodded as he chewed.

"How much is this project worth?"

"A lot. Enough that I wouldn't have to worry about money for a long time, several lifetimes, perhaps."

"Good. All right . . . Unless you get really lucky, you won't be able to hit him, much less just wound him, and you would need to practice for a month in order to get good enough to pull this off. So here is what I propose we do. Go to the duel in the morning, go through all the steps like normal, except that when you both turn and fire on the count of ten, I want you to turn a half second early and fire immediately. And I don't want you to hit him. I want you to fire just wide, on purpose."

Louis stopped eating and looked at her without expression.

"Are you getting all this?" Ramsay asked.

"I'm just curious about where this is going."

"I have a hunting musket, small caliber like a pistol, that I'm very accurate with, even at long range. I will position myself behind you on the small hill overlooking the orchard. When you shoot and miss, I will shoot and hit him in the shoulder, but we have to be careful. We must time our shots perfectly so that nothing is suspected, and we must fire just as he is getting ready to fire his ball. Because if we shoot before he is ready, he will have a free shot at you after he has regained his composure, and judging from his mood last night, I think he aims to kill you. The hill is on the west side of the orchard, so be sure you're facing east when you fire, otherwise I'll have to shoot him in the back."

"I like it," said Louis. "It's perfect, but what happens if our shots don't come at the same time?"

"They will. That's what we're going to practice for the rest of the day."

THE MORNING SUN was still below the horizon when they climbed into the carriage. Dark bags had collected under Louis's eyes during the sleepless night. He climbed into the coach and sat next to Ramsay and Serge without speaking.

"Here, have some," Ramsay said, offering a small silver flask. "It will help with your nerves."

"My nerves are fine," Louis said, looking out the window.

Ramsay shrugged and tipped up the flask quickly. "You're on your way to becoming a rich man."

"I just wish it didn't have to happen this way."

Ramsay rolled her eyes and drew on the flask again.

"Have you dueled before?" Louis asked.

"Yes, I've been in dozens of duels. Being a soldier, it comes up more often than you might think."

"Do you have any last-minute tips?"

"Yes," she laughed. "Mind you, don't get yourself killed out there this morning."

Louis looked solemnly back inside the coach at her.

"Don't worry," she said. "It'll all be over in a few minutes. I should get out here and find my position. The orchard is just over this hill." The driver stopped, and she hopped out. She wore shabby brown peasant's clothing and new brown leather boots. The driver handed down Ramsay's musket and equipment satchel. The gun was as tall as she was. "Don't forget to pick me up on the way back," she said before disappearing like a rabbit into the dense thickets beside the road.

The morning sun cut low through the rows of cherry trees, highlighting each white spring blossom, like votive candles in a church. The cool, still air was thick with the smell of the honeysuckle bordering the orchard. A double-doored coach stood at the edge of the trees. Three men milled around in the first row.

"That would be them," Louis said to Serge. "You remember the way Ramsay told you to check the pistols, don't you?"

"Yes, I practiced most of the night. I'm prepared," answered the valet.

"Good," he said, reaching over to squeeze Serge's knee. "Let's go."

They walked into the low trees to meet the three: Joubert, his second, and a referee who held a wooden case containing the pistols. Serge and Joubert's second shook hands and spoke softly before going aside with the third man to inspect the weapons. Joubert looked as tired as Louis.

"It's not too late to apologize, Monsieur Nehon," Joubert shouted over to Louis.

Louis turned quickly and looked hard at him. Joubert hadn't known his name, or so Louis thought. He despised him more than ever now. Only a coward could forgive such an insult as he'd received two nights ago. Louis took a deep breath. "I came here to defend my statements, not to grovel."

"Very well," said Joubert, his voice almost cracking.

"We're ready," said Serge, carrying a polished mahogany flintlock in his hands.

"Take your places, gentlemen," said the referee, motioning for Joubert and Louis to come over. The trees were planted in east–west rows. The sun shone brightly down their row up to the bramble-covered hill Ramsay had spoken about. "We'll draw lots to see who will shoot into the sun," he continued.

"That won't be necessary," Louis said quickly. "I'll shoot facing east, unless you object?"

Joubert shook his head and stepped into the middle of the row, cocking his pistol as he went. Louis cocked his and took his place back-to-back against Joubert.

"Gentlemen, I'll count off as you take your paces. When I reach ten, you may turn and fire at will. Do you both understand?"

Joubert nodded in time with Louis.

"Good luck. One, two, three . . ."

Louis squeezed the handle of the gun with each stride and scanned the sunlit hillside in front of him for any sign of Ramsay. He thought about her sitting out of sight against some short tree, bracing the long barrel for careful aim. He thought about her watching him at that very moment, counting the steps along with him.

"Eight, nine, t—"

Louis snapped around and fired his ball through a narrow cone of white smoke at the blazing sun hanging in the sky behind Joubert. There was only the sound of one shot, the way it had been during practice the afternoon before. Joubert took an extra step back then dropped to his knees, still clutching the pistol in his hand. The smoke cleared, and Louis's eyes adjusted to see Joubert kneeling with an astonished look on his face. A thin trail of blood trickled down from the small, perfectly round black hole over his right eyebrow. Louis looked on in horror as Joubert blinked three or four times and swayed on his knees. His pistol bucked wildly in his relaxed hand as he fell facedown on the short grass. Joubert's shot grazed Louis on the leg, just below the knee.

Louis fell to the ground clutching his leg and looked back angrily at the anonymous hillside. Serge rushed up to him. The referee came over after looking at Joubert. Louis was bleeding badly and had to be carried the few hundred yards through the gardens to the palace where a royal assistant surgeon attended his wound.

Louis tried closing his eyes against the pain as the surgeon worked, but every time he did, he saw only Joubert's pale, tired face and his blinking, unbelieving eyes against the backs of his own eyelids. He cursed Ramsay for killing Joubert. He visualized the satisfied look she must have had on her face at having made such a good shot. He should have seen it coming.

The surgeon closed the wound and wrapped the knee joint from midthigh to midcalf. Louis fell asleep halfway through the wrapping. He awoke late in the afternoon as Ramsay, now dressed in a red-and-black velvet gown, came in.

"How are you?" she asked.

Louis sat up gingerly in the large bed. "Fine. They say I'll probably walk with a limp, but . . ."

"Yes, but at least you're better off than Joubert. By the way, good shooting on your part. I didn't think you had it in you," she said, breaking into a smile.

"You bastard!" Louis exploded. "I should have known you'd kill him. I should have known you'd do it."

"What are you talking about? I didn't shoot. My musket misfired. You shot him."

Louis narrowed his eyes. "You're lying."

"Believe what you want, young one, but I'm telling you, I didn't fire. I have to go to Saxony on business, but I think you should know that the news of this is spreading quickly. As it turns out, the late Joubert wasn't quite as well liked as we thought. You're already somewhat of a celebrity. I recommend you get up and about as soon as possible, I think you'll have a lot of work to do. I'll see you around." Ramsay turned and walked to the open door where she was greeted by the tall, dark-haired Le Brun.

"Madame Ruebal, always a pleasure," he said, kissing her gloved hand.

"Likewise." She smiled at Louis before disappearing around the door.

Le Brun watched her walk down the hall before he entered. He carried an ornately carved, jeweled dragon-head cane in his hands. "How are you?"

"I'll be fine in a few days. I want you to know I plan to resume work as soon as possible."

"Yes," he said, opening a window. "I suppose congratulations are in order."

"What do you mean?"

"Come now. You know exactly what I mean. I just wish it hadn't come to this. I'm giving you the contract; you're the only qualified glassier left in France, as far as I know. But just between you and me, I'd have given it to you anyway. Here," he said, holding out the cane, "this is for you. The doctor says you're going to need it. The contracts are in my office waiting for you. Come by as soon as you're able. Good day, Monsieur." He left without looking back. Louis then held the cane and looked into the dragon's blue sapphire eyes as long as he could without blinking.

10

"Then I held the cane and looked into the dragon's blue sapphire eyes as long as I could without blinking," Poppy said, finishing her story.

"Did you ever perfect the mirrors?" I asked.

Poppy gave a slight start as if she thought I was asleep. "I did, but not in time to put them in the Hall of Mirrors. I did those by hand. They're not perfect, but they're close. I made my final breakthrough with the cast mirrors at the very end of the project. I took my final payment from Le Brun and helped start a factory at Saint-Gobain in France to mass produce this new glass."

"What happened to it?"

"It worked. It's in operation today, and I still own a nice percentage of the company."[15]

"What was the social scene in Versailles like for you after your recovery?"

"I was respected for saying what everyone else had always

---

15. Today, the Saint-Gobain is one of the largest companies in Europe with an annual revenue of forty billion euros.

wanted to but wouldn't. They were such pathetic creatures, but then again, they always are. I despised them, which of course made me all the more attractive in their eyes. Having the reputation for killing Joubert was another thing I didn't like. Each day, I wished I could tell the truth about what happened, but obviously, I never could."

"Did you ever find out the truth about who shot him?"

"Ramsay did it. Weren't you listening?" she said sternly. "Sure, she never admitted to it, but she did it. It's the only explanation for what happened. Speaking of which, Ramsay might be in Zurich when we arrive. Don't let her or anyone else know that I told you her name."

"I won't," I said in the middle of a yawn. I looked over at the cane again and stared at it as long as I could until I fell asleep.

POPPY WAS STANDING by the rail looking over into the open sanctuary below when I woke up. "Good morning," I said, looking for my underwear.

"Good morning." She turned and saw me searching. "They're at the foot of the bed."

"Thanks." I put them on and slid across the bed to where she was standing. Reaching out and grabbing the rail, I was able to pull myself up onto my right leg. The view was amazing. The sun shone through the glass with the same brilliance of yesterday morning, only now, from up here, the collage of random colors formed the same scenes from the panels on the hardwood floor below us.

"It's incredible," I said, looking over at her. She stood two steps back from the railing. She smiled at me then tentatively looked over the edge again. I hopped over and tried to put my arm around her, but she recoiled at my touch and walked over to the bureau. "What's wrong?" I asked.

"Nothing is wrong. I just don't like heights, that's all."

I sat back down on the bed and slipped my pants on as she

fumbled around in the drawers. I found my shirt at the same time I saw the round panel of stained glass above the stairs, the scenes now fully lit. At the top was a young woman in a ruffled blue dress standing in a crowd of people at what looked like a formal dance. To the right, a middle-aged man with a brown beard and round spectacles held up a brass syringe as if to purge it of air bubbles. It looked like the same one Poppy used now. At the bottom, a woman with long, red hair sat atop a white horse in the middle of a barren desert landscape. The next panel showed who I assumed was Graciela Cruz. She was portrayed in front of the doors of this church. In the center was a round panel of blue-tinted glass.

"I think I would like to go with you tonight. What is the name of this place?" she asked.

"It's called the Necropolis."

"I think I read about that place in *LA Weekly*. It's in an old movie theater, isn't it?"

"Yeah, that's it."

"Sounds like fun. What time do we go?"

"We'll need to leave at about ten thirty."

"I'll be ready. You can have Antonio and the car today to get whatever you need for our departure tomorrow."

ANTONIO DROVE PAST the burned-out warehouse on the way to the hotel. The gray outside walls still stood but were scorched black above each open window. Daylight shone through the second-story windows where the roof should have been. It was a complete loss.

The dingy outside of the Iowa Hotel looked dismal. The large front bay window was covered with a thin film of grime that made it look cloudy in the sunlight. The strong stench of urine and garbage crept out from the alley.

Four new transients sat on the couches and chairs watching

a gossip show as I walked in. Two of the four men playing cards
smiled at me and looked at my white bandaged foot as I limped
toward the stairs. The familiar dirty brown paint on the walls of
the hallway welcomed me as I approached my door. I hesitated
as I put my hand on the doorknob, and a funny feeling came
over me, like I might open the door and see myself still sitting
inside, still mired in the mental squalor that this place embod-
ied, still ignorant of this new reality I chased.

I opened the door slowly, leaving it open as I walked inside.
Driving by the burned-out warehouse hadn't felt like returning
to the scene of a crime, but being in this room did. The orange
extension-cord noose still hung from the light fixture, beckoning. I wasted no time in getting the rest of the money from my
stash from inside the hot plate. I kept looking back at the open
door, and couldn't help but feel like it was going to slam shut
and trap me back inside here. I quickly scoured the place for
anything I wanted to keep, knowing I would never set foot in
this room again. In the end, a few changes of clothing were all I
wanted from that life. I closed the door and quickly headed back
outside to the car. Antonio took the small laundry bag holding
my possessions as I got in.

"Where to, sir?" he asked, starting the car.

I looked at the hotel's weathered facade and watched the
shadowy, ghostlike forms of men moving behind the filthy glass.
"I don't care. Just get us out of here."

ANTONIO AND I DROVE around Los Angeles for the rest of the afternoon and evening, stopping only to spend the last of my money.
For seven hundred dollars, I picked up two suits, four shirts, four
ties, a belt, a pair of shoes, and a suitcase to carry it all. I laid them
all out on the guest bed and had cut most of the tags off when
Poppy walked in.

"Very nice. Are you going to wear one tonight?"

I almost laughed as I turned around to face her. "I don't think that would be very appropriate. I'm going to wear this," I said, modeling the black dress shirt I'd brought from the hotel.

"How appropriate is this?" she asked, turning around slowly. She wore a skin-tight, long-sleeved, black bodysuit that started at her ankles and ended in a high turtle neck. It made her thin figure look even leaner. Her glossy, straight black hair fell onto her shoulders and framed her face perfectly.

"It's perfect, and so are you," I said, holding my left arm open toward her for an embrace. She looked at me curiously with a slightly furrowed brow as though I'd confused her temporarily. She recovered quickly and smiled as she stepped forward to take my outstretched hand in hers.

"Are you ready?" she asked.

I felt awkward, as if I'd made some kind of mistake. "Yeah, let me put my new shoe on."

ANTONIO STOPPED THE CAR next to the front door where the block-long line started. The movie marquee jutting out over the entrance read, The Naked Kobolds: Saturday.

"What kind of music is this?" Poppy asked as we walked inside past the nodding doorman.

"You'll see in a minute," I said, enjoying the feeling of having her in my world for a change. I made my way through the crowd with her in tow. Henry saw me coming and pointed to the middle section of the bar.

"Okay, you two, time to go," he said to the two men seated in front of us. They grumbled as they took their drinks and left. "Well, well, look who still lives," he said, shaking my hand. "Who did you get to fix your foot?"

"She did. She used to be a doctor," I said, tapping Poppy on the shoulder to get her attention. "Henry, I'd like you to meet Poppy. Poppy, this is Henry." A strange expression came over Henry's face as he shook her hand. She shook his hand quickly and started scanning the interior of the club again.

"Well, tell me what happened," he said, barely able to keep his eyes off of Poppy.

"I'll tell you later. I'm thirsty."

He smiled. "A beer for you, and what does your lady friend want?"

"Vodka martini," she said without looking at him.

"He hasn't been in yet, has he?" I asked as Henry readied the glasses.

"No. Hey, I need to talk to you," Henry said urgently.

"Yeah, I know. I'm really sor—"

"No, not that, something else. Here you go," he said, placing the drinks on the glass bar. "I'll start you a tab," he said as he walked away.

"I like this place," Poppy said, sampling the martini. "Was he the friend you were talking about?"

"Yes and no. He is the one I called last night, but there's someone else coming who owes me money. He should show up around midnight. He'll be easy enough to spot."

She shrugged. "Where's the ladies' room?" I pointed her in the right direction.

"Henry," I shouted to get his attention as he walked by me. "What did you want to talk about?"

"What's the story with you and that girl?"

I told Henry what had happened the night of the fire, how she'd stitched me up and let me stay. And that was all I told him.

"You're right, that's a wild story," Henry said, "but I have an even wilder one for you. I know that girl."

"What?" I said, disbelievingly.

"Yeah, man, she lives in a church over in Commerce, doesn't she?"

"How do you know her?"

He shook his head, dismissing my question. "How well do you know her, brother?" There was a tone of concern in his voice.

"I know her pretty well." I felt comfortable with that statement. I had known her only three days but I already knew her better than I could know anyone else in my life. I just couldn't tell him why I felt that way. "Why do you ask? What the hell are you driving at?"

"She's bad medicine, man. You need to stay away from her."

I rolled my eyes to the ceiling as an all-too-familiar feeling started to come over me. *It's not his fault*, I told myself. *He could never understand.* "Go ahead with what you're going to say," I said, leveling my eyes at him.

He took a drink of my beer as he began. "Last year, after I lost my job at the Whiskey, I started helping my buddy Dominic with some drug deliveries, heroin mostly, but there was some coke too. I didn't do it for very long, but I needed rent money. Anyway, one night we're out together and he gets a page from his boss about some special drop he needs to do. 'This is a big one,' he says to me as he pulls into the parking lot of this gay bathhouse out on Vine called Members Only. He comes back five minutes later with an overnight bag under his arm. We drove from the bathhouse straight to the church, her church.

"Now, I can tell there's a swinging party going on because we had to park two blocks away. We go inside, and the place is hoppin'. The air was thick with smoke: tobacco, marijuana, opium, you name it. I peer into the main room and it's full of people grinding on a dance floor below the altar. Some out-of-town hardcore gothic band is blaring from the short stage behind the pulpit where the lead singer stood, while naked men and women completely covered in different-colored body paints are dancing in cages on either side of the band."

"That's bullshit," I interjected.

"No bullshit, man, you can ask her, but that's nothing. There we are, in the front of the church not believing what we are seeing, when this black man, the largest man I've ever seen, comes up to meet us. He must have been a professional wrestler or something, he's wearing baggy silk pants with a red sash for a belt and looks like the giant from that movie, *The Thief of Baghdad*. I just about shit right then and there, but check this out, it gets even better. He steps up to us, looks down, and asks us for our fish. Dominic and I just look at each other, then the giant points to the old stone holy water basin. 'Your fish, you know, for the party,' he says in a voice so deep it seemed to resonate through my whole body. Dominic and I lean over and look inside the dry bowl, and it's full of those fish-shaped Christian emblems you see stuck on the backs of cars all the time. There must have been a hundred of them, some were the plain outlines, some had *Jesus* written in them, others had Jesus's name spelled in Greek letters. He looks at us and says it's a Jesus-fish party, and that we have to go pull an emblem off a car and put it in the bowl in order to get in. Dominic asked for your friend Poppy, but it was no use. Gigantor wouldn't hear it and was just about to bounce us when Dominic said he brought a horse instead of a fish, holding up the overnight bag. The giant takes the bag and looks inside. 'Why didn't you say so,' he bellowed as he handed the bag back and let us pass.

"Your friend wasn't hard to find. She wore a backless black cocktail dress that showed off this wild-ass flower tattoo on her back . . ."

I watched his lips move and tuned out his words as I thought about the probability of his story. Very probable, but so what, she was due the latitude. After all, there were many nights I tried to quiet the memories with a bottle, and she had many more to quiet than I did.

"The weird thing was, I noticed a lot of people with the same black tattoo on their hands, the same tattoo your friend has. I never did find out what that was about."

"Really?" I asked.

"Yeah, lots of 'em. Anyway, about an hour later, she and Dominic come back downstairs. Dominic comes over without the bag and pulls me away from this yellow-painted naked girl that I had been dancing with after I let her out of a cage. We get outside, and just as I notice I've got yellow paint all over my clothes, he pulls out the largest stack of hundreds I've ever seen and peels off ten for me. Evan, she bought fifty grand worth of china for a fuckin' party, man, and you don't even want to know what Dominic said was going on upstairs. Man, I'm amazed any of them lived."

"So what?" I said defensively.

"So what?" he said surprised. "So what? So . . . be careful, all right," he said, softening his tone. He leaned on the frosted glass and looked at me, waiting for a response. The soft-blue glow lit his face from below, giving him a ghostly appearance.

I felt it welling up inside me like a hot spring from some unknown place. Hatred. I hated Henry for what he was saying. Each word out of his mouth was like a wedge driven between the two worlds I now straddled.

Out of the corner of my eye, I could see people raising glasses and bills trying to get his attention. He didn't flinch. "You don't understand," I said, glancing away, unable to look him in the eye.

"Okay, I don't understand." He leaned closer until our noses were inches apart. "Why don't you explain it to me, Evan?"

Looking at him was like trying to stare at the sun. Telling him should have been easy but it wasn't. I'd already told him a hundred times in my head, and each time he had rejected me. I swallowed hard on my anger and just spat the words out.

"I'm different, Henry." I exhaled a nervous breath as I watched his face for a reaction. It felt good to say the words, healthy, but hollow at the same time, like I should have said them months or even years before.

He smiled and shook his head. "That's it? *I'm different, Henry,*" he said in a mocking tone. "Dude, you're a professional arsonist. You're different. Tell me something I don't know." He held up his finger toward several people trying to get his attention at the end of the bar.

"That's not what I mean." Those first simple words felt like the first trickle of water slipping through a fissure in a dike. There were millions of gallons still behind it, eager to eat away at the breech. "I'm not like other—" I stopped when I saw him stiffen and look over my shoulder.

"Later," he said, going back to work.

Poppy put her hand on my shoulder as she sat down. I looked down into the frosted glass and tried to shake off what Henry had told me about her.

"Are you okay? You look like you've seen a ghost," she said.

"I'm fine," I said, putting on a smile for her. "My ghost isn't here yet."

The movie screen flickered to life with *The Planet of the Apes* as the band fired up.

"What time is your friend supposed to be here?"

"Any time now."

"I'll be back in a little bit," she said, kissing me on the cheek before disappearing into the crowded dance floor.

MARTIN SHELBY CAME IN MINUTES LATER. This time he wore a pale-gray golf shirt with black slacks and wingtips. "You're early," I said as he sat down.

"I had less trouble getting in this time," he said, looking around. I could tell he was nervous.

"Did they question you?" I asked, pushing my empty glass forward on the bar.

"Yes. Two different inspectors came by. They said there might be an investigation," he said anxiously.

"Don't worry, they always say that. If they had anything, you'd be in jail by now." I could tell that comment didn't help his nerves any.

"Can I get a drink down here?" Martin yelled impatiently.

Henry looked annoyed as he came over. "Chardonnay?"

"Whiskey sour," Martin said softly. I raised my finger, letting Henry know I wanted another beer. "You wouldn't believe the week I've had," he said as he watched Henry prepare his cocktail.

"You know, I just might."

"First of all, I've been nervous about doing this anyway, and then when it happens, I've got these pesky inspectors tooling around all the time, taking samples, taking measurements, asking questions. Lots of questions," he said, looking at me. "Then, on top of all that, my insurance company won't pay until their inspector comes out next week."

Samples and measurements, I thought. There would be an investigation all right. It had already begun. The police must have tipped them off to seeing me leave the scene.

"Eight bucks," Henry said sternly. Martin counted off eight one-dollar bills.

"And that's another thing, I lost my wallet in here last week along with all my credit cards."

"Oh yeah, I meant to tell you about that, Martin." He gave a slight start when I called him by name. I pulled out his wallet and held it out in front of him.

"What the hell?"

"I found it here after you left last week. I knew I'd see you again, so I kept it."

"Thanks," he said, reaching out for it.

I pulled it away just before he could touch it. "Ah, ah, ah," I said, shaking my head. "I believe you owe me some money."

The realization showed on his face, and he nodded solemnly as he pulled an envelope out of his front pants pocket.

"Not on the bar," I said, interrupting his movement. He checked his movement and handed it to me under the bar railing. I casually opened it and checked the bill count. I handed the wallet back to him but didn't let go as I looked him in the eye. "I think you should go now. You and I really shouldn't be talking to each other. Know what I mean?"

He nodded. He was nervous, more nervous now than when he came in. He stood up, grabbed his drink, drained it in one long swallow, and walked straight out.

"That was quick," Henry shouted over the band as I pocketed the envelope.

I nodded. "He's going to be a real popular guy before long. I don't want to be around him any longer than I have to."

"Why is he going to be so popular?" Henry asked, leaning closer to me to overcome the noise.

"That's one of the things I was going to tell you. I was seen leaving the warehouse the night of the fire. The cops chased me around for a while, then one of them shot me as I was about to get away. I was really close to losing the guy, then all of a sudden, *blam*, I was down. My first thought was to call you and have you pick me up, but Poppy found me and stitched me up."

"How did you get away after they shot you?"

"I hid in the alley behind her church."

He nodded thoughtfully. "Hey, man, I'm sorry about what I said before about her. I didn't mean to be that harsh. Tell you what

I'll do. The Palookas are playing at the Billy Club on Thursday. Why don't all three of us go, on me? What do you say?" he asked, smiling.

I wanted to. I knew it would make everything okay if I could. I just couldn't keep my feet planted firmly on both worlds for that long. "I can't, Henry. I'm leaving tomorrow for Switzerland, and I don't know how long I'll be gone."

"Switzerland, what the fuck?" I could see the change come over his face. It went from consolation to distrust. "You going with her?" he said, thrusting his chin toward the dance floor.

I knew then it was too late to tell him. If I was ever going to tell him, it would have been twenty-five drunken nights earlier, and even if I could manage the courage to tell him now, it would be completely in vain. I knew, or at least hoped, that I wouldn't come back from Zurich as the same person he'd known, and it felt like I was being forced to reap the harvest of secret seeds sown long ago. "Yes, I'm going with her."

"What's going on, man? You stay with her for what, three days, and now you're going halfway around the world with her?"

I grabbed my beer and tilted it back as I thought up a story. "I just hit it off with her. She is going there to see some friends and invited me along on her nickel." Each word felt like a ten-pound weight being placed on my chest. "It's no big deal. I just don't know how long we'll be gone."

He picked up a rag and began wiping the bar. "That's cool. Bring back a souvenir for me," he said in a flat monotone.

"I'm sorry, Henry."

"For what, not calling? Don't worry about it."

I shook my head slowly. "I'm just sorry." He raised his eyebrows as he kept wiping, as though he didn't know how to respond. "I'm gonna get out of here, man. How much do I owe you?"

"You don't owe me anything, but think about what I told you," he said, pointing to the dance floor. "And have a good time."

I forced a smile as I got up to leave. I walked away from the back bar as quickly as my three legs would allow and climbed the short section of stairs to a side platform overlooking the dance floor. Each step I took away from Henry was a step toward Zurich. It felt like I could go out the front door, make a right, and walk all the way there.

Poppy wasn't hard to find. She danced at the edge of the dance floor in erotic serpentine movements, holding her arms above her head to exaggerate the effect. Several people, men and women, looked on mesmerized as she swayed to the gothic rhythms of the band. I watched as she danced. Everything that was happening, all these changes in my life, were because of her. The spell over her was broken when the music stopped. She looked right up at me as though she'd known I was watching her. She smiled widely, showing her teeth. I motioned for her to meet me by the stairs.

"I love this music," she said, throwing her arms around my neck. "There's a place almost exactly like this in Paris. I'll show you."

"Sounds fun. Are you ready to go?"

She nodded rapidly. "Did you get your business taken care of?"

"Yes. Everything's finished here. I'm ready to leave."

ANTONIO STOPPED in front of the church but stayed in the car as we got out. "Come back at nine o'clock in the morning," Poppy told him as I walked up the steps ahead of her.

"Where is he going to stay tonight?" I asked.

"I keep a small place for him across town for when I want to be alone," she said, stepping inside. "Go on up, I'll join you in a bit."

She came up a couple of minutes later with a medical vial in her hand. "I think you're going to like this stuff. It's special, real mellow," she said, rolling it between her thumb and forefinger.

"No, thank you. I'm fine."

She looked surprised. "Suit yourself, but there's no need to be a prude about it."

"I'm not being a prude," I said defensively. "I'm just not into it." The vision of Henry's story kept running through my head. "Why do you use it?"

"I like it," she said matter-of-factly. "To me, it's the same as asking why you smoke. Because you enjoy it, right? Cigarettes will kill you the same as this," she said, holding up the assembled needle. "So what's the difference?"

"I just remember what it was like in Turkey. I saw it destroy a lot of people."

"Weak people," she said, pointing at me. "You and I and the others like us are different. The same rules don't apply. You had better get used to that. Besides, it helps pass time, you'll see one day." She held her breath and inserted the needle between her toes, exhaling as she pushed in the plunger. "Oh, yes, that's nice."

I turned away and searched for something to take my mind off Henry's warning. "Who's that?" I asked, pointing to the stone bust on the bureau.

"Her name was Teszin, and she was my first love, lover," she said, running her hand over my short hair. I rolled my head gently against her hand, exposing my neck, which she kissed as we laid down on the bed. She climbed on top of me and pressed her mouth onto my neck, sucking slightly.

"Harder," I heard myself whispering. I couldn't hear Henry at all now. I unzipped the top of her body suit and ran my hands over the soft skin of her buttocks as she ran her tongue along my collarbone. I gripped her tightly in my hands and gently probed her wetness with a finger. She let out a long, low groan that I felt more through her body than I heard from her lips. She rode up higher on me so I could reach deeper inside her. I visualized her erotic dancing as I tasted the salty skin of her breasts. I rolled her over and slipped the body suit down to her ankles in one motion. She pulled it off and slid her hand between her legs as she watched me undress. I knelt between her thighs. She grabbed me and guided me in as I lay on top of her. Time stopped again. She rose perfectly in anticipation of every thrust, never breaking her penetrating stare into my eyes. I had to look away first, and buried my face against her neck as I surrendered to the onrushing ecstasy.

I LAY NEXT TO POPPY running my fingers along her arm as I caught my breath. "What are the other ones like?"

"Like me."

"Do they use a lot of drugs too?"

"And then some. I'll admit that we indulge ourselves quite a bit compared to the social norm, but it all boils down to what we are."

"What are we?" I asked.

"Well, no one knows exactly. How are you supposed to know if no one has ever told you? Some think we are blessed to keep on living like we do, others think we are cursed because we can never escape this cycle."

"What do you think?"

"You really want to know?"

"Of course."

"I think we were created special by God and abandoned, spurned because of our hideousness, not unlike the creature created and neglected by Frankenstein, whose intentions were equally as noble.

"You see, no one ever told any of us why we are different or what to do about it. When we die there's no great revelation, no judgment day, no explanation, there is only another internment here. We just keep coming back over and over again. So eventually, you have to ask yourself, what is the point in being righteous or virtuous, if you'll just come back anyway? Your position never changes in the next trip. It doesn't matter if you were a murderer or a monk the time before. I've tried it. We've all tried it. That's why we indulge ourselves as we do. And why shouldn't we? That's what I meant when I said you saw opium break weak people. They don't know what we do. They can't know, even if they wanted to."

"How do you know normal people don't come back?"

"You misunderstand me. I think they do come back, just like we do. Have you ever heard them talk about feeling an unknown affinity or loathing toward someone they've just met, like they've known them before? That's because they *have* known them before. I think we are special not because we come back, but because we remember, because we know we have come back and will come back again.

"The trouble is, we live in a Christian society. The main goal of which is eternal life in heaven, or, put more simply, immortality. The doctrines of Christianity say you must have faith in a savior so that you will live again. What people really need is faith that they have already lived. That is the essence of immortality. You see, Christianity panders perfectly to their weakness and insecurity about this because it gives them some kind of false hope, some false heaven as a payoff for the squandered lives they lead. The horrible thing is that they are ignorant of the truth and that they will never know that they live a lie."

"What is the truth?" I interjected.

"The truth is not what you see when you look around. The truth is what you don't see. The truth is that you don't see men living the way they want to. You don't see them living naturally. Instead, they live their lives as they are told to. They live vicariously through this false spirituality, never having to take responsibility for their own existence so long as they believe in and are forgiven by an inattentive god. If that is not a sin, I don't know what is.

"The most frustrating thing is that we can do nothing for them, even though we know and live the truth. No matter how loud we scream, they cannot hear us. You want to grab hold of the bars and rattle the cages that hold them until they will listen, but when you do, you come away with only handfuls of ether. In the end, you realize there is nothing you can do. It's killing a legend, and how do you kill a legend? You don't. You can only replace it."

SECOND NOTEBOOK

"But why should not every individual man have existed more than once upon this world?"

G. E. Lessing,
The Education of the Human Race, 1778

11

The bark of the jet's wheels against the runway caused my pulse to quicken. The flight attendant announced in four languages that it was three o'clock local time. Gray clouds and drizzle hung low over the city, giving this new world a dark and foreboding air.

We spotted him at the same time as we walked through the sliding glass doors to the damp air outside the Zurich private terminal. He wore a black jacket and hat and stood next to a gray stretch Mercedes-Benz sedan, holding a white signboard with a black Embe on it.

"That must be for us," I said.

"It's not specifically for us, but we can take it. There will be a chauffeur here full time for the next day or so. Several others will be arriving before tomorrow night."

"What's tomorrow night?"

"That's when your Ascension begins," Poppy said, closing the door.

The car pulled away from the curb and out of sight of the terminal. The windshield wipers beat out a steady rhythm as they cut at the light drizzle. *Tomorrow night*, I thought. It's funny how life works. You can run in the same circles for months, years, even decades, then a change comes like a sudden storm at sea blowing you hundreds of miles off course, often forcing you to realize you had no course to begin with. I didn't know nearly enough about what I was getting into, but I was getting in anyway. I wanted to know more about them, and more about myself. I knew this would be a good change for me—it had to be.

Street signs printed in German lined the highway that ran into the heart of the city's old quarter. The driver exited onto the main thoroughfare that paralleled the slow-moving Limmat River. The city got older the farther he drove. Centuries-old church spires rose toward the heavens in front of us. Each narrow cobblestone side street opened for a split second then closed off its secrets as we rushed by. We crossed the river over an old stone bridge and turned down a twisting one-way side street only wide enough for one car. "Augustiner Strasse"[16] was painted in a rectangle on the wall of a building at the end of the block. The serpentine trail of wet cobblestones ended in front of a white-stone hotel, the Hotel St. Germain. We pulled into the circular driveway and stopped in front of the large black front door. I looked over at Poppy for some indication of what was going on. My heart was hammering.

"This is home. This is the Cognomina," she said, waiting for the driver to open her door.

I followed her. She pulled on a white rope that hung next to the door, ringing a bell inside. I set down my things, put my nervous hands in my pockets to keep them from moving,

---

16. Evan is likely mistaken in his recollection here, as there is no Augustiner Strasse in Zurich, but there is an Augustinergasse. Gasse means alley in German while Strasse means street. Augustinergasse is a narrow pedestrian street in the old part of central Zurich.

and rocked back and forth. I looked at Poppy, then looked at the door. Two deadbolts cleared their latches before the door creaked open.

A tall, thin, tuxedo-clad man appeared behind the door. He stood just over six feet tall. The tuxedo jacket hung loosely on his lanky frame. His narrow, chiseled face betrayed little about his age, but with the gray intermingled in his black hair and his tired posture, I would have guessed him to be about fifty. He didn't have the tattoo on his hand. He smiled when he saw Poppy. "Hello, Madame, so nice to see you again," he said in English with a thick German accent.

"Thank you, and how are you doing?"

"Very well, Madame. Thank you for asking." He turned to me and tilted his head back. "And you must be Herr Michaels." I nodded. "My name is Leopold Diltz. It is a pleasure to meet you. I'm the caretaker here. Welcome to the Hotel St. Germain. Please come this way, I've already had a suite prepared for you." He bowed slightly and turned back to Poppy. "Your usual suite is ready, Madame." He closed and locked the door, then walked ahead of us into the lobby. A large silver-and-crystal chandelier hung from the ceiling of the lobby and filled every inch of the room with light. Several oil paintings and sketches hung on the white walls above red velvet armchairs and couches.

"Can you show me this town tonight?" I asked Poppy in a whisper as we walked behind Diltz.

"Oh, sorry, love. I can't. I've got an appointment later tonight," she said, taking two quick steps ahead of me. "Have any others arrived yet?" she asked Diltz.

"Yes, about half, Madame," he said as he turned right down a short hallway with two doors on each side. He opened the first door on the right. "This is your room, sir. Dinner will be served in the dining room at eight o'clock."

Poppy stood behind him. I looked at her as I hovered in the open doorway. "Get some rest, Evan. I'll see you before I go out," she said and walked away.

"Don't hesitate to let me know if you need any attention for your injury, sir," Diltz said as he closed the door.

Alone again. The room's furnishings were old but pleasant. Dark wood paneling covered the lower part of the walls and was color matched to the parquet hardwood floor. I perused the books on the recessed bookshelf before I walked into the bathroom, filled the large bathtub, and climbed in.

THE KNOCK ON THE DOOR WOKE ME at seven forty-five. It was a young woman dressed in the black-and-white dress of the staff's uniform. "Your dinner will be ready in a few minutes," she said, struggling with the English.

I donned the dark suit along with a black shoe and sock and walked down the hall toward the lobby.

"Right this way, sir," Mr. Diltz said, sliding two dark wooden doors open, revealing a large dining room. The long, narrow table had twenty high-backed, carved wooden chairs around it. Each one richly inlaid with red-leather padding. A single white plate and table setting lay in front of the end chair. "Please be seated. I'll have your meal brought out promptly."

"Where's everybody else? Isn't Poppy going to eat?"

"The Madame has decided to eat with the others after you've finished." He exited out a side door and quickly reappeared with three staff women trailing behind him, each carrying a silver-domed tray. They sat the trays in front of me as two more women appeared carrying wine, water, and glasses. The flavorful aromas hit me one by one as they pulled the domes off. "Chicken Kiev, rare roast beef, and poached salmon with fresh dill, all with accompanying vegetables," Diltz said, taking a serving spoon from one of the girls.

"I'll start with the fish," I said.

He placed a fillet on my plate along with rice and steamed brussels sprouts. "Will there be anything else?"

"Well . . ." I hesitated.

"Yes, sir?"

"It's just that I feel sort of uncomfortable eating alone in this large room."

"Yes?"

"Would you join me?"

Mr. Diltz looked surprised and took a few seconds to answer. "Yes, of course." He sat two chairs down from the end. "Bring some rye rolls and seltzer please," he said to the girl standing next to the side door.

"Have you ever been to Zurich before?" he asked.

"No. This is my first trip to Europe since . . . Well, it's been a while," I stammered. The girl reappeared and sat the rolls between us.

"I'm sorry you have to eat alone like this. There's little I can do about it, but I'm embarrassed that I didn't think about it when I prepared for your arrival. Please excuse the oversight."

"It's all right. It was explained to me," I said. "You know why I'm here, don't you?"

"Oh yes," he answered.

"But you're not one of them, are you?"

"No, my position as the caretaker here is something different. You could say I'm an organizer, a secretary of sorts," he said, buttering a roll.

"How did you start here? I mean, why you?"

"I inherited the position. My family has a unique relationship with the Cognomina. The men in my family have been caretakers here for five generations. We are the only people in the world, besides each other, they can completely trust."

"How long have you been here?"

"I took over after my father's death."

I thought about his answer as I ate. "Poppy said the last newcomer, the last neophyte, to enter was in the 1920s, so you've never received someone like me."

"That is correct, sir. It's a first for both of us, you might say," he said, reaching for his drink. "Please, let me know if there are any inadequacies in the accommodations."

"Everything is great so far, but I might need you to make a map for me, something that points out places of interest nearby if it's no trouble. I want to explore a little, and Poppy said she had an appointment, so it looks like I'm solo tonight."

"It's no trouble at all. There are plenty of sights within a few blocks. This is the oldest part of the city. I'll make a map for you so you don't get lost—there are numerous unmarked side streets and blind alleys that can easily lead you off course."

I finished the meal and placed my napkin on the plate.

"Dessert?" Diltz asked.

"Later tonight, perhaps after I go out."

"As you wish, sir," he said, getting up to open the doors.

THE SUIT WAS RIDICULOUS. I had dressed up to eat alone. I closed the door to my room, took one of Poppy's painkillers, and laid down to rest. I drifted in and out of a light slumber, unable to keep my eyes closed because of the boisterous noises now coming from the dining room. Putting on a dress shirt and jeans, I grabbed the cane and walked into the lobby. Diltz stood in front of the dining room doors like a sentry. The shouting, laughing, and clanging of china behind him was distracting.

"Ah, Herr Michaels. I prepared the map you requested," he said, pulling a folded sheet of paper out of his shirt pocket. "It shows several points of interest in the area including a tavern or two. Would you like a car?"

"No, I'm going to walk tonight," I said, taking the map from him. The sounds of laughter and conversation became much louder as one of the doors slid open behind him. I caught a glimpse of two women and one man laughing on the far side of the platter-strewn table when Poppy came through the door.

"Did you send for the driver as I requested?" Poppy asked Mr. Diltz in an impatient voice.

"Yes, Madame. Your driver should be here momentarily," he said, reaching behind her to slide the door closed.

"Let me know the minute he arrives." She turned to me. "How are you? I'm sorry I have to leave you tonight, but it's very important that I see someone. Maybe we can get together later tonight."

"I'd like that," I said, smiling.

"I'll see you later then," she said, slipping back into the dining room between the sliding doors.

"Thanks for the map," I said to Diltz. "I'll be back in a while."

"I'll see you out, sir."

I heard both locks latch closed as I walked down the driveway. The rain had stopped, and the night air smelled fresh and new. A small sliver of moon hung low over the dark outline of the nearby rooftops. I realized as I wandered aimlessly through those ancient streets that I was walking toward the future. But try as I might to look forward, part of my mind still echoed back to Henry's warning. *Bad medicine*, he'd said. He was right about that. I knew that was where she was off to. But right as he was about that, he was wrong about the rest. He didn't know, he could never know. As much as I cared for him, he could never know about the mental strain of carrying around the hopes, disappointments, and loves of souls who should have been long dead, their voices infecting your thoughts like a virus. He could never know the disappointment when you realize you've been lied to on the grandest scale, and he could never know the hopelessness you feel when it starts to come together and you begin to see that there is no reward for being good and no punishment for being bad, when you see that there is only the loneliness of being. He could never know, but Poppy knew. And in time, I would know, whether I liked it or not. He was right about her indulgences, and they bothered me, but try as I might, I could not bring myself to begrudge her responses to the same hazards I could see on my own horizon.

I pulled out the map, found my bearings, and walked the four blocks to one of the taverns Mr. Diltz had marked.

The Fraumunster Inn was exactly what I had expected to find.[17] It sat on the corner of two narrow streets. Accordion music echoed down the cramped canyons of the neighborhood like a siren's song, beckoning all within earshot. I sat at the short wooden bar and drank alone with my thoughts.

THE WALK BACK TO THE HOTEL SAINT GERMAIN took an hour. My thoughts returned to the task at hand when the white two-story building came into view. I was less than a block away when the familiar gray stretch Mercedes sped past me and turned into the driveway. I picked up my limping pace so that I would arrive at the front door at the same time as the passenger.

The driver got out and opened the back door just as I walked up. The passenger stepped out into the light and looked right at me. He was slightly taller than me when he straightened up, and he wore a pullover tunic. It made his barrel chest and stomach look larger than they probably were. His brown, curly hair was thinning on top and ran down the sides of his head, meeting in a sparse beard that barely covered his full jaw and chin. His pale brown eyes stayed locked with mine as he stretched.

17. The Fraumunster Bar is near the Fraumunster Church on the west bank of the Limmat River.

"Hello there," he bellowed in a jovial voice. I stood dumb-founded, unable to speak. The tattoo showed prominently when he lowered his hands to his sides. "Are you sure you're in the right place, young man?"

I nodded quickly.

"I see." His baritone voice carried out into the anonymous night. He walked over and rang the bell. "Did you arrive today?"

"Yes," I said in a state of silent panic.

"Is this your first time here?"

"Yes."

"Well, it's a slow town all in all but it serves our needs nicely. Ah, here we go," he said hearing the locks slide free.

"You made it." Mr. Diltz said to him. "How nice to see you, sir. I was beginning to worry."

"I had a bit of trouble in Tangiers, but I made it, and look at what I found," he said, pointing to me.

"Yes," said Diltz. "That would be Herr Michaels."

"Ah, Nice to meet you," the stranger said, shaking my clammy hand. I nodded. "Here, let's go in." He motioned for me to enter first.

"Everything is prepared in your suite, sir," Diltz said to him.

"Good. What time are we eating tomorrow morning?"

"Ten o'clock."

"I'll see you then," he said, turning up the stairs that led to the second floor. "And good night to you, Mr. Michaels."

Diltz continued down the hall to my room.

I watched until he had climbed out of sight. "Is Poppy back yet?" I asked the caretaker.

"No, sir."

"Did she call?"

"No, sir."

My spirit sank slightly. "Would you leave a message for her for when she gets back?"

"Yes, of course. What would you like me to relay to her?"

"Tell her to wake me when she gets in. I would like to see her."

"Very good, sir. Your breakfast will be ready at nine o'clock. Is that satisfactory?"

I nodded, went inside, and picked up a book on the nightstand as I lay down. The fictional words were little solace for the genuine pangs I was feeling. Love is an indifferent affectation. It knows no right or wrong and doesn't care if you like it or not when it comes. If you feel it, you feel it. And I felt it there, alone on that bed in this strange new world. I read the same paragraph three or four times, unable to focus and control my own thoughts. I owed everything to her: my foot, my not being in jail, this trip, this family, even this new life itself. I closed my eyes and set the book aside.

SHARP KNOCKING WOKE ME out of a dead sleep. Sunshine highlighted half the bed. The knocking began again as I walked over to the door.

"Your breakfast will be ready in thirty minutes, sir," Diltz said, standing in the open doorway.

"What time is it?" I asked, half asleep.

"Eight thirty sir, in the a.m."

"I told you to have Poppy wake me up."

"Yes, sir, you did. Unfortunately, I was unable to deliver your message, as she has not yet returned."

I scratched my head. "She isn't back yet?" I asked, concerned.

"No, but not to worry, sir. It's not unusual. Come down to the dining room when you're ready," he said, and walked away.

I hopped to the bathroom and started at the stitches with a pair of small scissors and tweezers. The wound remained closed and itched less with the stitches out. I wrapped it tightly before making my way down to the dining room.

I ate alone, reading that day's London edition of the *New York Times* that Diltz had left for me. He came in as I finished.

"What time will it start tonight?" I asked.

"It will begin after dinner. We'll be dining at eight thirty sharp."

I nodded. I knew there was no way I could just sit there all day and wait for Poppy to return. "I thought I'd step out for a while. It looks nice outside."

"Sounds like a wonderful idea, sir."

"Would you tell Poppy to meet me here before supper tonight?"

"Of course, sir. I'll see you out."

The sun warmed my bones as I tested my foot. I ambled around for most of the afternoon, taking in several of the points Diltz had marked on the map; three museums, two churches, and an old battlement, anything to occupy time and take my mind off of Poppy and what awaited me tonight.

I WAS WALKING DOWN a café-lined boulevard next to the river when I saw it. It hadn't occurred to me that they would be here now in large numbers, and I was taken by surprise when I spotted a female hand with the now-familiar Embe tattoo on it. I noticed it twenty-five feet away. The skin color was too light to be Poppy. She sat in the courtyard of the Café Grossmunster reading a newspaper. I went in the front door, paid for a cup of coffee, and stepped out into the courtyard bordering the sidewalk. She sat alone. The newspaper obscured her face. Luckily, there were no vacant tables when I came out, and I limped over to her's.

"Do you mind if I join you?"

"No, not at all," she said in a Slavic accent that sounded a little like Bulgarian. She didn't lower the German-language newspaper.

Hanging my cane on the edge of the table, I took a seat. I

sipped my coffee and watched the river traffic as I thought about what to say. "Your accent, is it Bulgarian?"

She ruffled the paper slightly and shifted in her seat. "I am from Poland."

"Interesting," I said.

"What is interesting? Being from Poland? Not very," she said sardonically behind her white paper.

"No, I find the accent interesting," I said defensively. "I'm usually very accurate about them and I wouldn't have thought Polish."

She turned a page and continued reading. "Do you speak Bulgarian?" she asked in a mocking tone in Bulgarian.

I almost choked on my coffee when I heard it. "Yes, I speak Bulgarian. My name is Evan," I responded in my old native tongue.

She folded the paper neatly and placed it on the table. "Now, *that* is interesting. My name is Nadya," she said, offering her hand across the table. She was thin, and her tattooed hand felt bony in mine. She had a large, narrow, straight nose; cold, steely gray eyes; a wide, sloping forehead; and a strong jaw. She looked to be in her twenties, but I couldn't help wondering how old she really was.

"Nice to meet you, Nadya. I hope you don't mind me interrupting you."

"I do not mind. Your Bulgarian is excellent. I thought the only Americans that could speak Bulgarian would be with the CIA, but you do not look the part at all. Where did you learn it?"

"I lived in Bulgaria a long time ago," I said, smiling at her.

She gave me a curious look as though she were trying to figure it out. She reached for her coffee at the edge of the table then stopped. "Hello there, I remember this," she said, picking up the cane. She turned it from side to side inspecting it like an old friend you barely recognize. "Evan? Not Evan Michaels?" she asked.

"The very same. I hope it's not inappropriate to be so forward, but I saw that you have the same tattoo as Poppy and I just thought—"

"No. Welcome, Evan. Don't give it another thought. It is indeed a pleasure to meet you," she said, taking my hand again. "I did not think I would meet you until tonight. My real name within our family is Ramsay."

"Will you be there tonight, Ramsay?" I asked, sipping my coffee.

"I will. I am sitting on the panel."

"You're one of the five that will have the final say about me?" I asked, trying to mask my concern.

"I will cast one of the five votes, but it will be only one of five. I'm very much looking forward to hearing about you."

"I'm very anxious to get started. Is it against the rules for me to meet with you before this begins?"

"No, it is not against the rules. It is okay now, but we must not speak or be in contact after the Ascension has begun, not until a decision has been reached anyway. So you may be at ease.

"So you were a Bulgar?" she asked, smiling.

"Yes, the first time."

"What did you do in that life?"

"I was a farmer until the land was nationalized by the communists."

"1946," she said, astonished. "Is this only your second trip?"

"No, third."

"Lucky you. I can hardly wait to hear about it."

"Speaking of hearing about me, I was wondering if there are any tips you could give me that could help us make this easier."

"No. I am sure you can understand why I cannot. Poppy is to be your advocate, is she not?"

"Yes, she is, if she ever shows up."

Ramsay laughed. "Well, she does have a habit of doing that, but do not worry," she said, dismissing my anxiety. "She will be here, and she will be able to help you."

I nodded solemnly. "I have another question for you. What happens to a neophyte if he fails to win a majority vote in the affirmative?"

She shook her head. "Do not take a negative approach. I have every confidence that Poppy would not have brought you here and summoned all of us had she not believed you to be what you claim. If you are indeed one of us, we will find out. We are very thorough and we always find the truth. So relax, be at ease."

"Thank you. I will. I feel better already," I said, even though I didn't. My stomach was in knots. The strong coffee wasn't helping.

"How did you and Poppy meet?"

"I was shot behind her church," I said, raising my foot. "She found me and stitched the wound."

Ramsay chuckled and shook her head. "Normal people would say it is funny how a chance encounter like that can change your life, but I've been around long enough to know that nothing happens by accident."

I nodded and sipped my coffee, fascinated by her.

"As much as I would like to stay here and speak with you, it will have to wait until later. I must go," she said, getting up. "If you will excuse me." She left in a confident walk, not looking back.

I finished my coffee and walked a meandering route back to the St. Germain so that I arrived shortly before eight thirty.

"Has Poppy come back?" I asked Mr. Diltz as soon as we were both inside.

"No, but she did call and say she is on her way back."

"Back from where?"

"Luzern. She said she would be back in time to eat. Speaking of which, I thought I would dine with you tonight if you haven't any objections."

"I would like that," I said automatically, my thoughts preoccupied with Poppy.

"Good," he said, smiling slightly. "I'll send for you when it's ready."

POPPY WAS STILL NOWHERE TO BE FOUND when I met Diltz in front of the dining room doors.

"The arrangement is a bit different this evening," Diltz began. "We are going to dine in a side room at the same time as the others dine in here so that everything can begin immediately afterward. But we will need to fill our plates here first," he said, sliding the double doors open to expose a colorful cornucopia of steaming platters covering the long table. "Be sure to take enough now," he said, handing me a large plate. "They won't leave much after they get started in here."

I loaded my plate and followed him down the hall into the side room. A normal-sized wooden table sat in the middle of the plain, white-walled room. Wine glasses, salads, and refined place settings sat waiting for us. Mr. Diltz had just poured the wine when the bell rang. I watched from the side doorway as he unlocked and opened the door.

Poppy came through along with a short young man with dark hair and complexion. She saw me and walked toward me with her arms outstretched. "I'm sorry. Diltz here said you were worried about me."

"Worried about you? Don't flatter yourself. I'm worried about me. This thing is starting in a little over an hour, and I have no idea what in the hell I'm supposed to do," I said forcefully.

"There's no need to get upset about it."

"Upset?" I said, shaking my head. "*Upset* was last night, maybe even this morning. I'm beyond upset now." The calm, cool tone I used had little effect on her. "Where were you, anyway?"

Her face brightened. "I ran into Jea—" she checked her speech. "A friend." She pointed back over her shoulder at the handsome dark-haired man talking with Diltz near the door. He kept his hands in the pockets of his sport coat. "We ran into each other last night and started talking. Before we knew what happened, we were in Luzern."

"You know, that is just fucking great," I said, starting to lose my temper again. "I'm hours away from the most important undertaking in my life, in my lives," I corrected, "and you're off partying and chumming it up with your *friend*," I said bitterly.

"Whoa, whoa, whoa, take a second and relax. You're carrying on like you're going to face the Inquisition. I've been talking about your situation a bit with my friend and I've decided that it's best that you enter this process with a minimum of preparation so that all your responses will be automatic and sincere."

I could barely control the anger welling up inside me. I knew her story was bullshit. She hadn't thought of me or any preparations concerning me until she walked through that front door. I knew she was lying, a good liar can always tell, but what could I do? There was no way I could rebuke her. I was at her mercy and she knew it. I forced the bitter resentment back down into my stomach. "Maybe you're right," I conceded falsely.

"Are you excited?" she asked, smiling.

"I'm nervous. Mr. Diltz and I were just sitting down to eat. Why don't you join us?"

"Oh, I can't. I'm going to catch a quick bite with the others then I have to make some necessary preparations. I'll come and get you when everything is ready.

"We're not late, are we?" she asked Diltz.

"No, your timing is perfect, Madame. It's inside waiting for you."

"Great. I'll see you in a bit," she said, kissing me on the cheek.

I didn't notice Mr. Diltz walk up behind me as I watched Poppy and her friend enter the dining room. "Are you ready?"

"Huh?" I answered, distracted.

"Dinner, sir. Are you ready?"

"Yeah, let's eat."

I watched Diltz eat after I had put a few mouthfuls of food into my nervous stomach. The muscles in his long, gaunt jaws rippled as he chewed. The rumble of loud voices and the clanging of silverware on china crept under the door. "She's right about the lack of preparation being a benefit. From what I've been told, the Ascension is impossible to prepare for. It's like an IQ test. In the end, you simply know what you know. I've asked several of them about it, and they all told me the same thing."

I still thought she was lying. "It may be true but it's not very comforting," I said, picking at the plate with my fork.

"I understand," he said, starting on his lobster. "I'm not sure how much of a consolation it would be, but I'm available for you if you need anything."

"Thank you," I said, looking up at him. "Knowing that is some consolation already." I watched him eat for some time and noticed the sounds from the large dining room had died down somewhat.

"You said you spoke to some of them about the Ascension," I said, prompting him.

"Yes, but more specifically about a neophyte Ascension. I never thought I'd see one, so I wanted to prepare myself for whatever that might entail."

"Tell me, when you spoke with them about this did you ask them if anyone, any neophyte, has ever failed?"

"Yes, I asked about that."

"And?"

He took a long sip of wine. "As it was related to me, sir, there have been neophytes who have failed, but never has a failed neophyte come back and remembered failing." Mr. Diltz got up from the table to answer the gentle knock at the door. "It must be time."

12

"Hello," Poppy said, poking her head around the door. "We are ready."

"Very good," Mr. Diltz said, placing his napkin on the table. "I'll meet you downstairs." Diltz passed her as she entered. She wore a long, gray velvet robe with white trim at the cuffs and lapels. She looked regal, standing in the open doorway.

"I'm ready," I said, standing up, "but I should go to my room and put a suit on."

"Just put on your suit jacket, no tie. That will be fine." She walked ahead of me down the hall. The lights in the hallway were dimmed slightly. Our footsteps on the polished wooden floorboards were the only sounds I could hear. I looked through the open doors of the dining room as we walked past. The lights were off inside. The dim glow from the hallway reflected off the silver platters and domes that lay strewn amid the dirty dishes. The whole scene felt eerie, like a ship that had been hurriedly abandoned.

She stopped at my door. "I'll wait for you."

I stepped inside, closed the door, and went straight to the bathroom. Cold water blasted into the basin as I turned on the faucet. I bent over and put my hands on the sides of the sink. My stomach was turning over, my head was pounding, my legs felt like they would buckle under me at any moment. I cupped my hands under the tap, filling them. The shock of the icy water on my face began to calm me after the third handful. I readied a cigarette and primed my lighter before straightening and looking at my reflection in the mirror. It had no imperfections, no defects. The end of the cigarette flared orange as I took a long drag. My eyes rolled to the ceiling as I exhaled, then leveled straight into the mirror. I stared into those blue eyes, listening to the blasting water.

"Tell them the truth," I said, holding my own gaze. "You've been waiting all your life to tell the truth."

I took one last drag off the cigarette before dropping it into the full sink. Grabbing the suit jacket off the bedpost, I went back outside to meet Poppy.

"You look nice," she said, leading the way again. "Follow me."

To my surprise, she walked farther down my hallway. No one else had come down this way except me. She pushed open the last door on the left, walked inside, and stopped in front of the bathroom door. The room was laid out exactly like mine. She looked at me and reached out to straighten my collar.

"Just be yourself, Evan."

I smiled down at her, more curious about what was in the bathroom than nervous about what to do. She turned around and opened the door.

I could see only a faint glow of light on the floor of the darkened room beyond her. She stepped in, and the darkness enveloped her like a dense fog. I went forward and stopped in the doorway. When I looked for her inside, I saw only the white collar and cuffs of her robe moving below me. The faint glow I'd seen came from torches mounted on the stone walls of a long, descending staircase. I took a second to let my eyes adjust then stepped down, searching with my left hand for fissures, ledges, and handholds in the old stone masonry of the wall. The brass tip of the cane clicked and echoed downward with each step I took. We descended what felt to be between seventy-five and one hundred stone steps into what I assumed must have been an ancient grotto. The ghostly flickering of the last torches beckoned us to the bottom. Poppy held her finger in front of her lips in a motion for me to be quiet as I neared the landing where she stood.

The landing of the stairwell opened into a large cavern of a room. The high ceiling was supported by a dozen thick stone columns, each carved with intricate scrollwork at the tops and bottoms. The walls were made of the same rough-faced stone as the staircase, and the floor was a subtle mosaic of dark, smooth-polished granite that shined like the moonlit surface of a still pond. A simple wooden table and two chairs sat in the middle of the room. Both chairs were arranged to one side and faced a long wooden console resembling a judge's bench that hugged the back wall. A gallery consisting of two rows of tiered seats rose to the right of the lonely table. This gallery was positioned in front of a heavy black curtain that went from floor to ceiling and ran the vast distance of the room's width. The curtain seemed to mask even more of the grotto. Several large torches burned in freestanding silver-footed holders about the room.

I followed Poppy in. We were alone. I tried to place the cane quietly, but it was no use. Every sound, every shuffled foot or ruffle of clothing sent shocking waves of sound bouncing wildly about the room. She led me to the middle of the room next to the table, where an ashtray, water carafe, and glasses awaited us patiently.

"This is it," she whispered with a cupped hand. "They will come out there any minute." She pointed to where the long curtain met the wall near the judge's bench.

I looked around, trying to take in the immensity of the room. The thought of such a place existing underneath a modern city seemed fantastic, but there I was. I looked around until my eyes fell on Poppy. "Thank you." I mouthed the words without making a sound. She smiled and reached down to grab my hand. The echo of a heavy mechanical device broke the silence as the curtain pulled three feet away from the wall.

They walked out single file about five steps apart. The first five wore long white robes with black trim. They walked along the wall and stepped up one after another onto the bench. The others that followed wore normal clothing along with narrow black-and-red silk stoles draped around their necks and onto their chests. They turned one by one after exiting the curtain and took their places in the gallery. All of them moved solemnly without speaking. Their cumulative footfalls and movements built to a dull white noise and were a testament to me that these beings before me were real.

The five judges were settling into their seats when I saw the spear Poppy had mentioned mounted on the wall behind them. It was as long as a man, with a palm-size black spearhead and a flowing red-dyed horsehair skirt behind the metal point. The end of the white wooden staff along with the tip were coated with brown crusted blood. I stood mesmerized, unable to take my eyes off the spear until Poppy let go of my hand, breaking my trance.

The judge on the left end was the handsome young man I had seen arrive with Poppy before dinner. To his left sat a tall, rail-thin man with a long, narrow nose supporting wire-rimmed spectacles under a shock of thick black hair. He looked like an intimidating professor. In the center, under the spear, sat a weathered man in his sixties with long white hair and a long white beard to match. The deep wrinkles lay like plowed furrows cut onto his leathery face. Next to him was Ramsay from the café. She gave a slight smile when she caught me looking at her. On the end, next to the curtain, sat a gracile Asian with a shaved head. I couldn't tell whether he was a man or a woman.

The twenty seats of the gallery to my right were less than half full. A young man, dressed in the same robes as the judges, took a seat at a desk at the end of the gallery and opened a large, leather-bound tome and appeared to ready an ornate fountain pen. I assumed he would act as a scribe for the proceedings. The only faces I recognized other than Poppy were Diltz and the rotund man I'd met at the front door the night before. Diltz smiled reassuringly at me. The older man in the center was looking directly at me when I turned away from the gallery. The four others got situated, and one by one, they looked out at us. Poppy cleared her throat.

"I bring before you Evan Michaels," she said, addressing the whole panel, "a neophyte who claims to be one of us, a Reincarnationist. I believe his claim to be true and therefore have gathered you so that you may pass judgment on him. It is his wish to become a candidate for the Ascension." The remnants of her words floated about the room after she'd finished.

"Very well. Does the candidate know what is involved?" the old man asked, his tired voice echoing ominously.

"Yes. He has been informed. I will act as his advocate and as a witness for him."

The old man shifted in his seat as he addressed me. "Do you, Evan Michaels, wish to join our family and enter into the Cognomina?" His heavy, gray eyes looked as fathomless as time itself.

I felt every eye in the room on me. I knew what saying yes would mean to the life I'd known and to the life I saw around me in this room. "Yes," I said simply as I planted both feet firmly in this new world.

"Very well. Let us begin," he said, leaning back in his chair.

Poppy motioned for me to sit down. The young scribe's hand began writing in sweeping strokes on the blank pages.

The old man looked over and nodded at the professor, who tilted his angular head back and looked down his long nose at me.

The wooly hair on his head resembled the eraser of a thin pencil. "Let's start at the beginning, Mr. Michaels. How many lives do you remember?"

I looked over at Poppy for instruction.

"Answer him," she whispered.

I turned back to the panel and looked into the man's sunken eyes. "Three, including this one." I heard the scribe's pen begin to scratch across a blank page.

"When did the first one begin?"

"April 4, 1892, outside the small village of Voditza in Bulgaria.[18] It is about sixty miles west of Varna."

"Good, very good," the professor said. "The more detailed and exact you are in your responses, the easier this process will be.

"What was your name in this first incarnation?"

"I was called Vasili Blagavich Arda."

"What were your father's and mother's names?"

"Blag Ivanovich Arda was my father, and Liuda Poriskovna Arda was my mother."

"What were your brother's and sister's names?" asked the demanding professor as soon as I had answered.

"I had no brothers or sisters."

"When, where, and how did you die for the first time?"

I took a drink of water from the glass on the table. "It was in the fall of 1968. I was living in Istanbul. I don't know how I died or the exact date. I only remember that I collapsed on the floor of my room."

"What do you remember after that?"

"I remember being a little boy in Macon, Georgia."

"What was your name?"

"Bobby Lynn Murray."

---

18. Evan refers to the modern town of Vodica (also called Voditsa), Bulgaria.

"And your mother and father?"

"Judith Anne Murray. I never knew my father."

"When, where, and how did you die the second time?"

"It was in our home in Macon. I died in an accident," I said, hesitating.

"What manner of accident?"

"A fire," I said, staring forcefully at him. He looked down at his notes before he continued.

"How can you be sure about the date?"

"Because I went back to Macon three years ago to see his grave and to try to prove to myself that I wasn't mad."

"Are you?" interjected the androgynous Asian on the other end of the bench.

I paused and looked deliberately at each judge in turn from right to left. "No, I am not. But I wasn't sure at that time."

"Tell us about that time," the professor demanded.

I leaned over to whisper in Poppy's ear. "Can I smoke?" She nodded, and I lit a cigarette. "If you'll indulge me, I'll start from the beginning and work forward."

The professor nodded slowly.

"In the fall of that first strange year, I began having odd dreams and visions, most often when I was awake. They seemed random at first, then eventually, they began to form an order and make sense. They were memories. The first memories I had, Vasili's memories, were from the Bulgarian countryside. In that Minnesota winter, the visions, or memories, grew longer, more vivid, and more prolific. In time, I gained control over them, eventually reviewing them over and over until I was comfortable with things like language and music that I knew from this other person's memories. I began to question my grasp of reality early on when the memories first started to suggest a separate consciousness from my own. I questioned myself, but what was I to think? By that summer, I could read, write, and speak Bulgarian. The memories had become tangible. It was real.

"I couldn't go to Bulgaria as a seventeen- or eighteen-year-old and visit the places where Vasili had been. Though it was the surest way to prove to myself that those memories were real, that Vasili had lived at all. My opportunity at vindication and my peace of mind came with the second set of memories, those of young Bobby Lynn Murray. The memories of his short life came to me within a period of two weeks. They came after Vasili's memories. It was at the end of those two weeks that I left my home and parents to find the truth.

"I packed several changes of clothes, cleaned out my meager bank account, and took off on my motorcycle, headed for Georgia. It was eerie as I neared Macon. I started to recognize certain landmarks. I'd be riding along and suddenly know there was a bridge ahead, or I'd know which highway to take before I consulted the map. I rode through town unaware I was navigating until the bike coasted to a stop in front of Bobby's old house. The home came as a big shock. It was different than I had remembered, of course, as the original was destroyed in the fire. A new one was built on the old foundation and stood out from the older homes surrounding it. I recognized the neighboring houses and the school he had attended. I walked for hours around his old neighborhood in a daze, each building, each street, each crack in the sidewalk speaking to me like some long-dead, neglected ghost now begging for attention.

"I found Bobby's grave after a three-hour search in the municipal cemetery. It was a plain headstone, white with block letters and no scroll or artwork, the kind put up by the state when the next of kin can't afford anything better.

"That was it. All the proof I'd ever need was planted in the ground at my feet. There I was, alone in the cemetery with myself and my mother. The warm sun and fragrant air of magnolias invited me to stay. I touched her headstone as a son should and laid on the rich grass above Bobby as if to get close enough to reunite the memories with their bodies."

The scribe's fountain pen moving across paper was the only sound for some minutes after I'd finished.

"Where did you go after that?"

"Nowhere in particular at first. I wandered from town to town, working odd jobs for gas and food money. Eventually, I landed in Los Angeles."

"So am I to understand that you didn't realize you were a Reincarnationist until three years ago?" the old man asked, leaning forward.

"That is correct."

"So you remembered both your first and second incarnations in this life, your third life?"

"Yes," I said. The panel leaned back as one and began talking softly among themselves. "What's happening?" I asked Poppy. Her eyes were locked on the panel.

"Nothing. Your situation is unusual, that's all. You're doing fine."

They conferred for several minutes before the professor leaned forward and spoke. "We want to go over some details of what you've told us. It's sort of like coloring in an outline. Do you know what I mean?"

"I think so."

"I want to start from the ending. When you made your trip from Minnesota to Georgia," he said, looking down at his notes, "how long did it take?"

"About a week."

"Did you incur any traffic violations along the way?"

"No," I answered, somewhat confused.

"Did you incur any on your route from Georgia to California?"

"Yes, one for speeding in Texas."

"Where, exactly?"

"Slayton, Texas."

"Can you name any of the places in which you worked along the route from Georgia to California?"

"There were a lot of people I worked with for only a day, doing odd jobs, but I do remember the businesses that I worked for. The Farmers Co-op in Huntsville, Alabama; Masher Lawn Service in Lake Charles, Louisiana; The Bailey Cotton Gin in Amherst, Texas; Globeville Mining Co. in Globeville, Arizona; California Dreamin' Motorcycle shop in Barstow, California."

"What was the year and manufacture of the motorcycle on which you traveled?"

"It was a 1976 Honda."

"Was? You no longer own it?"

"No, it was stolen."

"Was it registered in your name?"

"Yes," I said, lighting another cigarette. He looked down at his notes as though searching for his next question. "It was blue, by the way," I said, putting my lighter away. "In case it turns up in the course of your investigation, I'd like it back," I said with nervous laughter. A few chuckles came from the gallery and panel. The professor smiled and continued with a series of rapid questions.

"What color eyes did your mother, Judith, have?"

"Blue."

"And hair?"

"Brown."

"Where did she work when you were a child?"

"She worked in a carpet factory."

"What kind of car did she drive? Tell me about your grandparents? Where did they live? Where did you go to elementary school? Did Bobby ever have any injuries?" There seemed no end to the professor's questions. The volley back and forth went on for hours. I focused my eyes on his mouth as he spoke, studying the gaps between his teeth in an attempt to stay alert. "Did you have any pets in Georgia?"

"No," I said automatically. I snuffed out the cigarette and dropped the butt in with the twenty-plus others.

"Did your mom have any lovers while you were growing up?"

"Huh?" I asked, snapping out of a daze.

"Your mother, Judith. Did she—" The old man in the center raised his hand to cut him off.

"Let's break for the night. It's a very good start, Mr. Michaels." His long, white beard danced under his chin as he spoke. "We'll pick it up here tomorrow."

Poppy led me out of the room while the others milled around and talked. "You look tired," she said, walking above me up the stairs.

"I'm exhausted, mentally. What time will it start tomorrow?"

"After dinner again. I'll come and get you when we're ready."

"I was hoping you would join me for dinner. I haven't really seen you since we came here."

"I . . . ah . . . sure, I could do that. I might have to leave a bit early though, for preparations."

"Great." I took several steps before continuing. "I have a question for you," I said up to her. "I have several questions, actually. First of all, is that spear on the wall the same one you told me about, the one they once used to kill candidates?"

She laughed. The sounds carried up the slanting shaft of stone stairs and shot back down at us. "You make it sound so morose, but yes, it is the same one."

"Why is it still hanging behind the panel?"

"I don't know, really. I suppose we keep it as a symbol of discerning the truth. Speaking of which, you did well tonight. I was thinking about halfway through the proceedings that this whole Ascension could go very quickly."

"Why is that?"

"Two reasons. It's relatively easy to verify historical facts these days. And number two, you only have two trips worth of material to account for. The last person who went through this in the 1920s, the one who was older than I, took months of sessions like that one tonight. That would be a real grind. I shouldn't think yours will take that long at all.

"The rest of your questions will have to wait," she said, opening the door at the top. "I'm going to sleep and I suggest you do the same. I'll see you later today." She walked quickly down the hall and up the stairs to her suite. I looked out the window in my room as I undressed for bed. Light purple and blue bands of light clung low to the city's morning skyline.

"WHAT TIME IS IT?" I asked Diltz on the way to the kitchen.

"Three p.m., sir. There's still some food left in the dining room."

"If it's no trouble, I'd like to have a driver for the rest of the day. I want to see the city, get some fresh air," I said.

"It is no trouble. When would you like to leave?"

"Right after I get a quick bite to eat."

He nodded.

"When do I need to be back?"

"Seven o'clock, sir."

"Oh, I almost forgot. Poppy will be dining with us tonight, Mr. Diltz."

"I'll make the necessary preparations, sir."

THE DRIVER KNEW EVERY PART OF THE CITY but less than a dozen words in English, and after three silent hours of alpine vistas, I was eager to get back and continue.

"How was your tour, sir?" Mr. Diltz said, opening the front door.

"Excellent. The scenery around here is wonderful. I think I'd like to take a cruise on the lake next time."

"I will make the arrangements, sir."

I noticed something peculiar as I walked in, and it struck me as odd that I hadn't noticed it before. There was no handle or latch on the outside of the door. There wasn't even a place for a key to activate the locks. The door could only be opened from the inside. There always had to be someone inside the building. It was never vacant, ever.

"We'll dine in the same room as last night. I spoke to Poppy moments ago. She'll be down to join us shortly."

We raided the pristine platters in the main dining room and then retreated to the side room again.

"I must admit, I enjoy dining with you like this," Diltz said, taking his seat. "I almost always eat alone."

"Don't you have a family?"

"No, I do not. My position here is a full time one and affords me little time to be social. Besides, the secrecy that I'm entrusted with doesn't leave much personal time."

I didn't know how to respond. I wouldn't say he was happy about his condition from the way he spoke, but he was disciplined about it. He was perfectly suited to his job, or his job was perfectly suited to him, I couldn't tell which. Probably both.

Poppy came in carrying a plate and a bottle of wine.

"How are they getting along in there, Madame?" Diltz asked her.

"Oh, fine."

"Thank you for joining us," I said, taking the bottle from her.

"It's pleasantly quiet in here."

"Yes, it is quiet, and it gives me an opportunity to ask a few questions we didn't have time for last night."

"All right," she said, taking a seat.

"What is the story behind that grotto we were in last night? It's enormous and it looks very old."

"It was once part of an old church. For hundreds of years, the Cognomina had access to the grotto by paying the church a tribute. When the church was destroyed by fire in 1743, we bought the ruin and built this edifice over the foundation and the grotto."

"How old is it?"

"No one knows for sure, but it was probably excavated by the Romans as part of an old temple. A Mithraic temple would be my guess,"[19] she said.

"It's beautiful," I said, staring at my plate of food.

"It's bigger, too, much bigger than the part you saw. You'll see it soon enough, I think. The festival will be held in the larger part."

I let my mind wander and fantasize about what was beyond the curtain. We ate for a few minutes in silence. I could tell Poppy was quite distracted by not being involved in the noise down the hall. "Is there anything else you wanted to talk about?" she asked.

"Yes, there is. I've been thinking about something you said the night before we left. We were talking about humanity as it relates to our condition, and you mentioned that you thought man lives unnaturally."

"Yes?"

"I think I understand what you're talking about, but I'm not sure."

"It's simple. Modern man lives in an unnatural world. He lives in a world dominated by dogma. Take Christianity or Islam for example, though any religion will do since they all work on the same principle. This devout man lives unnaturally because every day of his life he bites back on his desire and restrains himself from what he really yearns to do and say. And for what purpose? So it will get him

---

19. Mithraic temples, or Mithraeum, were common in all corners of the Roman Empire and were normally constructed in grottoes or caves to imitate the location where Mithra slew the sacred bull. (E. O. James, *The Ancient Gods*, 1960.)

into heaven? So that it will get his name in the book of life? Rubbish!" she dismissed with a wave of her fork. "You and I are proof that this is nothing more than a hoax, a farce. Each day that he bites back only propagates another day and another day and another day of the same mundane existence, the same unfulfilled existence that is so pathetic and weak. You know it's true. You ask any of these devout men what they would do if they knew the world would end at sundown of that day. The answers would astound you. Husbands wouldn't know their wives, mothers wouldn't know their sons, brothers wouldn't know their sisters for the answers you would find. You would find the true being that lives under the false exterior, shackled and estranged from the completely natural desires that flow like a strong, ancient river through the transitory and fickle sediments of dogma and religion."

Diltz placed his fork down. "These sentiments might very well be true, but I don't know if I would go so far as to call religion a hoax," he said.

"Islam, Christianity, and Judaism before that," she continued, "are the biggest hoaxes ever perpetrated on the human race. It robs man of his dignity and his freedom. People say that religion is the basis of our civilization. I say to you verily that it is a corruption of all that man is. Man lives his life in some socially engineered family unit and sells his time by the hour because he is too afraid to live in those hours. He is afraid to look beyond the veil that surrounds him because he knows no other way, because he is born into this bondage. And it is this way because some ancient text tells him this is how he should live. That is the corruption. That is man's true fall from grace. But man is told a lie about that even. He is told that his fall from grace happened because one man and one woman supposedly sinned at the beginning of time and that we are guilty simply by being men and women by way of that original sin. That is the least original joke ever told. Unfortunately for man, it is the most prolific."

Poppy continued, "The main tenet of Abrahamic faiths is that as men, they are estranged from God by their nature and they are made to feel ashamed to walk around naturally and act upon the impulses they feel. As men, they are told that the only way to overcome this estrangement is to seek salvation from a god that created them with godly desires, and then promptly orphaned them.

"But it's different for us, like I told you before we left LA, the same rules don't apply. You see, the enforcer to this entire hoax is guilt. You ask any devotee, and they will freely admit that. Their system simply doesn't work without guilt. But ours, Evan, ours is truly Eden. We run through Elysian Fields, free from their bondage, because in our world, guilt has no meaning or purpose or place. This is paradise," she said in a husky voice, looking at me with a raised wine glass, "and welcome, brother."

Diltz and I ate in silence, trying to digest her words along with the meal. Having thought some of these thoughts before, I understood where it came from. We were on the same line, a timeline. She was just further along it than I was, and once again I found myself unwilling to begrudge her any reaction to obstacles further down that timeline.

"What about Eastern religions?" Diltz asked.

"The Buddhists and Hindus are little better. Sure, they got it right that we all come back, but they have to taint it again with guilt, only they call it karma. You see, religion is universal in that it doesn't work without guilt. The tenet of karma states that if you lead a self-deprecating, self-abasing, virtuous life in this trip, that your position in the next will be improved and that your spirit will be cleansed and purified by wasting life after life. The idea that through such toil you will eventually reach nirvana is obviously as misguided as its western counterparts. We've all tried it. We have found by the most accurate methods possible that it doesn't work that way. And that method is experience.

"The idea of karma, the idea of retributive justice, is as silly as the story parents tell their children about Santa Claus keeping track of who's naughty and who's nice. Parents only tell children that in order to make them behave in November and December. It's the same principle at work, only on a larger scale. It is a hoax. There is no one in heaven or nirvana with a pen and pad keeping score on us. And if there ever was, he died a long time ago."

She drank the last of her wine and placed the napkin on the plate. "I should check to see if they're ready. If you'll excuse me."

Mr. Diltz and I looked at each other between bites, not quite sure how to start a conversation that could diffuse the charged words Poppy had left in the room with us. We ate without speaking until she came back.

THE MEMBERS OF THE PANEL and the gallery were already in place in the expansive grotto when Poppy and I walked in.

"Welcome back, Mr. Michaels," said the professor. "I'd like to start with some questions about your first incarnation, as Vasili."

I nodded.

"Tell me about your first memories as a child."

I leaned forward and began. "Vasili grew up on his father's farm. He played outside quite often, usually alone but sometimes with friends. He often played with three brothers around his own age that lived a five minutes' walk away."

"What were their names?"

"Hristo, Sorgi, and Thaxos."

"Last name and patronymic please."

"Siltykov, Hristovich," I said, pouring some water.

"Tell me more about that childhood," the man asked, leaning back as though he expected a long answer.

"There's not much to tell, really. Vasili lived with his mother and father on an eighty-acre farm near the village of Voditza. He worked on the farm, was homeschooled by his father, and took mass twice a week in town. It was that way until 1915 when the army was mobilized, and he left to begin military training."[20]

"You said you took mass twice a week. What religion?"

"It was simply the religion back then. I now know it to be Eastern Orthodox."

"Was your family religiously devout?"

"My father was, so everyone was. He was raised and educated in an Orthodox monastery near the Greek border. He taught me the language and the scriptures."

"You said you can read and write Bulgarian now?"

"Yes." I lit a cigarette as he conferred with the old man and Ramsay.

"You said you were in the military. Did you fight in the Great War?"

"I was in the Bulgarian army from 1916 until the armistice was signed in 1918."

"What did you do after that?"

"I returned home and helped my father with the farm for one season. I was in the process of acquiring my own land when my father died. I built a home for myself on the eighty acres and tended the land and my mother until her death the next year. That same year, 1920, I took a wife." I crushed out the cigarette in the ashtray.

"Go on."

"I met Vanya in Voditza. She was the daughter of the livery stable owner. I went into town to buy a horse and saw her. We were married four months later."

"What were your children's names?"

"We had no children."

---

20. Bulgaria entered the First World War in October 1915, with mass conscription and mobilization. (*November 1918* by Gordon Brook-Shepard.)

"Why not?"

"Infertility, I suppose. It wasn't for lack of trying, I can assure you. If any of you have ever tended a large plot of land, you know how valuable farm hands are."

The professor stared at me for what seemed like an eternity. "Were the babies lost, or were there no pregnancies?"

"She never became pregnant," I said, getting angry with his line of questioning. The young man with dark complexion to his right tapped him on the shoulder, breaking his concentration. I lit another cigarette as they whispered.

"I would make a motion that we change the topic for a moment. I would like to hear the testimony of the witness for the candidate," the young man on the end said.

"I concur," said the old man. Poppy straightened in her chair.

"Please begin," the professor said, nodding to her.

Poppy looked at the old man when she spoke. "It was at my home in Los Angeles—most of you know the place. I went outside to watch the fire brigades pass. I was closing the door behind me on the way back in when I heard the gunshot. I knew the shot was close but dismissed it, along with all the other shots I've heard in recent years. I wasn't concerned until my servant alerted me to a loud knocking on the basement door. Gun in hand, I went down to investigate. Evan Michaels turned out to be the source of the noise. He had been shot in the foot by the police while fleeing the scene of a fire." Poppy stopped to take a drink of water, and I noticed the rotund man I'd met at the front door the night before perk up and lean forward in his seat in the gallery.

"I was about to fire a shot next to his head to give him a good scare when he first tipped me off. I remember he had the most peculiar reaction when I leveled the gun at him. He became angry. No, furious is a better word. He shouted over and over at me to kill him. He had this crazed look in his eye that was unnerving. 'Kill me, kill me,' he said. 'I'll probably just come back again anyway.' Those were his exact words. That was my first clue, obviously.

"I took him in, attended to his wound, and encouraged him to stay, in the hope I could pursue my hunch."

"How, precisely, did you do that?"

"The second clue came the same night," she said reaching under her robe. She produced a pack of cigarettes and held them out toward Diltz, who came over and handed them to the man who had been questioning me. "Can you read the Turkish on that?" she asked.

He tilted his narrow head back so that the light from the torch on the wall behind him illuminated the pack. "'The Pride of the Turks.' Why?"

"It used to say 'Centuries of Flavor,' and Evan knew that, even though the slogan changed in the 1970s. I called the company the following day and checked. I found out later it was because he smoked those same cigarettes as Vasili while living in exile in Istanbul after the Second World War. Two days later, I took him to my funerary vault in Los Angeles and told him about myself. More accurately, he figured it out when he saw the concurrent dates on the monuments. That was the same day I called Diltz."

"What was his reaction when he figured it out?" the professor asked as though I were an inanimate piece of furniture.

"He was quite visibly shaken. He sat down and was motionless for some time. After he came around, he was very inquisitive about me and about this," she said, looking around the grotto.

"Is it your opinion that the candidate to your right is a Reincarnationist, like us?"

My heart quickened as the old man finished the question. Poppy turned to me as she answered. "Yes. He is one of us."

The panel was silent for several minutes before the old man spoke. "Let's take a short break."

"I want to know about the fire," the professor said, starting in again. "Is her story accurate? Were you at the fire she spoke of?"

I filled my water glass and took a drink as I weighed several different stories in my head. They were all underweight. I thought better of lying by the time I finished the glass. If I got caught in a lie about the fire, it could jeopardize this whole process. That's the trouble with lies, they have to propagate. They must procreate to cover each other. There is safety in numbers; one lie is never enough. "Yes, I was at the fire. I started it."

"Why did you start it?"

"I was paid to burn the building down." I saw the large man in the gallery come to attention again out of the corner of my eye.

"Paid by whom?"

"The building's owner, Martin Shelby."

"How much did he pay you?"

"Five thousand dollars."

"How did you encounter him initially?"

"He was referred to me."

"By whom?" he asked impatiently.

"A former client named Tom Preston."

Silence.

"So may we assume by this that you're a professional arsonist?"

"It is what I do for money, yes."

"How many fires have you started?"

"That I've been paid for?"

"How many fires have you started?"

I took a smoke from the pack on the table and primed my lighter. The tiny sprite flared as the cigarette started to burn. "Hundreds," I said, closing the lid on the flame.

Silence again.

"How did you first get started doing it professionally?"

I chuckled to myself. "It's funny, the way it got started. I was caught by the police—more specifically, one cop, a crooked one. He caught me leaving an abandoned apartment building in Los Angeles. He cuffed me and put me in the back of his squad car while he ran my ID for warrants. He didn't know then that I'd set a fire in one of the interior apartments. I had planned on watching the fire from across the street but ended up watching it from the back seat of a police car.

"I was nervous and fidgeted as wisps of smoke crept out of the small cracks in the plywood that covered the windows. Anyway, he checked his computer, but I was clean. Of course, that didn't stop him from keeping me there while he grilled me about what I'd been doing in an abandoned building at two in the morning. I remember him turning sideways in his seat to look at me and it taking every bit of concentration I could muster to make up a story and not get distracted by the smoke that was billowing out of the windows behind him. I told him I was scouting the site for a photography shoot. By the time I was near the end of my story, flashes of yellow were creeping toward the open front door. I knew that as soon as I stopped talking, the cop would turn around, and I'd be done for. So I kept talking. I saw flames starting at the upstairs windows and I kept talking. I was hoping I could keep him distracted. I never looked away from his eyes, even when the flames completely silhouetted his balding head. And still, I kept talking. My story had started to come apart, but I had no choice other than to keep talking. I guess I thought I could keep his attention until the whole building burned to the ground behind him. He must have seen the reflection of yellow flashes in my face or been onto my story about being *Rolling Stone*'s ace photographer and shooting Bruce Springsteen there next week, because he broke away from me and turned around slowly in his seat until the burning building was in full view.

"'Holy shit!' he yelled and then threw the car into reverse. He called in the address to the fire department once he had backed up to about half a block away. 'Photographer, my ass,' he said. He then accused me of starting the fire in the building. I told him he had no evidence, and he said he did not need any. I did my best to convince him I had saved the city money, they were just going to tear the building down anyway.

"He looked back at the fire for a full minute. 'Do *you* a favor,' he said, then he laughed and told me I had that part backward.

"He made it pretty plain, really, burn down his house for him, and I got to walk away. It took me about two seconds to make up my mind, and we made the plans right there in the squad car. He told me he was in the process of a divorce and that his wife was getting the house. The judge had determined that they would split the sixty thousand dollars' worth of equity evenly, but his wife couldn't dole out his half all at once without selling the house, which she wouldn't do. She was ordered to pay him a hundred dollars a month for twenty-five years, without interest. I remember the cop getting really pissed off just telling me the situation. But if his house were destroyed, by an accidental fire, for instance, he would get his thirty thousand dollars in a lump sum from the insurance company, and his wife would have nowhere to stay. He smiled at me in the rear view mirror when he said this. He took a key off his key ring and gave it to me along with a handwritten address.

"He told me I would get my ID back the next night in exchange for the key, but only if the place was burned. Otherwise, he said he would say he found my ID on the ground next to the burning apartment building and turn me in.

"I nodded that we had an understanding, and that was that. I did the job and met him just as we'd agreed. Everything was normal until about a week later, when I got a visitor at my hotel. The stranger explained that the boys in blue said I could help him and handed me an envelope containing an address and two thousand dollars. I had no idea what was up on the cop's end, but I took the money and did the job just the same. The first seven or eight jobs came like that. Later on, my name just got around town, I guess, because I've been doing it ever since."

"How many jobs have you done since then?"

"This last one, the one Poppy told you about, was my nineteenth."

"What was the officer's name?"

"Shirer."

"Did you ever see him again?"

"No. Not after that night in the diner when I got my ID back."

"What was the name of the hotel where the first man referred by Shirer came to meet you."

"The Altmore. I lived there until a year ago, when I moved to the Iowa Hotel."

The professor shuffled with his notes. I leaned back and stretched.

"How long have we been down here tonight?" I asked Poppy in a whisper.

"Only two or three hours probably. Are you getting tired?"

"No. I'm fine. I feel good. I've never shared most of these facts before. It's cathartic," I said as she winked at me.

Ramsay leaned over and whispered to the old man. They conferred for a minute before she straightened and fixed her pale eyes on me. "Mr. Michaels, I'd like to go back and cover the time you said you spent in the Bulgarian Army during the Great War. Please be as specific and detailed as possible," she said in that familiar Slavic accent. "When were you pressed into service?"

"In 1915, right after the attack on Romania. I was a stocky young man and was assigned to an artillery company as an ordnance handler."

"Did your unit ever see any action?" Ramsay asked.

"Yes, but not until the last week of the war. But I saw enough in one night to last me a lifetime."

"Where did you see action?"

I was about to respond when I felt Poppy place her hand on my arm. She leaned over and whispered close to my ear. "That one that is asking about the war, that's Ramsay, the one I told you about in France with the duel and the cane. I think Ramsay was very active in that war, so answer carefully. Part of the trick to being verifiable is your ability to tell the stories of your lives with uncanny detail and accuracy down to the slightest point."

I turned back to the panel. Ramsay was still looking at me, waiting for a response. "I fought against the French and the Serbs in the Vardar River valley in the autumn of 1918, but only for a short time, as I said earlier. The entire front collapsed very quickly for us. I was only involved in one battle."

"Who was your commanding officer?"

"Captain Eumen Hoxa."

A look of astonishment came over her face. "Tell me about Hoxa, tell me about the battle, tell me everything."

"It was a fluke. We shouldn't even have been there, which is probably the only reason why we surprised them and why we survived. When it happened, on September 18 and 19, 1918, the whole of the Bulgarian front had been in full retreat for three weeks . . ."[21]

21. Evan's description of the Bulgarian collapse is fairly accurate. By the third week in September 1918, the whole of the Bulgarian front had failed and was in full retreat. (*The Marshall Cavendish Illustrated Encyclopedia of World War I,* editor-in-chief Peter Young, 1984.)

13

Eumen Hoxa's legend was born on those days in September 18 and 19, 1918, when the whole of the Bulgarian front was in full retreat. Vasili wasn't a military strategist, but it didn't take one to realize the small triangle of land formed where the Cherna river flowed into the Vardar made a poor spot to make a stand, even if only for one night.

Vasili labored in the autumn sun, stacking the seventy-five pound, two-foot-long artillery shells in long rows three deep next to the gun emplacement. The five new Krupp 77mm howitzers stood a menacing vigil, looking south toward Greece and the two French divisions that lingered somewhere on the horizon. Vasili set down a shell to talk to the passing captain.

"How many rounds do you want to bring out of the wagon, sir?"

Captain Hoxa twirled at the ends of his thick handlebar mustache as he surveyed the surrounding Macedonian country-side. "Better bring them all out, soldier, just in case. And go help first squad when you're done," he said, walking down to the river.

Vasili arched his back and sighed before reaching back into the horse-drawn wagon for more shells. Two hours later he left his six neat rows and walked the twenty-five feet down to the next gun. The loader and breech operator shoveled dirt around the large steel-spoke wheels of the gun, bracing it. The first squad's ordnance man had unloaded only half of his wagon. His rounds lay in loose rows that leaned precariously.

"Thanks for helping," the ordnance man said as Vasili started handing shells down to him from the wagon. "Hoxa's been busting my balls all afternoon."

"Don't worry, we'll get it straight. But I'll tell you something, I don't like setting up here one bit."

"You know if we didn't have to hump these shells in and out every goddamn day, we'd be in Skopie by now, where we belong," said the smaller first squad man, straining to keep up with Vasili's pace. "Hopefully, he'll decide to use some of these rounds so we won't have to reload so many tomorrow morning. Besides, I've been dying to shoot some of these babies off in anger."

"You just might get your chance tonight, soldier," Captain Hoxa said, stepping around the wagon. "Now get your lazy ass back to work!

"All right, ladies, here's the drill," Hoxa shouted loud enough for all five crews to hear. "Have your positions and camps ready in one hour. Tie all the horses off next to the river. There will be only one fire tonight, the one that Verga is using to cook, and that will be snuffed before dark. We've got two full-strength French divisions sleeping in this valley with us tonight, so be careful."

VASILI PEERED OVER THE RIM OF HIS CUP at the worried faces surrounding him. The sound of twenty-two tired, dirty men sipping thin barley soup from metal cups reverberated as one continuous fifteen-minute-long slurp. The sun dropped quickly behind the hills on the west wall of the valley. To the south, the remaining sunset exploded beautifully along the leading edge of a storm approaching off the Gulf of Salonika.

"What do you think, Captain?" asked a lonely voice at the edge of the circle.

"I think it's going to rain. Brace yourself for a miserable night. Everyone keep a sharp eye for fires. The French won't be nearly as apprehensive or worried about us as we are about them."

"With a fire they'll be much more comfortable though," someone shouted, trying to break the tension.

"You know the French. They don't go anywhere if they can't go comfortably," came another voice from the circle.

"I hear they even have whores that travel with them, but only for the officers, of course," a young soldier said, looking at his commander.

"I think we should form a raiding party and plunder their camp of wine and women."

"A raiding party? Why not just attack them head on? A Bulgar is a match for twenty Frenchmen, if he's fighting for the right cause." The anonymous voice was met with boisterous laughter.

"Enough!" barked Captain Hoxa. "This isn't some church social. Be quiet and keep watch."

Hoxa climbed on top of the center howitzer and straddled the end of the barrel. He kept a firm grip on the muzzle as the operator cranked on the elevator control, raising the barrel toward the night sky. He scanned the horizon with his binoculars.

"Somebody saddle my horse," he said coolly from his perch.

"Do you see anything?" asked the corporal.

The captain shook his head yes.[22] "Lower the pitch so I can get off."

CAPTAIN EUMEN HOXA WAS A LEGEND in Bulgaria. He won the Order of Bravery, First Class, Bulgaria's highest military combat

---

22. This "Shook his head yes," passage is a subtle but interesting point. Bulgaria seems to be unique in Western culture in that they shake their heads side to side to indicate yes, up and down to indicate no. (*Culture Shock! Bulgaria* by Agnes Sachsenroeder, 2008.)

THE REINCARNATIONIST PAPERS

honor,[23] in the first week of the war. He single-handedly, and without authorization, took his company and outflanked a large, broken Romanian column in retreat from Petrila. He moved seventy men and ten artillery pieces thirty miles in one day and night. The encircling maneuver he executed was a masterpiece. His company opened up at first light and cut the column to ribbons, capturing four Generals of the Romanian High Command in the process. His courage was only outstripped by his detestation for rear area commanders, which is why he never advanced above the rank of captain. His reward for unshakable bravery and initiative was to be placed at the very front, facing a confident, fresh army.

VASILI WATCHED AS HOXA JUMPED DOWN off the end of the gun barrel, mumbling to himself as he walked to his readied horse. "Don't do anything until I get back," he shouted. He had planned to ride across the shallow, swift-running Cherna river toward the second and third artillery companies dug in over a mile farther north. Five silent minutes passed before the corporal jumped up and straddled the gun the way Hoxa had done.

"Can you see anything?" Vasili asked.

"Yes," the corporal replied, "fires, about twenty of them in one bivouac."

"You don't think he would fire on them, do you?" a nervous voice asked.

"No, of course not," the corporal said, still atop the howitzer. "He just wants to let the other squad leaders know."

"How far away are they?"

23. This was indeed Bulgaria's highest combat honor at the time, but stating that Captain Hoxa won the First Class of this Order is almost surely an exaggeration as classes for this Order were segregated by rank, with junior officers being assigned III or IV grades. (*World Orders of Knighthood and Merit* by Guy Stair Sainty and Rafal Heydel-Mankoo, 2006.)

"I'd say about two miles."

"Yeah, you're right. He won't attack, but we'll probably have to break camp and move out tonight."

"And reload all those goddamn shells too," said the first squad ordnance man. "What do you think, Vasili?"

"I've got a bad feeling about tonight. I have a weird feeling about this whole spot."

"But Hoxa's lived through too much shit to try something like this," the first squad ordnance man said, trying to convince himself.

Vasili reached into the empty munitions cart and pulled out his dirty gray uniform jacket. "That man is capable of anything."

AS QUICKLY AS HE HAD LEFT, Vasili spotted Hoxa riding back into camp. He jumped off his horse, handing the reins to the soldier closest to him. His eyes were ablaze with excitement. "The other companies are ready," he said, running up the riverbank behind the guns.

"Ready, sir? Ready for what?" asked the corporal.

"The reckoning," the captain answered, pulling a worn map from his pocket.

"You're not going to attack? I climbed up there. I saw them. There must be at least four-hundred men out there."

"At least," Hoxa said, getting even more excited.

"You can't do that, Captain. It's sui—"

The corporal was unable to finish his sentence before Hoxa whipped his revolver from its holster and pointed it at the end of his nose. "We are going to attack, by surprise, when the rain starts, and crush them in their tents. And anyone who has a problem with that order will hear the sound of this pistol." The corporal's eyes were locked on the end of the gun. "Now, everyone in their places. Start with high-explosive rounds, except for you," he said, pointing to Vasili and the other three men that made up second squad. "You prepare five white phosphorous rounds. We're going to target for the other two companies. They can't see the bivouac, but they'll sure as hell be able to see those shells exploding. We'll wait until their fires almost die out, then when they're asleep, we'll annihilate them," he commanded. Lightning began to flash, lighting up the open south end of the valley behind the French camp.

Vasili saw Captain Hoxa sitting astride the raised number three gun barrel. Hour after hour passed in silence. The air in the valley resonated with the claps of approaching thunder. Fat, cold raindrops began to spatter against the hard guns and dirty uniforms. Vasili could feel the level of apprehension in the camp rising along with his own every time that Hoxa made the slightest move. "Lower me," Hoxa said. He grabbed the end of the barrel for support. "Somebody give me a handful of mud." The members of the third crew looked at each other confused. "Mud. Somebody give me some mud."

"I know what he wants," the breech operator of Vasili's second squad said. He jogged down to the riverbank and brought back two handfuls of wet clay mud. Hoxa reached down from his perch and took a small amount with his fingertips. He shaped it into a thumb-sized roll, broke it in two, and inserted the mud plugs into his ears. Everyone else immediately imitated the captain.

"Raise me," commanded Hoxa.

The breech operator cranked slowly on the control that gently elevated the barrel.

"Second squad, raise to twenty-three degrees and load!" Hoxa barked.

Vasili handed a white phosphorus round to the loader, who carefully inserted it up into the open orifice at the back of the barrel. He withdrew his hand and the breech operator closed and locked the four-inch-thick, round breech door. The trigger man wrapped the cord around his hand twice to take the slack out. "Ready, Captain."

The wind blew strong from the south, running in front of the storm as a wave rises before a steaming ship. The lightning, thunder, and rain were directly on top of the French camp, exactly where Hoxa wanted them. "Fire for effect!"

Vasili covered his ears with gloved hands. The trigger man jerked hard on the cord that tripped the firing pin. A six-foot long tongue of orange flame jumped out of the barrel and into the night sky as the shell screamed toward the dying French fires. The echoes from the violent report had died down when the round impacted two miles away. Everyone in the company watched in awe. The exploding phosphorous ignited as soon as it hit, leaving ghostly white smoke trails as the burning fragments fanned up and out in long, graceful arcs like some obscene firework.

"Two degrees down," shouted the captain, binoculars still held up to his eyes. The crew reloaded. The breech operator made four quick turns on the pitch crank, and the barrel edged closer to the ground. "Ready!"

"Fire!"

The shell impacted after six long, eerie seconds.

"Everyone draw a bead on that burst and set for twenty-one degrees. High explosive rounds except for number two," Hoxa said, climbing down off the number three gun.

"Ready," cried each of the crews in turn.

"Fire!" barked Hoxa.

The five guns erupted as one. The muzzle flashes pushed at the darkness and lit up the entire camp as if it were day for a split second. The earth shuddered under the guns' collective recoil. The crews reloaded the guns as the first salvo of shells exploded in quick, white flashes. Hoxa stood between the second and third guns and held his riding crop high in the air, signaling to hold. A dull flash followed by a low rumble came from the west side of the valley behind them. First company's shells sounded like whistling tea kettles as they crossed overhead. Another volley came from the east flank a second later.

"They're in the game with us, boys. Fire!" Hoxa shouted and swept the crop down like a race starter.

The rain intensified with each barrage as though the shells were ripping holes in the bottom of the sky.

"Fire! Fire! Fire!" shouted the captain at the end of each loading cycle.

SHELLS RAINED DOWN mercilessly from three sides on the French camp. The sky lit up time and time again as if the whole south end of the valley were exploding.

The munitions handlers, loaders, and breech operators danced a frenzied ballet as they fed the ever-hungry guns. Each time a loader shoved a round into the gun, the operator slammed the breech closed, missing the man's hand by a fraction of an inch.

The cold, driving rain screamed and sizzled on the hot gun barrels like sausages on a griddle. It was the kind of rain that drives creatures underground and demands submission. Multiple flashes of lightning exploded fiercely over their heads, belittling the petty rumblings of men.

Oblivious to the elements, Hoxa continued to bark orders. "Fire! Reload! One degree up! Fire! Reload! Fire!"

Vasili grabbed the smoking spent shell casings as fast as they were ejected onto the churned-up mud behind the gun. His wet cotton gloves provided just enough protection to hold the searing casings for the second it took to throw them onto the growing pile down by the river. The five guns fired a salvo every ten seconds, just far enough apart for Vasili and the other handlers to pass the heavy rounds to the loaders and start the whole process again.

"Fire! Reload! Fire!" The shelling, the lightning, and the rain intensified as the night wore on. Vasili threw the hot casings over his shoulder one after another, ignoring the weather as best he could until, between salvos, he heard the splash of a shell casing as it hit the water.

The water, he thought, handing another shell to the loader. He grabbed another casing and threw it back behind him, watching this time. The shell splashed just before a bolt of lightning crashed to the left of number one gun, lighting up the area behind the camp. The shallow, swift-moving Cherna had swollen into a raging torrent. The brown, silty water moved like a giant undulating snake between the tops of the riverbanks. Vasili stood dumbfounded through two more close flashes and watched as the river seemed to rise before his very eyes.

"Vasili! Vasili!" shouted the loader. "Shell! Shell!"

He snapped to and rejoined the rhythm of the crew.

"The river is flooding. I saw it when the lightning flashed!" Vasili shouted quickly to the loader when he handed him a round. The guns roared as one.

"Those last three weren't lightning!" the loader screamed. "They're shooting back at us!"

Vasili was reaching down to grab a spent shell casing when another flash and explosion hit ten meters from number one, knocking him off balance.

"Reload, reload, reload!" screamed Hoxa, flailing his riding crop in the charged air. "Fire at will!"

The number one gun fell silent, but the rest fired in unsynchronized disorder as soon as each breech locked closed. Night turned into day as flashes constantly broke around them. The explosions from the incoming shells, the lightning, and the outgoing shells assaulted their senses as an indistinguishable, chaotic chorus of destruction. It sounded like the earth itself was being dismantled.

Vasili worked faster, keeping one eye on the dwindling rows

of ammunition and one eye on the river that swallowed the empty casings as fast as he could heave them.

Captain Hoxa made a quick circuit of the squads before climbing on top of the quiet number one gun, binoculars in hand. The trigger man for the silent gun lay facedown in the mud, the cord still wrapped around his lifeless hand.

Vasili's ears, partially deafened and somewhat adjusted to the constant explosions, began to pick up a faint yet distinct sound, a sound that shouldn't have been there amidst the tumult. Pinging. He concentrated on the sound in an effort to block out the fear that clung to him like a shadow. *Ping, p-ping, ping-ping, ping.* The ethereal sound got clearer and the chaos fuzzier the harder he focused. Adrenaline coursed through his veins. He grabbed each shell tighter and threw each casing farther as the sound of the surreal scene around him slowly went silent. Flashes came with concussions but no sound. Vasili kept an eye out for the source of the pinging while he worked, and the guns took on a comical feel as they silently bucked and blew fire. *Ping, ping, p-ping.* Each time a trigger man jerked on his cord, another ping. *Ping, ping, ping.* It was the spring-activated, thumb-sized firing pins striking the metal backs of the shells inside the guns. It didn't seem possible that he could hear them, but the striking pins rang out clearly, like a crew of blacksmiths working on an anvil at the edge of town.

"They're coming for us!" Hoxa screamed. His voice jolted Vasili back to the pandemonium around him. "They're coming!" Hoxa jumped off the wet gun awkwardly and landed spread eagle in the mud next to the fallen trigger man. He got up, seemingly undaunted, and slapped each remaining trigger man with his crop as he ran by. All four held fire, rubbed at stinging welts under their uniforms and watched the captain for orders.

"Raise your pitch to forty degrees, load phosphorous, and fire on my command."

"What is it?" shouted Vasili.

Captain Hoxa screamed out one long word over the incoming explosions. "Infantry!"

The breech operators cranked frantically on the elevator controls. The heavy, steaming gun barrels edged slowly skyward and trained in on the approaching troops. "Ready," each operator shouted in turn.

"Be ready to continue tracking them as we shoot!" Hoxa shouted. He raised his riding crop high. "Fire!"

The phosphorous rounds weighed less than the shorter high-explosive shells, allowing the handlers and loaders to shave a full second off their reloading cycle. Hoxa had given the other two companies orders to redirect fire any time they saw white phosphorous explosions, and as planned, larger white-and-yellow flashes sprang up around the first impacts.

"Up two degrees! Reload, fire! Up one! Fire! Up one!" It dragged on for what seemed hours as the tempest continued to rage in the valley. All the while Hoxa stood on a small mound between gun number two and number three, looking out through his binoculars, raising and lowering his riding crop like a band-leader each time a salvo screamed away.

The pitch of the barrels rose steadily, heralding the approach of the French infantrymen. The Cherna river had risen even higher, eliminating any idea of retreat. The gun angle rose from fifty degrees through sixty to seventy-five degrees. Each shell they fired exploded closer to their own position. The white phosphorous trails jumped out from the center like a blooming flower. Three and four at a time, the ghostly patterns leaped to life in front of them like giant white spiders, devouring everything caught underneath them.

Captain Hoxa continued to adjust fire while looking through the binoculars. "Up two degrees! Up one! Up one!" The operators raised the pitch until the guns were fully erect. Topped out, the shells arced a mile upward but landed a mere three-hundred yards away. Hoxa turned and looked up against the rain at the raised muzzles, disgusted that they would go no higher. He looked up to heaven as though he wished he could shoot the shells straight up.

"Ready!" shouted the four breech men at once. The hair stood up on the back of Vasili's neck. His eyes locked with Hoxa's just as a flash hit the number three barrel behind the captain's head, illuminating everything. Hoxa's face contorted as he mouthed the command to fire, his speech stolen. The deafening crash of thunder that immediately followed the lightning seemed to jump out of the captain's open mouth. Vasili stood transfixed by the scene, studying every detail of Hoxa's menacing face; the caked mud on his unwavering brow, the lean jaw of determination, the steady eye of wrath.

The blast knocked the breech operator and trigger man back several feet. The loader and ordnance handler were miraculously unaffected by the lightning strike. They stood stunned and confused about what hit them.

"Reload and fire at will!" Hoxa shouted before turning to monitor the exploding shells. "Hurry, boys! Hurry!" he shouted while looking through the field glasses. "It's going to be close!"

The explosions held three hundred yards out for several minutes as the neighboring companies brought all guns to bear on those pitiful acres. The captain scanned the hellish horizon, slowly panning back and forth with the binoculars. Vasili looked up and noticed the captain's attention had fixed on something. Hoxa dropped the glasses, whipped out his pistol, and took off running toward the curtain of fire, screaming and aiming with his pistol as he went. Vasili was the only one who noticed Hoxa leave. The other soldiers kept loading and unloading at the same feverish pace.

THE STORM EASED JUST AS DAWN BROKE over the ridge. The rate of fire slowed due to sheer exhaustion, then stopped altogether. The soldiers that still had their earplugs in removed them. It was quiet, and the scent of gunpowder lingered in the morning air. Survivors silently milled around the camp surveying the damage and the dead. Several minutes passed before anyone spoke. "Where's the captain?" asked a soldier. Hoxa was nowhere in sight.

"I saw him run that way," Vasili said, pointing to the blasted heath in front of them. "About an hour ago."

"We should look for him," the slumping corporal said. He pointed to Vasili first, then three other men. "You, you, you, and you, come with me."

The five of them fanned out and waded through the wet, knee-high grass and bushes. Vasili retraced Hoxa's path as best he could. One hundred fifty yards out, the landscape began to change. The grass, where there was grass, was flattened and scorched. Large, open craters littered the ground. The mud became too deep to walk through at one hundred seventy-five yards. The shells had punctured the earth, pounding it into a soupy, brown bog all the way to the smoldering French camp. A light-gray haze hovered over the churned-up ground. Upon closer examination they spotted and pointed out different body parts that lay in twisted, unnatural positions, coated and camouflaged in mud. The only thing moving, the only sign of life on the entire ruined plain, was a wet, shivering dog hopelessly mired in the muck, licking at the blood and the mud on what remained of a severed back leg.

Vasili turned away and slogged back through the mud toward the camp, leaving the other four to search for their leader. He stopped at the base of the small rise beneath the tired guns and picked up Hoxa's discarded binoculars. Reaching down and wiping the mud off the lenses, he draped them around his neck and trudged up into the remains of the encampment.

14

". . . Reaching down and wiping the mud off the lenses, he draped them around his neck and trudged back up into the remains of the encampment."

I could tell my story had gotten their attention. No one wanted to speak and break the silence that punctuated the end of the tale. I turned my head and saw Poppy looking at me with the same transfixed look on her face as the members of the panel. I continued.

"We fell back on foot that morning. The company's draft horses that had been tied up by the river were gone. We knew we wouldn't be able to pull anything, so we left the equipment and joined the first company. Luckily, news of the armistice came later that week."

"What became of Hoxa?" Ramsay asked.

"The other four came back covered in mud. They had searched for over an hour. There was no trace of him. Hoxa became a legend after that, even into the Second World War. They used to say that whenever a Bulgarian unit was pinned down, that Captain Hoxa's ghost would—"

"I'm familiar with the ghost stories surrounding Captain Hoxa," Ramsay interrupted.

"There was something said earlier about you living in exile in Turkey. Tell me about the events that led up to you leaving Bulgaria," the professor ordered.

"I stayed on the family farm with my wife through the Second World War until the communists took over and nationalized everything. We were arrested after we refused to surrender our farm. I served a year and a half in prison. She died shortly after she started a similar sentence. I escaped to Turkey the same year I was released and lived in Istanbul until my death."

"What was the name of the prison where you served?"

"It didn't have a name, it had a number: State Prison Number Four."

"When were you interned exactly?"

"December 1946 until June 1948."

"Where was State Prison Number Four located?"

"On the outskirts of Sofia."

"How did you escape to Turkey?"

"I walked."

"What did you do to earn money in Istanbul?"

"I found work in the open-air vegetable markets carrying crates."

"What did Vanya die of?"

"I don't know, I was in prison."

Silence.

"She was interned at the same time as you?"

"It was about the same time, within days probably."

The old man in the center leaned forward deliberately. The other members of the panel deferred their attention to him. "It's late," he said. "Let's stop here and take tomorrow night off. We'll pick it up the night after." The members of the gallery stood up and spoke softly among themselves as soon as the old man leaned back.

POPPY WALKED AHEAD OF ME UP THE STAIRS. The smoke from the torches was slightly thicker at the top. "Why did they want to take tomorrow night off?" I asked.

"They are probably using the break to verify the information you've given. It's to be expected."

"How can they check all that information in one day?"

"They can't. They will just get started on it tomorrow. The Cognomina keeps dozens of people at the ready to help with the required research."

"Is that how you had my medical records checked?"

"Exactly."

"What happens if someone goes to the police or calls a Crime Stoppers tip line once they learn about my arson activities?"

"Evan," Poppy said in a sigh. "Look around you. Do we look like individuals that would ever want the authorities involved in anything?"

"I'm not doubting you, I'm just careful, that's all."

"Don't worry, your past is safe with us." She opened the door at the top of the stairs. I walked around her quickly as she closed it behind us.

"I was wondering," I said cautiously, "if we could get together tomorrow, since we both have the night off. I miss you." I blurted out the last words.

Her eyes showed a genuine warmth I hadn't seen before. "Yes, let's get together tomorrow. Dinner is usually out on the town on off nights, so I'll have to catch up with you after that. Why don't you come up to my room? I should be in by midnight. My room is number seventeen," she said, stepping closer to me.

"You were wonderful down there tonight." She sprung up on her toes and kissed me. "Get some rest, Evan, you look tired. I'll see you tomorrow."

"GOOD AFTERNOON," DILTZ SAID as i walked down the hall in search of breakfast.

I smiled at him. "I'd like to get a ride to Lake Zurich if there's a driver available."

"There is, are you planning to take a day cruise?" he asked. I nodded. "You'd better hurry, the last day ship leaves at three p.m. It's a quarter till two now. You can just make it if you hurry. I'll prepare a quick breakfast for you to take with you."

"Perfect. Tell the driver I'll be ready in five minutes."

THE SAME DRIVER WAS WAITING in the car at 11 p.m. by the ramp when the ship pulled up next to the dock. I arrived back at the hotel by eleven forty-five.

"How was it?" Diltz asked at the door.

"Very scenic. Is Poppy here?"

He hesitated. His eyes darted quickly and nervously as he searched to find an answer. "Yes," he said finally.

"Great. I'm supposed to go up and see her," I said, stepping to the side to move around him. He shadowed my movement, purposely blocking me with his arm. We were inches apart. I could sense his discomfort at being this close.

"I don't think she should be disturbed right now," he said quickly, now unable to look at me.

I looked at him sternly until his eyes caught mine. "Did she tell you to tell me that?"

He hesitated again. "Well, ah . . . I wouldn't . . . No, she didn't . . . it's just that . . . Well, I think it would be a good idea if you waited until tomorrow to call on her, sir."

"I've been invited," I said, losing my patience. I nudged my way around him.

"But sir, sir," he called out behind me as I walked down the hall toward the stairs. I looked back when I placed the cane on the first step. His impotent, tuxedoed figure stood in the middle of the corridor. He stammered uncontrollably as though he wrestled with words he couldn't bring himself to utter and seemed completely unlike the man I'd come to know in the past three days.

I turned away from him and walked up the stairs, eager to see what the rest of this new home looked like. The stairs opened perpendicular to a corridor that ran the length of the hotel. A long, narrow Persian rug covered the floor to each end of the hall, and small crystal chandeliers hung above every set of opposing doors. The faint sound of classical music drifted from down the hall to my right. I walked toward the music, looking for Poppy's room as I went. The silver-plated roman numerals that were affixed above each door had no order about them; XI, XX, IV, XV, XXVI, II. The music came from XXVI at the very end of the hall. I found XVII halfway down the other end. I stood in front of the wooden door for a moment, then knocked lightly. The lingering music seemed to intermingle with low voices. My heart quickened when the doorknob turned, then sank as the door swung open.

A well-built, dark-haired man wearing a red soccer jersey opened the door. He was naked from the waist down, and his hairy legs were covered in random scars, scabs, and abrasions. I looked away from his erection and eyed the room beyond. It was different than mine. A large square bed dominated the room. The red felt wallpaper matched the luxurious bedspread. The headboard was a large, hand-carved wooden half sun that looked as if it rose out of the crimson bed. At least a dozen red-and-black pillows propped up Poppy's naked body as she lay on the bed. Another man, dressed only in a similar red jersey had his head buried between her thighs as two more kneeled on either side of her on the bed stroking themselves. She looked up at me as she zipped the brown syringe case closed. Her almond eyes were completely calm.

"I wondered when you would show up. Come in, we're just getting started," she said, breaking into a sly smile.

I felt the blood drain from my face. I thought I might collapse and probably would have if not for the rigid cane under me. My hand was shaking when I reached for the knob to pull the door closed in front of me. I closed my eyes tight and kept a firm grip on the door handle for some time, not wanting to take the chance that it might open again.

"Can I buy you a drink?" asked a deep voice behind me in the hall. I opened my eyes and turned toward him. Classical music still floated through the air. It was the rotund man from the gallery that I'd met. "I said, can I buy you a drink, friend? You look like you could use one."

I nodded slowly, not letting go of the doorknob.

"Come with me. I know just the place," he said, putting his large arm around me, escorting me away from Poppy's door.

"RED WINE, PLEASE," HE SAID TO THE WAITRESS standing by our booth. "And you?" he asked me.

"A bourbon and a beer."

The waitress walked off without speaking. The Fraumunster Inn looked much the same as it had two nights ago. She brought the drinks back and took the ten-franc note he'd laid on the table.

"Thank you," I said, raising my glass. "You were right. I needed this."

"To us," he said, clinking glasses with me.

I smiled.

"We haven't been properly introduced. My name is Samas," he said, offering his hand.

"And at the end of the Ascension, you will tell me your real name, right?" I said sarcastically.

"No. Samas is my real name, my name within the Cognomina."

I cocked my head and looked at him. "Why are you sharing it with me. I was led to believe the names were secretive, and that I would know them only after I was accepted."

He waved off my comment. "That's the normal procedure, but I look at that as a formality. I know what you are, and I know you belong here with us. It was obvious after the session last night."

His candor and openness were a refreshing surprise. His disarming personality was a welcome change. "Evan Michaels," I said, taking his hand.

"Nice to meet you," he said.

"And you, Samas. How did you come by that name? If you don't mind me asking?"

"It was my father's name."

"Your father?"

He nodded. "Samas was my father in my first incarnation."

"When was that?"

"1026."

My amazement must have shown on my face.

"Yes, I know, I'm an old man," he said, smiling. "But I feel I'm just entering my prime."

"Do you mind telling me more about yourself?" I asked.

He laughed heartily, his voice booming through the tavern. "On the contrary, it's my favorite subject. And, after all, it's only fair. I'll end up knowing everything about you by the time your trial is over."

The more I spoke with him, the less I thought about Poppy. I was feeling better. "Good. I feel like talking."

"Me too," he said, signaling the waitress for another round of drinks.

"Where do you live?"

"I live in the most beautiful place in the world, Morocco, by the sea. My home is right on the beach."

"Sounds nice. I'd like to see it sometime."

"You are welcome as my guest anytime you like, for as long as you like. Do you like Moroccan cuisine?"

"I've never tried it."

His eyes lit up. "Ah, my wife is an excellent cook. Her specialty is the native cuisine."

"You're married?" I asked, surprised. I never thought anyone as abnormal as I would ever enter into something so normal and everyday as marriage.

"Yes, I've been married to Zohra for thirteen years."

"Does she know?"

"That we're married? I hope so," he said, laughing. He looked at his tattoo after his laughter had eased. "Of course she knows. I told her. How can you be close to someone, love someone, and not let them know? It's impossible."

"What was her reaction when you told her?"

"I told her after we were married, so her options were somewhat limited." He chuckled. "She had most of it figured out by that time though, besides, she loves me and accepts me. Love is wonderful that way."

"Have you been married in your other trips?"

"I have."

"That's fascinating."

"Why?" he asked.

"It's just so different. I haven't told anyone since I tried to tell my parents. I guess I've never had the courage to open up and be close to someone."

He shook his head. "It's not courage so much as it is comfort. You have to be comfortable with what you are before you can share yourself. I was the same as you early on. Just keep in mind that time is on your side." He smiled.

"Do you and your wife have any children?"

A strange look came over his face. "No, of course not. How could I?"

I was confused by his answer.

He looked at me puzzled. "You don't know, do you?" he asked.

"Know what?"

"We're born sterile each time, all of us."

My eyes narrowed. "You mean, I can't . . . I can never . . ."

He shook his head.

"Why?" I asked.

He shrugged his shoulders. "It's the nature of being what we are, I suppose. It has just always been that way. I thought you knew, or at least that Poppy would have told you."

"I get the feeling Poppy didn't tell me a lot of things."

Samas looked at me. "That condition may seem like a shock now, but it's no great loss when you look at it in relation to what is gained. Almost everyone else on the planet would trade places with you right now. Besides, you can't miss something you've never had."

He was right. The reality sunk in immediately, as if I'd subconsciously known all along and I felt no loss or longing in receiving that knowledge. I felt he was also right about the envy, as right as Antonio had been.

"I'm curious as to what the relationship between you and I can become right now," I said.

"I don't understand."

"I met Ramsay the afternoon before my Ascension started. She told me I could have no contact with her after it had started, and there were certain things she was unable to discuss even then because she was to be on the panel. I understand why it's that way, but when you couple that with the way Poppy has handled my advocacy, namely, keeping me in ignorance, it becomes frustrating. The only person I can talk to is Mr. Diltz."

"He's a good man, his father too. I understand your position, Evan. I am not bound by any restrictions. I am here merely as a spectator. I have no official capacity at the Ascension. I came because I wanted to meet you. Each time someone new like you is found and confirmed, it's like gaining a new family member. It's a joyous and rare occasion. I wanted to see it. So as it stands, I am available to you. I am your kindred spirit, you may ask me anything you like. I've no secrets from you, Evan."

"I feel like I have a lifetime's worth of questions."

"Unfortunately, the tavern won't stay open that long." He chuckled.

"My biggest concern is that I have only a general idea about what I'm supposed to do throughout the Ascension."

"You couldn't have convinced me of that last night. I think you're doing well," he said.

"It's not that. I'm comfortable talking about myself, I enjoy it, actually. It's the first time I've been able to tell the stories to anyone other than myself. My worry is more a feeling of uncertainty due to the fact that Poppy keeps me in the dark about what's going to happen next."

"Your concern seems justified. I can't understand why she wouldn't tell you."

"She tells me, but it always seems to come as a description of what just happened. I want to know what's going to happen next."

"So would anyone else in your place. I think you have a right to know," he said.

"All right then," I said, looking into his brown eyes. "What's going to happen next?"

He smiled. "What's going to happen next is that agents will begin looking up obscure pieces of information. A judge in Texas will check to see if you were issued a speeding ticket in Slayton. A clerk in Georgia will check Bobby's mother's driver's license application to see if she really had brown hair and blue eyes. A party bureaucrat in Bulgaria will look up military records to see if a Vasili Blagavich Arda was with the 138th under Captain Hoxa in the fall of 1918."

"Who are these agents?"

"Individuals who we keep under retainer, for lack of a better term, for this exact purpose. There's no telling what or who we might need to know about."

"What happens after that?"

"Well, it's due to continue tomorrow night. There will be more questions, one more session's worth, maybe two, then there will be a break for a few days until the verifications filter back in from our sources. You and your advocate will be summoned, perhaps for more questions, and then the panel will deliberate in private and render its decision. At that point, all the Reincarnationists will be assembled, and the judgment will be read. When you are confirmed, there will be a festival in the other half of the grotto at which you will choose a name and be introduced, formally."

"What happens if I'm not confirmed?"

"No neophyte has failed in over two hundred years," he said, dismissing my comment.

"What happened to that candidate?"

He took a long drink of wine, finishing the glass. "We killed her," he said calmly. "But she never came back, so our conclusion about her must have been correct."

"Sounds reminiscent of the Salem witch trials. If you survive submersion, you are possessed; if you don't, you are pure, but still dead."

He laughed. "Yes, I can see how one could make that comparison." He offered no other explanations.

"Will I be killed if I fail?"

"Yes," he said, signaling for more drinks. "But if you believe in what you are, that shouldn't be a concern for you."

"What do you mean?" I asked, astonished that he would be so cavalier about my death.

"If you know that you have lived before and, more importantly, understand that you will live again, then the annihilation of death would hold no horror for you. Correct?"

"Poppy said to me that once you come back, you always will. If that's an immutable fact, then your assertion is correct."

He leaned over the table close to me, so close I could smell the alcohol on his breath and could make out intricate patterns in the light-brown irises of his eyes. "It's true," he whispered in a low voice. "I've come back sixteen times. That makes seventeen lives all told, and I remember the slightest detail from every one as if it happened yesterday. You will come back again and again, like the rest of us, each time stepping back up onto your own shoulders, standing a little higher, able to look out a little farther on the horizon and able to look back a little farther in time."

"Logically, I can't argue with you. I just don't know that my faith is there quite yet . . . but time is on my side, right?"

"Right," he said in one long low tone. He raised his glass. "To faith."

"To faith," I toasted. "Tell me something else. How does a candidate change advocates?"

He was silent for several seconds. "You're pretty angry with her, aren't you?"

"I'm not sure what I feel."

"Were you lovers?" he asked.

I nodded.

"I see. She'll be quite put off if you choose someone else."

"Her feelings are not of primary importance to me," I answered coolly. "Succeeding is."

"Well," he said in a sigh. "You can do one of two things. You can ask the panel to choose a new advocate for you, or you can choose your own, provided they accept."

I looked up into his consoling eyes. "Would you accept?"

"Are you asking me?" He looked astonished and honored.

"Yes, Samas, I'm asking you. Will you be my advocate?"

He thought for a moment. "I will. But I will not tell Poppy that there has been a change. That's your responsibility, agreed?"

"It's a deal." I shook his hand but began to question my decision as soon as I pulled away. He was right about the Ascension going well, and that was as much to Poppy's credit as it was to mine. I've just never liked being in the dark, that's how I've managed to stay ahead as I have. Most of the surprises that hit you in life affect you for the worse. That's what I feared most about her, justifiably so.

The entire ride home, I thought about how to tell Poppy, and how she would take it. Vengeance was a handy vehicle, but unnecessary. I wanted her and despised her. I loved her for what she was and hated her for who she was. But perhaps more importantly, I understood her and realized then that I didn't want to.

I AWOKE THE NEXT MORNING with a headache and an overwhelming sense of anxiety about confronting Poppy. Samas was sitting at the dining room table with Mr. Diltz and two others I recognized from the gallery when I walked in.

"Good day, Herr Michaels. Some coffee?" Mr. Diltz asked.

"I'm hungry, actually."

"I'll have some fresh rolls brought out," he said, getting up.

I smiled at the three and sat down. A thin, hard-looking middle-aged woman smoked next to Samas. Her black hair was pulled into a bun so tight it seemed to smooth some of the wrinkles around her small, bloodshot eyes. The young woman next to her looked no older than eighteen or nineteen. She wore an expensive men's two-piece business suit recut to fit her figure.

"Did you really watch that fire develop in the back of a police car?" the bun woman asked.

"Yep."

"I can picture that in my head. That must have been something," replied the woman in the suit.

"Very," I said. Samas was paying attention, but the woman in the suit looked bored and distracted as if I'd interrupted a conversation about me. Diltz brought a basket of rolls in and sat them on the table when I heard a door slide open behind me. Samas's facial reaction told me it was Poppy.

"Hello, Bando," Samas said.

"Hello, Juan," she replied snidely. The sound of her voice drained me of what little courage I had mustered.

"Can I get you anything, madame?" Diltz asked her.

"Coffee and croissant."

"Right away," he said, exiting to the kitchen. I still hadn't turned around.

"I have to go," Samas said. "Please excuse me."

"I'll join you," the other women chimed in at the same time. In a matter of seconds, I was alone with Poppy. She walked around the table and sat in the chair opposite mine.

She stuffed a cigarette into the silver-tipped holder. "Why didn't you stay last night?" she asked nonchalantly.

"I didn't feel li— I, ah— It wasn't what I was expecting," I said, averting my eyes to the basket of rolls.

"They weren't what I was expecting when I met them yesterday, but it doesn't mean you can't enjoy yourself. You should have joined us."

"Well, it, ah, just wasn't what I was expecting."

"And just what were you expecting?"

"It doesn't matter now."

"Then why the long face, love? Don't tell me your feelings are h—"

"Stop it!" I interrupted angrily. "You can keep your condescending attitude, all right! Here's the deal: I'm very grateful for what you've done for me. I don't know if I can ever repay that debt, but I can't do this with you any longer. I've asked for a new advocate."

She showed no reaction. "I see," she said coolly. "May I ask who is to be your new advocate?"

I lit a cigarette and drew in deeply. "Samas."

"They appointed you Samas?" she asked, astonished.

"No. I chose him."

She stood up and leaned over the table. "You be careful with him," she said.

I looked up at her, thinking of Henry. "You know, that's funny, I received the same warning about you."

I didn't turn my head to follow her as she walked around the table to the door. "I'll see you after the Ascension, if you make it," she said behind me, sliding the door closed.

Diltz came in seconds after she had left. "Where is Poppy?" he asked, holding a tray.

"She's gone."

He raised his eyebrows and sighed. "I did try to warn you last night," he said, setting the tray down. "How are you, sir?"

"I'm getting better," I said, still staring at her empty chair.

SAMAS WALKED INTO DILTZ's side dining room carrying two full plates of food. A lifeless lobster claw hung over the edge of the right plate and swayed with each step he took. "I thought I'd join you," he said.

"It's always a pleasure, sir," Diltz replied.

I was genuinely glad to see him. His mere presence was becoming a comfort to me. I smiled broadly at him.

"Did you get things straight with her?"

"Yes, I did. I think she left."

"How did she act?" Samas asked.

"Normal. Collected."

"Did she say anything?" asked Samas.

"Not really," I said, starting on my meal. I kept my thoughts to myself as we ate.

Diltz ate the way he lived; in ordered, measured amounts. And if Samas's eating habits reflected on how he lived, I wanted to know him even more. He ate like a man who lusted for food. He eyed the next piece of food on the plate while he chewed the one in his mouth, tackling the new one as soon as he swallowed. He worked as if he thought the meal might go bad before his very eyes. The sounds of pleasure he made with each new taste led me to think he was in the throes of passion instead of the main course of dinner.

Diltz ate as if oblivious to the show, but I was hypnotized by the display of emotions conveyed in Samas's facial expressions. He knifed off a thick slice of lamb and popped it into his mouth.

"Mmmm," he moaned. "Esmerelda should change her name to Rosemary, this chop is seasoned so well. Please pass on my compliments," he said with his mouth full.

"I'll pass it on. Try the mussels, she prepared those as well," Diltz said.

Samas grunted in acknowledgment as he took another bite. His pace slowed, and his enthusiasm waned after a full forty-five minutes, just as empty spots began to appear in the two plates. "Are they bringing the dessert cart by?" he asked.

Diltz nodded.

I couldn't resist it any longer. "You're going to eat more?"

"Yes," he said, still chewing. "I would eat it all if I could, Evan. And why not?" he bellowed, grabbing a handful of small mussels. "What is the purpose of life if you don't enjoy yourself? Simple pleasures such as Esmerelda's cooking are often the best." He pried open two shells and popped the contents into his open mouth. "Mmmm. What is that spice, dill?"

Diltz nodded.

"It's fantastic. Here, have some, and you'll see what I mean by pleasure." He dropped a half-dozen shells onto my plate. I pried them open as a woman came in with a stainless steel cart covered with colorful cakes, custards, and tarts.

Samas looked over the desserts like a jeweler inspecting precious stones. "I'll have the lime tart and the pavlova, and could you bring in a decanter of Armagnac, the '51 if there's any left," he said. Diltz and I both declined dessert. The woman reappeared with a crystal decanter and three glasses.

"I've been thinking," Samas said as he filled each of our glasses in turn. "I would like to ask the panel for a recess, two or three days. I thought we could go to my home in Morocco, spend some time in the sun. It would give us the opportunity to get to know each other, so we could work better together. Besides, it seems you could use a few days' worth of diversion."

"Can we do that?" I asked.

"Under the circumstances, I'm sure they would allow it."

"Let's go then. I could use a break," I said excitedly.

"It's settled," he said, raising his glass. "We'll leave tomorrow."

15

Each wide leather seat was open to us, as Samas and I were the only passengers in first class. I sat in a window seat and watched as the barren, brown North African coast rose out of the blue Mediterranean.

"Is that Morocco down there?" I asked.

"Yes."

"How much do I owe you for the ticket?" I asked. I had been thinking about the cost of a spur of the moment first-class ticket to Rabat since we took off.

"Don't be ridiculous, you are my guest. You owe me nothing."

"How much does a ticket to Morocco cost?"

"The cost of a ticket is unimportant when compared to the experiences it can bring us both. Money is not to be adored for its own sake, only for the richness it can bring to your life. It's the difference between potential and kinetic energies. Money is only useful when it's kinetic."

"Do you have a lot of money?"

He nodded. "More than I could ever set in motion, I'll put it that way."

"Poppy told me how it works—leaving money to yourself through the Cognomina, I mean. She told me how she came by her wealth."

"Yes, the infamous glassworks. That's a real money machine she has there. She was always industrious, good with jewelry, a real artisan."

"How did you come by your wealth?"

The engine throttled back as the plane began its approach.

"I'm a broker and a talent scout of sorts. I deal with art and antiquities. Art is my passion. Each of us has a passion; something that keeps us going on, life after life. It's the perfect line for me, really. I buy the fresh works of an era and sit on them for as long as it takes. In the end, I have to discard about ninety percent of them, but the other ten percent are priceless. I'm actually getting much better at discerning between the Melkmans and the Monets. It's probably around eighty-to-twenty now."

"Melkmans?" I asked.

"That's my point, no one's ever heard of him. He was in the ninety percent."

"Do you ever keep any for yourself?"

"Oh, of course. You always keep the best ones for yourself. I'll show you later tonight." Samas leaned close and pointed beyond the glass. "If you look along the coast as we land, you can see the coastal highway that leads to my home."

I nodded and looked out the window until we landed.

A PETITE, MIDDLE-AGED, DARK-SKINNED WOMAN ran toward Samas as we stepped out of the terminal into the hot, dry Moroccan air. She was engulfed in the embrace of his large arms, and he picked her up effortlessly.

"Mmmm, it's good to see you," he said, clutching her to him like a doll.

"I missed you, Habibi." She nuzzled her head in the nape of his thick neck. She spoke English with a British accent.

"Zohra darling, this is Evan Michaels," he said, placing her down and turning her toward me. She was beautiful. The brown skin of her face seemed to fade into her black hair and dark eyes. The few long, gray hairs sparsely intermingled with the raven black gave her a look of veneration usually reserved for men. She carried herself confidently, holding eye contact with me as she took my hand firmly.

"Samas told me about you on the phone. You are exactly as he described. My name is Zohra. It is a pleasure to meet you."

"Thank you for having me."

"The car is over here. Shall we go?"

"Please," said Samas.

"Are you hungry, Habibi?"

"I'm always hungry for your cooking."

"I'll take care of you," she said, looking at him warmly.

SHE DROVE THE WHITE JEEP down the narrow two-lane highway that bordered the craggy coast. I sat in the back seat looking at both of them. He was so different from Poppy that I wouldn't have recognized them as being the same thing had I not known. Poppy lived in the self-imposed exile of her church, with the doors always bolted. Samas lived like a popular general, always in the field among his troops. I liked his life, even though I knew my own was currently closer to Poppy's.

"There it is," he said, pointing to a large house nestled down by a small, sandy beach. The white stucco glowed in the bright sun. It went out of view when Zohra turned off onto a gravel road that wound toward the coast. The scent of the ocean was strong in the air. Two Great Danes—one black, one white with black spots—scampered up the road toward us. Zohra shouted something to them in her native Arabic.

"I'll get dinner started while you show Evan around," she said, pulling up behind the two-story home.

Their home looked like a museum inside. Every few feet a white pedestal held up a piece of the past. Greek, Roman, Egyptian, and Chinese artifacts rested under square protective glass covers. Numerous framed charcoal sketches covered the walls. Traditional furnishings were sparse so that all my attention was drawn to the ubiquitous art and artifacts. Perhaps it was designed that way.

"How long have you lived here?" I asked.

"I had this place built thirteen years ago, around the same time I married Zohra."

"Really? I would have thought you'd live in an older home."

"I have older estates, but I came here a while back to close a deal with a client who was purchasing a mint condition thirteenth-dynasty Egyptian sarcophagus. When the man died, I bought the property, tore down the standing home, and built this one."

"Why this place? Other than the beautiful location, obviously."

"There are two reasons. Let me show you," he said, smiling. He walked upstairs to the bedroom. The entire east wall of the bedroom was a series of sliding glass panel doors that opened to the Atlantic. It was an incredible view. He slid the doors all the way back until the room was completely open on that side. The breeze ruffled the mosquito net canopy above the bed. The sound of the ocean crept in slowly but steadily until every vestige of silence had been pushed back down the stairs.

"I've had a sleeping disorder in my last three lifetimes," he said. "Come over here." He pointed to a crescent of land that knifed out into the sea about a quarter mile up the coast. "That point," he said, "and that group of rocks down the coast form an acoustic chamber of sorts. It amplifies the sound. The constant sound helps me sleep. I actually have a recording of this sound that I keep in Zurich."

"This sleep disorder has followed you through three trips?"

"*Followed* is a good word to use. It only comes to me after I've started to remember my past. I never have the problem as a child."

"Was there something, some event, that brought it on?"

"No. It just happened, but it brought me to this wonderful location," he said, walking through the opening to the veranda.

"What was the other reason?"

"I was courting Zohra. Her family lives in Rabat, and I knew if I could keep her close to them, her decision about marriage would be easier."

I nodded then walked out to the railing and panned slowly, taking in the whole horizon. The sounds of the ocean seemed to come in stereo. *The most beautiful place in the world*—he had a good argument for that.

"Come, let me show you your room," Samas said, stepping back inside.

The guest room was downstairs facing the beach. The tan sand lay just beyond the single sliding glass door. A large mosquito net–canopied bed sat in the far corner.

"Do you have a problem with mosquitoes here?"

"Not them so much. We have biting flies this time of year." I looked at him somewhat surprised. "This is Africa, my friend," he said, laughing. "I'll show you the best part of the house after we eat. Come on, let's see how Zohra is doing."

The dining room was open to the kitchen. Three place settings sat around the small, black-lacquered table. Samas cleared his throat to get Zohra's attention. She was bent over, looking into an oven.

"Two minutes," she said, still embroiled in her preparations. "Be seated, please." The scent of roasting garlic and onions spiced the air. She brought it right from the oven to the table in a red clay tray.

"Zohra, you shouldn't have," Samas said when he saw the meal she had prepared.

"It smells delicious, what is it?" I asked.

"Roasted rabbits and guinea fowl with couscous. Samas's favorite."

"Indeed," he bellowed. "But that's enough talk. Let's eat," he said, starting on a rabbit. I imitated him and smiled at her. She brought out rice, unleavened bread, yogurt, and mint tea while we ate. Samas had finished the first rabbit and started on a guinea by the time she joined us. His vocalizations and gestures were as pronounced as they had been in Zurich.

"It's delicious," I said to her. Samas mumbled something to the same effect. I ate quietly, unsure of what to talk about, and about what I could say in front of her.

"Is this your first time in Morocco, Evan?" Zohra asked.

"Yes."

"Have you ever been in a Muslim nation before?"

"I lived in Istanbul."

"Ah, I've played there."

"Played?" I asked.

"Yes, I'm a cellist. I was with the Calais Repertory Company then."

"First chair too," Samas chimed in between bites.

"Was your stay in Turkey in a previous life?" she asked. I was unprepared for her question, for her knowing. I looked at Samas who nodded subtly as he chewed.

"Yes, it was."

"How long ago? If I might be so bold."

I smiled. "In the 1950s and 1960s."

"Where you a Muslim then?"

"No, I was not. Are you?"

"Yes, I am Sunni," she answered with pride. "You can often hear the call to prayer from here if the windows are open."

I took another rabbit and turned my attention to Samas. "What are your religious beliefs?"

He looked at me as if I'd said something in a language he didn't understand. "You're not serious? Religion is predicated on faith. You and I don't have faith, we have knowledge and experience. We have proof. The rules and tenets of religion do not apply to us. We have philosophy instead, of which I'm an Epicure."

"What's that?"

"A follower of Epicurus's teachings. In ancient Greece, he professed that life is to be lived, and that living for pleasure is the ultimate good.

"Do you remember anything between when you died both times and when you were born? They will ask you that at some point," he said.

"No, nothing."

"That's right," he said emphatically. "Nothing, nothing. More accurately, no divinity, just a return, right?"

I nodded.

"It's the same for all of us, no divinity. This, here and now, is all we have. This meal, this conversation, the friends and lovers you have, and the ideas you hold dear are all your world consist of. They are all that you have, they are all that any of us have. You and I are blessed, or cursed, depending on how you look at it, in that we know that these things are the makeup and extent of our world, of ourselves as individuals. We should therefore relish our time and move to enrich our lives as much as possible because in so doing, we enrich all that our world will ever be. I believe this is truer for normal people than it is for us because their time is much shorter than ours, in a practical sense. We have a consciousness that transcends death. We survive it as individuals, the same individuals or consciousnesses if you will. Normal people obviously don't do that or don't know they do that—either way, the outcome is the same. For those people, Epicurus's lessons should be all the more poignant."

"Do you buy that?" I asked Zohra.

"I don't have to buy that, I have faith," she said laconically, to which Samas burst out in uproarious laughter.

"Now you see why I love her," he said, still laughing.

"Poppy told me something similar, only her take on the whole thing was much . . . angrier."

"Poppy?" asked Zohra.

Samas pointed to his tattoo. "You've never met her. She's the one who found Evan." He turned toward me. "Let me guess. She damns all of them for their ignorance of what we know is fact. Is that pretty close?"

I chuckled. "Yeah, that's pretty close. You must have known her for a long time."

"Since the beginning. What she doesn't realize is that you can only be responsible for yourself and your own happiness. Take her, for example," he said, pointing to Zohra. "She believes that if she lives by the code set forth in the Koran, she will ascend to heaven after she dies. If it makes her happy, it makes me happy. And who's to say she isn't right? Just because it doesn't happen to us doesn't mean it can't happen to them, perhaps that's why she won't come back. That's the point. We cannot know, and that's why we should live in the here and now and bask in what it has to offer us. And that's why you should eat your fill of this fine meal, Evan."

I sat there, amazed by Samas. If Poppy was like me, then he was better than both of us. He was happy, content. I could see it in his eyes, the way they brightened and sparkled when he spoke of the surviving individual coming back. You could just tell he couldn't wait to come back. He loved it.

"Have you eaten your fill?" he asked.

"Yes, I have," I said, turning to Zohra. "It was wonderful. Thank you."

Samas stood up and walked into the kitchen where he grabbed a bottle of wine and two glasses. "Let's adjourn to my private gallery. I have a few things I'd like to show you. We can discuss the Ascension as well."

"Sounds good," I said.

"Thank you, dear. That was delicious, as usual." He bent down to kiss her. "It's over here," he said to me, leading the way.

He punched a code into the electronic keypad of the security system next to the white door, making sure I couldn't see. The door was thicker than I thought it should have been and made a distinctive *whoosh* as it opened, as though the darkened room inside had a controlled atmosphere. Samas turned on the lights, and the room exploded with colors and shapes. The walls were completely covered with a plethora of multicolored canvases hanging frame-to-frame. The differently sized, interlocking frames formed a giant jigsaw puzzle that continued around the four walls. The lighting inside was completely diffused and seemed to radiate from the sterile white ceiling and floor. The room had the feel of a medical laboratory. Two wooden chairs and a small white table waited in the center of the room.

"Come in, quickly," Samas said. I stepped in, and he closed the door behind me. "The sea air is horrible for them," he said, looking around. "It's very corrosive, it can dull colors in a matter of decades, but I think wine actually helps to restore their color. It does if you drink enough of it, anyway," he said, prying out the cork.

I examined several of the pieces as Samas poured. Each one had a small brass nameplate set into the bottom of the frame giving the title, artist, and date.

"This is the collection. We are standing in my favorite place in all the world." Samas held out a wine glass to me. "This is the best of the best. Centuries of culture and art. Dozens of lives, some tortured, some satisfied, but all fulfilled and all right here in this room with us."

I wandered about as he spoke, looking at the paintings and their tags: Cézanne, Bassano, Gauguin, Caravaggio, David, Van Dyck, and Manet were only some of the names I saw. "How much is this collection worth?"

"Whew. There's no way to know without putting it up for sale, but I'd guess any of these pieces would sell at auction for several hundred million pounds. I've had most of these pieces so long that most art historians consider them lost. That in itself would make them even more valuable. To my knowledge, this is the only privately owned collection of its kind in the world."

"Which piece is your favorite?"

He pointed over my shoulder to a two-by-three-foot bare spot on the wall. "The one I can't have, of course."

"Is there a piece that fits there?"

"Yes, but that's another story altogether," Samas said, offering me a glass of wine. "Let's talk about you."

"All right."

"I'll be frank. I can see a potential problem with your Ascension."

"Yes," I said, moving forward in my chair.

"You only have two trips' worth of information, one and a half really, when you think about it. That's where the trouble lies. The facts from your first incarnation are in Bulgaria. There are many places in the world where information flows freely, but your old homeland is not one of them. What records that do survive will be hard to get. But the real dilemma is with your second trip. The United States is the place in the world where information flows freest, but all the records could have theoretically been available to you beforehand."

"What are you getting at?"

"I'm just playing the part of the devil's advocate. This is how they think. I know, I've sat on the panel, and this is how I thought. What I'm getting at is that all the information you've given is suspect in their eyes. With that in mind, I think your cause is helped greatly if you give them something that can't be refuted."

"What do you have in mind?"

"They can't refute or invalidate emotions, specifically, your emotions on what this life is like for you. They can't argue with the way you feel, hence, they must accept it, and in doing so, accept you. It may seem like a small point, but I think it could make a difference in how they look at you."

I contemplated his idea as I let my eyes wander over the many millions of dollars on these walls. Any one of them would provide enough wealth to last several lifetimes. His idea made sense and more importantly, made me realize how far I had yet to go.

"Don't take this the wrong way," he continued. "I think your situation is good, especially with how you've handled yourself. I'm just trying to come up with ways to improve it even further."

"You know, this is exactly what I was talking about when I mentioned how Poppy was handling this. She never would have suggested something like that. I'm not sure she would have even thought of it."

"Well, she is a little different. I'm not saying that's good or bad, she's just different. This type of life obviously means different things to different individuals."

"I agree," I said, refilling our glasses. "This is a good wine. Where do you get it?"

"I buy it in Zurich, oddly enough. You can only buy wine in Morocco in special shops for foreigners that are ill stocked. It's Islamic law. I love this vintage, but I have to be careful with it around my wife. She is very devout. She won't even sit in the same room with me if I drink. It's barely tolerated in the house."

"You two seem an odd couple," I said, laughing. "How did you meet?"

"I was living in Rome at the time, that's a great place to be in the art business. She was touring with the London Philharmonic. I went to the symphonic hall with some Japanese clients in hopes of closing a six-piece deal. I saw her on stage in the string section and was captivated immediately. I arranged to be introduced to her at the reception afterward. She was cool at first, then went cold when she realized I knew nothing about music. But by the end of the night, I had gotten her to agree to a tour of some of the city's most exclusive galleries the next day."

"And you swept her off her feet with your art knowledge and charm? Something like that?" I asked, smiling.

He laughed. "It was nothing like that, my friend. Her contemporary art knowledge was almost as complete as my own. She was as cool and collected as a judge at the end of the day. That's when I knew I had to have her, whatever the cost in money, time, and emotion. I was already in love with her. In that sense, you could say she swept me off my feet.

"I found a touring schedule for the London Philharmonic and took in two shows in Florence the next week. I went only to see her play, watching from the anonymity of the crowd. I could hear her notes above everyone else's. It felt like she was playing for me alone, with all the others as mere accompaniment. I had gone to Florence to see if she still stirred me and I found myself saying yes to the same question in Trieste, in Belgrade, and in Athens.

"I met her backstage for the second time after a performance in Cairo. We spoke for about an hour and agreed to establish a correspondence. Five years, two dozen meetings, and one hundred and one letters later, she was my wife. I had offered, as a grandiose measure, to marry her in the Grand Mosque of Cordova, and she held me to it. It cost me a fortune and about a dozen political favors to pull it off, but it was worth every peseta."

"You really didn't tell her about yourself until after you were married?"

"Well," he hesitated, "not entirely. She knew about me, I told her I was different." He leaned back in his chair, looked at the ceiling, and smiled as though remembering gave him great pleasure. "I used to tell her stories about myself; nations I'd visited that no longer exist, events hundreds of years ago that I was witness to, descriptions of people I'd known. She thought they were fantasy at first, that I made them up as I told them or thought them out elaborately days before a scheduled rendezvous. She figured it out in the end. What I didn't tell her was that there was a society of us. She was angry at first, but when I explained the reason for the secrecy she understood, or at least accepted it."

I stood up to stretch my legs and examine more of the paintings. "Poppy mentioned something about what led to the secrecy. She said there was a member who got everyone killed."

"Yes," he nodded. "Brevicepts was her name, and that's exactly what happened. She got herself and the other four killed and caused our collective treasury to be looted, but more importantly, she threatened to do it again after they all came back. Brevicepts wanted to sack the villages that had turned on them. She felt it was our divine right as Reincarnationists to rule over humanity, she thought we were endowed as we are with that purpose in mind. The Cognomina had lost everything because of her megalomaniacal fantasies. The others beseeched her to moderate and live in comfort and anonymity like before, but it was no use. The other four had attributed her conduct to madness. And that madness had attached itself to the part of us that transcends, and it returned to her as soon as she began to remember. In the end, the other four decided that excommunication was the only option. The decision, they agreed, had to be unanimous. The old man, who sits in the center of the panel during your Ascension, do you remember him?"

"Yes?" I said, turning around to face him.

"He had to cast the final vote against her."

"What happened to her?"

"What do you think happened to her? She left and died eventually, and was reborn like us and died again and again and again. She's out there somewhere tonight, alone probably." There was no mistaking the remorse in his voice.

"Then you think the decision was unjust?"

"I think it was either unjust, or there is more to the affair than the original four are telling. Think about it, Evan, could you think of anything more punitive than to be permanently spurned by the only family you can ever truly have? They doomed her to wander alone. Imagine a thousand years living as you lived before you were found, only she doesn't have the bliss of ignorance that you had. She knows about us, what we are and where we are. I can't even contemplate the torture and horror that an existence like that would mean, if the term *existence* can even be used. I don't know. These days, the whole affair, as a rule, is not discussed."

I couldn't imagine an estrangement like that either. I've often wondered how I survived on my own to make it this far. Every day for those three years, I felt like a man wandering lost in the wilderness that is his own identity. The idea of being forced back into that dreaded wilderness, not lost, knowing all the landmarks and having to wander anyway, was too horrid a thought to hold.

"When do they expect us back in Zurich?" I asked, changing the subject.

"Two days."

"Two days off sounds good."

"That episode with Poppy rattled you, didn't it?"

It had rattled me, but pride wouldn't allow me to admit it to him. "It was a surprise. I certainly wasn't expecting what I saw."

"Well, it's certainly to be expected with her."

"What do you mean?"

"I don't know how to explain it other than to say that I know her."

"I noticed you called her Bando. Have you known her long?"

"Since the beginning. I found her, much the same as she found you, by accident."

"Tell me about it," I said, pouring more wine.

He took the glass and leaned back. "That's a long story, but a good one," he said proudly, followed by a dramatic pause, "Juan de Victoria was my name then.[24] I was a young man looking to start my fortune as a conquistador. I had been in the Cognomina for two hundred and fifty years, but I still struggled to keep up with the others and the wealth they had accumulated with their additional lives, so looking for the gold rumored to be waiting in the New World seemed a good idea."

"Did it work?"

"Yes," Samas stated with a touch of sadness in his voice. "But not without some loss. And that's where Bando—Poppy—came in," he said, correcting himself. "I remember the messenger was out of breath when he reached the steps that led up to the house of Victoria . . ."

24. Samas's account of his life as Juan de Victoria is interesting, as there was a man on Coronado's expedition by that name and the man was from Borgos, Spain. (*Fundadores de Nueva Galicia Guadalajara Tomo I* by Guillermo Garmendia Leal, 1996.)

16

Gripping the royal letter in his hand, the messenger was out of breath when he reached the steps that led up to the house of Victoria. The lean Moorish teenager had run all the way from the palace of the alcalde because the letter in his hand carried the seal of Don Antonio de Mendoza, Viceroy of New Spain.[25]

"Señor Juan de Victoria?" asked the messenger at the door to the house.

Juan looked at the lean teenager who smiled with the whitest teeth he had ever seen. He took the letter and studied it carefully, noticing the quality of the paper, the smudges from handling, and the seal.

It had been almost a year since he had written to Don Antonio in search of a commission in New Spain. A year of anticipation, stagnation, and sloth. A year wasted. He broke the seal and read aloud in front of the messenger and his housekeeper.

25. Antonio de Mendoza was indeed the Viceroy of New Spain at the time of this letter. (*The Conquest of New Spain* by Bernal Díaz del Castillo, translated and edited by Genaro García and Alfred Percival Maudslay, 1967.)

Nineteenth of August, the year of our Lord 1539

By the Authority of Antonio de Mendoza, Viceroy of New Spain, the services of Juan de Victoria are requested in Compostela, New Spain. You are to be commissioned as a lieutenant in the expeditionary force of Francisco Vasquez de Coronado. This letter allows you to gain passage on any of the King's ships to the New Spanish port of Veracruz.

Don Antonio de Mendoza,
Viceroy of New Spain for His
Majesty King Ferdinand

"Ready my possessions," Juan shouted to his servant. "I am leaving at midday."

"Yes, maestro," the servant answered with a slight tremor in his voice. "Will you come back?"

A smile opened in Juan's thick, black goatee. "I always come back."

THE *MARIA DE LA LUZ* WASN'T MUCH OF A SHIP but it was the only one leaving for New Spain in the next month, and Juan was leaving with her. He had reluctantly been granted passage from the ship's captain, Miguel de la Garza.

De la Garza looked to be in his midtwenties like Juan. He had a full black beard, cropped neatly, as was the fashion of His Majesty's naval officers. The wrinkled skin around the corners of his eyes reported to his years aboard ship, squinting against unfiltered sunrise and sunset. He had granted Juan passage because of the letter but had done so nonchalantly as though he saw them every day. Juan may have been under the commission of a viceroy, but it was understood from the beginning that they were going there on the captain's boat.

THE WEATHER WORSENED ON THEIR FOURTH DAY at sea, and it was on that day that Juan saw the lad for the first time. Juan first noticed him behind a pickle barrel at the front of the hold. The belly of the ship held the crew's quarters along with leftover barrels and crates that wouldn't fit in the forecastle and main hold. Juan's bunk was at the rear of the crew's quarters and across the stairwell from the first mate's. The hold had a single oil lamp suspended from a crossbeam, and that lamp swayed wildly and sent light chasing shadow around table, chair, bunk, and barrel as the ship groaned through twenty-foot swells.

Juan placed a folded pillow under his head, allowing him to see over the foot of the bunk. "I can see you quite clearly," he said. They were alone.

There was no response.

Juan knew every member of the crew was on deck wrestling with the wind-whipped rigging. "Do you know what the punishment is for stowing away under the Spanish flag?"

Still no response.

Juan stood up and walked slowly toward him until he could see that the shivering youth was the same Moorish messenger who had hand-delivered the invitation to come to the New World.

Juan sat down cross-legged on the floor of the hold in front of him, where the stowaway was shaking visibly. They sat silent, studying one another for several minutes before Juan spoke to the cowering figure. "Juan," he said, placing his hand on his chest.

The young African looked at him for some time and replied simply, "Bando."

TWO HOURS LATER, Juan had discerned that Bando spoke a bit of Spanish and had eaten nothing but pickles for the past three days. When Juan offered him bread, he devoured it immediately. Juan watched the boy eat with delight, but he couldn't help but wonder why this haggard boy had ventured so far at such great peril.

"Bando, why did you leave your village and your family?" asked Juan in Spanish.

"I left to find my first family," answered the young African, nodding his head as if to coax the Spanish words out of his mouth.

"Your first family?" asked Juan as he leaned forward.

"Yes, I left my second family to find my first family again."

Juan heard a footfall on the top step of the stairwell leading down into the hold. He turned toward the stairwell and saw Captain de la Garza's freshly polished boot. Juan's blood ran cold, and Bando was already scrambling for the cover of the barrels.

Bando began to panic. Juan began speaking loudly, "Goddamnit, boy, I told you to stay home. Do you realize what you've done? You could be killed for being here."

"He will be killed," came a voice from the stairs. "He *will* be killed now," said Miguel calmly as he stepped off of the bottom step and onto the floor of the hold.

"Captain, please spare the life of this boy. He is my squire. I left him in Cadiz, but he followed me aboard. I am obliged by his family to look after his safety."

"Then it appears as though you are errant in your duties, Señor Victoria," said the captain menacingly, as he stepped toward them, drawing his sword.

"Need I remind you of my travel letter, Captain?"

"Need I remind you of the punishment for harboring a stowaway on the king's ship?" shouted the captain. They stood nose-to-nose.

"No, Captain de la Garza, you do not," said Juan, stepping aside.

Miguel stood with his sword pointed at Bando's chest. "Stand up!" he commanded. Bando got up, knees shaking. Juan had untied his coin purse from his belt while Miguel had focused on Bando, and he deftly dropped the leather bag at Miguel's feet. It was the larger of the two purses he had brought with him. The captain stepped on it then stared directly into Juan's eyes. Juan returned the stare but said nothing.

"How can I be certain he is yours, Señor Victoria?"

"Respectfully, sir, you will simply have to accept my word as a Spanish gentleman."

"And no doubt, a *rich* Spanish gentleman at that," said Miguel, as he rolled his boot over the purse, trying to gauge its contents.

"I used to be," said Juan, looking at Miguel's feet.

The captain stopped moving his boot, looked at Bando, then at Juan. "He eats from your rations and sleeps in your berth."

"As you wish, Captain."

"I'll tell the crew," Miguel said, picking up the purse.

IT WAS A FULL DAY after the incident with the captain before Juan spoke to Bando. He found him belowdecks, behind the same pickle barrel. "Come out from behind there," said Juan without emotion. "Sit here," he said, pointing to his bunk. Juan sat beside him.

"Why did you save me?" asked Bando.

Juan leaned back, his shoulders hunched to fit the concave of the hull. "That is what you are going to tell me. I want you to tell me about your first family. What was your name?"

"In that place, I am called Nez-Lah. I am the gold shaper."

"Where does this family live?"

Bando shrugged his shoulders. "The place is called Latsei. I've tried to find it. I've looked for one season already."

Juan shook his head. "Do they look like you look now?"

"No, their skin is tan, like that of the captain, and their hair is black and straight like yours."

"Do you remember their language?"

"Yes."

"Speak to me in that tongue."

Bando looked up at the crossbeams of the hold for a moment and then began chattering unintelligibly. Juan noticed that when he spoke in this strange language, Bando took on a new cast. He seemed brighter, he smiled, and his eyes shined. He was remembering, Juan thought.

Juan did not recognize the language. He spoke thirteen languages and had heard over fifty more in as many lands. He knew the peoples of the silk routes to China and India. He knew the caravans of Africa and had heard their tongues as well. What Bando spoke was completely different.

Juan stood up and began to pace the length of the hold. Thoughts of the letters of Cabeza de Vaca and Pizzaro came into his head. It was copies of these letters that had provoked him to seek this commission. They told of strange and majestically painted heathens, all-powerful kings, magic, and gold. Perhaps these people Bando searched for lived at the edge of New Spain. "You said you were the gold shaper?" asked Juan, still pacing.

"Yes."

"Tell me about that."

"I make jewelry and plates for our people to use and trade. I made them from silver and gold from the mountains," said Bando.

"Gold?" interjected Juan, stopping midstride, his back to Bando.

"Yes, much gold," said Bando.

Juan turned around with his head down, looking at the tops of his boots. "Do you know where this ship goes, Bando? It sails to a place rumored to be full of gold. It could be your home."

"Will you help me look for my family?" asked Bando.

Juan turned and paced slowly toward the pickle barrel. "If we find them, will they let you shape the gold for me?"

"Oh, yes, I can shape as much as you like."

Juan stopped again midstride. A smile parted his perfectly shaped black goatee. "I will help you."

COMPOSTELA WAS A SMALL, SLEEPY TOWN at the very edge of the map, and one of the few that did not have a native heritage. Juan and Bando arrived to find a force of two hundred fifty cavalrymen and foot soldiers already there.

The formal send-off proceedings began with a sunrise mass at the eastern edge of town. The viceroy stood in front of his amassed force after the sacrament was finished and read a short speech extolling allegiance to God, king, and Commander Don Francisco Vasquez de Coronado. Each soldier then was required to place their hand on a cross and take an oath to uphold the name of God and King Ferdinand. Juan was fifty-third in line. When the last of the men had taken the oath, they formed ranks, unfurled pennons atop their lances, and rode off the map past a beaming Mendoza.

THE FIRST WEEKS STRETCHED INTO MONTHS as the expedition snaked north through river valleys and mountain passes. Juan and Bando and the other sets of scouts rode days in front of the armada, like so many probing, bony fingers. Bando began to recognize plants and cacti the farther north they traveled, and each afternoon the young squire would venture a little farther out in front of Juan before returning with game for their dinner.

Juan took the two rabbits from his friend and asked the young man a direct question. "Bando, do you remember how you died?"

"Yes."

"Tell me, please," said Juan as he began preparing the meal.

"I fell from the cliff above my village. I climbed up the face to meet Teszin, my love, in our secret place. She was very beautiful and she loved me, but she was to marry the son of another leader. It was arranged by her father. We met in the narrow rocks in the cliffs above the village many times to be together. I climbed up early that day to wait for her in our regular meeting place. I fell asleep and when I awoke it was night, and I was alone. I tried to climb down the rocks in the dark and I fell."

"What do you remember about dying?" Juan asked.

"I remember I slipped twice. I knew how high I was and I was scared. I felt the wind blowing. It was a cold wind." Bando's eyes glazed over. "After I fell, I forgot my family for many seasons."

They both sat in silence. Juan knew then that Bando was like him. It's always in the detail of the memories. Nobody remembers the wind blowing when they died unless it was. It was enough to convince him and would convince the others as well, he thought. Juan turned to Bando as the flames from their campfire licked at the roasting rabbits. "Bando, you spoke to me before of your first family. Did you ever speak to anyone else about this?"

"Yes, I told the elders at my village in Africa. I told sailors on the first ship to Spain. And I told you," said Bando.

"How did they react when you told them?"

"The elders made me leave. The sailors laughed at me. And you listened to me."

Juan smiled. "You and I are special, Bando. Those other people are not like us. They don't remember their other families. They can only remember the families they have now, and because of that, they don't believe us and they make us leave or they laugh at us." Bando sat bathed in firelight and stared at Juan as he continued to speak. "From now on, you should not speak of this to anyone else, for your own safety and mine. Do you understand?" Bando nodded solemnly. "When you die you will be born into a new family and you will remember this life as you remember your other life now." Juan leaned forward as if to make a point. "And in that next life, you and I can meet again in different bodies. We can be friends again and remember everything we did in this life, even eating two rabbits in one night."

Bando smiled. "I want to be friends over and over again."

"We will be, Bando."

EVERY DAY, BANDO PRESSED JUAN TO RIDE a little farther in search of some landmark he could recognize. They rode on arduous ridgelines in order to gain the greatest vista of the country beyond, and it was atop one of these ridgelines that they heard a salvo from the muskets of the main force. Five shots total signaled for all scouts to return.

One of the captains, Hernando de Alvarado, had found a city over the horizon.[26] He described it as a city on top of a city. It was without temples or battlements and was the first major settlement they had encountered in weeks. Coronado gave the order: in the morning they would ride on the city. A fever of anticipation ran through the ranks that night as each man speculated on his prospects for the next day. Talk of gold and jewels broke up the drone of stone on sword.

By midmorning, they were within view of the Zuni city of Hawikuh. The multistoried city of mud walls and crude ladders looked to offer little resistance and little gold. Undaunted, they rode forward.

26. Samas's identification of Hernando de Alvarado as being a captain in the expedition and finding the Zuni people of Hawikuh is accurate. (*The Journey of Coronado*, Fulcrum Publishing, 1990.)

Figures were visible frantically running about the compound. Two men ran out from a ground-floor room and began to lay down a narrow strip of ground corn flour in a circle around the complex in what appeared to be the city's only defensive fortification.

Coronado rode up to the edge of the corn flour strip and stopped. He dismounted along with four officers, and together they breached the circle of flour and approached the earthen walls. They were met halfway by a group of five half-clothed native men. The inside of the city bustled with activity as the two groups of emissaries gestured and shouted at one another. Then without warning, a single defender atop one of the walls let fly an egg-size stone at the intruders. It tumbled haphazardly and hung in the air for what seemed an eternity before it found its mark against the white-plumed helmet of Coronado, who was knocked to the ground by the surprise impact.[27] The officers dragged their dazed commander back across the corn flour defensive line and ordered the men to charge the walls.

The Zuni defenders shot arrows at the horses and rained stones into the main body of the force. The Spaniards returned fire with crossbows and muskets. It was over quickly and the remaining defenders, along with the women and children, ran off for the surrounding hills.

The victors entered the city to find meager stores of grain and a handful of carved stones. Bando rode around the corn flour perimeter, scanning the horizon. Juan wiped at his running nose, grabbed his notebook, and sat down to begin sketching the fallen city. He was putting on the finishing touches when Bando came riding in so fast that he nearly trampled the seated Juan.

27. Samas's dramatic firsthand description of the start of the battle of Hawikuh seems to be corroborated by author Neil Mangum, who described Coronado as likely having a bruised face after being hit with stones in the battle. (*In the Land of Frozen Fires* by Neil Mangum.)

"What are you doing?" shouted Juan.

"Follow me, I know this place," said Bando, as he spurred his white horse and took off like a shot for the northwest. Juan leapt up and hastily put his pad away. They rode at full gallop down a dusty foot trail that ended at a small lake. Juan sat up in his saddle and reined in his horse, but Bando kept going at full speed right up to the edge of the lake where his horse veered abruptly to the right, sending Bando flying high out of the saddle and headlong into the water. Juan, suppressing a laugh, dismounted, and walked to the water's edge.

The lake had a white circle of salt around the edge. Dark footprints lay scattered in the white crust along the bank.

Bando emerged from under the brackish water and began to shout and laugh incoherently as he splashed around. Juan's amusement had turned to confusion. "What is this place? What are you babbling about?"

Bando turned around and shouted enthusiastically, "Juan, I came here for salt with my father. Everybody comes here for salt. Juan, I have been here before. We are close!"

"Do you remember where to go from here?" asked Juan, loud enough to be heard over Bando's splashing.

"Yes!" shouted Bando, continuing to frolic.

"Well, which way?" asked Juan, who fought back a sneeze while he was envisioning the riches Bando said awaited him.

"That way!" screamed Bando in between laughs, "That way, that way!" He pointed to the northwestern mountains.

Juan walked along the crusty bank, leaving Bando to his moment. It was a moment that Juan knew. He knew that Bando must be feeling vindicated, finally realizing he was not crazy. Juan remembered the way it felt to have the tally of all that others told him wiped clean; how great it felt to step back in time and meet yourself, realizing who you are by remembering who you've been.

He hoped Bando was experiencing the unique kind of peace that could only be found by those like him, probably for the first time in his life. Juan could not help but feel a connection to Bando as he watched him float easily on his back in the salt water and look up at an empty blue sky.

CORONADO SET UP HIS HEADQUARTERS in the vacated city of Hawi-kuh. His plan was to send out reconnaissance parties to determine if any of the neighboring tribes harbored anything of value. There were two traveled footpaths leaving Hawikuh, one to the east and one to the northwest, Bando's route home. Juan and Bando volunteered to scout for the northwest path and received orders to leave four days ahead of Captain Tovar and the main body of the second reconnaissance group.[28] Coronado came to send off Juan and Bando. If Bando was right, Juan thought, he would never see Don Francisco Vasquez de Coronado or this group again. Juan realized if he wanted it all, they would have to return alone.

"How far is it to your village?" asked Juan as they headed out.

"Five days' walk. Two with horses, I think," said Bando over his shoulder.

"Is it on this trail?"

"No, tomorrow we go north off the trail and into the moun-tains. We are close," said Bando.

BANDO RODE HARDER into the afternoon of the second day, and Juan felt they were getting closer, close enough that he had to do one last thing for his friend, should the worst happen. Juan spurred his horse to catch up to Bando and then veered his horse in front to break

28. Captain Pedro de Tovar did indeed venture out ahead of Coronado in a northwesterly direction. He ventured all the way to the edge of the Grand Canyon. (*Coronado's Expedition in 1540 from the City of Mexico to the Seven Cities of Cibola* by Merrill Freeman, 1917.)

the young man's concentration from the narrow footpath. "Bando, if anything should happen to us, if we are separated or killed, I want you to know how to find me again. Do you understand?"

"Yes, I understand."

They rode two abreast. "Do you see this?" asked Juan, pointing to the tattoo on the back of his right hand between his thumb and forefinger.

"Yes, I see it."

"It is the symbol that all members of our new family use to mark ourselves. It is called the Embe. If we are killed, you will remember what I'm about to tell you, just like you remember this place and your first family. There is a city called Zurich next to a lake in the mountains of central Europe. All the members of this family always gather in this city on the longest day of summer. To the north of the lake and west of the river, there is a redbrick church. The back door of this church has this symbol on it," Juan said as he pointed to his tattoo. "This is where we meet, and if we are killed, it is where I will meet you when we both remember again. Do you understand?" Juan asked.

Bando nodded.

"We will meet in the summer when the days are the longest."

Bando nodded again.

"Good," Juan said, contented with his directions. "Good."

"What does this place look like, what are we looking for?" asked Juan.

"It is a city in the rocks," Bando said, pointing to the top of a bluff in the distance, "that rock."

The village came into full view past the next bend in the trail. At the base of the sandstone bluff lay a vertical community of some thirty buildings of different sizes built one upon another to make a three-story tall collage of stone walls and ladders perched beneath a great stone cliff stretching upward for one hundred feet.

Bando stopped his horse and dismounted. "This is the village of Latsei. This is my home." Bando's voice cracked as he spoke the words.

Juan tightened the leather straps on his armored breastplate and secured the chinstrap of his helmet. "Are you ready?" asked Juan nervously.

Bando nodded, not looking away from the village, "Leave the horses, we will walk from here."

THE VILLAGE STARTED TO BUZZ with activity as they approached. They had been spotted. Juan turned toward the village again, and Bando was already fifty paces ahead and walking briskly toward the gathering crowd of villagers, his head held high and his shoulders back. Fifty to sixty villagers gathered at the edge of the compound. Men, women, and children dressed in animal hides and adorned with silver and gold retreated into a semicircle around Bando as he approached them. The young African appeared as a black beacon in the growing crowd. The children fearlessly walked up and touched his ebony skin, then drew back and giggled. The taller children and some women reached out to touch his strange woolly hair. Bando turned around and Juan could see small rivulets of tears glistening on his face. Bando was too emotional to speak but he didn't have to. His eyes relayed the message to Juan as the crowd continued to close on him. When Bando spoke in their native tongue, the crowd took two steps back in unison as an older man with a wide golden neck collar shouted a sharp reply as he strode through the parting crowd.

Juan couldn't understand the words, but the tone was unmistakable. He placed his hand on his sword and started to slowly step forward when a clear female voice called out from the crowd. Bando spoke with this older woman in his remembered tongue as Juan carefully watched at a distance from the open part of the semicircle that surrounded his friend. Bandò spoke with her for several long minutes until she wiped the tears from his face and embraced him. They continued talking and hugging one another until the older man who looked like their leader stepped between them. He spoke directly to Bando, who listened respectfully before uttering a few simple-sounding words and touching the large gold collar the chief wore around his sinewy neck.

Juan watched from the edge of the village as the chief nodded and the woman led Bando out of sight into the maze of the rooms in the pueblo.

The chief locked eyes with Juan and began to walk toward him with the remaining villagers two steps behind him. Juan stayed calm but kept his hand on the grip of his sword as they approached. They slowly encircled him and marveled at his black beard. They approached in the same manner as they had with Bando, only with less apprehension, and reached out to touch the cold metal of his polished breastplate and helmet.

The chief stood in front of Juan and uttered one long, unintelligible sentence.

Juan stared at him without blinking and in that moment decided that he would say nothing. This had always worked before whenever he had ventured into lands that had never seen races other than their own. It always lends an air of superiority and piousness, he thought, which was better than looking like a scared stranger.

The chief spoke again, the syllables sounded the same as the ones before. Juan stiffened and threw his chest out underneath his polished armor. The chief looked puzzled and stepped halfway around Juan, looking at him as one might admire a sculpture. Juan followed him with his eyes only and stood completely still. The chief straightened in front of Juan and smiled. His teeth were yellow and irregular and looked as if they belonged to a man in his sixties, not the forty-year-old standing before him. The chief smiled broadly as he continued to speak at Juan.

Juan looked around and noticed the expressions of the faces in the crowd had changed from inquisitive to cordial. They began to talk among themselves and point at him as the leader continued speaking. Juan felt the corners of his mouth begin to curl upward, his hand still on his sword. He smiled out of self-preservation, still expecting an unseen arrow or stone to come at any moment. He forced a pensive grin back at the chief who grew brighter and showed even more of his yellow teeth. The chief stepped back toward the village and motioned for Juan to follow. Juan took a step and the crowd shadowed him all the way to the center of the village.

The chief stopped in front of a rug-covered doorway and then went inside. He returned with a woven blanket, which he laid on the ground in front of the portal to his house. He sat cross-legged on the blanket and motioned for Juan to do the same. When Juan sat, the bottom of the breastplate hit the tops of his thighs and pushed up uncomfortably against his chin. He forced the same stiff smile.

Two women appeared from the crowd with painted earthen cups and a large, hollowed-out yellow gourd. The younger of the two women sat the cups down on the blanket in front of them and began to pour a thin, milky-colored liquid from the gourd into the cups in equal amounts.

The chief raised a cup to his lips and drank deeply, finishing it in one long swallow. Juan mimicked the chief's movements, but when the cup was at his mouth, he inhaled deeply through his nostrils and immediately gagged in revulsion. It smelled like spoiled grain. Juan felt the crowd watching him. He exhaled sharply through his nose and forced down the concoction. The chief laughed as Juan fought to keep his drink down. The young woman filled the cups again before Juan could stop her. Juan turned green and blinked his eyes erratically. He knew he would never get another one down. But the chief covetously raised his cup again, beckoning the Spaniard to do the same. Juan watched as the chief finished his second cup and then placed his empty cup in front of Juan's full one. Juan took his cup and filled the chief's. Juan turned his cup upside down on the blanket and another man picked it up and presented it to the young woman who filled it. The chief and the second man drank again as the crowd stirred at Bando's reappearance with the older woman.

"Is everything all right, Bando?" Juan shouted in Spanish above the noise of the crowd. Everyone in the crowd gasped when Juan spoke for the first time.

"Yes, we are safe now," answered Bando as he appeared through the onlookers. "This woman," Bando said, reaching back for her hand. "This woman is Teszin. She is the one that I loved before. She remembers the things I did and said to her when I was called Nez-Lah. She is a good person and she wants me to stay. The chief does not like me. He thinks I am an evil spirit. But he does like you," Bando said, looking at Juan. "He thinks you are a good spirit because you wear the shiny metal like he does."

"What should I do?" Juan asked, looking at his squire for help.

"Keep wearing your armor and helmet. Do you see the gold collar he wears?"

"Yes," Juan replied.

"I made it for my chief when I lived before with these people. The chief says that if I can make another one in the same amount of time, then I must be telling the truth about who I am."

"Can you do it?"

Bando smiled broadly, showing his large teeth, "Yes, I can do it. They are letting me use my old workshop and supplies and they are letting me sleep there. You should camp at the edge of the village," Bando said, pointing to a clear spot under the edge of the overhanging cliff face. "I need to start on my work now."

JUAN SET UP CAMP ON A SMALL, BARREN RISE outside of the village, facing the overhanging cliff. He awoke the next morning to find the village already alive with activity. Women came close to his camp for water. Children played and shouted in small groups. He left to check on Bando at midmorning. A crude bench and stool sat in the corner of the workshop. Juan walked in without speaking and watched Bando work. His squire had exchanged his tattered shirt and pants for the deer-hide coverings the villagers wore. He sat hunched over his bench and worked very quickly, his hands reaching for stone tools blindly. The sound of stone on soft metal rang in the room and out the open door.

"Good morning," Juan said, startling his focused friend.

"Look, Juan, I am making it," Bando said with excitement as he showed off his progress on a wide band of gold. "I can still do it!"

Juan reached out a hand and touched the smooth surface. "It's wonderful."

"When I finish this collar, it is yours. That chief does not deserve two of them," he said with a smile. "I will shape others too, as I told you before," said Bando with a laugh as he reached for his tools again.

LATE AFTERNOON THE NEXT DAY, Juan walked out of Bando's shop with the second collar, a perfect copy of the chief's, weighing heavily around his neck. Bando and his model walked with a gathering crowd to the chief's door. The chief emerged from behind the tapestry with the original collar on and began to shout to the crowd.

Bando smiled at Juan as fresh tears welled in his eyes. "It is done. There will be a festival tonight."

THE MEN OF THE VILLAGE brought dead brush in from the surrounding area and prepared a bonfire in the center of the village. The chief lit the pile at sunset, and the villagers sat in a circle around the growing fire. Teszin, Bando, and Juan all sat as guests of honor next to the chief. Across from them sat five young men, each with a different sized drum. The young men and women of the village gyrated and undulated in unison as the drummers began their rhythm. Bando danced in perfect synchronization with the others, and Juan could only tell him apart by his physical appearance. The roaring fire threw gigantic dancing shadows onto the surrounding sandstone cliffs.

Bando danced around the fire to where Juan sat and pulled the conquistador into the circle. Juan joined in and mimicked the motions as best he could while being careful not to dislodge the new golden collar around his neck. He danced in the circle in front of Bando and behind the chief, keeping his eyes on the figure in front of him for cues to the strange dance. That was when he noticed that the chief was not keeping up with the others. The leader danced more slowly with each revolution, stumbling occasionally, until finally his tired legs gave out altogether on the fifth pass, and he collapsed facedown in the dirt, motionless. Teszin was on the ground at the chief's side in an instant. The drumming stopped, and Teszin rolled the chief over onto his back. He regained consciousness quickly but motioned that he was too weak to continue and that the festival should continue without him. Teszin and two of the dancers carried him back to his home, and the dancing continued until the fire died.

JUAN AWOKE THE NEXT MORNING to find the villagers clustered near the chief's door. He walked past Bando's open door on the way to the chief's. Bando was not at his bench.

Juan pushed his way into the chief's room and found Teszin kneeling beside him. She blew smoke into his face as she chanted.

The chief lay on his back with his tunic removed. His chest, neck, and arms were covered with thumbnail-sized white blisters. Bando stood behind Teszin. Juan leaned over and touched Bando on the shoulder, motioning for him to follow. They walked back to the workshop.

"What's wrong with the chief?" asked Bando.

"A fever has him."

"What will happen to him?"

Juan shook his head and mustered the courage to lie to his new friend. "It is difficult to say, perhaps it is best to leave him to the healers in your village." Juan knew the disease and he knew there would only be a few that would survive. He had seen it run through Samarkand, leaving only two thousand of the original thirty thousand inhabitants fumbling around in a vacant city. Half of the survivors were children, and it didn't leave anyone over the age of thirty-five.

"Yes, you're right. I'll get back to my work," said Bando, readying his tools.

"I'll be back later to check on you," said Juan as he left.

Bando worked quickly and tirelessly throughout the day and late into the night. The sound of his stone tools working was only interrupted when Teszin would bring in a basket of food. Later that day three more fell ill and awoke the next morning with the same white sores as the chief's.

BANDO CAME OUT TO JUAN'S CAMP at midmorning the next day. "The chief wants to see us," said Bando sullenly. He walked slowly back toward the village. Juan put his sketching materials away and followed him. They arrived to find Teszin with the chief again.

"How many complain today?" Juan asked Bando in Spanish.

"Twenty-two complain of the sickness," Bando replied and pointed to his abdomen to show the location of their pain.

The chief raised his head and spoke to Bando before motioning for Juan to come closer. He tried to speak to the Spaniard, but his lungs gurgled deeply before he could finish. Juan stepped forward but was careful not to touch him. Bando turned his head away and left the room as the chief spoke at Juan between increasingly shallow breaths. He wished he knew the language so he could know this man's dying words. Minutes later the chief stopped speaking and then stopped breathing altogether. He stared into Juan's eyes. Juan smiled. Breathless, the chief showed his irregular yellow teeth and closed his eyes.

Teszin folded the chief's arms across his chest and straightened his loose-fitting robe as Juan stepped outside.

Juan noticed as he walked back to Bando's shop that for the first time the village was silent. His young squire was inside working feverishly to distract himself, tossing his tools down as he finished, only to pick them up from the same pile when he needed them again. "What did the chief say, Bando?"

Bando was shaking visibly. "He thinks I came back for their souls, he asked that I take only his and go." He threw the curved stone he was working with against the wall. "He's wrong! Wrong, wrong, wrong!" he shouted angrily.

"I know, Bando, I know," Juan said, picking up the curved tool and handing it back to him. "Bando, it seemed to me that the chief didn't like you." Bando nodded his head, his eyes still cast down. "Well, now that he is gone, perhaps things will be easier for you here." Bando took back the tool without looking at him.

"I've seen this sickness before, in Asia," Juan continued. "It usually kills only the old and weak, like the chief. The others should recover in a few days, and in a few days we'll be gone."

Bando looked up at Juan, his eyes watering. "You will leave soon?"

"Yes, and I want you to come with me."

"I cannot," Bando said, shaking his head. "I traveled too far to find this place again."

Juan thought about his options. "Well, I must leave soon to meet Tovar and tell him that there is nothing here, so that he will pass and you can live here in peace."

"You would do that?"

"Yes, I will, but I need more of these to take with me," Juan said, holding up a piece Bando had just finished.

"I can make more in two days and two nights."

"In gold?"

"Some will be gold and some silver. I have supplies of both metals," Bando said, pointing with a stone hammer to clay pots in the corner of the workshop.

Juan walked over to the crude earthen pots and looked inside to see an amazing sight of gleaming nuggets and what looked like frozen spills of shining liquid metal. "Bando, how did your people get all of this?"

"We find nuggets for some, and sometimes we throw the shining rocks in the fire and collect the metal. This is only what they have found in the last few years. Is that enough for you?"

Juan kept his eyes locked on the shimmering metals in the simple pots. "Yes, it will be enough."

BACK AT HIS CAMP, Juan picked up the pad again and continued to sketch the outline of the buildings and the cliffs above. *If he left tomorrow and stayed away from the village, perhaps he could leave without contracting it,* he thought as he drew the details of two young men carrying a body to the edge of the blackened circle where the bonfire had been.

Bando worked late into the night, oblivious to the worsening condition of the stricken villagers. He slept in his shop and ventured out late the next morning to find seven bodies laid out parallel to each other near his door.

Juan sat at his camp, pad and charcoal in hand, occasionally looking up at his subjects. Juan looked up to find a weary Bando staring with disbelief at the seven bodies. They looked as if they might have gone to sleep on the ground next to each other, if it were not for the numerous blisters visible on their exposed skin.

Juan watched Bando look around at a city that appeared abandoned. Bando walked past a row of dwellings and saw a small girl peeking around the edge of a doorway. He remembered her from when he first arrived. Her hair was cropped short like a boy's, but there was no mistaking she was a girl. She looked to be about five years old. She had been one of the first to approach him. Bando slowly walked up to her and crouched down to match her size. She peered around the edge of the portal so that only half of her small face showed. Her tiny arm crept around the corner and clung to the outside of the stone wall. Bando placed his hand on the wall for support about six inches from hers. He looked at her for a few seconds and smiled. The girl smiled broadly so that a dimple appeared on her visible cheek. Bando moved his hand along the wall toward hers. Her dark eyes looked at his hand and then back at his white teeth. She let go of her hold on the wall and grabbed Bando's fingers. She giggled when she touched him. He breathed a sigh of relief and clutched her tiny hand.

Bando hadn't noticed the curtain rustling behind her and was startled when the girl's mother exploded from behind the tapestry and jerked the child back into the house, shouting all the while. In an instant, he was alone again. There was no activity in the village except for the rustling of other curtains.

Bando turned around and returned to his shop, which once more rang with the sound of his stone tools on soft metals.

TWO NEW BODIES had been placed at the ends of the other seven when Juan stepped into Bando's shop late in the afternoon. He had completed seven more gold bracelets and a silver medallion. Juan walked over to the newly completed pieces and donned one of the bracelets.

"How many more have died?" asked Bando, still working.

"Two," answered Juan, removing the bracelet.

"Will more die soon?"

"Yes, Bando, they might all die," Juan said, trying on another bracelet. "We might die too if we don't leave."

Bando stopped working and looked up at Juan.

"I'm going to leave tomorrow. It's not too late for you to come with me. It's probably safer than staying here," Juan said.

"To go where?"

"Zurich, to meet the others I told you about."

Bando walked to the open door and looked at the nine bodies. "No, I'm staying. I want to fix this."

"What's the point, Bando? There's nothing you can do for them now."

Bando pointed out at the corpses. "These are my people," he said, on the verge of tears.

Juan stepped in front of Bando and placed his hands on both sides of his dark face. "Come with me tomorrow. Let's leave this place together, like we came," Juan pleaded. "Bando, please, there is so much for me to show you, so much you don't know about yourself."

Bando looked into Juan's eyes but was not moved. He reached up and gently pulled Juan's hands away. "No, my home is here. I'm staying."

"Fine," Juan said, turning toward the door in frustration. "I'll see you again anyway."

Juan walked around the bodies outside Bando's shop and noticed that the latest one had a bracelet almost identical to the one he had tried on.

BY SUNSET, THERE WERE FIVE NEW BODIES laid next to the others. The wailing, which had been sporadic before, now came from all parts of the village. Cries rang out from every quarter, only to be answered in like kind. *I hope it's not too late*, Juan thought. *I've traveled too far not to get it now, and the gold would finally be enough to compete with the others in the Cognomina.* He could feel his opportunity was here, and tomorrow he would finally join their ranks as an equal.

THE COLLECTIVE LAMENTING OF THE VILLAGE finally stopped at first light. Juan sat up wide awake as the dawn broke brilliantly on the cliffs above Latsei. He had stowed most of his gear for the ride south when he caught sight of them.

There were a dozen of them, half women and half men. Some of them waved crude clubs over their heads. They moved in a cohesive group toward Bando's door. Teszin was not among them.

Juan began to walk toward the mob. *No, no, no, not today*, he thought, *any day but today.* "Bando, look out!" he shouted in Spanish.

The mob formed a semicircle around the entrance at the same time Juan drew his sword. The group hesitated a moment at the doorway before three men and a woman entered silently.

Bando was shouting at them as he emerged and struggled against the two men holding him by his upper arms. Juan broke into a full run toward the village. Bando tore free from their grasp and fell at the feet of the angry villagers. Bando got to his hands and knees and looked up in time to see the club blow that landed squarely above his left eye, knocking him flat again. "Teszin! Teszin!" shouted Bando in between kicks and club blows to his head.

Juan screamed, and the mob stopped attacking and turned toward the noise in unison. Juan was about fifty feet away and running rapidly while waving his sword menacingly overhead.

Bando got to his knees and looked out through the legs of the mob before crawling along the outside wall away from them. Juan slowed his pace when the group turned their attention on him.

The man with the club turned and saw Bando get to his feet and start running. He swung and caught Bando against the ear, knocking him off stride and into the wall. The rest of the crowd turned and pursued his black shadow around the corner. Juan could see that Bando had a ten-pace head start and was pulling away from them as he ran up a trail leading into the cliffs.

Juan stopped at Bando's empty doorway and bent over to catch his breath. Two small pools of blood dried into the dirt at his feet. He looked inside and saw the finished pieces. They were piled together at the end of the workbench, glistening brilliantly even in the dim light of morning. Juan couldn't help but step inside to get a better look at them. The pile was larger than he dared think it would be, heavier too. His mind raced between the tasks in front of him: the gold, the mob, Bando, the gold. He walked backward out the door, not taking his eyes off the pile. When he was clear of the doorway, he closed his eyes and threw his head back.

"Bando! Bando!" Juan's shouts echoed back off the cliffs. "Meet me by the horses and we go!" He shouted the words slowly so that each one had a chance to echo back before the next rang out.

He couldn't see Bando, but he saw that the crowd had stopped pursuing him up the trail. Confident that his friend had escaped, Juan reentered the shop, grabbed a rug, and began placing the finished pieces onto it. He worked as quickly as he could without risking damage to Bando's works. Taking another rug from the corner, he emptied the clay pots of their brilliant nuggets onto it, grabbed each of the rugs by their four corners, and left with his heavy makeshift bags.

Outside, Juan scanned the surroundings for the angry mob and did a double take at the nearest corpse. His eyes locked on the fibrous rope around the dead man's waist. He untied it and pulled at one end until the man's weight shifted and it came free. When the corpse rolled back into its original position, Juan noticed a silver bracelet on the man's wrist. He leaned over and spun it around on his arm, examining it, but being careful not to touch the clammy brown skin. Juan searched the bodies until he found another section of rope and removed it. Sword in hand, he quickly made a small buttonhole incision in each of the four corners of the rugs and laced the ropes through to increase the capacity of each bag. He listened carefully for the crowd, they were quieter now. He bent over the first corpse, removed the bracelet, and put it in the nearest bag without taking his eye off the necklace on the third woman over. He removed the necklace and stepped carefully to the next woman for her gold collar.

Juan was about halfway through the bodies when he heard a woman's shrill scream behind him. He turned suddenly and lost his balance, almost falling into the bodies at his feet. It was Teszin, looking up to the cliffs above the village.

Bando stood at the edge of the cliff, his black figure silhouetted against the blue sky. His deer hide shirt was torn off, and blood ran from his head onto his shoulders and chest. The wind atop the high wall whipped at his hair. Bando didn't respond to Teszin's shouting but instead stared directly at Juan who held a large silver necklace still partially draped around a dead woman's neck. Juan threw his head back and squinted against the bright-blue background to return Bando's stare. He smiled up at Bando.

"Are you ready?" Juan asked in a tone just strong enough to echo up to him.

Bando closed his eyes and pitched forward off his perch. He stayed aloft only for an instant, but he looked graceful and confident, as if he knew he could fly all along, and had waited patiently to demonstrate his unique skill. Juan saw him fly for that graceful instant then closed his eyes tight as Bando started his descent. Teszin let out a scream that echoed well past the impact. It took longer than Juan thought it should have for Bando to land, or perhaps his friend really had flown in that instant of grace.

17

". . . Or perhaps Bando really had flown in that instant of grace."

"Why did Bando jump?" I asked. The numerous faces looking out from the portraits on the walls seemed to want an answer as well.

"I've often thought about that myself. You'll have to ask Poppy."

"She spoke about you before we came to Zurich," I said.

"How so?" asked Samas.

"I asked her if the one that found her acted as advocate in her Ascension. She said no, and I sensed there was some animosity on her part."

"You're right about that. She's been hostile to me ever since the village. I'm accustomed to it by now. Besides, I understand where it comes from."

"Where does it come from?" I asked, wanting him to say it.

"Well, part of it is obvious, because of what I did that last day at Latsei. But there's something else, something with edges that don't dull with time. I think she feels responsible for their deaths. If she hadn't gone in search of them, they wouldn't have been exposed to the disease that was latent in both our bodies. No matter how you look at it, you cannot dispute the fact that she was responsible."

"You can't blame her for that," I said in her defense.

"No, no, no," Samas said, shaking his head. "Don't confuse culpability with responsibility. They're different. It's not her fault, but you can't deny it wouldn't have happened the way it did had it not been for her. She was responsible. That type of responsibility, no matter how you justify it, is your own in the end. You can't help but carry it around with you. My only transgression is that I was witness to hers. Is there nothing in your lives for which you have felt responsible in the same way?"

Samas's simple question cut to the very core of my being. At times it seemed as if everything I did could be reduced down to the lowest common denominator of reacting to the guilt I felt about the fire that killed Bobby's mother. It didn't matter that I'd inherited the guilt from unknowing benefactors. The feelings were as real as my own. They were mine now and equated to who I was and what I thought I—what I thought *we* were. "Are we evil?" I asked, looking at him.

"Which we? We humans, we Reincarnationists, or you and I, specifically?"

"We Reincarnationists. Are we evil for replacing the lives of those before us?"

A look of surprise came over his face. "I've never thought of it that way. Why do you ask?"

"Samas, I've wrestled with that same kind of responsibility and guilt for a few years. I've known for some time now that I could never absolve myself of those sins, and recently with meeting you and Poppy, it has occurred to me that there may not even be a need for absolution."

"That's right," he said emphatically. "That's the way it works. Personally, I think you're ahead of Poppy in that respect."

"What do you mean, ahead of Poppy?"

He leaned back as if exasperated that I didn't get it. "As Reincarnationists, we are burdened by the knowledge that we, and only we, are responsible for our actions. We know there is no divinity on whose shoulders we can lay the blame for any errors in our lives. Normal humans embrace the divine precisely because they can burden other shoulders with their sins. We know differently. But it's important for you to realize that we live in their world, not the other way around. So when you speak of absolution, you will eventually find that your desire for the quarter it can provide and your knowledge of the truth are incompatible. The only vehicle within which you can find solace is responsibility.

"Unrighted wrongs can haunt you like a specter. I believe they haunt Poppy to this day, which in some ways explains her actions. You may be haunted as well—only you know for sure. Ultimately, there is only one way to exorcise such a fiend; you must accept him." Samas leaned forward in his chair and stared at a painted face on the wall. "You must look him square in the eyes without turning away, taking in every unsightly nuance of his repellent face and say: 'Yea I know thee brother, and love thee as I love myself, for we are one and the same.' That fiend will have an unspoken, yet unassailable mastery over you until it is assimilated. It is only when you embrace that dark brother that you can know true freedom."

I absorbed the import of his words in a long silence.

Samas continued. "So when you ask me if we are evil, I have no choice but to answer in the affirmative. I must answer so, for we are evil, even if we only have the capacity for it. The evil is latent within us. It lives and breathes in that twin fiend. Does that answer your question?"

I nodded. "I think so. There is something else I'm curious about."

"What's that?"

"Why did you take the pieces off the dead bodies at Latsei?"

"Oh, dear Evan," he said with a sigh. "The answer is within your own question. They were dead, so what did it harm? Besides, they had no idea of the jewelry's value."

"That doesn't make it right."

He shook his head, disappointed. "Right or wrong is not the issue. I can live with it. That's my point." He finished the last of his wine in one long drink. "Let me ask you something. What would you do if a similar opportunity at fortune presented itself?"

He asked the question knowing I couldn't answer. "I can't say. I'd have to be in the situation."

"That's right, and that's the decision I made when I was in that situation."

"Fair enough," I said, refilling both glasses.

"It was the money from those artifacts that started all this," he said, looking around at the faces and landscapes on the walls. "It started *me*, you might say. It allowed me to become what I am now. There's something else you will come to know in time, and it goes back to what I said earlier. Life is not worth living unless you can fully enjoy it, and unfortunately, for most neophytes like yourself, amassed wealth is part of that. I don't have to tell you the difference money can make in your life, the way it sweetens it, the way it brings certain refinements into focus."

"This certainly *is* refined," I said, looking around at the walls.

"I told you this collection is my passion, what I didn't tell you was why."

"Go ahead," I said.

"All the pieces in this room have one thing in common, me. I commissioned all these works and modeled in several of them. I've had at least one portrait done in each of my last six lives. That's the kind of refinement I could not live without," he said with the resolve of a confirmed addict.

"What was there?" I asked, pointing to the blank rectangle on the wall behind me.

"A portrait of me. Done by Jan Vermeer in 1670."

"What happened to it?"

"It was taken from me, stolen from my home in Amsterdam by the Nazis in 1940. These two pieces were in the house as well," he said, pointing them out on the wall, "but the SS captain in charge took only the Vermeer. I searched for that one piece for five years, until the end of the war. Ramsay helped me and set an appointment with a Luftwaffe Colonel in Berlin to pick it up in the closing days of the fighting. The Nazis, as it turned out, hid a large portion of their plundered art in the tall antiaircraft towers around Berlin.

"The deal was ten thousand British pounds and a boat ride from Rostock to neutral Sweden for the colonel in exchange for the Vermeer." Samas sighed and continued. "I readied two hundred thousand pounds, hoping that maybe the colonel was sitting on more stolen works. I even had a truck at the ready to cart off everything I expected to find, but the Red Army beat me to him. I arrived in time to see them loading an eastbound truck with narrow crates. I sat huddled in a dense thicket nearby and watched them work, hoping to catch a glimpse of my portrait."

"Did you see it? Was it in any of the crates?" I asked him.

Samas continued, "Time after time, the soldiers would reemerge from the open portal at the base of the ominous concrete tower carrying yet another narrow crate with a black eagle stenciled on the side. The colonel's body lay in his bloody uniform at the base of the vacant spire. After an hour's labor, they removed the last crate, closed the truck, and retreated to the east."

I was already completely absorbed in Samas's story. I nodded for him to continue.

"It must have been another full hour before I ventured forth from my secluded vantage to inspect the scene. They had taken everything. I searched every corner in hopes of finding some lead to follow. Hours later, I found a manifest in handwritten German among the scattered papers littering the floor. It detailed everything that had been moved into the tower over the past three years, everything that I had seen being carted away in a mere hour. I wept as I read through the list. Evan, the contents of those crates made the collection in this room look like a show of freshman projects at a third-rate art college. My portrait was on the list.

"It took me twenty years to find it within the Soviet Union. It was in storage in the Hermitage along with all the other items on the German manifest."

"Where is it now?" I asked.

"In 1985 it was given by General Secretary Gorbachev to the government of Italy, along with several other pieces as a political offering. The Italians keep them leased out to various galleries around the world, though the dolts have it listed as 'doubtfully' attributed to Vermeer."

"Won't they sell it to you?"

"No. I've made a generous offer each year for the past three years. They've refused every time. I even left the last offer open, letting them put in whatever figure they wished, and still they were not interested. I never thought men could be so unreasonable," he said angrily.

I could see that the idea of his money not being able to buy something was poignantly irritating to him. "Is that not contradictory to what you said about wealth sweetening life? After all, you said this is your passion, what keeps you going," I said, baiting him.

"That's where you're mistaken, my friend. It is precisely my wealth that will bring the portrait back into my possession."

"How's that?"

"I'm going to contract someone to steal it. My life will be

sweetened, and the vehicle is still money, there are no two ways about it. Never underestimate the potential of kinetic money," he said, laughing.

"How much would it cost to have it stolen?"

"I would go as high as two million American dollars."

"That's a lot of money," I said, trying to match his cool demeanor.

"That depends on your frame of reference," he said, fixing his eyes on me. "It's a reasonable price for a part of your own identity. You'd do the same thing in my place. The point is that you must seize an opportunity when it comes, because it can last you several lifetimes. My situation with Bando at Latsei is a good example."

Poppy's episode with Joubert was a good example too. "I heard your story. I heard Poppy's story about the mirror concession, but the world is a different place today. Those opportunities are harder to come by."

Samas shook his head slowly from side to side. "Opportunity is everywhere, Evan. It could be in this room with us right now. It could even be on the wall behind you," he said, staring at me.

I turned to look at the blank spot. "Are you suggesting that I steal it for you?"

He held up a hand in objection. "Don't put words in my mouth. I'm not *suggesting* anything. My situation is this: I've tried to be reasonable with the Italians about a purchase and now I am at the point that I must contract someone for a handsome sum to procure it, a sum that will ensure I have plenty of interest. That in itself is an opportunity, and since I am merely contracting services, it is of no importance whom I contract, provided I have confidence in that person's abilities," Samas said, letting the words linger between them.

"I have confidence in your abilities based on who and what you are, so I'm offering it to you first, as a gift. You don't have to answer now, just think about it. Think about what two million dollars could do for you now and in the future."

I studied the wine in my glass and absorbed Samas's statement before speaking. "What is it about me that makes you think I am qualified to steal a painting?" I thought about my testimony in the grotto only days before, remembering the multiple criminal acts I had admitted to being involved in. "Do you think I am qualified because I've committed other crimes?"

"As have we all, Evan," Samas countered. "I just confessed to you that I have stolen from the dead. I think you are qualified because the job is an easy one based on vulnerabilities in their security system, and I know it would be easier for you than for others, based on reasons you likely haven't even considered yet. Listen," he said, leaning forward, "I'm going to have this done regardless of your involvement, so don't worry about my end. You just think about whether or not you want to participate. Any choice offered is always yours to accept or to reject, I just think back to when I joined the Cognomina and the adventures I chased in order to be able to keep up with the others. As I think back, I often wished I had been given a head start on the life I have now," Samas said, swirling his wine.

"It's getting late, and I want to go to bed," he said, walking to the keypad next to the door. "Are you ready?" he asked.

I nodded.

He punched in the code and we both stepped through in one motion. "I'll see you in the morning, Evan. Don't forget to use the mosquito netting, I'll have the windows open tonight," he said, walking away.

I ENTERED MY ROOM and walked straight for the sliding door. The air outside was cool, and the stars shone brilliantly in a black night sky. Samas's offer struck me as generous after the initial shock had worn off, very generous. Two million could certainly sweeten anyone's life, but there was something else it could do as well, something Poppy and Samas had both alluded to, perhaps without even knowing it. It could make me their equal.

I was a guest in his house now, but in time the disparity in our positions could no longer be ignored. I would be looked upon as an inept younger brother, incapable of living up to my older siblings' achievements. That's the challenge about entering into a new group, you automatically find yourself in a new peerage, and if I were to be confirmed back in Zurich, I knew I'd find myself at the very bottom of it, looking up at everyone else.

I walked back to the bed, parted the sheer netting, placed my roll of bills in a pile on the bed, and counted it. I had three thousand eight hundred and seventeen dollars out of the original five thousand. Stacked up, it was about an inch high. Funny, it would have seemed a large amount of money only two weeks ago. I began to see what Samas meant by having a frame of reference.

I assumed, upon confirmation, that I would have room and board at the St. Germain as long as I liked, but that was only a temporary solution. Eventually, after this small stack of money ran out, I'd have to either find some kind of income in Zurich or go back to my old world in LA, which seemed more perilous than Samas's proposition in many ways. In all honesty, criminality was not a major concern. He was probably aware of that as well. Perhaps that's why he made the offer in the first place. I knew the life I'd known before would welcome me back, waiting with open, atrophied arms.

I folded the stack of bills and put them back in my pocket. The faint, lazy notes of a cello crept into my room as I turned off the lights, drew the netting closed, and tried to quiet my racing mind until sleep came.

THE MORNING AIR IN THE HOUSE was thick with simmering spices. I awoke from dreams of Samas's offer. The colors of the guest room seemed duller than those of my dream world.

I found the source of the smell in the kitchen. Zohra stood on tiptoes peering into a large pot on the stove. "What are you cooking?" I asked.

"I prepare couscous three times a week and offer it to the poor at the mosque in Rabat. I made some pastries early this morning. They're on the table if you're hungry. Samas was awake a few minutes ago, he should be down shortly."

I took a pastry and walked around the living room, looking at the charcoal sketches on the walls. I stopped in front of a small sketch in a plain black frame. Its yellowing, cracked edges betrayed its age. In it, a young, semiclothed black man lay asleep next to a white horse. I studied it at length, looking for some seed of the person I knew, but try as I might, I couldn't put the two together.

"Hard to believe it's the same person," Samas said behind me.

"Yes, you're right."

"I liked her much better back then." He walked into the kitchen. "How long will you be gone?" he asked Zohra.

"Until late afternoon, but I left a rack of lamb in the oven for your lunch. Will you boys be okay this afternoon?"

"I think we'll manage," he said, peeking into the oven. "We have a few things to discuss."

"Good. I'm leaving. I'll see you later."

Samas came over to where I sat in the living room. "How did you sleep last night?"

"So-so," I answered.

"Did you have trouble with flies?"

"No. I was up most of the night thinking about your offer."

"And?" he prompted.

"I think it's very generous and very tempting. How long do I have to decide?"

"A while, until after the Ascension is finished, obviously.

Just give it some thought. I'll let you know before I offer it to anyone else."

"That's fair enough. Why is this one piece so important to you?"

He nodded. "I remember I first saw Vermeer's work in a bakery in the village of Delft in Holland. I was an Englishwoman living in Amsterdam at the time and was on my way to Zurich for the Sumerfest."

"Sumerfest? What's that?"

"It's a yearly get-together we have on the summer solstice. Gluttony and decadence are the rule of the day. In the old days, when the Cognomina first started, the original members would meet every summer solstice in the same location in order to stay in contact with one another. In time, the Sumerfest became a tradition."

"Is the Sumerfest still held today?"

"Yes, it just happened a little over a month ago. Anyway, back to the painting. I stopped in Delft for bread and saw an exquisite painting hanging behind the counter of the bread shop. It was small, but miraculous in its detail. It depicted a young woman seated at a table admiring a glistening loaf of fresh bread. The only way to properly describe it is to say that it looked like a modern color photograph. The shadow, the tone, the contrast, the detail, were all perfect. He was better than Da Vinci and even Caravaggio. The baker told me the man's name, Jan Vermeer, and that he lived in Delft. Vermeer, the baker told me, had offered him the painting for half a year's worth of bread but that had been a year and a half ago. I knew I had a real find in this sleepy town. The baker told me that Vermeer came into his shop every Monday, and I left word that I wanted to commission his services and would like to meet with Vermeer two Mondays hence at midday in the bakery."

"Did Vermeer actually show for the meeting?" I asked.

"I returned on the appointed day, eager to see the hand that could work such miracles. He was small in stature and wore his best threadbare clothing. An immodest man of meager means, he carried himself with the confidence of his art.

"'I understand you wish to purchase my services?' he asked in a mousy voice that matched his small frame. He looked to be in his midforties and had frizzy hair poking out from under his paint-smeared hat. I hadn't expected such an exquisite artist to look such a mess," Samas said with a chuckle.

"I asked him if he took commissions, and he told me he had not yet, but would hear my offer. I gave him my name, which at the time was Emily Restoud, and told him I would like him to paint my portrait and that I was prepared to offer him five hundred silver francs," Samas continued.

"Did Vermeer accept the offer?" I asked.

"Oh, yes. Vermeer accepted and asked when I would like him to call on me. I told him to come to my address in Amsterdam in one week and gave him a hundred silver francs for supplies." Samas smiled as he recalled the happenings of that day.

"He arrived exactly on time, canvas and supplies in hand. He was quite attractive in his paint-spattered clothes. Over lunch, he told me about himself. He'd studied with no one and had no explanation for his natural talent. We spoke until sunset. I put him up in a guest room so that we could begin early the next morning."

"How many days did it take him to complete the work?" I asked.

Samas replied, "The only problem with Vermeer was that he worked at a painfully slow pace and would keep me in the same position for hours on end. I really think he had no concept of time when he held a brush. That's probably what accounted for his mastery of detail. I had little patience to begin with, and modeling for him was close to unbearable." Samas sighed with a faraway look in his eyes as he recalled the next part of the story. "The whole painting took a week of ten-hour-long sessions to complete. I remember I would get tired after only half an hour in the same pose and would try to secretly adjust my position. Each time I did so, he would patiently set his brush down, stand up, walk over to me, and gently reset my position. His small elfin hands felt comforting, and in time I began to shift positions on purpose so that he would have to come over. My ruse worked in my favor, because by the fourth day, we were lovers."

I was beginning to understand why the painting was so important to Samas. I nodded for him to continue telling the story.

"He called the painting *The Rendezvous*.[29] It seemed appropriate. That was the only picture I have of myself as Emily Restoud, and I kept it hanging in my Amsterdam home for over two hundred and fifty years. I bought three more works in the fall of 1674 at five hundred silver francs apiece. He, of course, delivered them to me personally. He died the next year."

I leaned forward in my chair. "Do you have an attachment like that with all the pieces in your collection?"

"I have a history with all of them, and they are all very precious to me, but *The Rendezvous* is special, as special as Jan was. I loved him and I loved that portrait. It hung in the same room in which he painted it for over two hundred fifty years. I lost a part of myself when those bastards took it off my wall."

"Where is it now?"

"It's in Tunis," he said, brightening up. "The Italians have

---

29. The Vermeer described by Samas here and detailed by the author later in the notebooks as *The Rendezvous* does not match the description of any of the artist's known thirty-seven paintings, though nineteenth-century art critic Thore Burger details sixty-six additional works attributed to Jan Vermeer in an essay detailed in *Thore-Burger and the Art of the Past*. Burger is widely credited with having "discovered" the seventeenth-century Vermeer.

leased it to them for one year. I intend for it to be in my possession by the end of that year. Security in the Tunisian National Gallery is suspect."

"How will you go about finding someone if I choose not to help you?"

"There are several people I can contact. This certainly wouldn't be the first piece I've procured outside of an auction house," he said in a sly voice.

"Do you have a plan for how to do it?"

"Yes, I do." He smiled wide and leaned back. "Do you know much about security systems?"

"Some," I said, thinking back to the planning of dozens of arson jobs.

"I know a few things as well," he confessed. "But I know everything about the system in the National Gallery in Tunis."

"What are you talking about?"

"I have a master schematic of the security system as well as a floor plan to the building. I bought them from an inside source last month. That's how I know their security is suspect."

"All right," I said, smiling. "What does the place look like?"

"Wait here, and I'll show you." He came back minutes later, a tight roll of blueprints clamped under his arm.

I studied the blue-and-white paper over his shoulder as he rolled them out on the kitchen table. "It's not very big."

"I know. Small country, small National Gallery." He chuckled. "That works against us, really. It has been my experience that it's easier to steal something out of a large building than one of this size."

I noticed his use of the plural when he spoke, but kept it to myself. "What's that?" I asked, pointing to a small red sticker on the floor plan.

"That's where *The Rendezvous* hangs."

"How do you know?"

Samas turned his head and looked at me seriously. "Because I went there to see it, twice. I went to see it, but also to look for the cameras and sensors on this schematic."

"And?"

"And it's all accurate, right down to the guards' schedules. The piece hangs right here and looks the same, as though not a day has passed," he said, placing a chubby finger on the red dot. "But do you want to know what's ironic? It was taken off my wall in 1940, traveled God knows where on its way to Berlin, went to Moscow for forty years, and then went to Rome, New York, Singapore, Johannesburg, and finally Tunis. And after all that, it still rests in the same gold-painted oak frame I put it in as soon as the oils had dried."

"That's amazing."

"We're lucky about that."

I looked at him curiously.

"I put it in the frame and I know how to get it out."

"Is getting it out of the frame part of your plan?" I asked.

He nodded.

"Let's hear it."

"Basically the plan is to get in, get the portrait out of the frame, cut it off the internal frame, and get out."

"What security measures are in place to prevent a would-be thief from doing just that?"

"All the doors are alarmed, as are the windows and skylights. Two guards are on duty at all times and make rounds every twenty minutes. The entire floor plan is covered by motion detectors, and the paintings hang on pressure-sensitive mounts that are wired into the main alarm system."

"It doesn't sound very suspect to me."

"Believe me, it is. The only real problem is getting out of the building."

"I'm listening," I said.

"The first trick isn't getting in, it's staying in." A wave of child-like enthusiasm washed over his face as he began to describe the details. "The gallery closes at six p.m., Sunday through Thursday, and is only open for private parties on Saturdays. You'll need to go into the gallery about five or five thirty on a regular business day, carrying a small fanny pack with the tools you'll need. Minutes before six, you'll go into the women's bathroom and wait."

"Don't they check the bathrooms?"

"They do, but they only check them after the gallery is closed, and only one at a time. The guard will check the men's room first. When you hear the guard enter the men's room, quickly and silently go to the trashcan standing between the men's and women's bathrooms and climb inside. It has a top that will conceal you and is large enough for you to sit in comfortably for several hours. You should wait inside until dark, when the guards settle into their normal routine, then get out of the trashcan after you hear a guard pass. If they keep to their schedule, you'll have twenty minutes to get the painting and get out."

"How do you know they check the men's room first?" I interjected.

"Because I tried it. Besides, it's habit. When you think of going to the bathroom which one do you go to?"

I nodded. "I see your point."

"What about the motion detectors?"

He shook his head. "They're only for show. They can't use them because of the rats."

"Rats?" I asked.

"Yes." Samas laughed. "There is an ancient saying about the city of Carthage, where modern Tunis stands today. It's said that if the foreigners ever outnumber the original inhabitants of Carthage, the rats, that Hannibal will return from the dead to protect them. Hannibal still rests, they say, because the rats outnumber the humans five to one. I saw four inside the gallery as large as house cats, and if they're in there during the day, then there will be ten times as many at night. I do business with curators all over the world, and they all complain of the same problem with the types of sensors used in the gallery, the systems cannot be adjusted to discern between mice, rats, and humans. Modern systems use lasers that scan the room down to six inches above the floor to avoid the problem, but the Tunisians don't have that system."

"Okay," I said, conceding his point for the moment. "What about the pressure-sensitive mounts?"

"Ah." He held up his finger. "I had my source find out their manufacturer, then I called the company as a prospective buyer and queried the sales representative about the unit's shortcomings compared to their more expensive models. His sales pitch was quite enlightening. The gallery's units are sensitive to a positive weight, usually five to ten pounds. They are programmed to trigger the alarm if that five-to-ten-pound burden is removed but they won't trigger the alarm if they are burdened with more weight. This is how they can be overcome." He drew on the edge of the floor plan as he spoke. "We simply fashion a noose out of fishing line and drape it behind the frame. Once on the mount, you simply attach a ten-pound weight to the line and carefully remove the painting from the mount."

"It's so simple, it's ingenious," I said.

"Thank you," he said with pride.

"What's next?" I asked.

"The painting needs to be taken out of the frame. It's held in place with two small nails in each inside corner. They could be easily removed with a small hammer carried in your backpack. When you have it out, cut the canvas along the back side of the internal stretch frame. If you cut it so, it will leave enough material for me to have it restretched to its normal size. After that, you roll it up so that the painted surface is on the inside, and you leave."

"I'm sure the guards are just going to let me walk right out the front door," I said sarcastically. "Why couldn't I spend the night in the trash can?"

"I had thought about that, but it won't work. A new shift of guards comes on at midnight. They empty the trash and mop the floors just before the gallery reopens.

"Leaving is going to be the trickiest part, because no matter how it's done, you will set off the alarm when you exit the building. The upside is that you will already have the piece. It doesn't really make much difference, but I think this door might be best," he said, pointing to the floor plan. "It exits to the alley. From there, all you have to do is get to the harbor. I'll have a boat and crew ready to take you to that beach," he said, pointing out the living room window to the sea.

"What about the two million?" I asked.

"What about it? An account will be opened for you upon your confirmation. When I receive the painting, I will have Diltz transfer the money to you. You can call to confirm it if you want."

I nodded slowly. "Your plan seems easy, too easy for the two million dollar price tag attached to it."

"Well, of course, you would think so. The risks for you aren't the same as those for a normal person, but that doesn't mean you should do it for any less."

"Why would you say the risk is less for me?"

"This is what I mentioned last night. The two million is for someone who has a fear of incarceration if caught. You don't have that fear because of what you are. If you are caught, you need only to take your own life and wait to remember who you are when you come back. The money would be waiting for your next Ascension. Their prisons can't hold you. That's why it seems so easy for you."

It hit me then, it really was that simple. Their justice couldn't touch me. His offer became even more tantalizing, knowing it was within my power to commute any sentence if it came to that.

That kind of freedom was intoxicating. It was like a declaration of independence from *everything*. I began to see why Samas enjoyed this life as he did, and it made me yearn for it. "I like the way you think," I said, turning to the floor plan.

"Thank you. I've been working on this plan almost every day for three months. It's solid."

"I understand what you mean when you say that their justice can't touch us. But with that in mind, why don't you steal the piece yourself?"

He erupted with laughter as he placed his hands on his hips. "As if I could fit this girth inside a trash can. Besides, the sum I offer is affordable. It's no bargain, but it's not unreasonable to me. I've thought about stealing it myself and I think I would derive much more satisfaction if I could. But I can't ignore that the odds of success would be much higher if a more qualified man did it. *The Rendezvous*'s return will be satisfaction enough. What I really wanted was—" An abbreviated ring from the phone cut him off midsentence. He turned an ear toward it and waited for a second ring. It rang again fifteen seconds later.

"I know who that is," he said. He walked over to the phone. "Mr. Diltz, what a pleasant surprise," he said into the receiver before the caller could speak. "I understand. Thank you. Good-bye." A serious cast came over his face as he hung up the phone and walked back to the table. "They want us back tomorrow. They are close to a decision."

"That's quicker than you thought," I said.

"Yes it is, but it's probably a good sign. Diltz said they want one more session with you first."

"What do you think that means?" I asked.

"We're about to find out, Evan."

18

Familiar Zurich welcomed me as though it had been patiently awaiting my return. The nearer we got to the Hotel St. Germain, the more aware I became of the feelings I'd had since Diltz's call. Curiously, it wasn't fear or anxiety. It was confidence. I knew what I was and knew that I could convince them.

Samas stood beside me before the panel in the grotto. The gallery against the curtain was filled to capacity. Several new faces looked out at me. Poppy's was not among them. Torches crackled above the murmur of voices as the five members of the panel walked out from behind the curtain and sat down. Their expressionless faces told me nothing.

"Mr. Michaels," said the old man, leaning forward. "Are you and your new advocate prepared to continue with these proceedings?"

"Yes," I answered.

"Very well. There are a few things we still need to ask you," he said, nodding to the other judges.

"Hello, Mr. Michaels," said the professor, smiling warmly. "Welcome back." The gaps between his long, narrow teeth appeared like missing boards in a white fence. His unusual warmness boosted my confidence even further.

"Thank you," I said.

He nodded. "Let's jump right in. I want to know if you remember the name of the judge who convicted you, as Vasili, in 1946."

I took a drink of water from the tall glass in front of me. "I will never forget his name, Comrade Vlad Dukchov of the Committee for the People's Justice."

The professor circled something on his notes, while the members to his left and right looked on. "And the name of the commandant at State Camp number four?"

"Colonel Stohla."

"Do you remember the names of any of the guards?"

"I was only close to two guards, Similenka and Bukar. After I'd been there for three months, I mentioned to them that I'd fought with Captain Hoxa. Bukar and Similenka arranged for me to become a trustee so that I could work in the laundry and tell them stories about the captain."

"That's fine." He looked down at his notes. "There's one thing I'm curious about that we haven't touched on."

"Yes?" I said, preempting him.

"What happened to the relationship with your parents in Minnesota when you realized you were different?"

I looked over at Samas and pushed my chair back as I began. "There's a bird that I read about in school called a cowbird.[30] This bird secretly lays its eggs in the nests of robins. The eggs incubate and hatch along with those of the host bird. When they're young, cowbirds look

---

30. This was written as bird of the cow (птица член крава) in the notebooks. There is no word for this in Bulgarian as the cowbird is found only in the Americas.

like robins, so the hosts feed them, nurture them, and protect them as if their own. It is only when the young birds begin to mature that the parents can tell that the cowbird is different. At that point the host spurns the impostor, who is now strong enough to survive on its own. The impostor doesn't know where he comes from or why he is different; he only knows that he is. That's what it has been like for me, until now," I said, panning across the panel and gallery.

Several long seconds passed before the professor broke the silence. "Mr. Michaels, your first advocate told us she found you after you'd set a fire. Tell me about fire."

I shifted in my seat, feeling the watchful eyes of the panel. "She said all there was to say, really. I started the—"

"No, I don't want to know about a specific event. Tell me about fire, Mr. Michaels."

"I'm not sure I understand what you mean," I replied.

He leaned forward against the bench, all signs of his smiling friendliness gone. "You and I both know exactly what I mean."

I held his stare as long as I could, desperately not wanting to cave. I believe I could have, had the other eyes not tipped the scales to his advantage. I nodded in deference and lit a cigarette, carefully placing the still-burning lighter on the table in front of me. I looked at the flickering, wheat-colored fiend as I spoke. "The first time we met, it was an accident. I was unprepared for what it would do, unprepared for its appetite and its anger. Ever since it got the best of me in that first meeting, I have made sure that I always meet it on my own terms. I know exactly how it will act now. I honestly think I know it as well as I know myself. I keep bringing it back because I want to prove that I can beat it, to show it that I'm no longer the helpless child that cowered under the bed in fear. I had remembered it and knew what it was. And ironically, until now it had been the only thing that knew what I was, because it remembered me. It has been both my confidant

and my foe, and in a time of confusion, it was my only constant."
I looked up to find the judge smiling again.

"I've heard enough," he said, looking at the other judges.

"I agree," said the old man. "Let's take a short recess." The five
walked off the bench and past the curtain behind the gallery.

Samas stretched his legs under the table and turned to me.
"I must say, I think you did a marvelous job."

"Will they return with a decision?"

"Oh, yes," he said, looking over at the gallery. The fifteen
to twenty people had started to mill around and speak to one
another. Some appeared to be laying bets.

"Thanks for your help," I said to him.

"You're welcome."

"Hey," I said, tapping him on the arm. "What's this party
afterward going to be like?"

"That's the spirit," he laughed. "Oh, they're not to be missed,
but I warn you, there are some odd characters in our family."

"Where's Poppy? I thought everyone would be here for this."

"She will be here. She'll be in trouble if she's not." He turned
his bulk toward me. "Have you thought any more about our plan?"

"A little," I admitted.

He shifted back in his seat and looked straight ahead. "What
will you do after you're confirmed?"

"I'm not sure, probably go to Bulgaria."

"Have you thought about where you will go after that?"

"Stay here or go back to Los Angeles, I'm not sure."

"That money would surely come in handy no matter where
you go."

"You're not telling me anything I don't know. I'd just like to
make sure I have a home for the funds before I get them," I said
in a nervous laugh.

"We're almost there. It looks like they're ready," Samas said, pointing to the old man as he came through the opening between the curtain and the wall. The other four came through behind him and took their seats. Samas put his hand on my arm and gave me a quick reassuring wink. It was all I could do to stay still in my chair. My racing heart felt like it might burst at any moment.

The old man straightened in his chair. "I think it would be appropriate to apprise Mr. Michaels of our guidelines before we give our decision." Several groans rose out of the impatient gallery. The old man whispered to the professor, who stood up and spoke.

"Listen carefully, Mr. Michaels, as these guidelines are binding on anyone who enters the Cognomina. Members are sworn to maintain complete secrecy about our existence, our condition, and our collective. They are obligated to introduce any suspected new Reincarnationists into the Cognomina. They must agree to obey any summons the Cognomina issues to sit as a judge or juror. They are required to will their assets to the Cognomina, whereupon death, ten percent of those assets will be surrendered to a community fund for expenses and maintenance of our facilities, an accounting of which is given at the Sumerfest. They must agree to undergo a trial in each successive incarnation so as to prove their identity and reclaim their assets. They must agree to take a turn as administrator of Cognomina funds and activities. And finally, they must pledge eternal allegiance to the other members of the Cognomina. We are a family, Evan Michaels, and we care for each other as such. Are those conditions acceptable to you?"

I kept my mouth closed and nodded, half afraid that my voice would crack.

"Very well," he said, sitting down.

The old man stood up slowly, his weary voice echoing through the room. "By a vote of four-to-one, we have determined that the neophyte, Evan Michaels, is what he claims to be and will be welcomed into the Cognomina as our brother."

I exhaled a long sigh of relief. Samas put his arm around me and hugged tightly. A mixture of cheers and groans erupted from the gallery as wagers were settled. I leaned back and wiped at the tears welling up in the corners of my eyes. Mr. Diltz was the first to come over.

"Congratulations, sir, I knew you could do it. We're all so very happy to have you."

"Even the ones betting against me?" I laughed.

"Well, sir, they were giving quite long odds against you failing."

I smiled. "Thank you for everything, Mr. Diltz. Thank you both," I said, putting my arm around Samas. "I owe you both so much. I couldn't have done it without you."

"Don't underestimate yourself in this. You were marvelous, sir," said Diltz.

"I agree," said Samas.

I sighed again, trying to catch my breath and calm myself. "Let's get on with this party," I whispered to Samas. "I need to blow off some steam."

"As you have most likely been made aware of," the old man said above the gallery noise, "we all have a name that identifies us by our personality, intellect, and character." He lowered his voice as the crowd noise subsided. He looked at me as he continued. "These bodies we have now will wither and eventually fail us. They are transitory. When it dies, the name by which the outside world knows it dies as well. Every one of us will see each other in many different forms, but we will know the transcending, surviving individual within, and that is what our names are for. Do you have a name by which you would like to be called?"

I gripped the cane and stood up to address him. "I do. I choose Evan, for I start in this journey as the man I am now."

"So noted," he said. "Welcome, Evan."

The members of the gallery left their seats and walked toward me. Their collective voices came as one continuous greeting.

"Welcome home, brother."

"I'm glad you made it."

"Evan, I like that name. It suits you somehow."

"I've so looked forward to meeting you, Evan."

I acknowledged their comments as quickly as I caught them, trying to shake as many hands and greet as many faces as possible.

"Attention, can I have your attention please!" shouted the oldest judge. "Before we get carried away, I think it would behoove us to begin Evan's welcoming ceremony."

"Oh, that's right, I almost forgot," the bun woman said.

"Yes, the welcoming ceremony," came a voice from the back.

"Places, please," said the tall professor, motioning everyone close to the opening in the curtain next to the stone wall.

The crowd assembled in two parallel rows, like receiving lines. Three members of the panel came over, leaving the old man and the professor standing near their seats. I stood between the two lines, unsure of what to do. I looked back toward the panel for guidance but was distracted by the black, semiclothed figure that emerged from the other side of the curtain and faced me. He was enormous, standing almost a foot taller than me. His ebony arms were as thick as tree trunks. He wore only a pair of baggy, fire-red silk pants and a tasseled fez.

I smiled nervously and took a step back. He closed the distance between us just as I looked over and saw the tall judge with glasses remove the spear from the wall above the panel. I quickly moved away from him, but it was too late. The large man's black python arms enveloped me and in seconds I was immobilized with my arms pinned behind me. The tall professor, spear in hand, walked casually to the opening at the end of the lines as I bucked in a panic against the giant's viselike grip.

"What in the world is going on here?" shouted Samas behind me.

Undaunted, the man walked toward me with the spear until the point touched my shirt. I stopped bucking and remained still for fear of throwing myself onto the weapon. The sharpened edges of the polished steel tip reflected light from the flickering torches. I panted in excited, shallow breaths as I looked up into his eyes.

"I don't understand," I said weakly. "I thought I passed the Ascension."

He took a step back, as if to get a good thrust at me. "You did pass," he said, showing his irregular teeth. He took one more step back and swung the spear over his head and back toward the wall, severing a rope tied off to a cleat set into the masonry.

The heavy curtain raced toward the far wall with an echoing mechanical clamor that sounded as if the entire grotto were collapsing. The retreating divider revealed the rest of the room. Four long colonnades stretched into the dark distance. Crackling torches lit the near part of the expanse and showed off long tables overflowing with platters of food and pitchers of wine. Numerous large pillows lay scattered on large Persian rugs in front of a low, medieval-looking stage, complete with curtains and torch lighting. A large square swimming pool lay beyond the prepared banquet tables like a still pond.

The black giant released his grip, and I collapsed to the opaque marble floor in a nervous pile. The mechanical echoing ebbed to reveal uproarious laughter. I looked up to see the contorted faces in the crowd howling uncontrollably.

"Welcome to the Cognomina, Evan."

"What in the hell is going on?" I asked, rubbing at my strained shoulder.

"Sorry about that. I hope Chance didn't hurt you," said the laughing professor, motioning to the giant behind me. "Diltz told me that you were concerned about the spear, so we decided to have a bit of fun with it."

"They dragged it out of me, sir," Diltz said, his gaunt face breaking into a narrow, pensive smile.

"Don't forget about me," said Poppy, as she walked out from behind a column.

"Ah, yes, I almost forgot. Poppy was involved too. It was her turn to organize this," the spectacled judge said.

Poppy walked up to me seductively. The long, close-fitting black evening dress she wore reached past her feet and made her look as if she had risen directly out of the black marble floor. Its low-cut back showed off the colorful tattoo. "No hard feelings, I hope. Besides, you deserved it for being such an ass," she whispered.

"Brothers and sisters," she shouted. "Let the festival begin!" She clapped her hands twice, and colorfully dressed musicians walked out from behind the numerous pillars and began to play.

"Gypsies!" bellowed the giant behind me. He walked among them, taking a smiling young woman with a tambourine and spinning her like a top.

"It is almost the twenty-first century, Chance. They prefer to be called Romani," Poppy countered.

Other young women skipped about and sang while the men played guitars, violins, and accordions. They were dressed in multicolored layers of silk scarves and sashes. The men wore their best shabby suits over dingy shirts.

"Where did you find them?" asked a woman in the back.

Poppy turned around to address her, the silver-tipped cigarette holder in her black-gloved hand. "Ramsay has many Roma friends. I had a devil of a time getting them here on such short notice, since most don't have any legitimate government ID."

"But how?" asked the old man, concerned.

"Don't worry. I chartered a plane in Rome and had them

blindfolded until they got down here. They don't even know what city they are in," she mused.

"They don't look like they care," said the professor, admiring them as they joyfully played and smiled, walking in and out of the crowd.

"They shouldn't care, considering what they cost. I think you should find them quite entertaining."

"How wonderfully delicious," came a laugh from the back.

"Yes, they are here for our enjoyment, but they're not everything. There are more surprises, something for everyone, you might say."

"Even me?" asked the androgynous Asian from the panel.

"Yes, you too, Mr. Ing," Poppy shouted.

"Something for everyone," the black giant repeated in a bellow as he swept the tambourine girl into the air. "You've outdone yourself this time," he said to Poppy.

"Perhaps we should begin with introductions before this gets going," Samas shouted above the music.

"I second, and would like to be the first to do so," said the tall professor, stepping toward me. "I am Auda." He smiled warmly and stepped aside.

"I am Kress," said the woman I'd met in the dining room, her hair again pulled so tight into a bun it seemed to defy physical laws. "Welcome home."

"My name is Mr. Ing," said the mysterious Asian man.

"I'm Mara," said the beautiful young redheaded woman in the tailored business suit.

My pulse quickened when the giant spun his girl away and stepped in front of me. "My name is Hazard," he said in a French-Creole accent. "But everyone here calls me Chance." His bass voice boomed in deep echoes above the folk song.

"Nice to meet you," I said, taking his mammoth hand.

"No hard feelings, I hope," he said as he slapped me on the shoulder he'd strained.

One by one, they stepped forward to introduce themselves.

"I am Etyma."

"I'm Ramsay."

"Jens."

"Kerr."

"Nestor."

"Dilmun."

"Castor."

The fusillade of names and faces overwhelmed me. Their accumulated lifetimes rushed at me with each new handshake and embrace. I was awash in the attention and acceptance that for so long had eluded me. The empathy they showed brought forth in me a wellspring of emotion finally strong enough to subdue the fierce face of fanatic individualism I'd shown the world since I'd found myself to be different.

I wiped at the tears just as I saw the old man's silvery white hair and beard behind the crowd. They parted for him miraculously, as though they could feel his presence behind them. "Congratulations, Evan. I am called Clovis."

"Thank you, Clovis," I said, looking into the sorrowful gray of his eyes.

"I would say you don't know how happy I am to be here," I said, raising my voice to address everyone, "but of course, all of you do know, which makes this moment all the more precious. I don't know how to convey the way I feel right now, but as I look at your faces, I realize I don't have to. I'm home." I exhaled deeply and noticed that the musicians had stopped playing. The sound of breathing and crackling torches carried to the tops of the columns and bounced back.

"But most of all, I'm glad you didn't have to kill me," I

laughed. The uproarious hoots and howls were instantaneous. The musicians rejoined the commotion as the crowd edged onto the worn carpets encircling a red velvet chaise lounge in front of the crude stage.

Poppy walked up to me. "You're not home yet, junior. There's still the matter of the tattoo," she said, holding out a fingerless leather gauntlet which laced closed on the underside. She pried it open for me to slip my hand into, and I noticed the black ink worn into the edges of the Embe-shaped template on the top. I moved close to her as I slipped my hand inside.

"I didn't catch your name in the introductions," I said in a coy whisper.

She held the sheath firmly until my hand bottomed out, looking up at me as she turned it over to lace it. She pointed to the velvet couch. "Evan, you saw my name in my crypt. I am Nez-Lah, but everyone here calls me Poppy."

I sat down just as Auda emerged from the crowd carrying a well-worn leather pouch secured with three irregularly carved bones that acted as buttons. His long, brown, bony fingers unfastened the buttons and pulled back the top leather flap to reveal an odd assortment of ink-stained bone tools. They looked like alien toothbrushes. The slim wooden handles held rows of miniature, tiny, needlelike bone shards that stood up like plastic bristles. Unknown eons of black ink coated the tips of each tiny fang. He sat down and placed the tools on the red velvet between us then took my hand and inspected the leather-sleeved template before mixing oil and a dark powder in a black-stained, white ceramic crucible.

"Is that the ink?" I asked.

"Yes, it's my special formula," he said. "It's a blend of ash from a poplar, roasted and ground tamarind pits, and just enough poppy seeds to take the edge off."

"Will it hurt?"

"At first, but it will go numb after a while. Just lie back and enjoy yourself," he said, gently easing me back.

The crowd milling around me occupied itself in conversation as Auda took hold of my arm. He removed a small inscribing tool and dipped it into the crucible, bathing the white teeth in the tarry mixture. I turned my eyes away as he began and looked at a beautiful young woman in the band who sang in melancholy tones to the men strumming guitars, squeezing accordions, and playing violins. Her long, pleated, billowing skirt shuffled as she swayed to the song's slow rhythm.

Auda's first blows with the scribe came as a shock. The pain was acute, as if each small shard cleaved a nerve ending in two.

He worked quickly, breaking the skin over the whole area of the template. My right hand began to throb. He wiped the wound clean of blood and excess ink every few minutes with a tattered rag that looked as old as the rest of his tools.

"How are you doing?" he asked, reaching for a larger tool.

"I'm okay. It's starting to get numb."

"That's those magic seeds at work."

"Hey, can I get some wine over here!" he shouted above the end of the song.

The girl I'd watched earlier moved onto the short stage alongside six others. The men still wandered about the room, the sounds of their different instruments waxed and waned as the echoes bounced off the near and then the far end of the grotto.

One of the house staff hostesses I'd recognized from upstairs came through the crowd toward us carrying an urn and two silver cups.

"Right here!" shouted Auda. "And make sure mine is full." She obeyed and filled them both to the top. She bowed respectfully and walked away. "And don't forget where I'm sitting Leipshein," he said, spitting the words through clenched teeth.

He turned up the cup, finishing more than half in a few swallows. "Ah, that's better. I'll need a steady hand for the outside edges."

I took a long drink and turned to the stage as Auda went to work again. I involuntarily flinched at the pain from his larger instrument.

"Stand still," he said firmly. "We still have a way to go yet."

I nodded and stared back at the stage. The women's necklaces of shiny coins captured and reflected the torchlight flickering at the foot of the stage. Chance and several others danced on the carpets in front of them.

"How's it coming?" asked Samas, a large stein in his hand.

"Fine," said Auda, not looking away from my hand.

"How much longer until you finish? Clovis says we can't eat until you're done."

"I'll be finished when it's done," snapped Auda.

Samas peered over at his progress then mumbled and walked back to the stage.

"How old are you, Auda?" I asked as a song ended.

He smiled and kept working. "I'm older than dirt, but not as old as Clovis," he laughed.

"I heard he is the oldest."

"That is correct." He reached for his cloth. "I don't know exactly when I started. The years weren't recorded where I lived my first two lives."

"Where was that?"

"Scythia the first time, then West Africa. I would guess that was about seventeen hundred years ago."

"Do you make all the tattoos?" I asked in a wince.

"All except my own. Mara did this one. See where she messed it up?" he asked, pointing to a crooked edge.

"Yes. Who found you?"

"Chance did." He motioned to the giant.

I took another long swallow. "Really? What's his story? I mean, he's so big."

"He hasn't always been that size. Samas is the one who should have gotten a body like that," he said, laughing.

"How old is he?" I asked, watching the giant man's smiling face as he danced head and shoulders above the others.

"Old. It's rumored that he can read your thoughts."

"What?" I said disbelievingly.

"Yeah, that's what I say too. He claims he's been practicing since the Crusades, but I think it's a ruse. I think he says that to establish an advantage when gambling. He's quite the gambler.

"Anyway, I'm getting tired. Let's break for a minute. More wine!" he shouted.

"I'm curious about something," I said, looking down at the emerging tattoo.

"Yes?"

"Earlier tonight, you said we both knew what you were talking about when you asked me about fire. How did you know?"

"Easy," he said, craning his neck in search of the wine stewardess. "I knew there had to be a reason, Evan. There is a reason for everything. This is true for normal people too, only they don't know why they love or hate, why they feel they must rape, or kill, or why they must burn. But I knew that you would know why."

"I'd never told anybody why."

"I figured you hadn't. That's why I asked."

"I don't understand."

Auda turned and looked me in the eye. "Evan, it's important for you to be open with us, not because we want to know everything about you, but because you need to feel that there is no reason to keep anything from us. Take a look around you, man. This place is your home. These people are your brothers and sisters, your confidants. That is why we choose to associate with one another. Without that, we have nothing.

"You had all but passed at that point, Evan, I just wanted to draw you out of the shell I knew you were in."

"Do you have any compulsions like that?" I asked.

He chuckled. "They begin to pile up on you after a while, but fortunately they fade somewhat with time." He stopped another hostess who walked by with a large Middle Eastern water pipe. She uncoiled the mouthpiece from around the body of the pipe like a long slender snake. He placed the yellowing ivory tip between his teeth and sucked until air bubbles rumbled deep inside the pipe.

"Oh yeah," he sighed, allowing waifs of opium smoke to escape his mouth as he spoke. "There it is."

I shook my head when she offered the mouthpiece to me.

Auda grabbed his tool and went to work on my hand again. "What were we talking about?"

"We were talking about knowing the causes of compulsions."

"Yes. Their psychiatry would be obsolete if only they could remember," he said, pointing up to the ceiling and the world above.

He was probably right about that, but I thought he had underestimated how blissful some measure of ignorance might be.

"I was beginning to think you didn't like me," he said to the wine hostess as she approached and poured from her urn. She walked away with a stride full of indignation as soon as she'd finished.

"She doesn't seem to think much of you."

"Oh, she's just new," he said dismissively. "We can be a tough crowd." He took my hand and continued his steady rhythm with the tool. "What will you do after this?" he asked.

"After this festival, you mean?"

"Yes."

"I'd like to travel a bit, go back to Bulgaria maybe."

"Sounds like a good start. What will you do after that?"

"I can't say. Why do you ask?" I prompted back.

"Curiosity. This is a fresh start for you, at least it felt that way to me when I came in."

"Yeah, I know what you mean, but I'm not sure what I'm good at other than pyromania."

"It's not a question of ability, it's a question of want." He looked up into my eyes. "What do you want, Evan?"

I didn't have to think long for an answer. "I want to have fun, to travel and enjoy what this world has to offer."

"That's what I'm talking about," he said enthusiastically. "There, it's finished. Take it off, please," he said, tapping the hard leather of the sleeve.

I eagerly loosened the laces along the inside of my forearm. "That was quick."

Auda slowly tilted his antique wine goblet back until it was completely inverted. "Keep in mind, I've had quite a bit of practice."

I slid the sleeve off and marveled at the fresh figure on my hand. The black-affected area was inflamed and rose above the surrounding skin. The tattoo's crisp edges held the ink perfectly. "It's beautiful," I mumbled to myself.

"Be sure to get some ointment from Mr. Diltz later," he said, standing up. "I've finished!" he shouted. "Let's eat."

"Finally."

"It's about time."

"Not a minute too soon," came several grumbles from the crowd.

Poppy clapped her hands twice and the musicians took up a softer melody. The crowd moved as one mass toward the long banquet tables set up at the edge of the carpet. Samas was first in

line. Cane firmly under me, I walked over to the lengthening line
flanked by Auda and Ramsay.

"How did it turn out?" Ramsay asked.

I held out my hand as though my pride had manifested itself
in the form of that black symbol.

"It looks good."

"It usually does," said Auda, handing us plates.

I walked down the table, overloading my plate like the others.
I turned and found them taking seats on the carpet in front of the
stage. They sat in a semicircle around a makeshift chair fashioned
of gold-trimmed black pillows.

"They're waiting for you," Ramsay whispered. "The place of
honor is yours tonight." She pointed to the seat in the center.

I sat down to numerous smiles and salutations. They lounged
on large pillows and stuffed their mouths with food and wine like
Roman senators.

Poppy walked out onto the stage as the last ones settled in
their seats. "Your attention, please. Our entertainers for this
evening are, among other things, an acting troupe, and they wish
to present a play in your honor," she said, fixing her eyes on me.
"Ladies and gentlemen, the Brojka Performers."

I clapped politely along with the others as the actors walked
on stage. Their costumes looked much the same as their clothing:
bright and mismatched. They performed in their own language
and spoke their lines loudly to overcome the sounds of silverware
on white china and Samas's moans of delight. The cacophony
of clanging plates, clinking glasses, murmured speech, and bad
acting in an unknown language would have been an assault on
any normal person's ears, but to me, it sounded like angels singing.
I set my fork down, closed my eyes, and took in all the sounds,
visualizing each person in my head as I picked out their individual voice. I opened my eyes to see Chance reclining on a pile of

a dozen large pillows, his large fingers dropping small morsels of food into his open mouth.

"What is it they're presenting? I can't understand a word," Chance shouted back to her. The three men on stage increased their volume in response.

"*The Scarlet Pimpernel*, I think," replied the woman.

"How long is it?" asked Chance.

"It's dinner theater," said Poppy from a seat at the foot of the stage. "They will go on as long as we keep eating."

"Hurry up, Samas," said Auda and Chance at the same time. A muffled response came from his stuffed mouth.

The actors abruptly took their bows and walked offstage as soon as the last plate was sat down, and the people lounging around me looked at Samas as they applauded the exiting actors.

"Bring a dessert tray by, will you?" he said to a passing hostess, oblivious to everyone's stares. "And some brandy, a large bottle."

"I'm going to start a game before the actors come back," Chance said to Ramsay and Auda in a soft voice. "Who wants to play some cards?" he bellowed. Six voices called back to him in the affirmative. "Mr. Diltz, do you have a table we can use?" he asked.

Poppy stood up and walked onto the vacant stage. "Hold on a moment. There is still the matter of the gifts to be taken care of first."

"Quite right," said Auda. "Best do it now. We might be too far gone to do it in an hour. Don't forget what happened last time."

"Don't look at me," Chance said defensively. "I didn't start it. Hopefully, no one brought a pet this time."

"Enough," Poppy said sharply. "You will begin, Chance."

"Evan," she continued, "for centuries it has been a tradition to welcome a new brother with gifts. Each one offers something special."

Chance rolled over and stretched his arm out toward me. I

held my hand out underneath his ham-hock-size fist and caught a pair of small white dice as he dropped them.

"I had them carved from the bones of my last body. I was very lucky back then. They should bring you luck too."

"That's it?" asked the bun woman, Kress, in a belch of opium smoke. "That's not much."

"Hey, no jest. Those things will really bring luck. I should know."

"He might have a point there," said Samas.

"Let's see what you have," Chance said, challenging her.

Kress stood up and bowed to him in jest. "Gladly, sir." She walked over to me, almost stumbling twice. "I present to you, Evan, a unique gift of my own design, made with my own hands," she said, wiggling her fingers.

She removed a black watch from her wrist and handed it to me. The band was made of delicately interlinked polished black rectangles. Its smooth surface had an uncertain depth and seemed to absorb light. The ingeniously designed clasp concealed itself under the opaque surface when closed. The face was made of the same polished black with green arms of inlaid jade pointing to the four directions in the shape of a Maltese cross. It was fashioned to look like a watch but had no hands or movements.

"I don't understand," I said, puzzled.

"Time means nothing to you now," she said, leaning against a column for support. "You are no longer held captive in its irons. Beauty and pleasure are the only metrics by which our lives are measured."

"Here, here!" cried a voice from the back.

"This is beautiful," I said.

Kress smiled and staggered back to her pile of cushions.

"Samas, why don't you go next?" Poppy said from the stage.

"I'm a little busy right now," he said, eyeing a large tray of desserts. "Call on me later, please."

"Would you like to go next?" she asked Mara, the young red-haired woman in the tailored suit.

"And follow her?" she said, pointing to Kress. "Not likely." Several laughs rang out.

Ramsay stood up beside me and grabbed an ornate sword from the side of the short stage. "I have a traditional gift, one which many of you have taken advantage of in the past." She turned toward me. "Evan, you don't know my history the way the others here do, but I am a warrior who has fought in many battles. I have fought alongside most of the people in this room when they have needed my help."

"That's an understatement," Chance said, chuckling.

Ramsay handed me the sword, handle first. "Evan, I offer my sword as a symbol that I will fight by your side when you need me. I know it may not sound like much now, but as many in this room could tell you, at the right time, it is worth more than any fortune."

"That's no joke," said Mr. Ing.

"Thank you," I said, holding the polished weapon in my hand. "Hopefully, I won't have to use it."

"You're not living a rich enough life if you don't," laughed Chance, rolling his eyes toward me.

One by one, they came forward with an offering. The gifts were as varied as the individuals, from clay cuneiform tablets to use of a harem.

"Are you finished eating, Samas?" Poppy asked sarcastically.

"Yes, I am," he said, wiping his hands as he got to his feet. "I have already made Evan a very generous offer. It is with that that I welcome him into our company."

"What is it?" asked Auda.

He stood up as straight as a soldier. "Alas, it is still on the table, so discretion should be the rule of the day."

"Very well. That leaves you," Poppy said to Clovis.

The old man struggled to his feet. "I brought something from my homeland. A jambiya dagger with bejeweled silver sheath and rhinoceros horn handle. Be careful," he said, removing it from his waistband and handing it to me. "The Damascus blade is quite sharp."

The handle fit my hand perfectly. I removed the dagger from its sheath and looked at the blade in the flickering torchlight. The tip of the blade curved curiously down instead of up toward the thumb. "Thank you," I said, admiring it.

"What about you?" Ramsay shouted up to Poppy.

She smiled. "Not unlike Samas, I've already made an offering to Evan. It's the cane lying beside him, offered to me by Charles Le Brun on behalf of his Majesty King Louis of France."

"Nice. I remember this little dragon," Chance said, leaning over to pick it up. "Very nice."

"Thank you," I said to him, then nodded up at Poppy.

"That's everyone, isn't it?" asked Chance. "Is our table ready, Mr. Diltz?"

"Yes. It's set up by the pool, sir."

"Great. Let's play," said Auda, getting slowly to his feet. Several others got up and followed him over to the table as Poppy led the female quartet onto the stage.

I leaned over toward Ramsay and touched her on the shoulder.

"Yes?" she said, flashing her pale-gray eyes at me.

"I'm curious, the vote on me was four to one, who cast the descending vote?"

She shook her head. "We are sworn to confidentiality, but I will tell you it wasn't me. The Hoxa story did it for me. I think it's fantastic that you knew him. I wish I had."

"That's ironic," I mused, "everyone that knew him wished they hadn't." Our laughs were greeted by scowls from the four tuning their instruments on stage.

"Maybe we should get out of here," she said, looking over toward the game. "Have you ever had your fortune read?"

"No," I said, confused.

"Let's go, then." She got up and walked over to a small red-cloth-covered table set up halfway between the long banquet table and the poker game. Samas sat at the table across from a middle-aged woman from the band of musicians, her hair tucked neatly under a yellow scarf pulled tightly over her head.

She held a handful of oversized cards and nodded thoughtfully at him. "You are a very happy man, are you not?" she asked in a thick accent as we approached. He nodded. "But I sense something troubles you," she said, studying the cards. "It's a longing you've had for a long time, yes?"

"Yes."

"This goal will be attained very soon," she said in an exaggerated nod.

Ramsay placed her hand on Samas's shoulder. "That must mean you're finally going to lose that last fifteen pounds to get down to your ideal weight of three fifty."

"Three forty-five," he said, looking over his shoulder at her. "Why don't you see what she has to say about you?" He stood up and offered his seat.

"Sure." Ramsay sat down and held her hand out to the fortune teller.

"Madame," she said, taking Ramsay's hand, double taking on the black tattoo. "The other man had one of these too. What is it?"

"That is a private matter that I hope you can overlook," Ramsay said, holding out a fifty-franc note.

The string quartet began to play as the woman took the bill and folded it into her dress. "Palmistry or tarot?"

"Oh, palmistry, of course," Ramsay replied.

The woman took Ramsay's hand and studied it, looking down

her nose at the lines through crude, wire-rimmed spectacles. "You will continue to be very successful in your business endeavors. You will have more work than you can handle."

"Continue," Ramsay said, unconvinced.

"I see many men in your future."

"Really?"

"Yes, many men will fall under the spell of your charms, especially during the next twelve months," said the fortune teller, raising her eyebrows.

"Interesting."

"And you will live for a long time."

"How insightful," Ramsay said, winking slyly at me. "Why don't you take a shot, Evan?"

"Not for fifty francs," I said, taking a step back.

"Go ahead, it's on me." She laid down another bill.

The fortune teller took my hand and traced several lines with a long, yellowing fingernail. Ramsay placed a hand on my shoulder. "I'm going to check out the game. Come over when you're finished." She walked away, leaving me alone with the mystic.

"You've been alone for a large part of your life, yes?" the mystic said in the form of a question.

I nodded.

"You are in the middle of great changes happening in your life, yes?"

I nodded again, wondering if I wore my emotions on my sleeve.

"Many opportunities and adventures are open to you now, but you know this already, yes?"

I nodded.

"But still there is something that troubles you, yes?"

"Yes—"

"Don't tell me," she said quickly. "It is a tantalizing opportunity, but one you don't feel you're ready for or worthy of."

"Yes, but how did you—"

She held up a hand to interrupt me. "I sense that you're not a very trusting person. You are accustomed to depending only on yourself." She looked back down at my hand. "It shows that this opportunity, if taken, will change your life dramatically."

"What about money?" I asked.

"Oh, great wealth awaits you. I can see it right here," she said, tracing a long line on my palm with a bony finger.

Boisterous laughter periodically rang out from the game. Spectators stood in a circle around the seated players.

I'd heard enough. "Thank you," I said, withdrawing my hand. "Thank you."

I walked over to the edge of the crowd, thinking about what she had said. I peered over Samas's and Ramsay's shoulders to get a glimpse of the action. "What's going on?"

"No one has ever driven Chance from the table, but Auda is close. He hasn't lost a hand yet," Samas whispered.

"What did she have to say?" Ramsay asked.

"She said great wealth awaits me."

"Of course she did, young Evan," Chance crooned. "Why do you think they call it fortune telling?"

"I call your bet," said Auda. "What do you have?"

"Three queens," Chance said, his wide smile evaporating with each heart Auda turned over.

"Flush," said Auda, pulling a mound of different sized silver and gold coins toward him.

"Blast!" shouted Chance. "That's fourteen hands in a row."

"Maybe he's cheating," Poppy said to Chance.

"That's irrelevant," countered the giant. "Nobody cheats better than I do."

"You shouldn't have given your lucky dice to Evan," said Auda, goading him on.

Chance turned in his seat. Samas and Ramsay stepped aside to give him a clear view of me. "I'll give you one thousand dollars right now if you loan me the dice for a few hours," he said, a slight tinge of prideful desperation in his voice.

I went for my pocket and was about to say yes when Auda spoke.

"Evan, I'll give you two if you don't," he said.

Chance turned to his opponent. "You would," he said, sinking back into his seat. The impish cards were almost completely obscured by his thick sausage fingers.

Auda picked an oversized gold coin out of the pile and weighted it in the palm of his hand. "This feels about right." He tossed the coin up to me.

I looked across the table at Chance. "No dice," I said, pocketing the coin. Several chuckles and pats on the back came as they dealt anew.

A second staffer accompanied the wine pourer as they made another round. The new hostess offered fresh goblets as the other filled. I took a full one and marveled at the craftsmanship. The fresh goblets were made of silver with gold braiding inlaid around the rim. "How old are these?" I asked, holding it up.

"Who cares, so long as they still work," said Chance before emptying his in one long swallow. "Refill, please." He held his goblet under the large urn's spout.

"Darling, you found me," Auda said to the server. "Come over here and quench my desire."

"Give the poor creature a rest," said the man who had introduced himself to me as Kerr. He was young, but lean and hard looking with a long, scarlet scar slanting across the left side of his angular face.

I watched as the attendant approached with the water pipe again.

The string quartet continued to play on stage. Several couples waltzed among the columns, their counterclockwise turns delivering them back to a time when the music was new.

Ramsay tapped me on the shoulder and shoved the opium pipe mouthpiece into my hand. Her face contorted into a grimace as she held in a lungful of smoke. I placed the ivory tip in my mouth and inhaled without a second thought, the caustic smoke burning in my throat and chest. The tarry, stale taste stayed in my mouth long after I'd exhaled.

"It's good, isn't it?" she asked.

I felt its tingling effects as I stared into her gray eyes. "Yes," I said in one exaggerated syllable.

Ramsay laughed and took another draw off the pipe. "Oh, I want to watch this," she said in a stream of smoke. "They're going to dance." She motioned over to the women following the string quartet off stage.

"Wait," I said to the young woman carrying the pipe. "Don't leave just yet."

I floated lazily back onto the pillows in the center of the reclining crowd. Violins, tambourine, accordion, and guitars combined in a raucous rhythm as five young women danced on stage in gyrating, staccato movements. Their bright dresses and scarves blurred into colorful swirls as I struggled to keep my eyes focused.

"How are you doing?" asked a voice next to me.

I kept my eyes locked on the beauty in the center and didn't turn to see who was talking to me. "I'm feeling pretty good."

"Good for you. Say, do you see anything you like?"

"What?" I asked.

"The dancers, do you see any you like?"

"Yes, I like her," I said, pointing with an unsteady hand.

"Only one?" the voice whispered in my ear. "Don't be so modest. You're a young man. This party is for you, enjoy yourself."

"Okay." I felt my words begin to slur. "The one on the end is cute too."

"That's the spirit, that's the spirit," said the voice, trailing off into the background music.

I watched intently as the tempo of the music intensified, and they all danced at an accelerated pace, spinning and whipping their black hair in wide arcs. I remained focused on the middle one, taking another full wine goblet each time a staff attendant passed by. Cheers and groans periodically carried over from the shrinking crowd around the game table.

"They are lovely," said a tall, thin, dark-haired man after he'd fallen onto the pillows where Chance had laid. He wore a two-piece suit tailored of black leather.

"How did you do, Tobias?" Ramsay asked him, motioning back to the table.

"I lost about eighty-five thousand."

"That's not as bad as last time," she said.

"True." He grabbed the pipe carrier by the ankle as she passed and then took three long drags in a row off of the braided serpentine hose.

I changed my fuzzy attention from the dancer to the long, leather-clad man. "So what's your take on all this?" I slurred.

"My take," he repeated thoughtfully. He rolled over on his side to address me directly. "My take on this whole thing is that we are creatures inspired by a divinity that desires to question the authority of mankind's contrived Godheads. It is the only thing I've found that explains us. You see, or will eventually see, that slowly, imperceptibly, God and his hierology slips away from you until there is only the self. If there is no God, then there can only be the self. Selfishness necessarily supplants itself in the vacuum created by Godlessness, but this realization happens so slowly that the average man will never grasp it during his short earthly tenure.

That answers *what*, but it doesn't answer *why*. I think that eventually, we are supposed to enlighten the whole of humanity to this truth and lead them out of their self-imposed darkness."

"Believe me, they will be much happier in their own world," said Ramsay. "You and Poppy need to get those crazy thoughts out of your heads."

"It's more than just us," he said, turning toward her.

"Just remember, it's a moot point," she said sternly.

He ignored her. "That's my take," he said to me.

"Are you stirring up trouble?" asked Samas, walking up behind us.

"No. I'm just soliciting opinions," I answered. "Some more dangerous than others."

His large drunken form teetered precariously over me. "How ironic, I was just about to solicit an opinion from you about my offer."

His question brought anxiety to the forefront of my clouded mind. "It's too soon, Samas. I need some time to think about it and some space to breathe. I'll get back to you later, fair enough?"

"Agreed," he said with disappointment, before staggering off toward the ransacked banquet tables.

"What was that about?" asked Ramsay.

"A business proposal," I said, getting up. "I'll be back. I need to walk around for a minute."

I placed the cane under me and stumbled from column to column toward the back of the room. Auda and Chance were the only players left at the table. The wine server sat humbly in a chair next to Auda, a defeated expression showing on her face as she watched the game, uninterested.

Mr. Ing hovered around the table looking at the players' cards and perked up noticeably as Poppy walked toward him with a short, stocky woman next to her. I forced my eyes into a squint to make them obey. When they walked into the ring of torches circling the poker table, I saw that the woman wore a Russian policewoman's uniform, complete with its matching skirt that showed off her muscular thighs. Short blond hair poked out from under her high-peaked blue cap and was tucked neatly behind a combat-scarred cauliflower ear. All eyes in the room followed her as she strode confidently next to Poppy holding a portable defibrillator.

"Is she here for me?" Mr. Ing asked in an excited voice.

Poppy nodded knowingly as she motioned the policewoman forward toward him.

"Then you truly did bring something for everyone." Ing nodded knowingly. "Tell me officer, how can I help you?" he asked as he extended a pale hand out to her.

The short policewoman smiled, set down the resuscitation kit, and took his delicate hand in hers. She held his grip for a split-second before placing her second hand over his and spinning him up against the nearest column. She pinned him hard against the post with a loud grunt and then spun him around again on her way to throwing him high over her head toward the cushions in a well-practiced Judo throw.

Mr. Ing landed with a crash just as the cop clamped her athletic legs in a viselike scissor hold around his bald head. He turned his reddening face to Poppy and gave a panting groan. "Oh, she'll do nicely."

"Evan! Evan!" Kerr shouted hauntingly across the room's expanse. "We have a surprise for you."

I turned away from the tangle of Mr. Ing and his new friend and made my way back toward the noise, wondering if what my drunken eyes had seen had really just happened.

The music had stopped, and the entire crowd stood in a circle around the place of honor where I'd been reclining. I parted the crowd to find Kress standing over the two dancers I'd singled out earlier.

"They're for you," said Kerr. "They want to share something with you. Enjoy," he said, toasting me with his silver goblet as the dancers moved to both my right and left and locked their arms around my neck so that we moved as a line of three.

"Keep your foot up and let them lead you," Ramsay shouted to me.

The Romani musicians started playing as the two dancers began moving in time with the building rhythm. They stepped in unison and supported my weight on their shoulders as I tried to move my foot in time with theirs. I gave up after a minute of their increasing pace and just tried to hang on as their turns accelerated with the music, sending the entire room of new faces into a blurring spin. I saw Samas and Clovis and Auda and Kerr and I caught a glimpse of Poppy as she unzipped her syringe case next to Jean.

I looked around at each flashing face and saw a small reflection of my own as I danced to their cheers before I crashed into a heap on the cushions with the two dancers.

THIRD NOTEBOOK

"If a man dies, shall he live again? All the days of my appointed time will I wait, till my release should come."

Job 14:14

19

I awoke to the faint echoes of splashing water. The dancers were gone. Several semiclothed men and women lay sleeping among the strewn pillows and toppled glasses. The torches flickered weakly as they burned the last of their fuel. I was the only thing moving, except for the splashing water.

I got to my feet, bracing myself against a column. My cane was nowhere in sight. I made my way over to the pool, limping from pillar to pillar. My head pounded unmercifully. I peered around the last column just as Clovis was climbing out of the water. Tiny rivulets of water trickled off his gray beard onto the sagging skin of his naked body. His long hair lay close to his head like a wet blanket. He looked up at me and smiled.

"Welcome back, Evan," he said, wiping beads of water off his face with a wrinkled hand.

"How long was I asleep?" I asked.

"A few hours."

I rubbed at my temples.

"How do you feel?"

"I've been better, I just can't remember when," I answered.

"You should eat. Are you hungry?"

I nodded gingerly.

"Good, so am I. We will have Diltz prepare something for us," he said, covering himself with a thin robe. "Did you have a good time last night?"

I turned and looked at the motionless bodies littering the floor. "I think so, but I would probably get a more informative response if I asked that question of you."

He walked up and looked me square in the face. He was my height. His gray eyes penetrated me. "It seemed like you had the time of your life."

"That's good," I said, looking away.

"Where is your cane?"

"I don't know."

"It should be here someplace. You had it last night. I will help you look for it. Can you walk without it?"

"I think so. I need the practice without it anyway." I followed him back over to where I'd slept, my limp becoming less pronounced with each step.

"Here it is on the stage. It seems to be none the worse for wear," he said, handing it to me.

"Thank you."

Clovis stood on the stage and looked down on the unconscious men and women lying randomly on the floor. "Look at all the fallen soldiers, the heroes of our times."

"Shut up," groaned an anonymous, muffled voice, his face buried in a pillow.

Clovis smiled at me. "Let us eat."

"GOOD EVENING, GENTLEMEN," SAID MR. DILTZ as we entered the dining room.

"Evening?" I asked looking at both of them.

"Yes, it is night," said Clovis.

"I guess the next question should be *which* night," I said, laughing.

Diltz gave a courteous grin. "Would you gentlemen like something to eat?"

"Baked fish, please," said Clovis.

"And you, sir?" he asked, looking at me.

"A cheese omelet and a glass of tomato juice."

"Right away," he said, disappearing into the kitchen.

I sat down across from Clovis and hung my cane on the back of the chair next to me. The dagger he had given me dug into my abdomen as I sat down. I removed it from my waistband and looked at it under normal light for the first time. Red rubies and yellow sapphires punctuated the polished silver scabbard. I studied it for several minutes before I spoke.

"I couldn't really appreciate this in the poor lighting of the grotto. It's amazing."

He smiled humbly.

I ran my fingertips over the raised silver characters around the handle. "This writing is Arabic, isn't it?"

"Yes. It says *Death to the foes of Islam.*"

"Are you a Muslim?"

"No," he chuckled. "I am no Muslim, though if I were not what I am, I believe I would be."

"Why?"

"It is the most virtuous of the western religions and holds men to the strictest path of righteousness."

"Do you think there is a divinity that awaits those who adhere to the strict path of righteousness laid out in the Koran?"

Clovis sat back in his chair as though evaluating an answer. "I do not, but I do believe the Koran's strict path of righteousness leads to divine men, and the world needs as many of those as it can get."

I nodded and looked back down at the strange weapon. "Last night you said this is from your homeland. Where is that, exactly?"

"Arabia on the Red Sea coast," he said with pride.

I removed the knife from the scabbard to inspect the blade. I couldn't imagine ever having a use for it, but marveled at its quality just the same. "I would like to meet the craftsman who could do work like this."

"I am afraid that is impossible. He died two hundred years ago."

"Oh, I didn't realize this was an antique," I said, sheathing it.

"Neither did I," Clovis confessed.

Mr. Diltz came back in carrying a basket of rolls along with one glass of tomato juice and one of water. "I have messages for you both." He turned to Clovis first. "Chance said he is flying to Bali in a few hours and would be happy to drop you along the way, unless you would prefer your usual route."

Clovis took a drink and set the glass down. "Tell him that I must get back to my garden quickly, so I will not have the time to sail. Tell him I accept his offer and will be ready shortly."

"Very well," said Diltz, turning toward me. "Samas had to meet a client in Bern and will return in the morning. He told me to tell you that you are welcome to return to Morocco and stay with him as long as you like. He said he is returning to Rabat tomorrow afternoon, via Tunis."

"Thank you," I said in a sigh.

"Is there any message in case he calls?" asked the caretaker.

"No. I suppose I'll just see him tomorrow," I said, wishing I had some time to myself.

"Very well. Your food will be right out, gentlemen." He retreated back through the kitchen door.

The old man grabbed a roll and broke it in two. "You act as if you had just received bad news instead of an invitation. Is his hospitality as bad as that?"

"No, that's not it at all," I said quickly.

"Well, what then?"

"It's just that I have a lot to think about right now."

He nodded thoughtfully. "There is something I am curious about."

"What's that?"

"Samas's gift to you last night."

"What about it?"

"Is his *generous offer*, as he called it, what is burdening you?"

"Is it that obvious?"

He shook his head. "No, but I can tell it has you occupied." He shifted back in his seat. "When someone first enters the Cognomina, there is a tendency for him to be awed by or enamored of those who welcome him. In such a context it is often difficult for that newcomer to stand up, or say no to someone who he perceives to be his senior. I want to assure you that this need not be the case. We are all equals here."

I knew that wasn't true by the deference the others had shown him. "Thank you, Clovis. I appreciate the concern, but that's not it really. I don't have a problem with telling him no. I'm leaning toward yes, actually. It's a matter of timing more than anything else. He is very excited about recovering something very dear to him, and I'm trying to catch my breath from the changes that my life has undergone. I can't blame him for his enthusiasm, but . . ." I said, ending the sentence with a shrug.

"Perhaps a period of introspection would be in order."

"Yes, I agree."

"But you believe such a period would be tainted if you were a guest in his home."

"Yes," I said, making a mental note of Clovis's acumen.

Two staff girls carried in our plates, I recognized one as the water pipe hostess from the night before. She gave me a sly, knowing smile as she set my plate down.

"I think I have a solution to your dilemma," Clovis said, as soon as we were alone again.

"What's that?"

"I invite you to leave with me tonight and stay in my home, where you can reflect on this with the unbiased consideration it deserves."

"That's very kind of you. Are you sure it's no trouble?"

"Not at all. It is a rare occasion that I have a visitor. I relish the idea of having you stay with me, Evan."

I sat and thought about getting away. I thought about freedom. It would be as easy as standing up from this table and joining him. It could be the first choice I made for myself as this new man. "I want to join you," I said, returning his smile. "I can be ready in half an hour."

CHANCE FILLED THE SEAT next to Clovis when I walked back into the dining room. I left my bag by the door and took a seat across from them.

"Clovis tells me you're coming with us," said Chance.

"Yes. Do I understand it right, we're going on your plane?"

"That is correct."

"Do you fly it yourself?" I asked.

"Yes," he said, puffing even larger with pride. "I got my license last year. You can join me in the cockpit if you like."

"I'd like that, unless you want to," I said to Clovis.

The old man chuckled. "No, I will not be riding up front."

"He'll be asleep," said Chance. "He hasn't gotten used to traveling in airplanes yet."

"Nor automobiles."

"Speaking of which, perhaps we should say goodnight before we leave here," Chance said to him.

Clovis nodded. Chance drank the last of the coffee in his beer-stein-size cup, and I looked on somewhat bewildered as Clovis pulled a plastic syringe and two medical vials out of his small yellow carpet bag.

"I still cannot do this," he said feebly as he handed the assortment to Chance.

"Yes, I know," he said sympathetically. Chance manipulated the vials in his thick fingers as a jeweler handles tiny precious stones. "Let's see here, it's this one." He successfully inserted the needle into the vial on the fourth attempt then turned it toward the old man. "That damned Poppy is never around when you need her," he said as he injected Clovis in the arm. "Count back from one hundred, please."

Clovis blinked his tired eyes rapidly. "Ninety-nine, ninety-eight, ninety-seven, *devyanosta shest, devyanosta pyat, jewla . . . jewla khan, jewla . . .*" His chin dropped to his chest, and he remained motionless.

"You forgot to say goodnight," I said, smiling.

"Oh shit, you're right." Chance put the syringe away.

"What did you shoot him with?"

"A sedative, he'll be out for twelve hours or so, or until we wake him with this," he said, holding up another vial. "Are you ready?"

"Yeah."

"I'll carry him if you'll grab his bag."

I took both bags and watched as Chance hefted Clovis's limp body like a sack of grain. "Does he really dislike flying that much?" I asked.

"Poor chap, it's not his fault, really—the world has passed him by a long time ago," he said, ducking through the doorway into the hall. "Now he doesn't like traveling in anything that doesn't involve a horse or a sail."

"Are you gentlemen departing?" asked the tuxedoed caretaker as he unbolted the front door.

"Yes, we are, Mr. Diltz. See you again soon," said Chance.

"Evan," Diltz said as we walked out. "Is there any message you want to leave for Samas?"

I stood under the green awning above the front door and looked out at the sleepy skyline. "Tell him I'll call him when I'm ready."

"Very well," said Diltz, closing the door behind us.

THE DRIVER PASSED THROUGH THE SECURITY GATE leading to the private planes and stopped the Mercedes next to a small blue-and-white twin-engine jet.

"Is that yours?"

"She's a beauty, isn't she?" Chance said, stepping out into the cool night air. I followed him and ran my hand over the wing's smooth surface as he opened the door.

"How much does one of these babies cost?" I asked, bracing myself for a number that would hint at what my new monetary goals should be.

"I wouldn't know exactly. I didn't buy it, I won it."

"How?"

"Playing baccarat. A gentleman I periodically play with wagered it against my home and lost. That's why I learned to fly."

I shook my head in amazement. "Samas told me you were quite the gambler."

"Did he?" asked Chance, looking at me. "That's where he is wrong. Gambling doesn't describe what I am, it describes what I do. What I *am* is a winner, and that is what makes all the difference," he said, returning to the car for Clovis.

Chance, his arms filled with strength, carried the old man like a bride over a threshold, like Isaac before the altar. Clovis's listless head flung back inanimate, his open mouth aghast. Chance climbed the steps into the plane, being careful not to bang Clovis's head or feet as he entered. I carried the bags in right behind him.

Chance's massive body filled the fuselage. He gently placed Clovis in a rear seat and buckled the belt around him. I placed the bags in the front seat and stepped back out of the plane when I saw Chance, unable to turn around in the narrow confine, begin to lumber, butt first, back up the aisle. He stopped for a moment in the open doorway above me and waved off the driver. "Are you ready?"

I nodded.

"Let's go then." He slid his upper body sideways through the cockpit door. The pilot's seat had obviously been reset just for him. It was six inches lower and farther back than the other one, as well as being twice as wide.

"What do I do?" I asked as I settled into the smaller seat on the right.

"Here, put these on." He handed me a set of headphones. "Just sit back and enjoy the ride."

Chance dwarfed everything in the cockpit. He spoke German into a small handheld receiver as he flipped switches on the control panel with his littlest finger. He seemed the perfect picture of modernity as he eased the jet down the runway. His dialogue with the Swiss air controller crackled in my headphones, and the sound of the engines rose to mimic the roar of a raging fire as the plane accelerated across the asphalt. Chance's bass voice speaking German into the headphones and the drone of the jet lulled me to sleep as we floated up into the night sky.

A NUDGE FROM HIS HEAVY HAND woke me out of a deep sleep. We flew toward the morning sun hanging low on the horizon.

"Hey," Chance said, making sure I was awake. "There it is." A narrow strip of land divided the blue sea from the sky.

I rubbed the sleep from my eyes. "There is what?"

He held an accusatory finger out toward the brown strip on the horizon. "Yemen."

20

Numerous buildings of the small town passed under us quickly as Chance circled the jet for an approach at the lonely strip of asphalt in the sand. Clouds of dirt and sediment boiled up at the edges of the runway as the plane touched down. I waited until the engines went silent before I spoke.

"Where are we?"

He inspected several instruments and switches on the control panel. "Al-Mocha, in the Arab Republic of Yemen."

"Does he live here?" I asked, pointing to Clovis's slumped figure in the back seat.

"No, he lives about ten miles down the coast. Don't worry, it's a nice place. I need to make some quick notes before I take off, could you go back and wake him?"

"How?" I asked somewhat confused.

"Shoot him with ten CCs of the bottle labeled Tennler. It will be in German."

"I'll give it a try," I said, climbing out of my seat. I went to his yellow bag and fished out the needle and vial. "Where do I shoot him?" I asked back into the cockpit.

"In the arm is fine."

Needle in hand, I walked to the sleeper in the back of the plane. I rolled up his sleeve and ran my fingers over the flat side of his arm. The spotty skin had lost all its elasticity but the muscle underneath was still surprisingly firm.

"Don't forget to purge the needle of air bubbles," Chance shouted back to me.

"Thanks." Holding the needle up, I pressed on the plunger until a thin stream shot up onto the ceiling. Clovis's snoring became erratic as soon as I plunged the syringe into his arm.

"How long will it take?" I asked over my shoulder.

"Did you shoot him already?"

"Yeah," I called back.

"Then he should be coming around any time now."

I watched his furrowed face for signs of life. His eyes darted in quick movements under their lids, then flickered to life.

I moved my head from side to side trying to catch his wandering eyes. "Good morning."

The disorientation showed in his face. "Where are we?" he said in a yawn.

I motioned out the window to the small town appearing through the clouds of settling sand. "Look for yourself."

"Mocha," he said, resting his head softly against the small oval window. "Help me up, please."

"How was your nap?" asked Chance as he pulled himself through the cockpit door.

"Good, I think. I had strange dreams."

"Well, I'd love to hear all about it, but I've got to get you off and get out of here. The Yemeni Air Force has closed the national airspace, so I had to land illegally. Is there anyone in town with a telephone?"

"Yes, there are two or three. Why?" asked Clovis.

"They will have no doubt called the authorities with the low pass we made." He turned the latch and swung the door open.

"Oh, that heat, it's horrible. I don't know how you can stand it," Chance moaned.

Clovis ignored him and stepped into the sunlit doorway. "We should start walking before the midday sun is upon our backs," he said to me.

I followed him out onto the runway and turned around just as Chance reached for the door.

"Good luck, Evan. I'll see you again soon. Good seeing you again, old man." He slammed the door closed and latched it tight before either of us could respond.

"He is right. We should leave, the authorities will be on the lookout for activity here," Clovis said.

The jet engine whined and roared into the sky above as we walked along the hard-packed dirt road that led into Mocha.

MULE-DRAWN CARTS RUMBLED DOWN the streets of the sleepy town. Giggling children played in the middle of the wide, unpaved boulevard that disappeared into the desert at both ends. Their mothers swept at the endless dirt in front of simple mud construction houses and periodically snuck glances out at them from behind black veils. Everything about this land looked ancient, as if the world somehow turned more slowly under Yemeni skies.[31]

"This way," Clovis said, walking toward a larger building at the end of the street. The Arabic script above the barn-size double doors faded unintelligibly into the earthen wall. From the way the reclusive villagers huddled in their numbers in front of doorways,

---

31. Evan's dismal description of modern-day Mocha appears to be confirmed by noted Yemen researcher and author C. G. Brouwer, who describes Mocha today not as a vibrant port but as a forgotten place largely in ruin. (*Al-Mukhā: Profile of a Yemeni Seaport* by C. G. Brouwer.)

I assumed few visitors ever frequented the town. Snorting horses answered Clovis's loud raps on the small, wooden side door.

A middle-aged, dark-skinned man opened the door, his close-cropped black hair contrasted against his long beard. A curved dagger like the one Clovis had given me was secured in the waistband of his leather blacksmith's apron. His long beard parted into a white smile as he embraced Clovis and they exchanged greetings. The Arab then pulled Clovis inside by the hand, who motioned for me to follow.

The livery stable inside could have been an exact copy of the one I'd been in a hundred times in Bulgaria as Vasili. Clovis pulled back on the man's hand and positioned him in front of me where he introduced me in Arabic.

"This is Nusel," Clovis said to me. "His younger brother works for me when I'm gone."

He shook my hand and spoke what I assumed to be a greeting, his head checked halfway through a bow as he noticed my fresh tattoo. Clovis placed his hand on Nusel's shoulder and walked over to a stall holding a thin, weary-looking brown horse. The horse stirred at his approach and brushed its muzzle against Clovis's head, who spoke to the animal in a soft voice as he rubbed its neck.

"Is this horse yours?" I asked.

"Yes. Nusel doesn't know what to do with him. Poor guy, he is unsettled if I am not around." He turned and spoke to the Arab stableman, who nodded every few seconds.

"It is too late in the morning to reach my home before midday. I suggested to Nusel that we relax with coffee until the sun's zenith has passed.

"We should arrive at my home just before dark, in time for dinner. Are you hungry now?"

"Yes, very," I said.

Clovis put his hands together and gave a slight bow as he

spoke to Nusel. The stableman nodded and bowed deeply, then withdrew out the open side door. Nusel returned minutes later with three tall glass cups of black coffee along with bread and a large sugar-covered pastry. I mimicked Clovis's bowing gestures as Nusel set the tray down between the stools on the dirt floor. Undaunted by the thick stench of manure hanging in the stagnant air, I broke off a section of the pastry and began to eat.

Clovis spoke at length with Nusel in Arabic, periodically translating for my benefit. The temperature rose relentlessly inside the barn as the day wore on. Of the three of us in the circle, I was the only one sweating.

"How are you holding up?" Clovis asked after the second cup of coffee.

"I'll be fine."

He leaned over to check the progress of the shadows visible through the open door. "We should leave." He turned and spoke to Nusel, who stood up and began to round up pieces of tack hanging on the walls. Clovis motioned for me to help the stableman as he led the lean horse out of the stall and toward the back door of the barn. The sun dominated a cloudless blue sky. I carried the weathered leather yoke out to Nusel, who backed the horse up to an old, black-painted wagon. Clovis immediately began work at the leather straps that confined the animal.

"Put your bag in the back. We are leaving," he said.

I placed both of our bags behind the seat and climbed up onto the bench. Clovis stepped up and sat next to me before taking a water-soaked leather bottle from Nusel's outstretched hands. The reins cracked against the horse's back, and we rolled out the open side gate. Nusel waved enthusiastically behind us as Clovis turned the corner. He turned south onto the wide boulevard, passing several abandoned buildings that had been half consumed by the relentless sand. The wagon's wooden wheels reported of every small bump in the road.

"What's the story with that town?" I asked Clovis.

"What do you mean?"

"It looks like it's dying," I answered.

"It is dead compared to what it once was. Take a look behind you, Evan. That is the town of Mocha, it gave the world coffee."[32]

I turned and looked at the ghost town getting smaller behind us. "Al-Mocha is the same as the coffee mocha?"

"Yes, the highlands just above those inland dunes were the finest coffee growing regions in the world for many generations, but the beans were stolen and replanted in the tropical soils of Indonesia and the New World. Those lands proved much more fertile and eventually lured the trading ships away. The town has died a little more each decade since the Dutch and English ships left. It's hard to believe that twenty thousand people lived there at its height."

"How many live there today?"

"Less than a thousand, and they are mostly fishermen."

"What happened to the rest of it?"

Clovis glanced back over his shoulder. "It was reclaimed by the desert. There is a saying in these parts, cities that rise from the sands too quickly, soon sink back into them."

The bumps in the road smoothed to a dull vibration as he coaxed the horse to a gallop.

"Can I ask you a personal question?"

"Surely," answered Clovis.

"Why are you so averse to flying?"

He leaned forward on the bench, folded the leather reins over in his hands to take up the slack, and cast his eyes down at the hard dirt road skittering past underneath us. He looked up at

---

32. Mocha has been synonymous with coffee since the Islamic hermit al-Shadhili reputedly discovered the drink and its stimulating effects around 1200 A.D. (*The Devil's Cup* by Stewart Lee Allen, 1999.)

the horizon as he spoke. "I have been around for over nineteen hundred years, Evan, and in all that time, I have never wanted to travel faster than a good horse could carry me. I have gotten around that way for all of my lives. Right, boy," he said, cracking the reins across the horse's back.

"Have you ever been in a plane or a car without sleeping?"

"No. What is the point of it? I am more comfortable with this. Last night was only the third time I have traveled in their machines, and I did it then only to meet the modern timetables to which the others now adhere. No, my friend, that way is not for me."

He pointed to the right in the distance where the road turned and paralleled the sea. "From here on in is my favorite stretch of road in the world. I think it a sin to travel it any faster than necessary."

I smiled and took in the beautiful scene. "They told me you are the oldest of us. Is it true?" I asked.

"They say quite a bit, do they not?"

"And not enough sometimes."

He looked over at me and smiled. "Yes, it is true. I am the oldest."

"How many members like me have you found in all this time?"

"That I have found personally?" he asked, looking at me.

"Yes."

"Six. I found Chance, Kress, Ramsay, Jens, Tobias, and one other. I actively searched for many, many years, but that was a long time ago. In some ways, it was easier back then. One of the things I used to do was seek out any new spiritual leader. These were often men or women who spoke in strange tongues or possessed some new knowledge unknown to the other inhabitants of their city or village or tribe. In a few instances, these people turned out to be Reincarnationists who knew not what they were, save that they were different and took it as a sign of divinity. I found Chance, Tobias, and Jens that way. I think it much more difficult to find such individuals today. When enlightenment can be peddled in the marketplace alongside loaves of bread and cuts of meat, the voices of those truly divine become muffled. The world used to be a much simpler place, Evan."

I eased back on the seat and watched the waves roll onto the empty beach as we passed. White gulls and black frigate birds plied the waters for their quarry. Not only were we the only people in sight, but were it not for the hands that packed the dirt on the road, I would have thought we were the only ones who had ever been there. Time passed quickly in the isolation, and the waning sun rested on the tops of the crests of the approaching waves when I saw it. The small spire rose out of the timeless sands like a soldier on post and stood vigil against the azure expanse of ocean and sky.

"Is that a lighthouse?" I asked.

"Yes."

"Does this road go past it?"

"No, it stops at it. It is my home."

"You live in a lighthouse?"

"My home is at the base of it."

"Does it still work?"

"Oh, yes, I am the keeper."

The tower stretched higher into the evening twilight the closer we came. The road wound down onto a narrow point of land that jutted out into the sea and supported the stone blocks of the lighthouse. Waves, subdued by the ebbing of daylight, licked at the shore on both sides as we approached.

"As much as I enjoy the views on that ride, I am always happy when it is over," Clovis said to me.

I assumed from that comment that his butt was as sore as mine. Clovis reined the horse to a stop next to the back door of a small stone house dovetailed into the larger tan blocks of the tower. A tethered gray horse grazed on the sparse grass lying close to the ground.

"Aye, Sayedee!" cried a young alto voice from the high railing circling the glass dome at the top of the spire. The young Arab on the walkway looked surprised at my presence.

Clovis waved and called back up to him. "That is Drusel, younger brother of Nusel," he said to me. "He has been manning the light during my absence."

Clovis called up to him and climbed down off the wagon. "Bring your things inside, Evan. I will show you to the guest bed." The young man at the railing above watched me until I reached the door. The setting sun's last rays reflected off the silver handle of the dagger tucked into the belt around his waist.

"This way," said Clovis, opening the rough-finished wooden door.

I followed him in and hovered within the shallow perimeter of light in the doorway. He struck a match and lit a brass lantern sitting on a polished wooden table in the center of the room. He turned up the wick and took hold of a small rope dangling above the table. The room filled with light as he pulled and hoisted the lantern up close to the rafters.

"A Yemeni chandelier," he said, tying the rope off. The roughly hewn stone blocks of the walls were barren, and huge timbers from some remote corner of this treeless land held up the thatched roof. A large open hearth stood in the far corner, its edges blackened from untold years of usage. Two chairs sat at the rectangular table, the polished surface of which held dozens of round, dark knots, scattered like constellations. Two more chairs hung from the crossbeam above the lantern.

"You can set your things in the bedroom." Clovis pointed to an open door opposite the hearth. "You will be on the right side."

I stepped in and waited a moment for my eyes to adjust. Two

small mats lay rolled up against the far wall. I sat my bag in front of the right one.

"I am going to start a stew."

"Sounds good," I said back to him. Lingering in the bedroom, I noticed three leather-bound books next to the other bedroll. The lettering on the spines and covers had long since worn off from handling. "What are you reading?" I asked as I opened one. Handwritten Greek letters covered the thick, brittle pages.

"Those are Diocletian's garden journals. I found them again a few years ago."

I walked out with the dagger tucked proudly into my waistband. He looked up from his preparations at the smaller table in the recessed kitchen.

"Ah," he said, smiling as I approached, "look at you. You will fit in perfectly here."

I peered over his shoulder at the preparations. "Can you grow things in this soil?"

"With some effort. I have to bring fresh loam down from the highlands each winter. I keep a garden between here and the well up on the hill," he said, pointing with his knife. "We will eat from its bounty tonight."

My next question was cut short by a loud, uninterrupted mechanical clatter from above that sounded as if the tower had just collapsed into the sea. Clovis went on chopping, undisturbed.

"What's that?" I shouted over the noise.

"That is just Drusel resetting the light's pendulum weights," he shouted back. "The revolving lens is driven by a large clock mechanism. It has to be wound each night to last until morning. I will show you tomorrow." His shouts carried loudly as the clamor abruptly stopped midsentence. "Ah, there," he said in a normal tone again. "I will show you tomorrow."

Drusel came through a door next to the hearth that led into the tower. Clovis called him over and introduced us. Drusel clasped my right hand with both of his and looked at the fresh black of the Embe. A white grin appeared under his young, sparse beard. Clovis spoke to him and motioned to the iron pot he stirred. Drusel reluctantly let go of my hand and grabbed a bucket next to the hearth on his way out the back door.

"Does he know?" I asked.

"Know what?"

"About this," I said, pointing to my tattoo. "He smiled as if he knew."

Clovis shook his head as he stirred. "They know it is a sign of something special, but they know not what exactly, though there is no scarcity of speculation. I should not think it unusual that they would treat you with the same curiosity and reverence as me."

"I noticed Nusel showed you quite a bit of reverence."

"Well, I have lived in these walls for a long time, and because of that, I am a bit of an oddity to the remaining villagers. Drusel's grandfather did not know me in this body, but he did know me by this," he said, pointing to his tattoo with a wooden spoon. "To the villagers, the lighthouse has always been manned by a mysterious foreigner with the same mark on his hand. It is only natural for them to be intrigued by another one. They are a simple people, Evan, beautiful in their simplicity. Being an object of curiosity and reverence seems an equitable trade for the pleasure of their company."

"Don't any of the other Reincarnationists visit?"

"Oh, not in a long time. My lifestyle is too . . . introspective . . . for most of their tastes."

"I noticed that about you. You seemed uninterested in the festivities of my Ascension. Why is that?"

"I look at things differently. I do not mean to sound pious, but there comes a time in your life, Evan, when you realize you have done everything that can be done. Neither Bacchus's fruits nor the sirens of the sea can captivate you as they once did. When that day came, I knew the time for simplicity was upon me."

Drusel waddled back through the door, his hand straining on the rope handle of the coal- and dung-filled bucket. He sat it down next to the hearth and began arranging the fuel on the floor of the fireplace's black mouth.

"It is ready," Clovis said, carrying a small cast iron pot over to the hearth. I followed and held my lighter to the pyramid-shaped pile before Drusel could light it. Clovis hung the pot from a hook set into the masonry then spoke to Drusel and pointed to the chairs hanging from the rafters.

The Arab nodded and walked over to take down a necessary third chair. He stretched to reach the dangling legs then gently lifted it off its resting hook. As he lowered it, his eyes widened in amazement at the accumulation of dust on the seat. The sediment lay on it in a uniform thick layer. Bewilderment showed on his face as he held it and looked over at Clovis.

Clovis walked over and took the chair from his hands. "That is life in Arabia for you, an endless battle with dust." He carried the chair outside and cleared the seat with his hand. He set it at the table minutes later. There was more dust on the chair than could be cleared away with a single hand—it betrayed long stretches of solitude accumulated within the sediment, and Clovis seemed embarrassed by the abundance of both.

I sat in one of the other chairs and watched as Clovis returned to the pot. He finished cooking and ladled three carved wooden bowls full, placing each of them on the table without speaking. Drusel mumbled a prayer over his bowl before he ate.

"It's good," I said, breaking the silence.

"Thank you. I agree," Clovis said, smiling. "It is a shame I do not cook this more often. My habit is to cook more simply when dining alone."

"Why do you live this way, Clovis?" I had planned on waiting for the perfect moment to pry a question under his protection of repose. "Don't get me wrong, I appreciate your hospitality and I think this is exactly what I need right now, but still, this place is so isolated, so solitary."

"Exactly," he said, looking up at me.

I looked up at him, confused. Drusel ate, oblivious to our conversation.

"It is comforting to me," he continued. "As I said, I prefer a slower, uncomplicated life. This quiet corner of the world affords me that. My home here allows me a refuge from the maddening changes going on in the world."

"What changes are those?"

He raised his eyebrows as though I'd missed his point entirely, then began again. "It is a matter of perspective, I suppose. Funny, for over sixteen hundred years I saw mankind build its society on the experiences of the past, and then suddenly, as though at the behest of some unseen catalyst, within a few generations of the Renaissance, society began to continually rebuild itself on anticipations of the future. It was then that virtue became based on the promise of the new, instead of the traditions of the past. I came here and stayed shortly after that."

"But look at the advances made since then."

"Oh, yes, there were changes to be sure, too many changes to possibly fathom. The Renaissance marked the emergence of the empowering engine of youth and their thirst for change, but I am a youth no longer and care not for their change."

"Is change really so bad?"

"It is not change per se, but the heated, cavalier manner in which it comes. It is the same story told time after time. A new generation is always coming to power in the world. They live their lives and achieve all that they can, but when their time wanes, and they see the coming generation eager to step into their shoes, they become alarmed at the prospect that this approaching legion will not respect the standards and traditions which they had so painstakingly established. Thus begins the eternal conflict between the old and the new."

Clovis had a faraway look in his eye as he continued. "These untiring, youthful legions are full of enthusiasms and dreams and they rebuild the world anew in their own image, not caring if the standards of those who came before are swept asunder. The older generation invariably cries out with concern, but the new one will say it is necessary to raze the dilapidated, out-of-fashion structures, to begin anew on the same foundation. To the new, there is no loss, only progress, but what they do not realize, what they cannot realize, is that their sword of progress has two edges, the second of which awaits them in the hands of their successors. So the question presents itself, who is right and who is to be trusted? Dreaming youth, eyeing the future, or their conserving elders who cast a longing glance at what once was. For me, I chose not to live in that world of tumultuous change and came here. I have been very lucky in that time barely touches this land. I should think the Bulgaria of your youth must have been much the same."

I nodded. "It was. That's why Istanbul was such a shock, but not necessarily an unwelcome one."

"As I said, it is a matter of perspective."

I took several wooden spoonfuls of the cooling stew. "Why here, Clovis, why this place?"

"Fate brought me here and asked that I stay."

I remained expressionless in the hopes that he might elucidate on his cryptic answer.

"You see, I built this tower. One might say it was my penance."

"What do you mean *penance*?"

He poured a stream of light-brown water into a glass from

a clay pitcher and watched the sediments settle to the bottom as he began. "I used to be in the same line of work as Ramsay, only it was different then. Soldiering was still an honorable trade in those days. I came to this corner of Arabia under the banner of Ali Abdul Pasha, who wanted to consolidate his late father's territorial gains against the Ottomans. He hired me out of Damascus. He appointed me sharif of Mocha and charged me with its protection and security. I was completely content with the responsibilities and handsomely commensurate pay, that is, until Ramsay showed up commanding a brigade of English dragoon fusiliers bent on capturing the port and the coffee-producing highlands."

"You fought against Ramsay?"

"No, it did not come to that. Do not forget the oath you took, Evan. Ramsay took it as well. Our first loyalties are to one another.

"I remember they eased into the harbor in a tall three-masted clipper, the *Trade's Increase*, decked out under Union Jack.[33] The villagers amassed around the dock in the normal fashion for receiving an English trading ship. It was only when the ship dropped anchor broadside to the dock and brought her guns to bear, that they realized something was wrong. A young messenger was sent to my quarters in the stone citadel at the heart of town. I took two lieutenants and made my way to the scene. Ramsay stood at the foot of the gangplank, flanked by a dozen red-jacketed soldiers holding long, bayoneted muskets. I parted the crowd and stood at attention in front of them. Ramsay turned around to greet me and flushed completely white.

"'I had no idea,' said Ramsay in German, so that his troops couldn't understand.

---

33. The *Trade's Increase* was the ship of English trader Henry Middleton, who having been taken prisoner by Islamic authorities in the area months before, had escaped and returned to Mocha to wreak havoc on the city. (*The Honorable Company: A History of the English East India Company* by John Keay, 1991.)

"'Nor I,' I said.

"'I, ah, I don't know where to begin.'

"'You could begin by telling me why you are here and why those cannons are pointed at my town.'

"Ramsay swallowed hard and struggled to look into my eyes. 'The captain has asked me to present the local official with terms of surrender for the port and city of Mocha.'

"'And those terms are?' I asked as I noticed one of the soldiers looking at my tattoo, then back at Ramsay's.

"'Is there someplace we can discuss this?'

"I nodded solemnly, turned on my heels, and barked off an order for my lieutenants to clear a path through the gathering crowd. Ramsay whispered to a sergeant next to him, then followed two paces behind.

"I motioned for my men to remain at the entrance of the stone citadel as we went inside. I led the way up four flights of stairs to the roof. The smart, black-trimmed red jacket fit Ramsay's gaunt frame perfectly, and its rows of brass buttons blazed in the sun.

"'What in the hell are you doing out there?' I asked, pointing to his ship.

"Ramsay demurred, then began, 'The first thing I'm going to do is resign my commission, effective immediately. I will not bring arms against you. The second thing I'm going to do is still beseech you to surrender.'

"'What are you talking about?'

"'I don't ask you as an adversary; I ask you as a brother. Do not resist. You haven't any idea of what you're up against, Clovis.'

"'It would not be the first time I have been outmanned, and underestimated.'

"Ramsay shook his head. 'The game has passed you by, old friend. You speak of being outmanned—you're outgunned. With what are you going to defend this place? Your sword? Your dagger?'

he asked, pointing to my side. He turned away and walked to the stone railing at the edge of the roof. 'Will these be your defenders?' he asked, placing a hand on one of the two short cannon mortars guarding the port.

"I told Ramsay that my fellow Yemenis would be my defenders, but he was insistent that I would lead them to their doom." Clovis had a far-off look in his eye as he continued. "I told Ramsay that the streets of Yemen had seen enough bloodshed to drain his precious England dry, but he insisted I listen to him. He said he was talking about the dispatching of men en masse. I was unmoved by his pleas and continued to try to find a compromise," Clovis continued.

"Did you end up finding terms you could both agree to?" I asked him.

"I asked Ramsay what his captain's terms were, and he told me the captain demanded that all municipal functions be surrendered immediately, and all means of transportation were to be commandeered as property of the Crown, including beasts of burden. Worst of all, the captain demanded that all stores of coffee and all future coffee production be sold to the Crown. The city of Mocha was to be annexed as a British protectorate," Clovis sighed deeply, as if reliving the defeat he surely felt in that moment so many lifetimes ago.

"Did you agree to the terms?" I asked him.

"No," he replied. "I could no more allow the British here than I could raise my own flag. I told Ramsay the terms were unacceptable and I would not allow it."

"How did that turn out?" I asked, urging him to continue.

"Well," Clovis said, "Ramsay insisted that the town be put under British rule, saying that was the only way his captain would have it. I told him it was nonnegotiable. He accused me of being willing to lead my troops to their deaths, solely for my own intransigence," Clovis paused for a drink of his water. After a long drink, he said, "I told Ramsay he was in no position to question my motives, to which he replied that he was, however, in a position to question my actions. I told him to stop being so self-assured."

I nodded, completely enthralled in the story.

Clovis continued, "Ramsay asked me if I would like to relay any messages to his captain and I told him he needed to be careful. I knew he would be charged with cowardice or maybe even treason if he resigned. I invited him to join me on the side of the righteous, but he had his heels dug in. I told him to tell his captain he had one hour to leave or we would throw his red coats into the Red Sea. I thanked him for the warning, and we wished each other good luck as he headed back to his ship. That was when I began preparations."

"What happened?" I asked, setting my spoon down. "Did they leave?"

Clovis took the glass of water and drank, being careful not to stir up the layer on the bottom. "No, Evan, they did not. Ramsay was right. They overpowered us easily, shooting any man in the streets with a saber or dagger. Eighty of my hundred-man volunteer force were gunned down in the first minutes of fighting. They forced the rest of us back into the citadel, which they then razed with volleys of cannon fire. I organized a retreat when there were only six of us left, and we escaped to the well up on that hill," he said, pointing out the open door. "We camped there for two nights. The remaining five men all wanted to slip back into town and avenge the deaths of their fathers, brothers, and sons, but I held them back. At the end of the second night, I could no longer dissuade them. They saw the fight in me was gone. I awoke alone on the morning of the third day and bided my time for a week, living off of mollusks and water. I slipped back into town under the cover of darkness and stole a British wagon, which I secretly loaded with stones from the collapsed citadel each night until I had enough to build this tower."

"How long did it take?"

Clovis shrugged. "A penance is measured by effort, not time."

"What happened to Ramsay?"

He swallowed the last of his stew and sat his spoon on the table. "He was put in irons and taken back to England in the belly of that ship, where he was hanged for refusing to engage the enemy."

"And you?" I asked.

He sighed and sat back in his chair. "And I, I lived here."

"When did this happen?"

"A long time ago," he said, getting up from the table. "Can I take your bowl?"

"Yes," I said. "Thank you for the meal. It was delicious."

He nodded curtly and took my bowl. I could tell he was finished talking, and perhaps even felt he had said too much. Drusel placed his bowl on top of the others and carried them outside. "Drusel will sleep in here. I will prepare our beds," he said, drifting into the side room. I followed him in and helped with his preparations. "I am sorry that I do not have a private room to offer you."

"Don't apologize, Clovis."

A smile graced his lips as he fluffed his pillow. Drusel turned down the lantern and lay down in front of the hearth. The deep ticking of the clock mechanism atop the tower echoed through the silence.

"Thank you for telling me the story, Clovis," I said into the darkness.

His blanket rustled as he turned to look over at me. My ears strained against the ticking for several seconds. "Thank you for asking."

Dust danced in the beams of morning sun that cut through fissures in the thatched roof like tiny spotlights. Clovis was gone, and his bedroll lay curled up neatly against the wall. I left the cane behind and limped out into the brightness of day. Drusel's gray mare was gone.

Clovis stood on the beach silhouetted by the white foam of the lapping waves. He held a sword in his hands. I sat on the edge of the short ridge below the lighthouse and watched as he moved in graceful, measured steps along with each practiced parry and thrust. His twirling, curved saber caught the light as he moved through timeless forms of choreographed attacks, and his tired frame became miraculously lithe with each step. He whipped his sword through the air and his face contorted menacingly with eyes ablaze, as though striking down long-dead foes.

"You look like you're pretty good with that thing," I shouted down to him as soon as he'd finished.

He turned, startled, and quickly scanned the horizon until he found me. "I am still the best in these parts," he called back. "Come down here!" He motioned me down to the beach with the sword.

"You're not going to run me through, are you?" I said jokingly as I walked up to him.

"No, I want to show you where to fish. I keep three poles over by that rock," he said, pointing them out. "I usually fish with all three. This place below the tower and the point over there by the rocks are the best locations."

"Great. I haven't been fishing since I was a child."

He pointed to the edge of the surf. "Split those black mollusks apart for bait."

I nodded and motioned to the sword that hung at his side. "What's the story with that?"

He clasped the blade with his left hand and ceremoniously offered me the handle. "You said in the Ascension that fire was your confidant. This is mine."

I placed my hand around the sweaty grip and took it from him. "Do you practice every day?" I asked.

"Yes."

"When was the last time you used it, in anger, I mean?"

"Against Ramsay's British dragoons."

"Not since then?" I asked.

He shook his head and began walking back up the beach to the lighthouse. "No, Evan, that was the last of the fight in me. Their guns made it too easy to kill. Fighting lost its virtue for me when a man could no longer blow his last breath in your face. Since then, I have led a much more simple existence here. I found to my surprise that it is much better suited for us than the lifestyles most of the others embrace."

I looked up at the tower and thought he probably had little choice in the matter. He was bored of living as they lived now and was now left alone in his boredom because the others had resolved not to come to his same end.

"When is the best time to go fishing?" I asked.

He looked up at the sun then back at the tide level. "About now is good. Go ahead if you like, but do not forget to shield yourself from the sun. Tonight, we will eat whatever you catch," he said, stepping up onto the shelf of dry earth above the sandy beach.

I returned for the poles and prepared the bait before settling in to fish for dinner.

I WALKED THROUGH THE DOOR later that afternoon carrying the three fish I'd caught, only to find Clovis sitting at the table, inked brush in hand above coarse brown paper. "Set them by the pot," he said, looking my way only for a moment. "Beware the thin silver fish, it is not healthy to eat it."

I set it aside. "Are the others okay?"

"Yes," he said, concentrating on a series of complex strokes. I wiped my hands on my pants and peered over his shoulder. "It is an apology and a warning, but it is really an exercise about perfection," he volunteered before I could ask. "Calligraphy, not unlike gardening, is a practice in patience." Strange Japanese characters emerged effortlessly onto the page from the end of his slender brush. He filled the paper from top to bottom. He dipped the brush into the short bottle of ink and quickly scrawled a line of Arabic across the bottom of the page. "There, it is done. Let us have a look at your catch."

"Is there anything I can help with?" I asked.

"Is your foot well?" he countered.

"Yes, I've been walking today without the cane, and it feels fine."

He handed me a large leather bag. "You may go for water then. The well is beyond the garden. There is a footpath to show you the way. Go now, before it gets dark."

The sun was on my back as I followed the meandering path up away from the shadow of the tower. Clovis's garden was larger than I had expected. Small drifts of fine sediment breached the border of roughly hewn stones enclosing the darker, fertile earth of the garden. Short stalks of rich green and withered brown twitched in the breeze.

The well beyond was nothing more than a deep, water-filled hole circled with stones even more worn than those of the garden and tower. A thin rope slanted into its murky, uncertain depths. I raised the rotting, porous bucket at the end of the rope and filled the leather bladder with brown water. The empty bucket hit the water with a hollow thud. I hefted the water bottle onto my shoulder and limped back toward the beach. The lighthouse spire stood black against the soft pastels of a Red Sea sunset.

Clovis waited for me in the open doorway. "I was just about to prepare the light. Would you like to see how it works?"

"Yes, I would."

"Set the water down and follow me." He grabbed a lantern and went through the door leading to the tower. "I started the fish already. It should be done by the time we are finished," he said, starting up the circular stone stairs set into the masonry of the walls. Two heavy black chains dangled lifeless in the center of our ascending spirals. The stairs emerged onto the narrow catwalk I'd seen Drusel on the night before. The brilliant purples and reds of the sunset were so close it seemed I might stain my hand if I reached out to it.

A cupola of window panes surrounded the clear, beehive-shaped lighthouse lens. Clovis opened a narrow door set into the framework of glass and motioned me toward him. He stepped in and walked around the lens until he found the small, hinged glass door that opened to reveal the soot-covered brass burner inside. Clovis ran a rag over the inside surface of the dome-shaped lens and wiped at the fine black powder that always tells of fire.

"Hand me that bottle, please." He pointed toward a clear bottle half filled with yellow oil.

"One small flame can provide enough light?" I asked.

"It is not the brightness of the flame but the power of the lens." He took the cork from the bottle and poured a small measure of oil into a reservoir below the charred wick. "May I use your lighter?"

"Here, let me," I prompted as I slid my hand in next to his.

"All right. Apply the flame there," he said, pointing.

I lit it and withdrew my hand as he closed and latched the small trapdoor.

"Do not look at the light, for it will surely blind you. Go to the railing and look at the sea," Clovis said in a fatherly tone. I obeyed and turned back only slightly when he worked a large crank beside me, starting the same mechanical clatter as the night before. We were both bathed in warming white light as he placed his hands next to mine on the railing. A fresh beam cut at the dark and washed over us every ten seconds.

"As much dim distance as a man perceive, from a high lookout o'er a wine-dark sea."

"Is that yours?" I asked.

"Oh, no," he mumbled. "It predates me. It is from Homer's *Iliad*."

I looked out to sea. "It's nice."

"Yes, it is," he said, starting down. The lantern he'd left at the bottom of the tower illuminated the nautilus-like spiral of stone stairs below us.

"What's in there?" I asked, pointing to the narrow wooden door opposite the one leading into the house.

"Stored goods and supplies." He put a hand on my shoulder. "Come, let us eat."

THE HOT DAYS PASSED QUICKLY. Clovis left me alone to my fishing and walks along the deserted beaches while he ceaselessly tended his garden, swept at the ever-encroaching dust, and practiced his calligraphy and swordplay. He spoke only at meals and in passing around the house. I felt he did so out of habit more than courtesy. Either way, I relished the solitude and the opportunity to live his slower pace of life for a while. Clovis came out to see me on the morning of the fifth day.

He sat on the beach next to me. "Any luck?" The three tall, thin poles of polished bamboo stood erect in the sand.

"Not yet."

"Do you mind if I try one?" he asked.

"Please, show me how it's done."

Clovis pulled up a pole and retreated back up the beach until the baited hook showed on the end of the clear line.

"These poles look fairly new, where did you get them?" I asked.

"They were a gift from Nusel's father. They are easier than using nets." He drew the pole back over his head and cast it off to the right in a sharp whipping motion. "I always have better luck farther down," he said, settling onto the sand.

"Clovis, I want to thank you for allowing me the time to be alone these past days."

"It is my way."

"I'm glad you suggested this. Thank you for inviting me."

He nodded curtly and readjusted the pole in his hands, and I sensed that my thanks somehow made him uncomfortable.

"By the way, how are you coming with your demons?" he asked.

I turned toward him, surprised by his direct question. His stone-like profile remained locked on the spot where the fishing line disappeared into the swells. "I'm still wrestling with them. How about yours?" I countered.

"Mine?" he asked, the visible corner of his mouth curling into a wrinkled smile. "My demons," he mused. "I have spurned them all, and held my demons close; lest I fall, and they lose their host." He turned and faced me. "That one is mine," he said with a wink.

"Do you still feel that way?"

"What way?"

"That you must spurn them," I said, pointing across the sea as though the rest of the world lay in wait beyond it.

He nodded slowly for several seconds. "Evan, ours is an inherently lonely existence, because of what we are."

"And what's that?" I asked quickly.

He turned toward me as though surprised at my question. "Why do you ask that question of me when you already possess the answer? We are the singers of goat songs. We are Zeus's Dioscuri sons,"[34] he said, his voice rising with emotion.

I narrowed my eyes at him, confused.

He shook his head impatiently. "We are their victims, their hostages," he said, pointing beyond the sea as I had done. He faced straight ahead and took a deep breath to collect himself. "It is all so different now, Evan. At times it is difficult to know where we stand in a remade world. Yes, quite difficult.

"The Greeks and Egyptians of my youth believed in the transmigration of the soul, they believed in us, or at least the possibility of us. But those days are gone, and now the true tragedy is that their beliefs, which served us so well, have failed *them* so miserably. That failure is because the standards of those beliefs were too low, too tangible. You see, if their godly goals are not high enough, then the common man can stand on tipped toes and touch the top of the portico, dwarfing all gods within. At that point, the

---

34. When Clovis uses the term "the singers of goat songs" he is likely referring to the origins of tragedy, specifically the ancient Greek meaning which is *tragōidiā* contracted from *trag(o)-aoidiā* = "goat song" from *tragos* = "goat" and *aeidein* = "to sing."

"We are Zeus's Dioscuri sons." Here Clovis is likely referring to a little-known fact about the Greek gods and twin brothers Castor and Pollux (the Dioscuri), in that they spent alternate days as gods on Olympus and as deceased mortals in Hades.

system becomes valueless and without hope. In the end, those men who, through courage, had stood as tall as their gods, eventually showed cowardice and slunk away from the mirror, not in fear, but in loathing, for their once lofty gods now showed the same tangible flaws as their aspiring worshippers.

"Their problem with our limited divinity, if there is any divinity within us, is that they will see what we have as too modest a goal. Lately, I find myself wondering if they are not right."

I lay back on the warm sand and looked up into the endless blue as I absorbed his words. I looked back up the beach to the lone tower of the lighthouse and wondered if this hermitage was his answer to them.

"Is seclusion the answer?" I asked him and then offered an answer before he could reply. "Indifference seems to be the way most of the group deal with it, barring the doors of their ivory towers against the normal world."

"Held hostage in those towers, of stone or ivory," he said, nodding toward the lighthouse.

"If a hostage in a tower, why not of ivory?" I asked.

"Why not indeed, why not of gold?" he countered. "Are you still not within the confines of a tower? But this cuts to the heart of your quandary, does it not?"

Even after days of idle contemplation, Clovis could still see the conflict in me. "Looking at it simply, I suppose it does. If I have the opportunity to choose the material of my cell, why would I not?" I wanted to tell him that the conditions of his exile, though beautiful, were as unacceptable to me as those of the Iowa Hotel, but I checked myself and continued. "I simply want to live as comfortably as possible."

"And who should blame you? If your quandary is as rudimentary as that, then you toil for naught." His tired eyes met my questioning glance. "Why would you put yourself at peril?" he challenged. "Surely, the risk in Samas's offer is the only thing that has deterred you up until now."

"Yes, but the risks do not apply to me—"

"And the rewards are great and immediate," he said, finishing my sentence.

"Yes," I conceded.

Clovis sat up and adjusted his pole a few inches. "It is true that bodily peril holds only a limited terror for us, but there are other hazards best left untried. I know your youthful blood runs hot with want, but keep in mind that Samas knows that too. Why chance it, Evan, when all that is required of you is patience?" He stood up slowly, looking at his twitching line. "Yes, patience."

He pulled his pole just as the line jumped. The top of the polished cane arched toward the water in quick, jerking motions. Clovis fought his way back up the sloping beach until a red-and-yellow fish the size of my thigh emerged from the sea.

"Grab it!" Clovis shouted.

"It's big enough to feed a dozen of us," I said as I pinned it down with my knee.

Clovis ran up to remove the hook. "This is a rare treat, my friend. These fish are delicious. This is the largest one I have brought to land in a long time," he said, beaming with childlike excitement.

"It looks like my services won't be needed for a while," I joked.

He grabbed the fish under the gills and hefted it up. "You can prepare it if you like."

"Sure," I said, pulling in the other two lines. "What do I do?"

He held the gasping fish toward me. "Here take him. Scale and clean him, then rub salt inside the body cavity. The salt is in the storeroom. We will roast him later tonight."

I took the catch from him and started back up the sand. "What are you going to do?" I shouted back. He was already naked and waist-deep in the water.

"Swim!" he shouted back, before diving underneath an approaching wave.

THE FISH STOPPED TWITCHING halfway up to the house. The horse tied off to the post sniffed us both as I passed. The head and tail of the fish draped over the ends of Clovis's short kitchen table. The curved blade of the dagger effortlessly laid open the pink flesh. Flies materialized as if from nowhere as soon as the first handful of fish entrails hit the bottom of the bucket. The sound of their frenzied buzzing filled the house. I brushed them off the fish as I worked, then hurried through the door to the tower toward the storage room for the salt. The dry hinges squealed in protest as I forced the door open.

Rows of warped wooden shelving lined the walls to the back and bent around the corner out of sight. Open-top burlap sacks sat on the floor holding stores of various grains and seeds. Tethered, drying plants hung down from the ceiling, and one could have easily thought they had grown down naturally from errant seeds that had taken hold in the accumulated sediment on the rafters.

I stepped in and began checking the clay jars resting nearest the door. Tilting the empty vessels over one by one, I noticed a short bottle hanging precariously on the shelf above and caught it just as it tumbled over the edge. It was clear glass streaked with black on the inside. The black-smudged cap over its wide mouth read *India Ink* in English inside the Arabic script running around the perimeter. It looked much the same as the squat jar I'd seen Clovis using with his brush.

I noticed my fingertips were blackened as I stepped up onto a grain sack to put the ink bottle back. My eyes crested the top shelf to find a row of similar empty bottles close to the edge, each smudged and streaked in the same manner. I reached back to place the bottle behind them only to find more. On my toes, I could see them. The two rows of bottles beyond the first were shorter and looked hand-blown from cobalt-blue glass with narrow, fluted necks. The three rows beyond those were small, crude clay vessels, thick dust cloaked the stained black around their long-desiccated cork stoppers. All the rows stretched down around the corner.

I stepped down off my perch and navigated through the sacks and boxes farther back into the room. Several small wooden crates lay close to the wall on the floor and bottom shelves. Halfway to the corner, I found one open. Scattered pages lie on top of its contents. As I picked it up, the obscuring dust rolled off the page in tiny avalanches to reveal Clovis's Japanese calligraphy. I couldn't help but smile as I thought of him, both a prisoner of the past and fugitive from the future. He seemed the picture of patience and perfection, writing stanza after stanza of his epic, each day taking only a page-length measure.

I fanned through the pages beneath in bewilderment, unable to break away. I could not interpret the Japanese characters filling each sheet, but noticed they seemed unnaturally similar to one another. An uneasy feeling came over me as I inspected them, like shuffling through a deck of cards expecting to find a normal variety of suit and rank, only to find the two of spades following the two of spades following the two of spades. The margins were the same on each page, and identical characters appeared in exactly the same place as though they had been copied from a template instead of from memory. *From memory*, I thought as I stood up and stepped around the corner.

Empty ink bottles ran down another ten feet of shelves to the back. I reached down and raised the dust-covered lid of another short crate. The brittle, yellowing edges of the pages cracked as I thumbed through them, again, each one the same. Clovis didn't put down a single page from a larger work each day but instead stroked the same stanza every day, for countless days stretching back decade after decade.

My head began to swim as I counted dozens of identical crates filling the shelves around the corner. *Had his solitary existence shuttered from the world for centuries devolved to this?* I asked myself in vain as I tried to comprehend any meaning from the madness that screamed out to me from the piles of pages.

My eyes darted from clasp to clasp on the crates, wanting but unable to open them. I sat the ink bottle down, stooped to close the open lid, and folded the page gently into my pocket. The storeroom door creaked again as I pulled it closed.

I walked back to the kitchen and lengthened each successive limp as I tried to outpace the anxiety that followed me out of the storeroom. I veered off to the right for the bedroom and immediately packed my possessions. I had no thoughts then except to leave that place and pursue a different future.

My bag landed in the back of the wagon with a *thump* that startled the grazing horse. My breath seemed to compress in my chest as soon as I stepped back into the house. The noonday sun glowed through the thatched roofing. I grabbed the dagger that I had left next to the lifeless fish and placed it snugly in my waistband. Cane in hand, I stood in the open doorway looking for anything that I'd forgotten. I forget nothing.

I recalled memories from Vasili's time with horse-drawn equipment then slipped the crude bridle and simple yoke onto the horse in the same fashion Nusel had done. The beast instinctively walked to the wagon and backed up to the hitch. I strapped him in, climbed onto the seat, and cracked the reins, sending us both into the hottest part of the day.

I saw Clovis as I turned the wagon onto the road toward Mocha. He stood naked on the beach, knee-deep in a wave that ebbed away from him. I opened my mouth but found nothing to say. I faced forward, aligned my head with that of the horse, and snapped us both to a gallop.

I DIDN'T LOOK BACK, but I could sense the lighthouse and the trap of his broken existence getting smaller behind me. The sun was intense and sapped the energy from me as I rode on. After several hours, the heat began to induce a strange feeling of communion with myself, not unlike that I had so often summoned through arson. The vast, lifeless expanses of sand and sea on either side seemed an appropriate metaphor for the road I was on.

I slumped back on the bench seat, letting the reins go slack in my hands as the blazing sun and constant vibration from the road lulled me into a strange trance of acute, yet passive lucidity.

I SNAPPED OUT OF MY TRANCE when the wagon lurched to a stop in front of the livery stable. Both brothers came out to tend the laboring animal. After five long minutes of gesturing, I managed to have Drusel take me to an operating telephone. Half an hour later, Samas's voice crackled weakly through the line in a warm, full-bodied hello.

"I'm ready," I shouted into the receiver. "Let's do this."

22

The bark of the tires against the Tunisian runway broke the shield of determined concentration I had donned when I left in the wagon. I had not thought about Clovis since then.

I assumed that Drusel would take the wagon back to him, but what would I say when I saw Clovis again, what *could* I say?

I walked out of the airport straight into the back of a dingy taxicab. I unfolded the note in my pocket and read aloud the name of the hotel Samas had given me over the phone. "Hotel Majeet."

The young, smiling cabbie turned in his seat to face me. "I know the place." He pushed out his lower lip in disapproval. "I take you to a much better place. Very nice, many foreigners like you."

I looked at the note and read the name aloud again.

"Okay, okay, but I think you like the other place better."

I remained silent and stared out the open window as he pulled out into traffic. He navigated his tiny car through the narrow, unmarked streets like an experienced ship captain who knew his maps by heart. The passing buildings of simple brick construction with their brightly hand-painted signs would have been at home in Istanbul.

He stopped in front of an anonymous brown building with a simple Arabic inscription scrawled over the arched doorway. He looked up in the mirror and repeated the name I had read to him. "Hotel Majeet."

The script above the ignoble entrance seemed to say *go away* to anyone not invited.

Not caring about the cost, I peeled off a twenty-dollar bill and handed it to the cabbie, lingering only long enough to notice his approving reaction. I had taken no more than two steps away when the cabbie took off, engine racing and tires squealing around the corner and out of sight. Resting white gulls took flight at the commotion and looked down on me with curiosity. The low drone of heavy machinery growled up from the nearby port.

The old woman waiting behind the high counter of the front room eyed me as suspiciously as the gulls had. Deep wrinkles crept out from the corners of her thin mouth and exaggerated her natural frown. Undeterred, I strode in proudly, set my bag down, and placed both hands flat on the blue-tiled countertop.

"I would like a room, please," I said, fully expecting her not to understand a word. The credibility of everything Samas had told me about the job seemed to hang in the lengthening silence before her response.

"What is your name?" she asked in a cold voice. Her English came without effort as though she spoke it every day.

I smiled wide. "Evan Michaels."

"Here, you're already paid for," she said as she placed a key and a sealed envelope on the counter between my hands. "It's through there." She pointed a crooked finger down the hallway to my right.

A feeling of confidence washed over me as I took the envelope and key. "Thanks," I said, walking past her. "I think," I mumbled once I was down the hall and out of earshot. The match to the number six on the key chain was at the end of the hall.

The room was spare in its furnishings, but its bare, sterile walls looked clean. A single small nightstand rested next to the white-quilted bed. A wooden chair flanked the bed on the other side. I placed the bag on the chair, stood the cane in the corner, and sat on the edge of the bed as I tore the letter open. Samas's booming bravado-filled voice echoed in my head as I began to read.

> *Welcome to Tunis, Evan. It was so pleasant to finally hear from you. I only hope you are as eager to begin as I. I suggest you start by becoming familiar with the painting and the layout of the gallery. It is on the same street as the hotel you are in. Proceed toward the sea, the Tunisian National Gallery is the first building before the promenade. Please familiarize yourself with the route from the gallery to the dock. The boat,* The Panta Mine *is moored in slip number fifteen. Its captain is a Welshman named Flynn Coogan. He is waiting for you and has most of the supplies you will need, anything else can easily be found in the open-air bazaar down the street from the gallery. Everything else is in your hands. I eagerly await your return.*
>
> > *Good luck,*
> > *Samas*

THE OLD WOMAN SAID NOTHING when I walked past her on my way out. The clock above her graying head showed three o' clock. I stepped onto the sidewalk, placed the cane under me, and started toward the sea.

The Tunisian National Gallery was set back from the street to make room for the two life-size carved-stone elephants that guarded the entrance. I walked past, feigning disinterest while taking in every detail of the building's facade: the flowering colors of the low planters between the granite pillars, the clock set high in the wall under the peaked roof, the ubiquitous white stains of the loitering pigeons.

The surrounding city was abuzz with the kinds of activities that surface after the heat of day and before the fall of night. Men and women, old and young, burdened with all manner of goods, walked in and out of the breach in the storefronts that served as the entrance to the indoor bazaar. I noticed several other foreigners as I entered.

The inside was organized chaos. Each merchant ruled over a ten-foot square of concrete floor under the high, sheet-metal-roofed iron superstructure, and their wares were as varied as their weathered faces. Brass pots lay stacked next to caged monkeys, next to six-foot-tall mounds of onions and gourds. Old women constantly fanned sides of beef and racks of lamb with long palm branches to beat off the swarming flies, their steady rhythm wafting the scent of spoilage into the stagnant air.

I stopped on the square of a T-shirt vendor just beyond a young couple arguing amongst their piled guitars. I picked a shirt hastily emblazoned with a mural of racing camels. The young boy watching the stand took the twenty-dollar bill from my hand and crammed a wadded handful of Tunisian bills in its place. He giggled when I pulled the shirt on over my sweat-soaked white button down. I couldn't be sure if he laughed at my choice or my gullibility in not contesting or even counting my change.

I took two steps back to the neighboring square. "How much for a guitar?" I shouted into their heated squabble.

"Thirty dinars," they both said in bright smiles.

"Does the case come with it?"

"Yes!" "No!" they answered at the same time before immediately jumping back into their argument.

I flipped through the wrinkled wad of bills before fishing another twenty out of my pocket. "Enough?" I asked, holding it out.

"No," he said, just as she snatched the bill out of my hand in a motion almost too quick to see. They rejoined the fray as I closed the case on top of a guitar and walked off. Sufficiently disguised, I made my way back out to the street, fighting the inflow of merchants at the entrance, each one carrying a bundle on his back like so many foraging ants.

I slipped between the elephants and pushed open the glass door at the front of the gallery. My heart rate quickened as I walked past the guard station in the middle of the foyer. The uniformed Arab at the desk kept his head in a book as I passed.

The main room of the gallery was even smaller than I thought it would be. I started at the left wall so that I would take in everything before reaching the Vermeer. I eyed each piece in a thoughtful pose, thinking only of the red dot on the blueprint I'd seen on Samas's kitchen table. I ambled around the room from station to station, stopping to inspect the bathroom and take measure of the trash can. Two large rats scurried from underneath it when I lifted the lid to inspect the inside. The nearby patrons, mostly Europeans, were not as happy to see them as I was.

I felt like the people gathered around the Vermeer somehow violated my privacy as I stepped before it. I had imagined that I would be alone when I first saw it. Standing before the painting, I marveled at the detail in the reclining figure; the white, angelic skin, the wide seventeenth-century hips, the now-familiar black tattoo. The artist had captured everything in the opulent room; the red velvet curtains, gilded statutes, even the other paintings on the walls of Samas's Amsterdam home. I stood in front of *The Rendezvous* until the familiar feelings of cold, businesslike loneliness, those feelings that had served me in this situation so many times before, returned to me. It came over me slowly as I swayed in front of the image of my contractor. And though unseen, what I felt next was unmistakable. Want drifted into the portrait like a phantom, supplanting cold reason and eclipsing fear. I pictured myself in the same opulent surroundings as those in the painting and knew then that I stood there no longer out of obligation, but out of anticipation. I narrowed my focus to Samas, the form might have been different, but that sly, knowing smile was no doubt the same. Imagining him in this voluptuous form made me smile. I moved closer and listened carefully to his barely audible whispers to me of promise and pride.

"It's lovely, isn't it?" asked a large Englishwoman behind me.

"Yes," I said, turning around to survey the lay of the exits. I looked down at the inert watch Kress had given me and smiled. The four green arms remained motionless. "What time is it?" I asked her.

"A quarter till six. My word, they'll be closing shortly. Jules, dear, it's almost time to go," she shouted after her missing husband.

Until tomorrow, I thought, as I moved away from the Vermeer.

One guard stood at the front desk, his back to me, the other milled around the front door looking out at the bustling street. I slipped unobserved past the open archway of the foyer where they stood and walked back down to the twin bathroom doors. Looking around for eyes looking at me, I ignored the silent protests of the skirted silhouette on the door and entered the women's bathroom.

The simple stalls had brown curtains in place of western doors. The harsh fluorescent tubes flickered with a low hum. Small one-inch square blue, red, and yellow tiles formed a random collage of color on the floor. I had just put my hand on the water faucet when I heard the creak of the men's room door. My heart in my throat, I picked up the case and the cane and eased the women's door off its jamb enough to see out.

"Where have you been, Jules?" the squat Brit asked of her husband.

"In there," he said, pointing over his shoulder to the men's room. "Good Lord, can't I get a moment's peace from you? We're on holiday, for heaven's sake." He stormed off toward the foyer.

I left the bathroom and followed on her heels as she chattered after him. I averted my eyes from the guards as they locked the door behind me.

A crowd of people beyond the elephants enveloped me immediately. I turned at the end of the block and wandered down the alley behind the gallery, again taking note of where the doors were. My eyes were watering uncontrollably from the rotting stench of garbage by the time I emerged at the next cross street.

I had no more lifted my cane into the air before a small blue-and-white taxi screeched to a stop in front of me.

"Where you go? I know best hotel in town, pretty girls, pretty boys, good restaurants—you tell me," spewed the young driver.

"I'm going to the docks."

"Good, good, good, get in, we go now."

"Take the shortest route," I said, slamming the door closed.

The short ride down the narrow cobblestone streets allowed me just enough time to ready another twenty-dollar bill. I held the bill in front of him when he stopped at the water's edge, then tore it in two. "Wait here for me," I said, handing him half. "I'll be right back."

"Okay," he yelled behind me as I walked toward the docks. "But hurry, there is much business now."

I waved my half in the air and kept walking. A dried crust of yellow-white salt coated the edges of the gray wooden dock planks. A small white motor yacht bobbed in the water of slip fifteen. The man sleeping in the deck chair next to her stirred out of his sleep as I tapped the planks with my cane. *The Panta Mine* was stenciled in bloodred letters across the boat's stern.

"You Michaels?" he asked from under his frayed straw hat. His thick Welsh accent only hinted of English.

"Yeah, you Coogan?" I asked, mimicking his tone.

"Been expectin' ya." He stood up and readjusted his hat to expose the brown spotted skin stretched tight over his strong gaunt facial features. He stuck a bony hand in mine and smiled wide. "Trust you got the letter I delivered."

"I'm here."

"So you are," he nodded. "So you are. I have somethin' for ya." He stepped on board the boat and rummaged in the confined cabin. "Ah, here 'tis." The small, blue-nylon bag in his hand bulged at the zipper. "The boss said you'd know what ta do with it."

"The boss?" I asked.

He pointed a gnarled finger at my tattoo as he handed me the overnight bag. "Yeah, you know."

I set the guitar down and unzipped the blue bag.

"How long ya played?"

"Excuse me?"

"The strum box," he said, nudging the case with a sandaled foot, "how long have ya played it?"

"I just picked it up, actually," I said through a stifled grin.

"Hmm," he mumbled.

I opened the nylon case to see a hammer, a small flashlight, a utility razor, a lead-weighted wire noose, and a snub-nosed pistol. "What's this?" I asked, holding the gun up.

"That's a revolver. Don't get caught with it in the city. That's big trouble here."

"No, I mean what's it doing with these other supplies?"

"Don't know. I'm just here to deliver it, and deliver it I have. He said you'd know what to do with it. Oh, yeah, and I'm supposed to take you to his house whenever you're ready."

I shoved the gun back in the bag and zipped it tight. "I'll be back late tomorrow night. Be ready to go. We might need to leave in a hurry."

He settled back into his folding chair. "I ain't going nowhere."

The cab driver revved his engine impatiently as I walked back onto dry land. I handed the other half of the bill to him as I got in.

"Where you go now?" he asked as he compared the two halves.

"Take me to one of those nice restaurants you mentioned, the best one. I have some celebrating to do."

23

Heavy throbbing in my head recounted each glass of wine from the night before. I changed into my cleanest clothes, grabbed the guitar, and slackened the strings until they could easily be pulled back from the round acoustic opening. The instrument begrudged a low, sour note as I ran my fingers across it. I thought the guards might recognize the ornate cane, so I left it hanging on the back of the chair in the hotel room. Grabbing the guitar and blue-nylon case, I closed the door behind me. The old woman gave a look of contempt when I set the guitar case down on the counter.

I put on a smile for her benefit. "I'd like to stay another night."

"It has already been paid for. You're paid for as long as you want to stay."

THE DAY PASSED SLOWLY as the anticipation built toward my late afternoon rendezvous. I went through the plan over and over in my head while visualizing every detail inside the gallery down to the height of the painting on the wall, the depth of the trash can, and the sound the guards' shoes made against the polished granite floors.

I stopped in the market and paid twenty dollars for a small

red canvas backpack just large enough to hold the contents of the
blue bag Coogan had given me. Lunch was at an open-air café
across the street from the two elephants. A new set of vacationers
passed between them every twenty minutes or so, by the clock
high above the gallery's front doors.

At five thirty I crossed the street and walked around back
into the alley. Taking a deep breath, I braved the barrage of buzzing flies and wedged the guitar case into a three-foot-high pile of
refuse next to the back door of the gallery. I pulled up pieces of
garbage around it so that only the inconspicuous handle showed.
The alley was empty as I placed the last camouflaging sheets of
newspaper over it. I shoved my arm through a strap on the red
pack and walked back around the corner.

I pushed open the glass door and walked in painful strides
through the foyer, past the guard desk, and into the gallery. Both
guards watched a small television sitting next to the blank security
monitor. Neither of them noticed me as I passed, then lingered in
the open hallway behind them. Their gray uniforms and pistols
instilled an automatic fear in me that curiously waned the longer I
secretly stared at them. The confidence that had so often been my
ally slowly flowed back into me with the simple realization that
the two men before me did not know.

I stood as a stalking wolf in their presence, the very air
around me thick with larceny, and still, they did not know. They
deserved the contempt I silently heaped on them. Standing
there, I couldn't help but feel that my swelling bravado mocked
them and the order they represented. I smiled and chuckled
to myself, having almost forgotten the inherent advantages all
assailants enjoy.

I turned away and hovered around the sculptures, standing in the center of the room so that I could keep one eye on
the guards and the other on the prize. I watched the vacationers

as they milled in front of the Vermeer, their idle conversations barely reaching my ears. They would be the last ones to see it before it returned to the blank spot on Samas's wall. The two elderly women, arm in arm, the young couple with their sleeping baby, all three sunburned, would tell stories in their nights to come about how they were the last to see *The Rendezvous* by Jan Vermeer, that they were there the day it was stolen. And I, unknown I, standing in their midst, would be the cause of it. I was the anonymous individual they would admire for what I was about to give them. *Take a good look*, I thought.

Out of the corner of my eye, I saw the fat guard struggle out of his chair and stand vigil by the door, starting the process of my crime into motion. I walked in backward steps, never losing track of the guards. Once against the rear wall, with the whole room in view, I edged over toward the bathrooms. I slipped off the backpack and slid it silently through the sprung metal lid into the trash can. Unobserved, I snuck another peek inside to be certain I would fit.

The few remaining patrons ambled toward the entrance as I slipped undetected into the women's bathroom where my ears immediately caught the sound of whistling where there should have been none. I crouched down and peered under the brown fabric curtains to find a pair of legs spanned by elastic hose in the second stall. I bolted upright, tiptoed to the last stall, and pulled the curtain closed. The toilet flushed minutes later, and I leaned forward to catch a glimpse of her through the gap in the curtain. The heavyset blond woman touched up her lipstick and pulled at the pantyhose under her ample black skirt before washing her hands and disappearing back into the gallery. I stepped out seconds later and walked back to the bathroom door.

The voices near the gallery entrance were barely audible when I put my ear next to the jamb. Their parting musings slowly declined to reveal the unmistakable sound of leather shoe soles landing on polished granite. It was the guard, it had to be, probably the fat one. Each of his footfalls sounded closer than the last, and I knew that the entire plan now hung on the simplest of assumptions, that he would instinctively walk into the men's room first. I clenched my fists tight as he approached and wished that I had kept the gun with me instead of putting it in the guitar case outside in the trash pile. The guard's strides wavered for a split second before he pushed open the men's room door.

I stepped out into the gallery just as the men's room door came to a rest in its frame. The dimmed lighting in the empty gallery seemed to subdue everything but my nerves. Instinct took over, and within several seconds I was inside and looking out on the room from the narrow slit in the lid of the garbage can. The door opened, and the guard passed in front of me as an eclipsing shadow on his way to the women's room. That door opened seconds later. His dark figure shrank away as he walked back toward the lit foyer and out of sight around the corner. Faint tidbits of a television program echoed back to me. I parted my lips next to the crack and breathed from the fresher air outside, stopping to peer out every few seconds in nervous anticipation of his return.

My shoulders filled the cramped circumference of the can, and the ache of immobility crept into my joints after the guard's sixth or seventh circuit. In the long sabbaticals between each pass, my mind drifted to thoughts of my impending fortune; a Black Sea home, a flat in Istanbul, liberation from this confinement that had been my limited life so far.

The initial rustling scratches at the steel below my feet came just as night fell beyond the two small skylights visible through my fissure. The first big rats came in quick sorties, running along the walls one by one. But within the next three guard passes that measured an hour, the floors were being crisscrossed by them, the constant flashes of the red dots on the motion detectors betraying their nightly invasion to the uncaring defenders.

I could see it was dark enough to start the job and I resolved to go after the guard's next pass, but before he could come, I was startled by another visitor in the can with me. A young rat had slipped through a small hole in the bottom and scrambled about, unaware, or uncaring, of the giant above him. I felt him scurrying around from morsel to morsel and I concentrated on the gnashing of his tiny teeth in an attempt to ignore the stiffening ache in my knees and back. My little friend not only ate but jealously guarded the small entrance as well, biting at any strange nose poking in. The drama playing itself out at my feet made me laugh. There we were, both of us rats, earning our living in the trash. "If only you had the chance to better your condition," I whispered down to my friend. I wondered if he could possibly know that he would eventually become too fat to leave and would be trapped inside the can. Probably not.

The roaming rats scattered with the approaching footsteps of the guard. I readied the pack of supplies beneath my feet and clutched my fists as he passed close, the danger palpable, the reward tangible.

I eased off the top of the can and carefully stood up, stretching my legs slowly until the blood began to flow again. My eyes never wavered from the entrance hallway as I set the pack down. Faint television noise still flowed into the dark gallery. I had to use the bathroom very badly and cast a longing glance at the small male silhouette on the door before taking my first catlike steps toward the back wall.

I snuck around the rear of the gallery until I reached the enlarged shaft of light that projected onto the back wall from the fluorescent tubes above the guard desk in the foyer. The ten-foot wide beam of cold, white light exposed me as they came into view around the corner. Both of the guards' backs were to me as they watched the small, flickering screen. The street traffic was visible between the elephants, beyond the glass doors. Two quick steps would have easily taken me across the gulf and back into darkness, but I hesitated and hovered in the bathing light, emboldened for a moment by the sense of vulnerability. It seemed if I lingered long enough, I might even the odds. Several dark rats, enlarged with shadow, braved the breach along with me. I stepped back into the cloaking darkness on the other side and glided over to the waiting portrait.

Stooping to one knee, I unzipped the pack and, one at a time, laid the tools out on the floor: the razor knife, the thin wire noose, the small flashlight, the weight, and the hammer. I stood up slowly and approached the painting, noose in hand. Vermeer's incredible attention to detail was apparent even in the dim darkness. I turned to search for the back door, visualizing a path of escape through the slumbering statues, then I opened the noose and draped it over the top of the frame. The wire slipped behind it effortlessly, catching on the alarmed mount a third of the way down. I remained motionless for a tense moment, easing my head around toward the lit hallway in search of alerted guards who never came. Cautiously, I maneuvered the rest of the noose over the gilded frame until it hung in a thin line under the center of the portrait. The curious rats investigating my tools scattered as I reached for the weight. I adjusted my stance so that I faced the shaft of light as I placed the hook of the weight onto the wire. Then slightly, ever so slightly, I lowered my hand, incrementally burdening the wire until it hung free. And still, there was no shadow or sound of stirring from the guard desk. Every square inch of my skin tingled with excitement; with that same intoxicating mixture of danger, guilt, and power that a child feels the first time he steals or disobeys as he ventures out onto the thin ice of his own morality for the first time.

Standing up, I placed both hands gently on the frame and slipped my fingers in behind it. I looked at Samas's smirking face from his previous life and exhaled deeply before gently lifting. It was light and came up easily off the mount. I held it in my hands, two million dollars. Almost there.

I glanced again toward the hall then placed the painting face down on the floor, exposing the frame fasteners. Flashlight and hammer in hand, I started prying at the first nail. The low, groaning squeak barely carried above the collective footfalls of the scurrying rodents. On the second nail, the flashlight caught and highlighted a faded handwritten message scrawled onto the back of the canvas. The third and fourth nails came out easily, and the painting itself popped out after several silent strains with my thumbs against the corners of the canvas. And still, after all that, the unknowing guards did nothing.

I took the razor knife and laid a long incision just outside the crude metal staples holding the fabric to its wooden skeleton frame. The thin blade clicked with each aged strand it cleaved in two. The brittle canvas immediately frayed at its fresh edges, and the yellow, unpainted border of the liberated painting crackled as I rolled it in my hands.

I left my tools on the floor and was halfway back to the shaft of light when I heard the now-familiar sound of the heavy guard's footsteps. I dropped to the floor and froze instinctively. His elongated shadow slowly grew on the floor until he stood fully silhouetted at the end of the hallway. The flashlight in his hand darted wildly about the room, cutting at the dark in a narrow beam. I could smell him and wondered if he could smell me. My eyes followed the dancing light, willing it away from the empty frame at the foot of the weighted wire. The floor was cool against my chest and seemed to absorb the hot tremor running through my body. If I could just calm myself, I knew I could concentrate hard enough to make the light stop moving. Unfortunately, it stopped before I was ready and came to rest on the hammer lying on the floor twenty-five feet away from me. I held my breath as he took two cautious steps forward, his light finding the empty frame and bare wall. I turned my eyes toward the darkness on the far side in search of the door just as he shouted above the television noise to his partner. The high-pitched shrill of an alarm split the air a second later. Powerful strobe lights pulsed from the ceiling in a rapid staccato, exposing us both. In the corner of my eye, I saw the guard retreat around the corner in a series of six interrupted white flashes. The rear door was visible in the intermittent play of light and dark. I jumped to my feet, gripped the rolled painting, and bolted for the exit. The silver-painted door frame of the rear emergency exit reappeared closer with each successive flash until I was through it and back into the comfort of night.

The strobes had filled my night vision with floating white globes, ruining it. I plunged my hand into the garbage pile, pulled out the case, and took off in a running limp down the alley. The guards did not follow. I shortened my strides to a trot as I neared the cross street. Backing up against an unlit wall, I opened the case, pulled the slackened guitar strings to one side, and inserted the rolled painting through the round hole into the body of the instrument, being careful to lay it against the edge of the cavity and out of sight. The constant wail of the alarm rose above the alley and spread out over the city. I had done it. The excitement felt tremendous as I placed the small pistol into the waistband of my pants.

I slid down against the wall for a second to take weight off of my shaking legs. The running had triggered painful messages from my foot again. Taking deep, regulating breaths, I closed the case, got to my feet, and walked around the corner, skirting the edge of a gathering crowd that circled the stone elephants. I limped toward the long line of taxicabs bordering the curb and nodded to the one in the front.

"American?" the driver asked.

I nodded.

"Where to? I give you good price. I like America. You tell me where."

"The docks," I said, climbing into the back with my guitar. "Oh shit, the cane," I mumbled to myself. "No, driver, take me to the Hotel Majeet first."

"Okay," he said, steering wide of the approaching blue-and-white police vans.

I held the case tight as they passed and couldn't help but feel I'd set in motion the gears of a large machine that now silently worked against me. I knew the onus would be on me to keep ahead of it.

"I went to America once," the cabbie said, distracting me from new dreams of comfort and travel.

"What?"

"I said, I went to America once, twelve years ago. My brother drives a taxi in New York."

"That's nice," I replied disinterestedly.

"Are you from New York?"

"No, I'm not, but I am in a hurry. How long will it take to get there?"

"We are here," he said, stopping across the street. "Five dollars, please."

I placed a twenty in his hand. "Wait for me, I have to get something."

"Okay," he said behind me as I crossed the street, guitar case in hand.

The woman behind the counter looked up as I walked past, then turned back to her book. I fished the key out of my pocket and inserted it into the lock with an unsteady hand.

The room inside was dark and my nose caught the scent of cigarette smoke as soon as I'd closed the door behind me. I moved my hand under my shirt and onto the butt of the gun just as the night light next to the bed clicked on. I whipped out the pistol before I had a firm grip on the handle and I accidentally fumbled it across the floor toward Poppy, who sat in the chair next to the bed, cigarette in one hand, the cane in the other.

She raised her eyes from the gun. "That's not for me I hope. You forgot this," she said, tapping the cane on the floor.

The accumulated adrenaline coursing through my veins turned to anger as I stood there confused. "What the fuck are you doing here!" I shouted. "You scared the shit out of me. How did you know I'd be here?"

She stood up slowly and walked over to me, gracefully stepping over the gun. "You still don't understand how all this works, do you?"

"What are you talking about? Why are you here?"

She crossed the room, crushed out the cigarette, and placed the cane in my empty hand where the pistol should have been. "I'm here for vengeance," she said, looking into my eyes.

I stared back. "Vengeance? What have I done to deserve your vengeance?"

She laughed out loud. "Don't flatter yourself, junior. My vengeance is not for you. In fact, I'm here to help you." She looked down at the guitar case. "Clever boy. Is it in there?"

"Is what in there?" I asked defensively.

Her face cracked into a sly smile. "How much did he offer you for it? One million? Two?" she asked as she moved closer to me, running her hand over the front of my pants.

"Two," I conceded.

"He certainly saw you coming." She unzipped my fly and slipped a hand inside in search of me. "He'll pay twenty," she whispered, before lowering to her knees.

I gripped the dragon and dropped the case as she took me into her warm mouth. "Wha— What are you suggesting?"

She pulled off after a few seconds. "I think you'll like what I can do for you."

24

"Evan," Poppy whispered as she shook my shoulder. "Evan, wake up. We need to go now."

It was Poppy. I hadn't dreamed her. "What time is it?"

"Almost morning," she said, slipping her high-heeled shoes back on.

"Go where?"

"To make delivery," she said, before pointing to the unrolled painting laying on the floor in front of the open guitar case. "How were you supposed to make the drop?"

I slid to the edge of the bed. "At the docks, right after I'd finished."

"Word has already reached Samas then that you're over-due and were most likely unsuccessful. That bastard is probably on the phone to his next prospective helper by now." She knelt down and rolled up the painting, taking notice of the hand-written message on the back. She translated aloud. "'To my dearest Emily, the only woman I have ever loved. Your favors have become the star that I steer by.' Ugh." Poppy exhaled in disgust. "How saccharine." She looked at the portrait for several

seconds. "I just can't picture it, can you?" she asked, holding it
up for me.

"I prefer not to think about it."

She inserted the roll back into the guitar and closed the case.
"Are you ready?"

I leveled my eyes at her. "Are you here to help me with this?
Because if you're not, I'm going through with this as planned,
down at the docks."

Her face was devoid of emotion as she stared at me. She
picked up the case, walked over to me, and placed it on the bed
next to my leg. "You can do whatever you like. I believe I can help
you, Evan, and I believe you can help me. What you need to ask
yourself is whether or not you can trust me."

"*Can* I trust you?" I shot back.

Poppy looked up at the cracked plaster ceiling for a few
seconds before answering. "Yes, you can trust me. I will protect
any financial interest you have in this. In fact, I will better his
offer and take it from you now if you like."

I was shocked by her offer. It was tempting. If I accepted, it
meant that I could walk out this door a multimillionaire, unencumbered by the stolen piece. Her exotic eyes burned charcoal
black as I mulled it over. She wanted this more than I did, and
now I wanted to see why. "I appreciate your offer but I think I'd
like to see this thing through to the end, with you."

Her face burst into a bright smile. "Oh, I hoped you would
say that. Get your clothes on, we're about to make a killing."

HER DRIVER STEERED THE WHITE SEDAN onto the airport tarmac
toward a small, lone white jet. *Fabric des Glaces St. Gobain* was
stenciled across the fuselage in French red, white, and blue.

"Rabat," she shouted into the cockpit as she entered the plane.
"I think he'll be surprised. What do you think?" she asked me.

"He'll certainly be surprised to see you," I said, then mumbled to myself, "I know I was."

THE LOWERING WHINE OF THE ENGINES woke me as they throttled back for a descent. My arms still clutched the case close to my chest. Poppy spoke French into a telephone from her seat in the back. She came forward to see me as soon as she'd finished her conversation.

"Good morning. There's a car waiting for us on the ground. Do you know how to get to his home?"

"Yes, I remember the way."

"Good," she said, looking out the window at the approaching earth. "Good."

THE COARSE GRAVEL IN THE DRIVEWAY crunched under the car's tires as we rolled to a stop behind Samas's beach home.

Poppy surveyed the residence over lowered sunglasses. "How quaint, it looks like a carriage house. Are you ready?" she asked, reaching over and placing her hand on the case's handle.

My first instinct was to shout out in protest. Everything rode on this. I mustered a stern look from my tired eyes and spoke. "I am choosing to trust you."

"I know that," she said through an innocent smile. "Let's go."

The sad notes of a cello hung in the air as we approached the open front door. I knocked softly on the wooden door jamb and stepped cautiously inside, Poppy right behind me, case in hand.

Zohra sat in a kitchen chair, her eyes shut tight in concentration. She cradled the singing cello between her legs like a wooden lover.

"Zohra," I said in a soft tone.

Her eyes snapped open in shock. A sour note escaped both her and the cello as the bow slid wildly off the strings.

"It's you," she gasped. "We thought that you had . . ." She left the sentence unfinished as she noticed Poppy's Embe tattoo.

"Where is Samas?" I asked.

"Upstairs, on the balcony," she answered, still somewhat disoriented.

I smiled at her and walked down the hall. The sound of the amplified surf rolled down the stairs toward us like an invisible waterfall. We climbed to find Samas filling a lounge chair on the balcony overlooking the ocean.

He placed the telephone handset back into its cradle as he heard the approaching footsteps. "I don't like this at all, love. The woman at the hotel said he left with—" His jaw dropped open as he turned around and saw us. "You!" he growled at Poppy.

"Hi there," Poppy said cheerfully.

"What the hell are you doing here?"

"That would seem to be the question of the day," Poppy said, glancing at me. "And one I very much want to answer." She walked over and placed the guitar on the railing. Samas seemed to hold his breath as she opened the case and removed the canvas roll. Gripping it by the top edge, she let it unfurl in front of her, exposing the image to him. His face flushed white then red with the realization that she had it, not me.

"What's the matter, Juan? You're not laughing this time," she said, with a sly smile that betrayed her enjoyment of this perverse pleasure.

He reluctantly turned toward me, barely able to take his eyes off the long-awaited painting. "Why have you done this?"

"Evan did nothing," said Poppy. "I took it from him for my own reasons. This is between you and me now."

"You don't mean to tell me this is still about Latsei?" he asked, getting to his feet.

"Of course it is, how can there be *forgive* when there is no *forget*?"

Samas shoved his hands deep into his pockets and stepped to the railing. "What is it you want?" he asked, looking out to sea.

Poppy reached into her purse for a slim, gold cigarette lighter. "Oh, it's simple, really. I want to see the look on your face when I burn it."

My blood ran cold as I weighed the possibility of her actually doing it.

"You wouldn't," he said. "Besides, Evan has a financial stake in the piece's return. If you destroy it, you will be stealing from him."

"Oh, I fully intend to make him whole. In fact, I think it will be some of the best money I've ever spent. By the way, don't you think two million is a rather modest reward, even for you, Samas?" She clicked her sleek gold lighter, striking a small flame on the second try.

"Poppy, please don't," Samas pleaded. "What will it take to satisfy you?"

She looked up at him and shook her head in disbelief. "You're incorrigible. You still think you can get out of this, don't you?"

My eyes stayed locked on the tiny sprite as she edged it upward, ever closer to the dry, frayed border of the painting.

"No, no, please, I beg you!" Samas shouted.

Poppy held the lighter in place. The small flame that blackened the bottom corner threatened to awaken and consume the canvas at any moment. "Perhaps you should offer a more handsome sum for it, one that would force me to reexamine my ability to reimburse Evan."

"Yes, yes, good idea," he brightened. "What say, three million?"

"Twenty," she answered coolly.

"Twenty?" he retorted, his eyes in a squint as if the mere mention of such a number pained him. "I don't—"

"Don't be so fucking coy," she shouted. "I know you have it, and you know it's worth twice that."

"But I—"

"Well, here goes nothing," she said, moving the flame closer.

Samas shot his arms out in protest. "Okay, you win, Poppy," he blurted out. "Twenty." He exhaled in a throaty groan as Poppy clicked her lighter closed, snuffing the sprite.

"A fifty-fifty split of twenty million, how does that sound to you?" she asked me.

"M-more than fair," I stammered.

She shook her head disapprovingly. "Don't set your standards so low, junior. Lest scoundrels like this continue to prey on you."

"I guess you have a deal," she said to Samas as she handed him the canvas. "Get on the phone to Diltz. I want to know it's done."

Samas, his large frame now somehow smaller with resignation, tucked the painting under his arm and picked up the phone.

"What will you do now?" Poppy asked me in a whisper as Samas dialed.

"Travel, I guess. Build the life I've wanted. Go away for a while. That's what we do, isn't it?"

"Sounds like a good start. Would you like a ride back to the airport?"

I nodded. "Thank you," I said behind a cupped hand.

She smiled. "It is I who should thank you, lover. Oh, that was fun."

Samas's voice cracked as he spoke into the receiver. "I need to effect a transaction, Mr. Diltz. Into the accounts of Poppy and Evan, ten million American dollars. Yes, each." He hung up the phone without saying goodbye and lay back in his chair, clutching the roll. "It is done," he said, defeated.

Poppy looked at me and nodded toward the stairs.

I walked over and placed a hand on his shoulder. "Thank you for the opportunity. Sorry it turned out this way. You can keep the guitar, for Zohra, I mean."

Poppy suppressed a snicker and took my arm as we walked out.

"Hey," Samas called out over his shoulder to Poppy. "Does this make us even?"

She stopped at the top of the stairs and thought for an instant. "Why not, life is cheap."

Zohra sat on the bottom step wringing her hands. She started nervously at our presence, then bolted upright and sprinted up the stairs past us as we descended. Poppy rested her head on my shoulder and squeezed my arm as we walked silently back to the car.

"Where are you off to now?" I asked her as the driver wheeled up next to the jet.

"Back to France, then Los Angeles. What about you?"

"Zurich first, I need to get my finances in order."

She stepped out into the noonday heat. "How does it feel to be rich?"

I plunged a hand into my pocket and pulled out the last of my money. "I wouldn't know yet. I'm down to my last fifty bucks. Speaking of which, I was wondering if you had any cash, enough to get me to Switzerland, maybe?"

"Sure," she said, walking across the tarmac to the plane. "Will ten thousand francs be sufficient?"

"I think so." I followed her up the steps into the jet. She opened a polished wooden panel against the back wall and removed ten wrapped packs of bills from a pile of more than a hundred.

"Here you go," she said, handing me the blue bundles. "I'd like it very much if you would come to see me whenever you are back in Los Angeles." She moved closer and gave me a quick kiss. "Take care, Evan."

I STOOD ALONE IN THE HOT, blasting jet wash as the plane taxied away, the stack of bills in one hand, the cane in the other. I watched the jet until it slowly rolled behind a hangar then I turned and began the long walk across the open expanse of asphalt to the commercial terminal.

The money showed in a lewd bulge as I waited nervously in the ticket line.

"Your destination?" asked the woman behind the ticket counter.

"Zurich," I said as I removed a bundle. "First Class."

I WAS THE FIRST TO EXIT the plane when it rolled to a stop. The now-familiar Zurich terminal visible beyond the narrow exit cause-way looked different somehow. The colors seemed more vibrant, the floors cleaner, the people more promising. I studied their passing faces as I stepped over to the roped-off area around the customs desk.

"Do you have anything to declare?" asked the customs agent in a low monotone. His partner asked the same question to the woman behind me. A third man in a different uniform sat at an adjoining desk.

"Only cash and this," I said, holding out the cane in my right hand.

"What is your business in Switzerland?"

"Banking."

He glanced quickly at the dragon, then fixed his eyes on the new tattoo. "Detective," he said, getting the attention of the third man behind the other desk.

The officer stood up, grabbed a file, and walked toward me, the brass badge pinned to his brown uniform read *Interpol*.

"Is there a problem?" I asked the customs agent nervously as my windpipe constricted with apprehension. I looked over at the approaching agent in time to see him close the file and nod to the customs man, who snapped a cuff around my outstretched right hand. I recoiled, pulling the other end of the handcuffs away from the stunned officer. The Interpol agent dropped the file and tackled me to the floor. I wrestled with him over the spilled contents of the folder. He clasped the other cuff around me just as I saw myself in the black-and-white photographs littering the floor. My own face, firm with concentration, looked back at me in image after image. I had been captured in each flashing strobe; first hiding on my stomach, then getting to my feet, and finally, running toward the gallery's back door. The fresh tattoo showed clearly in each one.

25

Money meant nothing now, and the events of the next two weeks following my arrest showed me quite clearly just how tenuous my purchase in the world had been, as though cruel fate, weary of countless snubs, lunged at me from the shadows like a hungry tiger, eager to capitalize on any misstep. But of course, whenever you have to mention fate, you already know it's been cruel. I saw then that life is everything that happens between the narrow getaways. That life was now over.

From the airport holding cell, I was taken to a Swiss detention facility in downtown Zurich, surely no more than twenty blocks away from the Hotel St. Germain. But that was only the first small taste of what awaited me.

THE FIRST FEELING YOU GET upon entering a prison in chains is one of regret, not for doing what you did, but for the now obvious error in the doing. The second feeling you get as the first door closes behind you is the presence of an order higher than your own. When you stand inside the first door looking back, that sense of helplessness seems to have its teeth only in the outer layer of your skin and you still harbor the fantasy of bolting back through that door toward freedom, like a lucky rabbit escaping the jaws of the higher fox. But as you are led farther and farther inside the thing, past a second, a third, then a fourth and a fifth door, some primordial instinct of self-preservation alerts you to the fact that your chances of escape are halved and then halved again with each door latching closed behind you. And when you are led to the last and smallest room, the guards close that last door and take your last reserve of hope with them. You inevitably find resignation waiting for you on the simple steel bunk. I sat as a supplicant and wondered why I had not struggled, and how I had been led here so easily.

That first taste of incarceration, though initially bitter, would itself eventually become the fixation of fantasy as my condition of confinement became more barbarous and inhumane with each successive stop, first in Italy, then back to Tunisia.

THE FIFTEEN-MINUTE MEETING in a side room of the Tunis city jail that passed for my trial, proved to be nothing more than a parade of gesticulating accusations in Arabic, a comparison of my now-bruised and swollen face with that in the photographs, and a sentence, translated into English, twenty-five years without parole. I later discovered I had been tried on the same day, in absentia, in Rome, and had been given a twenty-five year sentence there as well, *to run consecutively* the letter said, *for my refusal to coop-erate in the recovery of the Vermeer.* By that time it didn't matter, they would never find the painting, and I had already found my resolve, or so I thought.

The next morning, after a sleepless night filled with the wails of other men being interrogated, I was led onto an old, rust-colored bus with steel plates welded over the windows so that the other five passengers and I had no view save that of the stoic, machine-gun-carrying soldiers. I braced myself as best I could with cuffed hands as the bus pitched and bucked over crude Tunisian roads. By midday the heat had robbed the oxygen from the sealed vehicle, and I concentrated on microscopic particles of dust as they filtered up from the road and danced in the narrow shafts of light penetrating through what looked like bullet holes in the roof.

Just before sunset, the bus came to a lurching stop. I was the first prisoner off the bus and the first one to see the place. The ancient, menacing, brown-brick fortress was the same color as the endless, featureless sands that lay siege to it. More armed soldiers prowled along the tops of the wall, their young faces twisted into angry scowls at having to be in this miserable station.

The lonely dirt road that wound back into the distance, that wound back toward everything, would be the last vestige of humanity that I would see with these eyes. I stood beside the bus in my bare feet as the others were led off, my shoes draped around my neck by their tied laces. I visualized myself walking down that road on bare, blistered feet back toward the world, *would that not be penance enough for them?* I would never survive it, no one could, but there would be a goal, a promise of something before I met their justice. Anything but inside. I wondered if they would shoot me if I just started walking home. The guard grabbed me by my shirt and shoved me in line with the others as they filed willingly through the open steel gate. Again, I went quietly, my head down, looking at the hardened, bare, brown feet of the Arab in front of me.

I knew immediately that it would be rough. The guards spoke to their countrymen and treated them with apathy, where I received a shout and a harsh shove. The first stop on the inside was a delousing shower of white lime. Each of us stripped naked and walked through the white dust cloud, breath held and eyes covered. I was held back and forced to go last. A new set of red-and-white-striped cotton prison fatigues awaited me on the other side. No shoes or socks were provided.

"Hey, what about shoes?" I asked and pointed to my feet.

The unseen baton blow behind my knees knocked me to the stone floor. The pain curled me into a defensive ball as they delivered more blows across my back and head.

"Yala!" came a barking command from behind the circle of blue-uniformed soldiers. I fought to force air back into my bruised body as soon as the blows ceased.

"Get up," said the sergeant in two thick syllables. His blue uniform was stretched tight across his large, distended stomach. Faded yellow chevrons were stitched onto his short sleeves. A dense shadow of black stubble lay on his full, tanned cheeks below the small, sadistic eyes that looked out from under the woolly line of his single eyebrow.

I struggled to my feet and stood in a slumped posture. He stood before me, silent as a statue, sizing me up, yet showing me his size at the same time.

"No talking," he said with loud confidence. "Understand?"

"Yes," I answered between shallow breaths.

He opened his fat slab of a hand and slapped me across the face, again knocking me to the floor. Through my ringing ears, I thought I heard the surrounding younger soldiers laughing.

"No talking," he shouted. "Understand?"

I got to my feet quickly and licked at the salty blood trickle running from my nose. He opened and clenched his fists repeatedly as he waited for my answer. I nodded in a wince.

"Good," he bellowed. "You go there," he said, slapping me down a long, dim hallway lined to the end on both sides with close-set riveted steel doors. The caravan of slapping, clubbing, and catcalls ended as I landed in a heap in front of the last door. Cell number 145.

The fat sergeant jingled his keys in the lock. The door creaked open to reveal a small gray cell, the open ceiling crisscrossed with iron bars, the crude wooden cot complete with a reclining African man. Four guards each grabbed a limb and heaved me forward onto the dust-covered floor. I lay motionless as the door slammed shut behind me. The sound of their laughter slowly died as they walked back down the hall.

I looked up to find the man on the cot looking at me, his red-and-white fatigues faded into a striped combination of pink and dingy gray. The pant legs were tattered to rags below the knees, and the sleeves were ripped off to expose his sleek black arms. His wild eyes shined with the intention, or perhaps the result of a mischievous spirit. Taut muscles rippled under his skin with the slightest movement. Deep lines of worry crossed his brow and separated his hard face from his smooth, ebony head, shaved as clean as a billiard ball.

"The joke of it is, they think we're the bloody savages," he said in an English Cockney accent. "My name's Reginald. What's yours?"

I blinked at him in disbelief for several seconds before I measured my response. "I'm Evan Michaels, at least, I used to be," I said, turning my eyes toward the bars above.

"Don't fret it," he said, getting up. "We'll get you cleaned up in no time." He walked over to a small, dog-size steel hatch set low in the wall next to the door. I watched as he opened the lid on a wooden bucket and stuck his hand inside, pulling out a striped, wet rag that looked to be the remains of one of his sleeves.

"They've made a mess of you, friend." He sat cross-legged on the floor in front of me and swabbed at the open wounds dotting my face. "I don't want you to take this the wrong way, but I'm very glad to see you. Well, I'm glad to see anyone, to be more specific. They keep the foreign prisoners together, infidels they call us. That's rich. The bloke before you was Dutch. And for the last . . ." He left the sentence hanging as he looked up and tallied the chalk marks on the wall above his bunk. ". . . seventeen months, I've been alone. I enjoy the extra space and all, but the lack of conversation can be maddening." His face exploded into an emotional expression as he spoke.

"What happened to the Dutchman?" I mumbled through swollen lips.

"He died. Dysentery it was. He made a real mess of it in the end. He gave it to me too. Can't you tell? I must have lost thirty pounds. What am I talking about, how could you know," he laughed nervously. "Never mind me. I have a tendency to ramble, at least that's what Steen used to say. He was the Dutchman we were talking about. I'm just excited at the possibilities of conversation, especially with an English speaker."

"I don't feel much like talking right now."

"Oh, that's okay. You just listen and rest for now," he said, cleaning blood-matted hair away from a scalp cut. "But I do look good for what I've been through, don't you think?"

I had no idea what his eyes had seen, but looking around, it wasn't hard to imagine. And through it all, he had been deprived of such a simple and basic comfort as his own reflection in a mirror. I knew that's why he asked, and why I lied. I nodded and slowly laid my head on my arm, surrendering into a fitful sleep under the stream of his ramblings.

THE FIRST SUNLIT RAYS OF DAWN lit the streets of the Istanbul I had known. Thousands of peddlers stood watch behind their wares that covered the sidewalks on both sides of the street. I walked down the middle of the narrow cobblestone avenue, the cane tapping out a rapid rhythm beneath me. The brass tip on worn stone and my own shuffling footfalls provided the only sound to the scene, as though the milling merchants on either side operated in a muted vacuum. They remained oblivious to my presence, mouthing unspoken words and clanging silent pots.

It was only when I walked past the first of them that they took notice and began to move out toward me. They approached from behind at first, struggling to keep up with my quick pace. Women came forth offering up platter after platter of goods, their weathered and aged faces pursed into narrow-eyed pleas. Their old husbands, hats in hand, reached out for me and mouthed nodding words of praise through silent, toothless smiles. The small crowd of eager sleeve-tugging followers attracted the attention of other vendors farther up the street, who stirred to life in a mass preparatory ambush. I strode quickly in an attempt to outpace them, but they converged on the center of the street like waves crashing in from both sides. Their heads disappeared below the innumerable platters they offered up, each filled with spongy, mold-covered fruit or gray, maggot-ridden meat. They swarmed around me, jostling, sometimes violently, in order to make the best presentation. Platter after platter of spoilage was passed under my nose as I struggled to make my way through them. I shouldered my way as best I could and swung the cane overhead menacingly only to notice the crowd ahead had exploded into a seething mass of bodies, three to four deep, filling the boulevard into the distance, each one climbing over the one below, their hands outstretched toward me.

I drew in a deep breath and was about to let out a scream at them to leave me be when the muezzin's lonely call to prayer echoed over the silent, crawling chaos.

All heads slowly turned as one toward a lone needlelike minaret on the horizon. The pilgrimage started immediately.

They meandered through the streets as one long, amorphous snake of bodies, beckoned by the haunting melody and I, stuck in the middle of the thing, had no choice but to follow. Their offerings were gone, and I was no more to them than another pilgrim in the procession. The song grew louder, and the tower taller the closer we came. The head of the long line emerged into the open square below the spire and wound to the right around it in a long coil that eventually met the tail. As my part of the snake entered the square, I stopped struggling to free myself. It had been where I was headed from the beginning. I looked up and squinted against the first rays of the dawn. A cold chill ran down my spine as my eyes found the blue-and-white bathrobed muezzin leaning her petite figure over the thin railing. It was Judith, Bobby's mother. The veins in her delicate neck bulged as she strained out the mysterious, ancient words. She smiled and pointed me out in the circling crowd at the end of each exhausting refrain, her black eyes laughing.

THE CALL TO PRAYER STILL SANG OUT as I gasped myself awake. Cool, gray light filtered down through the bars.

"It's their idea of an alarm clock," said Reginald from his bunk on the other side. "It comes five times a day. Go back to sleep, Evan. It's better that way."

REGINALD HAD SNAPPED OUT OF A SNORING SLEEP and scrambled to his feet in front of the small trapdoor before the guard had finished yelling his Arabic command. He put the lid back on the wooden chamber pot and shoved it into the anonymous set of hands reaching through the opening. A fresh one was handed back along with two stainless steel bowls and a brown disk of unleavened bread.

"Here we go," said Reginald, handing me a cup. "The Outpost's finest."

"Is that the name of this place?"

"That's what Steen called it, I guess that's the name he was told. He said it used to be a French Legionnaire outpost."

"Is this the only meal of the day?"

"No, there is one more in the afternoon. It comes with a pomegranate every other day," he said, almost boasting. "What are you in for, Evan Michaels?"

I tore a strip off the loaf and dipped it into the bowl of thick gruel. "I stole a painting."

"Are you an art thief?" he asked, wide-eyed.

I shook my head as I swallowed the tasteless mush. "No, I'm not . . . I don't know what I am."

"How long did you get?"

I looked into his eyes while I mustered the courage to say the words. "Twen . . . twenty-five."

"Years?" he asked in disbelief.

I leaned back against the wall and rolled my eyes up toward a guard as he paced along the catwalk above the cell bars.

"Whew, bloke, that's a stretch. Have you been inside before?"

"Yeah, in Bulgaria."

He raised his eyebrows curiously. "Well, Yank, you sure work in some strange places. What was the Bulgarian jail like compared to this place?"

"I don't know yet. Do we work? Do we ever go outside, or is this it?"

"Oh, we go out, two hours a day, but that's the good news. The bad news is the infidels' time in the yard is during the heat of midday. But they don't work us and they only beat us until their arms get tired," he said, laughing. "Sorry, I suppose I shouldn't joke about it. Seriously, they tire of the abuse after a while. It's better if you don't fight back. The only rule I have is that you not use the chamber pot until nightfall or early morning, otherwise you'll soil the water, and we'll have nothing to drink. And when you do get thirsty, drink from the rag, it's safer. I don't want another episode like before with Steen, especially now. I'm a short timer," he said in a toothy grin. "Eight more months of this, then it's *fuck you, Saheeb*, and I ride a camel out of this place."

"How long have you been here?"

"Almost three years. I got three and a half for possession of hashish and pornography. Both violated the word of Mohammed, the judge said. I've got some words for Mohammed and I'm going to scream them out loud at him just as soon as I'm back in jolly old England."

I chuckled and raised my cup out toward him. "Have a pint for me, eh?"

He smiled wide and clinked my cup. "Surely."

BY MIDDAY, THE SCENT OF URINE AND FILTH soured the stifling air above the cellblock. The constant, ghostlike murmur of other captive voices was broken by the haunting wails of Muslim prayer and Reginald's endless chattering. He filled any empty moment with one-sided conversation, as though he had an enmity with silence.

The cell door flew open without warning around noon to reveal the sergeant, club held tightly in his grimy hands.

"Time to go," said a joyful Reginald as the fat Arab sergeant walked in.

"Go where?" I asked.

"No talking!" shouted the sergeant as he stepped forward and laid a baton blow across the instep of my bare left foot.

I cried out, gripped my foot, and rolled onto the floor as he drew back for another go. I bit hard on my tongue and lay defenseless before him. To my surprise, it was not the guard's baton that landed on me, but Reginald's hand. He placed one hand on my shoulder and one up toward the guard in my defense. I lay still as my cellmate spoke in smiling, apologetic nods. The Arabic rolled off Reginald's tongue effortlessly. I couldn't understand, but knew from his appeasing tone and posture that he pleaded on behalf of my ignorance. Reginald cowered to the floor next to me as the sergeant drew back again. The young guards in the hall laughed as the fat man spat on both of us and walked out.

"Can you walk?" whispered Reginald.

I nodded.

"Come on. We have to go. I'll help you," he said, lifting me up.

The open courtyard was little more than a square of barren earth bordered by four stone walls. Uniformed guards paced along the tops of the walls, each one's rifle at the ready. A smaller square of low, whitewashed stones lay just inside the walls.

Reginald placed his arm around me as we entered. "Come on. It will feel better if you walk it off."

The desert air was a refreshing change from the cellblock, and the open expanse of sky seemed to lift my mood by some small fraction.

"What's the line of white stones for?" I asked.

"That's the proverbial line in the sand. It is forbidden to go beyond it. If you do, those guards up there will shoot you dead with no warning. I've seen them do it twice, headshots both times. Turned the poor bastards off like flicking a switch. How's the foot?"

"Better," I said, looking up to lock eyes with a passing guard.

THE TEMPERATURE IN THE CELLBLOCK DROPPED dramatically as the sun slipped below the horizon. I sat on my bunk trying to ignore the stench and Reginald's ramblings on everything from cricket strategy to Irish autonomy. I nodded and grunted in agreement just often enough to keep his attitude even.

"What's that?" I asked, pointing to a cardboard box tucked under his bunk.

He leaned over and slid the box out into the dim light. "This is a collection of crap sent by the Red Crescent. They come here every six months and bring care packages like this. Let's see here," he said, tossing the contents onto the floor one by one, "an English language version of the Koran, fucking useless, a little Arab skull cap hat, fucking useless, and notebooks of empty paper and pens for writing letters, fucking useless," he said sarcastically.

"Why are the notebooks useless?" I asked.

"There's no mail here, no pickup, no delivery. We have no form of communication with the outside world. If whoever you have on the outside didn't know you got in trouble here, then they won't know anything of what happened to you until you get out. That's the thing that weighs on me the most, Evan," he said in a serious tone. "Back in the West End, I left a beautiful young wife and a one-year—" he checked himself for a second, "a four-year-old boy. They know nothing about what happened. They probably think I'm dead, and I must remain so for another eight months. Each day I wonder if I'm still in her thoughts. Each day I wonder what proxy lies between her legs and acts as father to my son."

I laid back against the wall and felt a part of my spirit leave. It was the part of me that still clung to that last hope that I could leave this place alive. The realization then came over me quite effortlessly that if no one else could help me to commute my sentence then, as Samas had said, that responsibility naturally fell upon my own shoulders.

"Well, it's about that time," said Reginald as he got up and placed the open chamber pot at the foot of his bunk.

"Time for what?" I asked.

He stepped up onto the edge of his bed and peered into the open bucket. "The lowering of the colors," he said as he unbuttoned his tattered trousers and dropped them around his ankles. He aimed his penis with his right hand and held his left high overhead like a conductor about to set his orchestra in motion. His head was cocked to one side as though waiting for some starting signal. He began to relieve himself a split second after the muezzin began the evening call to prayer. The sound of his urination, exaggerated by his elevation, splashed loudly into the hollow bucket and echoed beyond the confines of our cell into the length of the cellblock, testing even the most faithful. He struggled to keep the stream steady as he set his left hand into motion and conducted himself in a loud whistling version of "God Save the Queen." The urination continued, but the song faltered as his face broke into smiling laughter.

"I trust you'll torture them with your 'Star Spangled Banner' after I'm gone," he said in a chuckle as his last trickling drops landed in the bucket.

I laughed aloud, but only because Reginald did and only because I couldn't help but enjoy his small snub. But the laughter escaping me rang hollow as it began to sink in. It was no accident that I was there. Whether through aspiration or desperation, everyone eventually finds their own level, and I knew that I had found mine.

DURING MY LIMITED TIME OUT OF OUR CELL, I found myself fascinated with the line of white rocks in the prison yard. I walked that line every day, and with each new day, I began to see them as the true boundaries to my existence. As the days began to run into one another, and time started to pile up behind me, a strange phenomenon emerged. My mind, unencumbered through hour after unending hour of idle emptiness, started, of its own volition, to pay attention and take note of every tiny detail in my surroundings. For the first few weeks, I played with my heightened senses as a novelty, passing whole days tracing every crack in the floor back upstream to its main tributary or counting my own breaths up into the thousands. It was only later that this sharpening, this intolerable sharpening, began to reveal edges to all things as though a giant lens had brought everything into a crisper, clearer focus than man had been designed to endure. Day by day, week by week, the edges continued to sharpen, until it seemed one blow might be enough to cleave one thing from another and shatter the entire existence around me. But that blow never comes and that unbearable clarity progresses until you begin to see your own edges against the larger background. At that point, the clarity supersedes the prison and thus becomes the object of escape.

Shortly after that is when I reached into the box under Reginald's bunk for the notebooks and pen and began to set down this story. It's ironic, I had read several autobiographies before this episode began, and with each page turned I would always think of the author and wonder where he sat as he penned out the story of his life, what photographs sat on the desk, whispering to him of long-forgotten laughs and losses, and what trophies rested on the mantel as a testament to toil and achievement. I write mine from the confines of cell 145 in an unnamed Tunisian desert prison.

Chronicling these events over the past months has helped to focus my idle mind away from these ever-refining powers of observation that plague me. It has helped me come to an understanding as to how I arrived here. But having done so, I must confess I no longer know if this is the epilogue to the story or if the preceding pages are but a lengthy prologue to what I might become.

The torture and beatings are less frequent now than in the first weeks, but lately, it seems that each new abduction and obligatory all-night session is more thorough and earnest than the one before. Their questions, if they even bother to ask them, roll off me, and their blows affect me not to their ends, but instead to my own. Reginald is awake and waiting each time I'm dumped back into our cell. And each time, he cleans me up and tells me I look fine. I don't believe him any longer but I can appreciate why he says it. I lie in bed at night, and the sound of my own breathing sounds ridiculous to me, as though someone else is mustering the will to see it done.

Sometimes, usually after a session with the sergeant and an interrogator from Tunis, I reread the first parts of these notebooks and marvel at the change they have brought about in me.

Blow by blow, blight by blight, the attacks pile up against you, and you are forced again to remuster your dwindling mental resources and tighten the defensive perimeters of your servile mind. Slowly, one mental rampart after another goes undefended, another post falls to the enemy, and another flag is lowered in the face of their superior numbers until even those tattered remains of what you once were become too scattered to hold together. Standing in the wings of lucidity, master of nothing you survey, a decision is made and it makes perfect sense, but then it had to, even to be considered in the first place. Salvation is seen in a release from the bonds of this life, to rise above the conditions you've sunk to, to dissolve life here before it dissolves you. At that point you stand as the agent for all desperate men and as such, are compelled to action.

But I know better. I know the promise of peaceful death lingering just below the prospect of such a release is a false one, for I exist and live now only because the person I was before is dead, which means that I cannot exist without having replaced someone, even if that someone is who I once was. And if that is true, then like the caterpillar that surrenders itself to the moth, suicide must be seen as a life-giving act. The day they helped me figure this out is the day I found the faith to become myself.

Most people think that faith has to do with religion, and religion with divinity, but I tell you that any man who has the courage to take his own life, any man who can choose the hour of his own death, any man who can stand at the very threshold of himself and step through, that man stands as close to divinity as any ever will. For if death is not a prelude to another life, then this time now is nothing more than a cruel mockery.

At times, I wonder if my increased acumen has afforded me too close a scrutiny at my own edges. But secretly, I know the fact that I have resolved myself to this end does not matter, for I am at this end and I realize that such resolution is but a pale preface to the eventualities. What matters now is the doing, not the petty preamble of forethought. I have been in the minority of extant men long enough and I now long to slip into the welcoming arms of mankind's silent majority.

REGINALD IS BEING RELEASED IN TWO DAYS and he has agreed to take the notebooks with him. It occurred to me to have him contact the Cognomina for me once he is outside, but the oath of secrecy I adopted with this tattoo precludes me from exposing him to that truth. Because of that oath, I have written the notebooks in Bulgarian so that he won't know. I have asked him to hang on to them, in the hopes that some stranger might come for them in around eighteen years. That person, I will tell him, might not even know exactly why they are at his door, but he is to give that young man or woman the three notebooks and to tell them about me if they ask. As I write these last words to whomever I will be, I am no longer able to fight them as they come to me slowly and faintly: the low, steady, maddening sound of my own heartbeats as they echo back to me from the walls of this fatal room.

I sing the song of a deathless soul,
Whom Fate, which God made, but doth
   not control,
Placed in most shapes . . .
For though through many straits and lands I roam,
I launch at paradise, and I sail toward home;
The course I there began shall here be stayed,
Sails hoisted there, struck here, and anchors laid;
For the great soul which here amongst us now
Doth dwell, and moves that hand, and tongue,
   and brow . . .
This soul, to whom Luther and Mohammed were
Prisons of flesh; this soul which oft did tear
And mend the cracks of the Empire and late Rome,
And lived when every great change did come,
Had first in paradise, a low, but fatal room.

From *The Progress of the Soul*
by John Donne, 1572–1631

AUTHOR BIO

D. Eric Maikranz has had a multitude of lives in this lifetime. As a world traveler, he was a foreign correspondent while living in Rome, translated for relief doctors during a cholera epidemic, and was once forcibly expelled from the nation of Laos. He has worked as a tour guide, a radio host, a bouncer, and as a Silicon Valley software executive. *The Reincarnationist Papers* is his first novel, which has been adapted into the Paramount Pictures film *Infinite*.

CONNECT WITH
D. ERIC MAIKRANZ

For exclusive bonus content to
The Reincarnationist Papers
and to invite Eric Maikranz
to speak at your book club, visit
www.EricMaikranz.com

Twitter
@ericmaikranz

Facebook
Facebook.com/DEricMaikranzAuthor